"Every curve, every twist takes you further down the rabbit hole.
Sharon Doering has written a crackling debut
that should be on your 2020 list!"
SAMANTHA DOWNING

"If you love Gillian Flynn, you will love this book"
Manhattan Book Review

"An explosive, darkly comedic thriller that belongs on every to-read list.
Scrupulously plotted… *She Lies Close* is a live wire of a debut"
MARY KUBICA

"Grabbed me from the first page and wouldn't let go. A fast-paced, taut,
psychological mind-bender that hits all the right notes"
D.J. PALMER

"Dark, searing, and raw… A no-holds-barred debut that builds tension and
suspicion, culminating in an ending that will shake you to your core"
SAMANTHA M. BAILEY

"A chilling twister of a thriller…
Smart, compelling, and darkly funny"
LISA UNGER

SHE
LIES
CLOSE

SHE LIES CLOSE

SHARON DOERING

TITAN BOOKS

She Lies Close
Print edition ISBN: 9781789094190
E-book edition ISBN: 9781789094206

Published by Titan Books
A division of Titan Publishing Group Ltd
144 Southwark Street, London SE1 0UP
www.titanbooks.com

First Titan edition: September 2020
10 9 8 7 6 5 4 3 2 1

This is a work of fiction. Names, characters, places, and incidents either are the
product of the author's imagination or are used fictitiously, and any resemblance to
actual persons, living or dead, business establishments, events, or locales is entirely
coincidental. The publisher does not have any control over and does not assume any
responsibility for author or third party websites or their content.

Printed and bound by CPI Group (UK) Ltd, Croydon CR0 4YY.

Did you enjoy this book?

We love to hear from our readers. Please email us at
readerfeedback@titanemail.com or write to us at
Reader Feedback at the above address.

TITAN BOOKS.COM

For Marc,
my muse

For Jon, Sam, and Ed,
my heroes

PROLOGUE

He'd brought a spade instead of a shovel. It had been a stupid, panicked mistake. There'd been a gang of dirt-breaking tools, all wood-handled and rusted, leaning against the wall in the garage, and he'd grabbed one without thinking.

Mud made for stubborn digging, and the spade would only stretch the work. As he thrust the square blade into sludge, his back muscles twitched and his pulse thumped in his neck. Rain dripped into his eyes, stinging.

He'd been crazed and incoherent an hour ago, his throat still felt clawed from screaming, but now his mind felt strangely calm. Hollow.

He wanted to pull the blanket away.

Don't.

The night was cold enough for his breath to cloud the air, and his clothes clung heavy with rain, yet his skin itched with heat. Inside his gardening gloves, his hands sweat.

Don't look.

Here among the trees, the rotting stench of detritus was

thick in the back of his tender throat. And he was hearing *too much*: the sizzling, frying-oil sputter of rain; chirping crickets; and his own breathing, heavy and animal.

Don't look under the blanket.

Tilting the spade and pitching mud into a pile, he felt something come loose from the back pocket of his jeans. He reached back, trying to catch it, a muscle memory reaction from always carrying his phone in his pocket, but missed. It hit the forest floor with a subtle *thump*.

What had he dropped?

Blue moonlight filtered through the leaves of scrappy young trees. He wiped sweat and rain from his eyes with his shirt sleeve and squinted.

A small slip-on shoe, red and sparkly.

1

TEENAGE BOYS DESCEND UPON ME

My mind is a snow globe in the hands of a toddler who's shitfaced on apple juice. I keep waiting for the white flakes to settle, but they remain a perpetual, furious blizzard.

Exhausted and wired, I sprint through muggy darkness. Baby monitor in one hand, cell phone in the other. My cheap foam sneakers pound cement sidewalk, and my unsupported arches stretch and twinge. I suck the humid stink of late-summer compost deep into my aging lungs. *Why does life smell so bad?*

I corner the block, and the white-noise static of the baby monitor zaps to silence.

Out of range.

I run faster. If I push it, I can run an eleven-minute mile. That's one lap around my block. My heart bangs against its cage, and salty tears slip onto my tongue. Crying is part of my routine too.

My neighborhood, Saint's Crossing, was built quick and

11

dirty thirty years ago. At least that is what a plumber told me when I hired him to fix the second-floor-bathtub-leaking-onto-my-kitchen-table problem.

Houses on my block are modest and cozy. Or small and ugly. Depends on your perspective and mood. In daylight, their colors are typical midwestern drab: tan, sage green, and pale yellow. Trees dotting small lawns and parkways are too large and too many. Tricycles and coffee tables are occasionally left on curbs, offered for second-hand use. Saint's Crossing is a neighborhood of families, young and old, but most of all it seems down-to-earth and safe.

Or so I thought when I moved in several months ago.

I reach the furthest point away from my house. This is when fear and guilt sink their nails into the back of my neck because I've left my sleeping children home alone.

Well, Hulk is with them. She's a Boston Terrier. Think tiny dog with pointed, upright ears and bug eyes. Of course she has no thumbs to dial 911, but she would get in a few good barks if an intruder broke a window. Before he offered her food.

This is when I worry my three-year-old has woken up and is wandering the house, rubbing her chubby little thumb along her square-foot blanket, tears streaking her irresistible cheeks.

This is when I agonize most over Leland Ernest, my next-door neighbor.

A mosquito buzzes my ear, and I smack it.

A towering lamppost casts shadows of trees onto the sidewalk. A slight breeze gives the leaves breath and shapes the branches into yawning monsters. My shadow, a twelve-foot giant, tramples these sidewalk beasts.

Leaving the lamp's glow in my wake, I run toward a long stretch of houses whose owners zealously oppose porch lights.

A low branch whips my chest and spikes my pulse. I didn't see it coming. These late-night sprints around the block are a rush. I never know what's going to smack me in the face or if an uneven sidewalk crack will snag my shoe and take me down.

Homestretch—exactly fourteen houses away—I pump my legs harder.

Strides ahead, an obese pine tree overruns the sidewalk.

As I sidestep the pine, a black shadow erupts from high in the tree and, swooping down, claws at my neck.

The impact throws me off balance. I fall onto dewy grass, and I piss my shorts. Sounds of static and clicking scatter into divergent points of noise overhead.

What the hell hit me?

Felt substantial, like a squirrel.

But that makes no sense.

Bees. Had to be bees.

Bees make sense because pin-prick points along my neck and shoulder sting and burn. My fingers search my neck for stingers, but only slide along wetness. Sweat. Maybe blood?

I picture a swarm of bees crashing into me, fleeing their hive because some old guy pesticide-bombed the co-op they'd built near his front door.

But... do bees screech?

As I sit in my piss-shorts in the grass and breathe in an

13

effort to prevent hyperventilation, two teenage boys descend upon me, touching my damp back and shoulders with their nicotine-rubbed fingers.

"Dude, are you alright?" His voice is part hilarity, part grave concern. *Oh please, call me anything but "dude". Have I lost all markers of femininity?* My eyes work to make out his face and shape. He is teenage-skinny, has a boy's crew cut, and strikes me as military-confident. "That was sick. *Way* sick," he says.

His friend, wearing a baseball hat over shoulder-length hair which feathers beautifully, shakes his head silently, mind blown.

I run my fingers through cool, wet grass, searching for my belongings. Beyond their cigarette-smoked clothes, fabric softener laces the air. Someone is running their dryer.

"I'm OK. I'm not sure what happened," I say, embarrassed at the extent of my disorientation and glad for darkness. Even if they catch a faint whiff of urine, they can't see my wet shorts. "I think I got stung by bees."

"Dude, those were bats. Like, twenty little fuckers. They came out of nowhere. *Swoosh*. Went that way." He points across the street as if it matters, as if we could see anything in this darkness. As if the bats were waiting on cue for an encore.

Bats? Is he kidding?

If there is one thing I can't stomach at this moment in my life, it is to be fucked with.

I consider the situation. Whatever hit me had bulk. I consider the quality and tone of the screeching. Maybe I heard flapping. I can't remember, it happened too fast.

I gaze up at him, checking if his lips curl up at their corners.

14

No curl. His lips are parted. He's out of breath too.

Not fucking with you. It was a pack of bats. Pack? Roost? Colony?

His quiet friend with feathered hair is still shaking his head, no sign of stopping.

"I didn't know bats sounded like radio static," Crew Cut says. "Can we call someone for you?"

"I'm OK. Really. I live a few houses away."

Getting knocked over by small flying things while pursuing physical fitness is embarrassing. I feel geriatric and uncoordinated and smelly, and desperately want to slither into darkness. I stand and take a few rubbery steps, then shift into a jog.

His voice already a house behind me, he calls, "If you get a craving for blood, you know why."

I swallow, but my throat is dry, and it doesn't take. Hot wind blows at the scratches along my neck, drawing a sting.

Shit. Bats carry rabies.

2

THAT SAC WAS THE WORST OF SURPRISES

Hulk is thrilled by my pee-shorts. As if someone finally understands her disgusting compulsions.

I shower and pull on yoga pants and a T-shirt. Wet hair dripping down the back of my shirt, I grab my laptop and google, "attacked by bats".

Five minutes online and I'm bleary-eyed, brainstorming my eulogy. Without immediate treatment, rabies is fatal nearly one hundred percent of the time, and, for some cracked reason, the upscale neighborhood north of mine currently has a bat problem. The flying, pug-nosed vermin have been found inside homes, and sixteen bats have tested positive for rabies this summer.

I'm about to call my mom, but stop. It's hours past her bedtime. I mentally scroll through a short list of friends. Liz lives thirty minutes away. *Too much to ask.* As for the others, I haven't seen or talked to them in how long? Weeks? Months? I tell myself not to worry, not to question friendships. All these women are busy juggling work, children, cooking, and cleaning and have neglected their friendships, their sex lives, and, occasionally, their basic hygiene.

Valerie is only fifteen minutes away and never misses a text.

-Valerie! I know it's super late, but I need you to watch my kids for 30 min.

-Booty call?

-Funny, no. Bats. I need a rabies shot.

-You're joking.

-No. Need go to ER asap.

-Seriously?

In lieu of response, I send her a photo of my neck.

-Be there in 20. Need to find glasses.

Valerie arrives at my door wearing her glasses slightly crooked upon her nose, flannel PJ bottoms, and flip-flops. Her threadbare Eminem T-shirt stretched tight over her belly and breasts reveals she hasn't bothered with a bra. One nipple lands a solid inch lower than the other. I am all too familiar with this boob asymmetry, and it makes me love her more.

"I'm sorry to pull you away from Dan on a Saturday night," I say.

Bugging out her eyes, she makes a raspberry noise with her lips, and a sphere of spit lands on my arm. "Oh please," she says. "He's eating hummus from a spoon in his boxers, watching *Curb Your Enthusiasm* reruns. I'm not into *any* of those things."

"Thank you."

See, your friendship hasn't missed a beat.

She makes another raspberry noise. "Seriously, it's nothing. Let me see your bite."

"They're scratches, I think." I bend my neck so she can see. "I need to get the vaccine just in case."

"Wait! Are they in your house? The bats?"

"No, no. I was outside. I was jogging."

She raises her eyebrows. "You left the kids home alone?"

"I only did one lap around the block," I say but I am caught. My brief, late-night parental negligence has been secret. Now my impropriety will be *known*, will be questioned.

"I should go," I say, hiking my purse over my shoulder. "Chloe and Wyatt are sleeping in their beds." I go for the door, then turn around. "Listen. When I leave, keep the doors closed and locked." I dig my keys out of my purse and rattle them, stalling, considering what I want to share with Valerie. "My neighbor is a suspect in a criminal case."

Kidnapping.

Although, at this point, five months in, it has probably turned into a murder case. But I don't want to say *murder*. I'm not ready to say *murder*.

My disclosure feels stagy and unnecessary, but my neighbor's criminality has been a cloud of noxious fumes—something godawful like burning PVC—trapped inside my mind for days, and I have been desperate to vent. And Valerie *should* keep the doors locked. What if she was planning to lie on my couch with the front door open, warm summer breeze breathing through the screen?

"*What* criminal case?"

18

"Ava Boone."

"Oh my God, Grace. *Ava Boone?* Oh God. That poor angel." Valerie claps her hands to her cheeks and drags the skin down, nudging her glasses straight in the process. "That poor baby should be starting kindergarten like my Max. This is *crazy*. Why didn't you tell me?"

"I only found out a few days ago."

"Why is your neighbor a suspect?"

"I don't know all the details," I say, which isn't exactly a lie. "He's probably innocent. They haven't arrested him, right? He's probably a good guy." I'm trying for optimistic, I'm championing devil's advocate, but my voice wavers because he's *not* a good guy. "I'm just being on the safe side."

"Safe side? Ditching your kids to go for a jog? What were you thinking?" She's not patronizing me or being a dick. It's a fair question.

I have several answers, each of them honest.

1. Thinking? I was barely thinking. These past four days my mind has been sticky with cortisol spooge and desperate for an eleven-minute brain-bath of dopamine clarity.

2. I have not slept in four days. I was hoping physical exertion would lead to sleep.

3. I haven't had sex in six months and needed some form of physical release.

4. Chloe took a photo of me last week. Actually, she took twenty-five. A series of snapshots beginning with sneaking my phone off the counter as I washed dishes and ending with her getting a purely joyful tickling on the couch. I thought I was pulling off forty. These photos were a slap in the face, twenty-five of them. The first few photos showed my ass sagging in gray yoga pants and the outline of my underwear inches below where said ass is supposed to end. The next dozen photos highlighted underarms so pale, doughy, and mottled, they made me want to give myself plastic surgery with a butter knife. The final shots showcased my oily, creased forehead and greasy hair and this lumpy scrotal-like sac under my jaw I had no idea existed. That sac was the worst of surprises. That I appear happy in the photos, deliriously happy, as I tickle my pint-sized trouble-maker, counts for nothing. The ugliness her photojournalism displayed whites out everything. I remind myself, *Mom* ranks as "most searched" on porn sites. Doesn't work. Nothing will boost my ego. Bottom line: exercise was needed.

I go with the easiest answer. "I haven't slept in four days, Val. I was trying to knock myself out."

"They got drugs for that. Or why not polish off a bottle of wine? That's what I do." She shakes her head, dumbfounded, same as the long-haired teenage boy. "Didn't you check the neighborhood before you bought?" There is support and concern in her voice, but also judgement. *What kind of idiot mother are you?*

"I checked the predator site, but what else can you do? Go door to door, asking if anyone's a suspect in a kidnapping? He's not convicted of anything. She's still missing."

"*Missing?*" she says. "You know seventy-six percent of kidnapped girls are murdered in the first three hours."

Seventy-four percent, according to my Google search. "I know. I should go, Val." She's put me on the defense, which I hate. And my neck stings. Images of the water-fearing, rabies-infected Indonesian teenage boy I saw on YouTube resurface.

"You're right, you should go," she says. Then, "Do the kids know?"

"Not yet, no."

"OK, you go." Avoiding the mangled side of my neck, she hugs me quickly, but generously. A good hug. One that makes me realize I am in serious need of adult contact.

Wyatt's eight-year-old hugs are few and far between, and when he gives them, he turns his face away from my eyes and my clothes as if the smell and the sight of me is unbearable. Before the hug even begins, he is pulling away.

Chloe's three-year-old hugs are communion, all fluttering butterfly hands and moist skin, but they are also greedy. Chloe is known for holding my face between her grubby palms and squeezing hard. If she can't reach my face, she is on my leg, her small hands grabbing the cellulite on my thighs.

Kids are takers. They poke their little straws into your Capri Sun soul and they suck.

I drive myself to St Joe's hospital with my window down. Warm breeze blows at my face, cooling my cheeks, but my scalp is sweaty and tingly.

Hospitals make me nervous. It's a phobia, really. Driving to one is akin to nearing the front of the line for a haunted house. Not a cutesy haunted house targeting a wide-eyed middle-school audience, but one that indiscriminately employs thirty-year-olds with criminal records and runs extension cords to power real chainsaws.

The last time I went to a haunted house, I elbowed a zombie in the jaw and knocked him over a coffin. I hope I can keep my hands to myself at St Joe's.

3

SHRINK THIS WOMAN

The soapy, metallic scent of Betadine is up my nose.

I am on my back, shirt off, bra on, shivering. The hospital air is chilled. Plus, I'm anxious.

The ubiquitous white tissue paper crinkles beneath me as I wiggle slightly on the narrow bed. My ER room is partitioned by a modern sliding glass door behind a curtain.

"These don't look like bat bites. More like scratches," the woman doctor says. She told me her name a minute ago, but I've forgotten. Blue gloves on, she wipes my broken skin with Betadine, which is shockingly cold, and sets the yellowed cotton ball refuse on a tray.

My doctor is slender and has straight blond hair with seemingly natural highlights. Like a child. Her gorgeous hair is swept back into a ponytail so smooth and flawless, I am mystified. She is not conventionally beautiful and has no curves to her body, but her complexion is clear, her teeth are white, and her nose is petite. These features—natural highlights, dainty nose, small pores—are the bland features women like me covet as we get older and have to exert effort to keep masculinity from creeping into our faces.

"Yes, scratches," I say. "That's what I was thinking."

"You could get rabies if one of the bats had saliva on its claws and that bat *also* had rabies," she says. "Those are very low odds. Only six percent of bats have rabies."

She finishes cleaning and bandaging my neck, then palms the garbage and throws it away. "Sit up, please," she says, lifting the top of my gown off my lap and holding the arm-holes open. I do as I'm told. I sit, then slip my arms through.

She pulls a penlight from her lab coat pocket, clicks it on, and aims it at my eyes. "Follow my light. You say they attacked you?"

"I know. I know," I say, tracking her light, "it sounds nuts. I must have been in their way as they flew by."

"Hm." She clicks her light off and slips it into her pocket.

"Two teenagers saw it happen." Why do I feel like a child trying to prop a lie?

She shrugs like maybe she doesn't believe me, but also doesn't care. She finishes the standard six-point inspection checklist (respiration, pulse, eyes, ears, nose, throat) while she continues, "A dozen bats in the area have tested positive for rabies so we need to be on the safe side. We'll give you the first vaccine tonight along with an antibody shot to prime your immune system. This is all standard post-rabies exposure protocol. You will make appointments before you leave for follow-up shots. You need to get them all within one month." She makes eye contact and widens her eyes. Sclerae as white and healthy as her teeth. "I don't want to scare you, but untreated rabies is

24

fatal. If you finish the series of four shots, you will be fine. Do you understand?"

"Yes."

"Have you ever had an allergic reaction to a vaccine?"

"Not that I know of."

The nurse who typed my information—name, birthdate, reason for visit—into her laptop minutes ago starts typing again, presumably recording my answer. The nurse is my age, maybe older. Her hair is curlier and messier than the doctor's, the skin around her jaw and neck is sagging, but she has the same clear, efficient, kick-ass look in her eyes as her colleague.

"Have you ever been diagnosed with cancer?"

"No."

"Heart disease?"

"No."

"Have you ever had surgery?"

"No."

"What medications are you currently taking?"

"Adderall."

"For attention deficit?"

I nod.

Shame slides in like a sliver under a nail. It's small, but poignant.

If I were on a cholesterol-lowering drug, would I feel ashamed by the profuse globular fat molecules bobbing slothfully through my blood? If I were taking asthma medication, would I feel ashamed by my melodramatic bronchioles?

I'm not sure, but I don't think so. Lungs and blood are just lube and gaskets. The brain is a window into a person's soul, their true state of being, internal strength, trustworthiness, and integrity. My brain, stripped down, without meds, is inadequate.

"How often do you drink alcohol?"

Would this question ordinarily come later in the questionnaire, but she moved it up in the queue in light of my attention deficit admission?

"Once a week, tops."

"When you do drink, how many do you consume?"

"One or two glasses of wine, I guess."

"Any other medical issues you worry about?"

This question bloats inside my head.

This would be a good time to tell her I haven't slept more than a few hours in four days. This would be a good time to tell her that when I gazed out the window over the kitchen sink yesterday morning, the tip of a blue spruce tilted thirty degrees toward the ground before it righted itself. That hours ago when I was sitting on the toilet lid while the kids took a bath—with their ear-piercing laughing and shrieking amplifying off bathroom walls and water tsunami-sloshing out of the tub and onto a mess of towels and balled clothes on the floor—something inside me, some working part that's supposed to remain fixed, free-fell for a moment. That I sense the vibrating strings interlacing the universe on the verge of ripping apart.

If I said these things, the doctor might document some tidbit that could force me to undergo some sort of mental therapy for which I don't have the money or time.

You just need sleep.

"I haven't been sleeping well lately so I don't feel myself."

She waits, in case I want to reveal more. When I stare dumbly at her, my shoulders slouched, she says, "You can talk to your primary about a sleep aid like Ambien, but there are side effects. If you think your sleep difficulties are temporary, I would stick with Benadryl for a short-term solution. Always knocks me out."

"Me too, but if I take Benadryl, I'm hungover in the morning and can barely make a sandwich for my son's lunch."

She smiles politely, but this is the ER. It's all about turnover and, like a waitress already thinking about her next table's tip, she wants me out. She rolls off her blue gloves and tosses them in the trash to indicate we are almost done here. "I'm going to grab the syringes, and then you'll be all set. Do you have any questions?"

"I teach preschool. Can I go to work Monday?"

"Yes. You'll be scabbed over by then. To be cautious, keep your scratches covered with bandages." She smiles. "Were you hoping I'd ban you from work for the week?"

"No." Her joke draws a nervous sweat from my skin, cutting to my insecurities regarding how I am perceived. Do I give off that white trash vibe? "Are the shots painful? In the stomach?" I've heard urban legends about rabies shots.

"No. Rabies shots haven't been given in the stomach since the eighties. Just a shot in the arm. And I'll inject antibodies near the wound. You'll do fine." She taps my knee once. "I'll be back in a few minutes." She pulls open the curtain, then the sliding glass door. She exits quickly, graceful as a dancer.

My kids' vaccines are always injected by a nurse. That the doctor is preparing my vaccine makes the situation seem dire. Iodine soap stink hangs heavy in the air. My stomach is tight, my skin is cold and clammy. The ER is *freezing*.

"I am not making this up," I say to the nurse.

She smiles and gently backhands the flab on my upper arm like we've been sitting at a bar together for hours. "You wouldn't believe how many times we hear that in the ER. Guy came in last week with a peanut butter jar up his ass. Said he *fell on it.* Swore up and down he wasn't making it up."

My eyes go wide.

"It was a sixteen-ounce jar, but still. Men. They're sick, I tell you."

"The bats weren't attacking me, per se. I think I was in their way."

"I believe you," she says. "I heard they found bats *inside* several homes in Arbor Ridge Ponds. I bet some deranged, bat-loving lunatic is behind the population climb, roosting them in his house, carving bat houses and setting them about his yard, fantasizing he's going to become a vampire. Bats are supposed to be dying off, I thought. White-nose syndrome, my ass."

I smile, and tension eases in my shoulders. Even though hospitals and their staff make my skin crawl, women like this make all of life's problems manageable. I need to shrink this woman and put her in my purse so she can blurt amusing aphorisms throughout my day and depreciate my worries. *Politicians and diapers should be changed often and for the same reasons!*

In forty years, thousands of old ladies will be running around with tattoos!

She continues, "People are crazy, I tell you. My neighbors, I've known these people ten years; I've shared an ungodly number of wine bottles with these people, as you do with neighbors. Last month my neighbor lets it slip they're into suspension." She smacks my arm flab again. "Like, suspending from their body piercings." She's shaking her head. "This couple, they're in their fifties. You think you know your neighbors, but you don't."

My stomach clenches. Inside thirty seconds, I come up with four unlikely but possible scenarios resulting in one of my sleeping children dying, and I have a fifth idea in the works.

I want out of here. I hoist my purse into my lap and reach inside for my cell phone, overwhelmed by an urge to check on Valerie and the kids.

4

THE SKIN PEELED BACK

The kids are sleeping, same as when I left.

Of course they are. Why would you expect otherwise?

After Valerie leaves, I stand over Chloe's bed and listen to her breathe. She's on her front with her knees tucked under her chest, balled up like a baby, and I match my breathing to the rise and fall of her small, curved back. I hover too long, waiting for her rhythmic breathing to falter, waiting to catch her case of sudden unexplained death in childhood, SIDS's ugly cousin. I reluctantly retreat and peek in Wyatt's room. The pale bottom of his big foot, soft and flawless, sticks off the end of his loft bed. I want to kiss it.

Healthy and safe, I tell myself in the voice of a seasoned cop who is trying to calm a frantic parent. I head into my room, grab my laptop, and climb into bed.

It's going to be another restless night. My pulse is acute, and my worries are rolling downhill like a cartoon snowball, gaining bulk and urgency.

I open my laptop and search Leland Ernest. Nothing comes

up. Well, three obituaries pop up, but those are unrelated to my neighbor, obviously. My neighbor has no online presence. No Facebook, Twitter, or LinkedIn. No school history, work history, or reported arrest. I've searched online the past few nights, hoping the Kilkenny police will report on suspects, hoping someone will mention my neighbor.

My *neighbor*.

When you buy a house, you have a pre-made list of questions—How long is the commute? How much you will have to spend on repairs? How old is the roof? Has there been mold? How much traffic is there on the street out front? How many showers? Does the house emanate a pleasant feng shui vibe?—but the huge question mark, the major unknown, the one thing you absolutely can't control or fully investigate is your neighbors.

To each of your days, they can add sudden, unexpected joy or debilitating terror. They can provide an onion in a pinch or they can steal your sense of freedom. Since I moved into this house months ago, I've only talked to five or six people on my street. Creepy Leland and Scary Lou are two of them. While I managed to nab a house with two bathtubs, my neighbors suck.

It's been five days since I met Lou.

I'd been fetching Wyatt's bicycle from down the street.

Wyatt's chain had twitched off, and he'd fallen. He'd abandoned the bike and limped home with scrapes on his palms and knees like mashed strawberries.

Damn second-hand, third-rate bike.

I was stretching the bike chain back onto the chainring, my

fingers and palms sticky with gear grease, grass pressing into my knees, when a man said, "Hey," his tone loud and crotchety like he was going to let me have it.

Feeling at once bold and exhausted, I turned toward him. "Yeah?"

He wore slides over black socks pulled up high and a white T-shirt tucked into khaki shorts. His old man outfit clashed with his turquoise sweatband, which cinched his flyaway, graying hair. He must be a sweater. The hair above his sweatband lifted a little in the evening breeze. I didn't peg him for an expressive guy who wanted a splash of color to mix things up. Had to be a penny-pincher who'd found a use for his wife's decades-old sweatband. His hand was bandaged. I aged him around sixty so I assumed he'd had a biopsy of a suspicious mole.

His dog barked behind the screen door, everything dingy and shadowed inside the house. It was a husky mix of the lean, wolfish variety and sounded like it wanted to pick a fight. Hands on hips, the man said, "Your next-door neighbor is a suspect."

Talk about going in rough and dry. This guy had no foreplay talk, and it took a moment to get my bearings. "Suspect of what?"

"You know, that Boone girl."

I had been all too familiar with *that Boone girl*. I'd watched her YouTube video so many times, it was already playing out in my mind. Ava's mischievous smile showcasing her missing front tooth, the flesh soft and swollen as fruit pulp where a new tooth was breaking the skin, her smooth baby face hinting at angular beauty, and her voice, unsettling in both its husky tone and nuanced maturity.

"Which neighbor?" I said, getting to my feet. The afternoon sun was too harsh. I was squinting, wishing I'd brought my sunglasses. The air was burnt and ashy, like someone's dinner gone awry. "What did they do?"

"The guy to your right." The old man had cold eyes; two black marbles squeezed tight. "He was flirting with her right before she went missing."

I cringed. *Flirting* with a five-year-old? How was this man comfortable saying something so obscene without at least dimming his voice?

I knew the neighbor he was talking about. I'd helped Leland move a dresser up his stairs five or six weeks ago. My creep radar had been gonging, but I'd convinced myself I was being a snob.

"I wanted to tell you the day you moved in, but didn't… well, I…" he bit the inside of his cheek, "I didn't want to ruin your day. I'm Lou, by the way." He nodded, but kept his hands on his hips. His dog's barking, hoarse and snarly, persisted.

Oh. That's why he'd started the conversation bluntly. Since the day I'd moved in, Lou had probably been biting the inside of his cheek, sweating into his sweatband, wanting to tell me about Leland Ernest, but didn't want to ruin our move. Lou had shaken the can so many times, he couldn't pull the tab slowly to let it fizz; it was bound to explode.

My irritation eased. As rude and peculiar as Lou seemed, I

appreciated his directness. No one else had bothered to warn me about Leland.

He said, "I got a wife and daughter. My daughter, Rachel, she's seventeen." He sighed, and I couldn't tell if he sighed because he was almost in the clear, his daughter had almost aged out of kidnapping, or if he felt more weighed down that she'd entered prime rape age.

"Nobody told me," I said. I sounded weak and grouchy, which matched how I felt. I considered all the people who could have told me: my realtor, the guy who sold me the house, my neighbor Brooke, whom I'd actually met before I bought. She could have warned me. The word *community* formed in my mind, hard and jagged as shattered glass. *Well, maybe they didn't know.* I picked up Wyatt's bike and walked it to the sidewalk. "How do you know?" I said.

"Secretary at my work, her brother is a cop. Your neighbor Leland was hired to paint the Boone house, but he was, well, too friendly with the girl." When I said nothing, Lou said, "I'm a screw mechanic."

His husky's bark was still loud, but too repetitive; it had lost its angry edge.

"Wait," I said. "Wait. He was just being friendly? That's it?" Raising a boy brought out the defender in me. Wyatt was friendly. I didn't like the idea that he might be suspected of wrongdoing for being simultaneously friendly and male.

Lou worked his jaw, then inhaled so big his chest puffed. His nipples hardened under his thin T-shirt. "He followed my girl while she walked home from the bus stop. Drove his

34

car behind her, asked her if she wanted to go bowling at the mall." The way he said it, "mall" sounded vulgar. "This was when she was thirteen."

My stomach twisted. "What did you do?"

"I don't have money to hire a lawyer, and I know how these things eat up tons of money and never go nowhere." I believed him. The divorce was still a bitter pill in the back of my throat, tasting of dollar bills marinated in filthy fingers.

It looked like money was tight for Lou. His roof was rotting, his driveway was ridden with potholes, and he had no landscaping, not a single bush. "What we did was, we got a dog, and my wife drove Rachel home instead of her walking." He bit the inside of his cheek, considered something, then said, "I rang Leland's doorbell and told him, if he talked to my daughter again, I'd slit his throat."

I pictured flesh opening, blood oozing from its center. Goosebumps lit the back of my arms. *Chilling.* It was chilling that he said that. I wanted to get away from this shark-eyed man, yet it was like I was looking into a mirror. His protectiveness was fierce, borderline repulsive.

"Well, so, that's what we did," he said quietly, almost to himself. He brushed his sandal against something in the grass, schoolboy shy, regretting the throat-slitting admission.

"Do my other neighbors know?"

"I told the ones who have kids."

Assholes.

I started home, trying to keep my greasy fingers splayed and away from Wyatt's handlebars. The teeth edging Wyatt's

35

bike pedal tripped my shin, and the biting pain brought my attention forward. The pedal left me with four horizontal indentations, the skin peeled back, a dot of blood welling in each hole.

"Looks like you got yourself a piss-poor bike chain," Lou said.

"Yes, *that* I have." I tried to laugh, but my laugh dribbled. "I'm Grace, by the way," I said, walking quickly away, panic suddenly on me, harassing me like yappy pooches nipping at my heels, pawing at my shins.

That panic, it's still there. It hasn't eased, hasn't quieted, since I talked to Lou.

Now my fingers glide over the small scabs on my shin and I wonder about Lou. I imagine an old shark, skin cadaverous, wearing a turquoise headband. I picture his jaw working, the mystery bandage on his hand.

I have never seen Lou's wife or daughter, *never.* Maybe Lou was diverting attention away from himself for a reason. And maybe the thing between Leland and Lou's thirteen-year-old was a misunderstanding. Thirteen is an age where fantasy and confused reality collide, like the extraordinary border where saltwater and freshwater meet, yet stay separate.

Maybe, but I doubt it.

I spend another hour on my laptop before I open Ava's YouTube video, what I consider to be the finale of my web-surfing. Ava is the last thing I will see before I close my eyes. Ava is one last potato chip in my ritual of greasy worry-gorging until my stomach feels queasy and bloated.

Every time I pull up her video, I expect it to have been removed, taken down from YouTube for violating some law related to an ongoing crime investigation. A few days ago, I recorded the video on my phone in case this very thing happens.

But no, her video is still here. The family posted this one minute and nineteen second video of their daughter weeks before she went missing, and now the video has over four million views. If her parents posted with aspirations for Ava's fame, I bet they regret it.

5

A GAME OF HEDGE-CLIPPER TAG

Wyatt, Chloe, and I are outside on the back deck by 9:00am. They are eating from their bowls; I am drinking tea. Morning sun is low and glorious, and a comfortable September breeze twirls the wind spinner we hung in a small crabapple tree. On mornings like these when the kids are outside, sitting still, listening to birds and observing neurotic squirrels jump from tree to tree, I try to toss my mental garbage out to the curb. All my worries, all my bad decisions.

Moments like these—when I get to watch Chloe's gossamer eyelashes lower and lift as she gazes up into the tree, when I get to witness Wyatt smile at his little sister as if no one is watching him enjoy her—are bliss.

My neighbor will be deemed harmless, but will still move away.

I will not die of rabies.

The children won't feel abandoned or unloved or guilty because I divorced their father.

I will win a small amount of money, which will allow me to dig myself out of debt.

I will get this yard under control.

I can fix broken things in a house.

I will catch that nasty chin hair the very morning it sprouts.

"Mom," Wyatt says, gazing up, "you know how birds fly in a V?"

"Yeah."

"How do you think they decide who's the leader?"

"No idea, Wy. Let's look it up during Chloe's nap."

"I'm all done with naps," Chloe says, pissed off.

"That's nice," I say. "Who wants to swing?"

Everybody's a sucker for the swing set. Ours is two swings and a slide framed by wood that is splintering and stained moss-green, but still sturdy. Chloe swings on my lap, then Wyatt's lap, then she swings solo on her tummy, her downy, white-blond hair puffing and hanging mid-air before her body pulls it the opposite direction.

We pick wild raspberries off prickly brambles behind the shed and pop them into our mouths without worrying about dirt or microscopic worms.

Don't look at his house. Not a single glance.

The kids migrate to the sun-faded, hole-ridden sandbox under the slide, and I discreetly slip away to unlock the shed. It is a circular combination lock, and the motion of my fingers rotating past the numbers brings back an angst associated with the memory of rushing my high-school locker open.

The heat and odors pouring out are both suffocating and nostalgic. Hot grass, thick oil, and decay. There is a faint buzzing in the dark, cluttered back corner. I imagine a small cluster of carpenter bees working on a home. They haven't bothered me yet, and the kids don't go in the shed because it's always locked. Coaxing bees to relocate is a concern for another day.

I grab hedge clippers, gardening gloves, a big shovel for me or Wyatt, and a plastic hand trowel in case Chloe insists on *helping*.

I hack weeds that have grown too solid, too tree-like to pull. My shiny clippers gnaw at their thin trunks. Mosquitoes aren't too bad, but the heat and humidity are relentless. Plus, I'm wearing a turtleneck; I didn't want the kids to come in contact with my scratches.

I peek at the kids every few minutes. Still in the sandbox. Wyatt still patient even though his sister ruins every damn thing he builds. Nevertheless, his bucket of patience is small and will soon be empty.

My yard-work timer is short. I have fifteen minutes, tops.

I swear I weeded here a week ago. Look away, and things spiral out of control. Gnats buzz the corners of my eyes.

Inside the house, the landline rings.

I feel obliged to answer the landline because the answering machine is set too loud and I hate hearing my recorded voice at such an irritating volume. I have been meaning to change the volume on that thing since we moved in. I glance at the kids, drop the clippers in the grass, and peel off my gloves.

Inside, air-conditioned coolness blasts my skin and feels amazing, like a cold beer slipping down my throat felt a decade ago. "Hello?"

"Hi, Grace. This is Chuck. Sorry I didn't get back to you yesterday. I'm catching up on phone calls this morning from home."

At the sound of his voice, my skin prickles and my throat quivers.

Chuck is the representative for Whisper County State's Attorney's Office. We have become strangely familiar these past five days. During our previous two conversations, I drilled him with questions about Ava Boone's case, driving my raw emotion across telephone wires.

He has not enjoyed talking to me. I am a mosquito buzzing his ear, but he empathizes and that's why he hasn't blown me off. I haven't asked him, but I'm guessing he has kids. He is also Liz's neighbor. He knows I work with Liz so it's just as possible that he doesn't have kids, but doesn't want to be a dick to his neighbor's pesky friend.

I stand at the screen, watching the kids. Still in the sandbox, still getting along. A small lottery.

"I'm sorry to keep bugging you," I say, not sorry at all, "but I need more details about Ava's case." It's difficult to even say her name. It feels indulgent or shameful or careless or maybe all of these.

Don't consider what she's like, that she's a girl with an easy joy in her eyes, generous with her candy, mortified of bees, and will stand her ground when it comes to brussels sprouts and hairbrushes. That she has a bad habit of picking at the dry edges of scabs on her knees. That she dances and twirls even when there's no music. That she loves cats and horses and anything you can sniff: markers, lip gloss, lotions. Don't dare contemplate what she might have gone through. What she might still be going through.

"Well," I say, "not about the case, but why Leland Ernest is a suspect."

"Listen, Grace. Like I said before, my hands are tied in what I can tell you because the investigation is ongoing."

We have gone through boring, rehearsed generalities before. I need more. I need gossipy details that will give me a feel for my neighbor's state of mind and why the police consider him possibly dangerous.

Don't let him off the phone until you get at least one detail.

"Chuck, I need to gauge how dangerous this guy is. I mean, my kids are outside. They're in the sandbox right now. Should I let them outside?"

He ignores this question. Of course he does. He maneuvered around most of my questions during our previous conversations, maneuvered himself off the phone, which is why I left him another message, which is why we are talking again.

"If the detectives had evidence that Leland abducted a child, they would have charged him," he says. "But there is *no case* against him. Ava Boone is, well, it's not a court case; it is a police investigation. All I know has come from talk around the office. The police department is your best bet for information."

"I have called the police department. Many times. They won't tell me anything." He knows this.

I check the sandbox. Two heads? Affirmative.

"Chuck, I have a little girl outside. I don't have a fence. My door is, I don't know, twenty, thirty feet from his, nothing

42

between our doors but grass and trees." I gaze at Leland's backyard. There's a cluster of saplings at the end of his lawn, his own little forest. "If Leland is, was, a suspect, doesn't that mean there is some concerning evidence on him?"

This is another question that will get a vague answer, but I need to keep the conversation rolling. I need to wear him out, I need him to feel bad for shutting me down over and over. I need to nudge him into an emotionally charged state of mind where his sympathy outweighs routine and protocol.

"Someone can be considered a suspect without physical evidence. If they had a motive or opportunity." His coolness raises my pulse. My forehead feels tight.

"So, they have nothing on him? Leland is this innocent guy, and his neighbor, *me*, is going out of her mind for no reason?"

"That could be the case." He sighs. Condescending.

The next time you call, he's not going to call you back.

The helplessness I feel ignites my nerve endings, and sparks sizzle and race across bundles of neurons heading for my brainstem.

"Huh. I just realized something," I say, my voice clipped and cynical. "You don't know anything about this case. Not a thing. Detectives haven't shared information with you. The guy down my street knows more than you. He said Leland was flirting with her." I shove the word *flirting* off my tongue like Lou did, head high, shoulders back, but inside I'm quivering. "Why didn't you just tell me straight you knew nothing? Why waste your time, my time?"

I cringe at my poor manners and cruel accusations, and

hold my breath. I am crossing my fingers that he's embarrassed for me and he won't mention to Liz that her friend is a douche.

He sighs again. Not condescending, but annoyed. "Off the record. This is *off* the record. Ava's dad told detectives Leland took an interest in the girl. They hired him to paint interior walls, the kitchen and bathrooms, I think. He was there, painting, for a week and he talked to Ava a bunch of times. He was trying to teach her to whistle."

My breath catches. His casual tone is like steel wool rubbing against my tender eardrum. *He was trying to teach her to whistle.* It sounds innocent, yet it sounds lewd. I gnaw at wet, rubbery skin along my thumb, biting tiny pieces off, willing myself to not interrupt.

"He asked her what she wanted for her birthday. Asked her what color her room was painted. One day he gave her a Happy Meal toy. A Shopkin character."

Chuck definitely has a kid. No other reason to know about Shopkins: plastic, thumb-size figures which personify food items or accessories. A happy, wide-eyed root beer float. A winking, long-eyelashed ice cream sundae. A coquettish handbag. Chloe has about thirty of them.

"Ava's dad let her keep the toy, but he didn't like the gesture. She goes missing a week later," Chuck says. "They interviewed Leland once and didn't get anywhere. That is *all* I heard."

Dang, Chuck. You didn't even make me work that hard.

Maybe because it's the weekend and he's working from home. Maybe he's barefoot, sitting on his deck, sipping coffee. Maybe he's in his boxer shorts. Maybe he's hungover.

But I'm pretty sure it's because I called him an out-of-the-loop loser, and it got to him.

I open my mouth, ready to probe into what else Ava's dad might have told detectives, but I glance at the sandbox.

Empty.

Wyatt is on the swing, gazing into the tree canopy. The other swing is bare.

"Thanks, Chuck. I've got to go." I try to open the screen, but it jams. I fixed the damn thing last week. I knock the screen door off track and, as I run into the grass scanning for a pink T-shirt, the screen crashes onto the deck behind me.

"Chloe! Wyatt, where's Chlo?"

I am running toward the side of the house.

Oh God, if she ran to the front yard! She doesn't have the no-street-thing down. *Oh God.*

"She's over there, Mom," Wyatt says, unworried, pointing toward the shed.

I breathe, Wyatt's calm voice lulling me back, and turn.

There she is, smiling beside my daylilies, hedge clippers in her small hands. My heart stops. Sunlight accentuates the blade's sharpness as she opens and closes the clippers. If those things can cut a small tree, they could easily slice off one of her fingers. Or pierce her neck.

"Baby," I say gently, trying not to alarm her or make her run and trip, but my voice cracks. "Baby, you're helping Momma with gardening. You're so sweet. Let me get you a shovel so we can dig weeds." Her eyes sparkle with mischief. It's likely she's considering turning this into a game of hedge-clipper tag.

Every moment feels a millisecond from disaster.

"A caterpillar! Look, Chlo," I point to a bush and swipe the clippers from her hands.

"Where's a caterpillar?"

"It was just there," I lie. "Maybe he crawled under the leaf. Let's look."

Don't be mad at Wyatt. He's not your babysitter.

"Where is it?" As she peeks under leaves, she trips on who-knows-what in the grass. I catch her by the armpit before she falls.

"Let's take a popsicle break," I say, my body already anticipating ten minutes of calm. My children eat popsicles with utmost focus and silence. Like surgeons excising a sticky, pervasive tumor.

Wyatt mumbles sarcastically. Something about it being early for a popsicle break.

Letting my guard down, I glance over at Leland Ernest's house.

He is standing on his small cement porch, sipping from what appears to be a juice box with a small straw. Head tipped back, he's gazing up at the sky. No, his eyes are closed.

I have only seen him a handful of times since I moved in. Unfortunate for bad stereotypes, he *looks* like he walked straight out of a Flannery O'Connor novel. He is mid-thirties. His skin is the white and doughy shade of someone who stays inside. His belly is soft and stretches his shirt. His hair is straw blond.

Each time I have seen him, I've greeted him in a conservative, but friendly, neighborly way. But that was before I knew.

He glances toward my house now. His lips release his juice box straw, and he waves at me.

He was trying to teach her to whistle.

I picture Leland licking his lips, puckering them, and blowing softly. I picture him watching Ava's mouth as he instructs her to do the same.

My belly feels slippery, full of squirming fish, their silvery scales flashing as they whisk. I consider marching over there and telling him I know what he's done even though I know nothing. I consider giving him the finger.

"Momma, I want them juice box too."

Ignoring his wave, I gaze down at my daughter.

"What's wrong, Momma?"

"Nothing. I'm fine, baby." I smile and, through my blurry eyes and under bright sunshine, her white-gold hair shimmers like jewels on water.

These past five days I have told myself, *This is not a big deal. He is only a suspect. Don't let his proximity hold your peace captive.* Today I told myself we have had a gentle morning, a good morning, but it is a lie.

My children are playing twenty feet away from a man suspected of kidnapping a small child.

She's been missing five months. Murdering *a small child.*

He has had my heart squeezed in his grubby palm the whole morning: while we picked raspberries, while we swung, while I watched Wyatt smile and Chloe giggle.

Like the bees in my shed, he hovers in the dark composting

corner of my mind. His presence is a subtle but frightening vibration, a hum.

I look over at my neighbor's house again. His cement slab of a porch is sunny and bare, holding nothing more than a chair and a plastic pot of marigolds. He is nowhere in sight.

The doorbell rings inside my house.

6

PEACE BE WITH YOUR VAGINA

My ex. Nate.

If he'd have cheated once, I would have stayed. Five times, he was wiping his ass with my soul.

He's wearing green scrubs and his forehead is shiny. It doesn't matter that he's glossy from sweat, his healthy glow and career's importance emanate from him like an aura. Standing on the other side of my dingy screen door, he seems out of place, simulated and artificial.

Comfort and nostalgia wash over me because he knows me, intimately. Understands me. He is my best friend.

The warm and fuzzy feelings don't stick.

Desperation emerges and power-washes nostalgia to smithereens. I want to be rescued *so bad*. Financial woes are elbowing to the frontlines of my brain along with a list of half-broken appliances needing strong hands and patience. I have neither.

Desperation is as fleeting as nostalgia.

Anger blooms and strangles desperation until it wilts. *We*

have rules. He broke the rules, coming here unplanned. Kids need consistency, not more confusion. And damn him for tearing our lives apart.

As if my emotional spectrum is not maddening enough, blood rushes to my center. I miss his fingers skating down my stomach. I miss the rough brush of his jaw stubble against my neck in the morning. I miss his smell: harsh soap and a touch of woodsy aftershave.

Nate is intelligent, friendly, compassionate, and handsome. All terrible ingredients for fidelity.

His hair is sandy blond and falls into a casual sweep across his forehead. His eyes are dark and mischievous. A long time ago those eyes lured me and, on so many occasions, his playful eyes got him out of trouble.

I open the screen and try to smile. "You should have called first."

"I know," he says, his eyes scanning my turtleneck, "but I heard about your ER visit and wanted to make sure you were alright."

No need to ask how he heard. He works at St Joe's. I figured word might get to him.

"I'm fine. You should have called instead."

As if cued, their sneakers stampede the hall behind me. Chloe screams with excitement, "Daddy!"

"Can I come in?" he says.

I give him a look—like I have a choice?—and step aside.

He walks in and catches Chloe, pulling her into a swinging hug.

"Hi, Dad," Wyatt says and gives Nate a good hug from the side.

Nate musses Wyatt's hair and kisses his forehead. "Hey, Wy." Nate could be an amazing parent, the best actually, if he wasn't always at work. GI surgeons occasionally live at the hospital.

Can't stay home when I'm trying to save the world one colon at a time. Got to go put my fingers in someone's belly button.

That used to be his joke. He'd tickle the kids' bellies as he said it. The joke used to be tired but good, something to rely upon, but became unbearable when I found out he'd been putting his fingers inside several nurses as well.

After the superstar greeting is over, Wyatt disappears (TV calling), and Chloe walks up the stairs. Beyond the staircase spindles her little legs and bare feet trek arduously.

Where did her shoes and socks go? She was just wearing them.

"Daddy, I'll hide," she says. "You come find me."

"Sure thing. I'll count to twenty. Go hide." To me, he says, "How did it happen and where did it happen and who was with the kids?"

All his questions are rich with concern, but punctuated with accusation.

If I answer honestly, I am bound to be found guilty of bad parenting. If I tell him I left the kids home alone for eleven minutes, he'll be pissed. Which makes me furious. He wouldn't stand a chance of taking care of them around the clock, so what gives him the right to judge?

"It's not a big deal. Valerie was watching them." It's only a lie if put into context. "As for my neck, it's a few scratches. The ER doctor—"

"Erica," he says. He's probably fucking her too. Hospitals

are big fuckfests. Everyone working nights, already in their pajamas, close-call adrenaline rushes every few hours, limbs brushing against limbs as they squeeze past portable equipment and beds in tight rooms.

"She said I'd be fine. She gave me the first vaccine."

"Can I see?" he says, reaching for the lip of my turtleneck. His finger grazes my skin, and I pull away. I can't handle his touch. Even after a long night working in a nasty, bacteria-laced hospital, his lingering aftershave and testosterone smell is alluring. His proximity makes my skin tingle with need.

"I don't want to redo my bandages. I'm fine."

He sighs, staring at my face.

Worried my eyes will reveal how much I miss his touch, I gaze down.

Dog hair has rolled itself into balls and taken residence along grimy molding. The oak floor, scratched and faded, is speckled with black, sticky-looking patches. That can't be gum, can it?

"Make sure you get the full series of four shots," he says, condescending. "But let me know the minute you have side effects. Rabies vaccinations can mess with people."

At the bottom of the stairs, he sings, "Ready or not, here I come," and pounds his shoes slowly and loudly upon each stair for ambience.

I follow him up. "What kind of side effects?"

"Anything from dizziness and nausea to vertigo to neurological issues. Reflex and sensory changes, spinal infection..."

But some of those symptoms are normal for me.

Of course I can't tell him. If I have health issues making me incompetent, he could take the kids from me. If I seek treatment for mental health issues, he could take the kids from me. If I move the kids next door to a suspected kidnapper, which I accidentally did, he could take the kids from me. Every thought of mine has to be filtered by my internal lawyer before I speak.

Chloe is naked in the tub. She's already turned on the water and plugged the drain. The kid is three going on ten. She'll be asking to use the stovetop by kindergarten. A tiny pink spoon in her hand, she stirs water in a plastic teacup.

Nate says, "Hey, pumpkin-head, I thought you were going to hide."

"I'm taking a bath because I didn't want to get sand in my bed. I was playing in the sand." On the narrow ledge of the tub, she lines up plastic teacups and dinosaurs, then fills the cups to the brim with water. All those balancing cups, the floor will be soaked in minutes. I toss down a towel.

While she plays in the tub, I sit on the toilet lid and I tell him about my run-in with the bats. Leaning against the door, he listens, stone-faced and skeptical as a police officer, as if I'm trying to lie my way out of a ticket.

"I'm all done," Chloe says, already climbing out. I wrap her in a towel. She turns back toward the tub. "Look at all the sand. My vagina made the tub all dirty," except she pronounces vagina *bagina*.

It would have been funny and adorable had I not felt wobbly. Instead, my feminist, protective, angry momma kicks in.

Your vagina did nothing wrong. Nothing is your vagina's fault. It's not dirty. It's healthy and exactly as it should be! It is not the source of any man's problem. It is part of your body and will let you become a mother if you want. Love your vagina. Peace be with your vagina. Your vagina is full of rainbows and sunshine!

I say, "You had sand in your diaper and between your toes, didn't you? And all that sand got rinsed off your skin into the tub, and now your skin feels happy."

Chloe ignores my proper explanation and flees, naked and giggling, out of my arms. For a half-second before her feet reach carpet, I worry her wet feet will slip on the ugly vinyl the scrap of bathroom rug couldn't cover. "Don't run; you'll slip," I call, my voice rising and trembling. I follow them into her room.

Nate sings "Three Blind Mice," Chloe's favorite nursery rhyme. He's marching and clapping, and she's naked and jumping on her bed.

I stand in the doorway, watching them, wishing we could go back to that time when we were a family, whole and unfractured.

Nate raises the blinds (cordless, of course), and my pulse hitches.

"Oh no," I say. "Keep the blinds closed."

"Who's looking? It's morning. Sun's out." He points at the blue sky as if I were an idiot.

My voice lowers a register. "Please close the blinds."

He tilts his head at my request. "Are you taking a higher dose of—"

"Nate." Quick and sharp. This is all I have to say. We've

had this discussion before. No open talk about medications in front of either child.

Wyatt crosses the hallway into his room, a Goosebumps book in his hand. Chloe continues jumping on the bed, singing, "*See how they run.*"

"Close them," I say, but movement beyond Chloe's window catches my attention.

Behind my neighbor's second-story window, a small hand presses against the glass at the bottom ledge. Above the splayed fingers, brown curls frame a little girl's face. Her cheeks are soft and round, still holding tight to baby fat. Her lips are slightly parted; she was going to say something, but forgot. Air shimmers before my eyes as if it hangs above an asphalt road on a hot day after a steamroller pressed new oil. I blink. Her fingers are so small. I rub my palms into my eyes and blink again.

She's gone. The window glass has a slight ugly green tint, a characteristic of energy-efficient windows. *Even if someone* had *been there, you wouldn't be able to make out detail through the tint. You're seeing things. You've been here before. You just need sleep.*

Nate lowers the blinds and softens his tone. "You seem anxious, Grace. Everything OK?"

Skin along my back and shoulders tingles. Heat is coming off me. *Why, yes! Everything is dandy since you fucked a handful of nurses and I moved into this crumbling house next door to a possible child killer and several times a day I feel the floor drop an inch away from me and now I'm seeing things. Everything is fabulous, dear.*

I smile. "Everything's fine."

7

FERRET OUT THE ASSHOLE

Even though unpacked boxes still linger in corners—as if I'm expecting them to eventually cave and unpack themselves—I seriously consider selling my house. After Nate leaves, I dig out my financial statements and punch numbers into a calculator.

It doesn't take long for me to realize I can't do it.

My mortgage is underwater or upside down or fucked sideways. Whatever derogatory name bankers use for crummy mortgages as they stare condescendingly down their noses, that is my mortgage. The housing market has dipped since I bought. I have accrued debt from the divorce. I swear my lawyer charges me if I even think about calling her. Also, I make a hair above minimum wage. Money-wise, caring for people's most beloved cargo, stimulating these small children's brains, teaching them manners and kindness and important life-coping skills, ranks just above dropping a wire basket of frozen French fries into boiling oil.

Yes, my ex is a surgeon. But the student debt he amassed is massive, and his salary has chipped it to a smaller, yet still nauseating size. Three more years of student loan purgatory and he will be free; birthed, wet and shiny, into upper class. To my shaky mind, three years sounds like eternity, abstract and useless.

I have no financial safety net. My two living relatives are working stiffs.

Mom is sixty-seven, works as a receptionist in a cancer screening center, and has far less money saved than she'd ever envisioned. My father's Alzheimer's and lung cancer combo lasted too long, required too much at-home care, and ate away at their retirement at the steady, persistent pace cancer ate away at his innards and Alzheimer's at his memory.

My older sister works as a night auditor at a Holiday Inn to support her out-of-work-electrician husband and their four kids. She has been doing the zero-interest-rate-for-the-first-six-months credit card musical chairs game for years. At my mom's house on Easter, she joked about holes in her underwear. I mailed her underwear and socks on her birthday as a joke, and when she called to thank me, she laugh-cried.

Even if I had enough money to sell, how could I do that to the next family?

I am furious at the guy who sold me this house and have considered (several times in the middle of the night) hiring a PI to track him down. I have fantasized about spray-painting "soulless" on the front door of his new house.

Tony Durtato, the roofer.

I met Tony's three teenage daughters: thirteen, sixteen, and seventeen. If he moved to get away from the freak next door, how had he sold this house to me, a woman with a daughter?

Tony met Chloe. I held her on my hip, her sleepy head on my shoulder, a pacifier in her mouth, her security blanket cushioning her soft baby cheek. While we stood on his back deck and gazed at the swing set he'd built, he touched Chloe's little socked foot with the thick, callused knuckle of his forefinger, smiling and seeming to take in the moment. "I miss that stage," he said.

"So," I said, trying to sound casual, "are you moving because of a job change?"

"No," he said, still smiling at Chloe's sock.

"Why *are* you moving?" I said, upbeat, airy, eyebrows lifted.

He looked down at the deck, his eyes drifting to my right. I followed his gaze to a greasy stain he probably wished he'd covered with a pot of flowers. "Change of scenery," he said, his eyes lifting to me and Chloe. "We bought a house that has a little more space. My younger ones have always shared a room." His answer made sense and didn't seem rehearsed. Wanting more space was a good answer.

How could he have allowed me to think I was lucky, getting this house for such a great deal, when there's a copperhead den steps away?

Because he was out of his mind. Desperate. Not thinking.

The spray paint job is nothing more than vengeful daydreaming. I don't have money to ferret out the asshole.

Doesn't matter. Your neighbor is not *dangerous.*

In high-profile cases like child kidnappings, there are probably two or three dozen suspects. Leland Ernest gave a

Happy Meal toy to a girl who later went missing. Untimely generosity and kindness were his crimes.

Yeah? What about Lou's daughter?

Maybe a misunderstanding. Lou seemed easily triggered, which might make him prone to misunderstandings.

I shouldn't have bought this two-story, three-bedroom house. Yes, the rooms are all tiny, but still, it was indulgent. I should have bought a two-bedroom townhome. I just, well, I wanted a yard for the kids. When I was a kid, I had a yard.

Back home from grocery shopping, I sit Chloe in front of the TV so Wyatt and I can bring in the groceries. He brings in the milk, but gets distracted by Chloe's show, *The Backyardigans*. Wyatt loves the songs. I don't bother nagging him because it will take too much effort. Besides, they're sitting side by side on the couch, their shoulders touching, and that gives me a sense of peace. With the cheery backdrop of cartoon music, I bring the groceries inside and put away the food. I set a pot of water on the stove. Spaghetti night. Most nights are spaghetti night.

"Hey, Chlo, would you like a piece of cheese while you're waiting for dinner?" I say, turning on the flame.

She doesn't answer.

"Yoo-hoo, Chloe?" I sing, trying to up my game to compete with the TV. "Chloe, are you hungry?"

No answer.

I walk to the edge of the kitchen and scan the TV room.

Wyatt is upside-down on the couch, his head resting on the carpet. Chloe is gone.

"Where's Chloe, Wyatt?"

"What?" he says. "She's not here?"

Relax. This happens all the time. But my heart is racing as I move to the stairs. "Chloe, are you up there?" I say, keeping my voice even and upbeat as I take the stairs two at a time. She's not in her room. "Chloe?" Ditto for Wyatt's room, my room, and the bathroom.

"Chloe, please answer me. I'm worried." I don't bother keeping it upbeat anymore. I move down the steps too quickly, slipping on a stair near the bottom. I grab the handrail and keep my balance, but feel a quick twist in my back muscles and wonder if tomorrow it will be hard to move.

I jog to the kitchen.

The sliding glass door is open.

How did I miss that before? She must have walked out when I was making a trip into the garage for more groceries. That was ten, fifteen minutes ago. My pulse is drumming and my neck is slick as I imagine the danger a three-year-old can get herself into within the span of fifteen minutes. Fifteen minutes is like a lifetime. Like the end of a life.

I rush out, no need to slide the screen because I busted that off the track yesterday and it's still leaning against the siding.

Chloe's on her belly on the swing. Her legs dangle, and she's bent her knees so that her bare feet don't touch the ground as she swings. *She's fine. See. You don't always have to go apeshit. Things are almost always fine.* Trying to catch my breath, I cross the grass to her. She has something squeezed tightly in her hand. It's sticking out from her closed fist.

A metal-on-metal gliding *swoosh* catches my attention, and my eyes follow the sound to Leland Ernest's back porch. His glass door sliding open. He's stepping inside. My eyes catch his bare calf and bare foot, skin pale, before he's gone. His glass door *swooshes* shut.

My heartbeat picks up again. "Hey, Chloe, what do you have there?"

"Nothing," she says, her mouth full, her saliva crackling.

Her dirt-dusted toes push off against the ground. There's a wrinkled candy wrapper there in the dirt, the waxy paper white and brown, and her toes graze it.

"Can I have a piece?" I say.

Lifting her face to me, she smiles. She loves sharing. "Sure, Momma." She opens her tiny sweaty hand and holds out three Tootsie Rolls for me. I take one.

The Tootsie Roll always struck me as an inferior candy. A cheap candy that grandmas kept in lidded bowls, uneaten, uncoveted, hardening over months, years. A chocolate-bar wannabe. A rugged, unmeltable, unbreakable candy suitable for war and being whipped down onto asphalt like a Pop-Its snapping firecracker. If I were a deviant, if I were mentally warped, if I were a suspect in a child kidnapping, the candy I would always have handy in my pocket? The fucking Tootsie Roll.

I don't keep Tootsie Rolls in my purse or my house. It's possible my mom does. It's possible that Chloe's got a stash of

Tootsie Rolls in her room, courtesy of Grandma.

"Thank you for sharing," I say sweetly, my heart jack-hammering. "Did you get those from our neighbor?"

"Uh-uh." She shakes her head. "I'm not supposed to take candy from strangers." She looks up at me, her eyes wide and questioning. She's testing me. *Fuck.*

I smile and say sweetly, "Where'd you get it, then?"

"I forgot."

"Did you get it from your room?" This is altogether possible. I have found chocolate chips inside Chloe's jewelry box, crackers and crumbs in one of her little kid purses, and a sandwich bag of Dum Dums under her pillow.

The Fourth of July parade was two months ago. It seems unlikely that she'd exercise the restraint to keep a small bag full of candy. It seems entirely likely that she lost her bag of parade candy in her cluttered room and recently discovered it. There's nothing more joyous than finding something you thought you'd lost or better yet, forgot you'd lost.

Her face is aimed down again as she swings. Her wispy, blown hair is snow white and shiny as the silky, moist seeds bursting from a split milkweed pod. Air breathes through her hair, lifting it, letting it fall. Her little toes arch and press against the oval dirt patch below the swing where grass won't grow. "I think so," she says.

"Is it the candy from the parade we went to?" I sound steady, but my shoulders quiver.

"Probably," she says, her voice rising to a question.

"Did you talk to our neighbor?"

She gazes up with questioning eyes and says, "I'm not supposed to talk to strangers."

"That's right, but you can tell me if you did. Did the man in that house," I point, "come over and say hello?"

"I don't think so," she says.

Fuck. I shouldn't have asked her leading questions. I put ideas in her mind and gave her an easy way out.

What upsets me more, brings me to the verge of tears, is that I've failed her as a parent. She's either scared of breaking the rules or scared of the repercussions so that she, as a tiny three-year-old, doesn't feel at ease speaking the truth. *She's only three.*

"Chloe, can I take those other two candies and save them for after dinner?"

"Sure, Momma." She hands me the other two candies, and I put them in my pocket.

"Thanks, Chloe. It's fine if you play in the backyard, but you need to tell me before you go outside. OK?"

"I know," she says, a stubborn bossiness creeping into her voice.

I open my mouth—about to ask her well then why didn't she?—but stop. They tune me out when I talk too much. I turn toward the house, unwrap the one she gave me, and pop it into my mouth.

I am checking for a chemical taste, for a taste that's anti-freeze sweet or rat-poison bitter. I am assessing if I should rush her to the hospital. *If it's poisoned, then you've poisoned yourself too.*

It tastes fine. Fresh. Better than I remember Tootsie Rolls tasting. When's the last time I ate a Tootsie Roll? A decade ago? Two decades ago?

I bite into it, severing it with my teeth, not sure if I'm comfortable with the fact that I'm probing for a small bit of razor or some sickly oozing poison that he injected inside. My teeth sink into firm chewy chocolate with a hint of plastic. No razors. No bitter poison.

She found the candies in her room or in the car or in Wyatt's room or behind the couch. That's the obvious answer. No adult is going to walk over and give a toddler candy. Not in this stranger-danger, food-allergy-aware, personal-space day and age.

Of course he didn't give her candy. Of course he didn't. You need to calm the fuck down, Grace. It was a complete coincidence that he was outside at the same time as Chloe. What, your family is the only one allowed outside? It's a gorgeous day, sunny, not hot, slight breeze, no mosquitoes. If anyone were going to sit outside, this would be the day.

Still, I gaze one more time at my neighbor's house. *If you talk to my daughter again, if you give her candy again, I'll slit your throat.*

We eat spaghetti and a big bowl of peas for dinner. I fight the screen back onto the door's track. We play hopscotch in the driveway.

I try to tell myself, *It has been a good day. The kids are happy and healthy. You get to be with them way more than Nate does. You have done nothing to deserve any of it, yet here it is,* but it doesn't stick. My breathing is jagged.

With the bathroom door open, Wyatt relaxes in the tub: humming, creating bubbles between his fingers, and blowing a bird whistle. When he's finished, he hangs his towel on the hook instead of tossing it on the floor to mold and—bonus— he brushes his teeth.

"Mom," he says, standing outside the bathroom in his robe, "I can unload the dishes before I go to bed."

"Thank you, kiddo, but I'll take care of the dishes." I press my lips to his warm, moist forehead. I hold his cheeks and smile at him. "You're such a good boy."

After one book in the rocking chair, Chloe tells me she loves me and falls asleep quickly.

Occasionally I think I have the most amazing kids.

Just wait. They will turn on you. Under pressure, they turn into monsters. Under grave pressure, most people do.

8

I KNOW MORE THAN I SHOULD

The papers mentioned, offhandedly, Ava Boone is *such* a lovely name—*a great actress's name!*—but all I could think of was the cheap flavored wine we drank in college. *Boone's Farm Strawberry Hill.* I swear we got a bottle for a buck and a quarter.

To bottom-shelf hyperglycemic drinkers like me, Ava Boone sounds trashy. Makes me want to believe this girl lives on the edge of the city near the flat-roofed warehouses and railroad tracks. Makes me want to believe her hair is matted with knots, she's playing unsupervised in the street, and she's never been to the dentist. I would like to picture her dad in prison states away, and her mom having too many visitors (stringy women and dirty-jeaned men).

But this isn't Ava. Her parents are married, her family is well-rounded and whole, a crisp-apple family. Railroad tracks are closer to my house than hers. In all the photos, she has a buoyant, genuine smile on her face and her hair is clean and combed. Solid middle class, borderline upper class. Cute slate-blue ranch-style house with an octagon window in the cathedral foyer. Clean vinyl siding. Two-car garage. Skyline cedar playset in the backyard with one of those yellow-and-blue striped canopies over the platform slide.

A sweet, shiny-apple family.

It happened on a Friday night. Ava's older siblings, Mason and Lila, were kicking off their spring break vacations by having sleepovers at friends' houses. Ethan and Natalie tucked Ava into bed around 9pm and when they woke in the morning, the little girl's window was open, the screen was cut, and Ava was gone. No sign of a struggle. Carpet near the window wet with rain, puddles on the sill.

No one heard anything or saw anything.

There was a small party next door, maybe a dozen kids. Teenagers walking in and out the front door, vaping on the curb beside the car-crowded street, hugging and handshaking, all long arms, poor posture, and quick movements. Their quiet talking punctuated by eruptions of laughter.

There was a larger party across the street. Adults drinking sweet wine and bottled ale around a fire pit in the backyard, talking loudly, moving slowly. Kings of Leon playing in the house where the women who couldn't get warm huddled, gossiping in their socks and sweaters, stuffing vegetable sticks in their mouths, fingering the little decorative rings hooked to the foot of their wine glasses so they could tell their glasses apart.

Both parties broke before midnight because it started raining.

Police interviewed everyone who attended the parties. Nothing peculiar was reported.

Strangers account for less than five percent of child abductions. Statistics point to family members in most cases.

Kilkenny police never mentioned they suspected the parents, but everyone knew they did, *assumed* they did. *It's always the parents.* Except police didn't find evidence indicating Ethan or Natalie. If they had, something would have happened by now. As far as we knew, neither Ethan nor Natalie had a motive. The Boones were a happy family. No skeletons. No prior run-ins with the law. Squeaky clean. A waxy, light-reflecting, perfect apple.

Ethan Boone is a middle-school social studies teacher in Talilah, the town west of ours. He coaches girls' basketball. On the news and in the papers, his co-workers and students described him as humble and goofy, two key traits to being well-liked by mercurial thirteen-year-olds.

Natalie Boone is a social worker. She counsels troubled teens at a non-profit organization called Talilah One-Eighty. Part-time, so she can be around for her kids. Ava, 5. Lila, 13. Mason, 16.

The papers painted Lila as a straight-A student, a basketball star with a good group of friends. They portrayed Mason as a C student. A little bit of a troublemaker, but in a good-natured way. He got an occasional detention in order to draw a laugh from a schoolmate.

Natalie Boone has a sister, Sarah, who lives an hour south and works the night shift as a hospice nurse. She worked that Friday night, providing in-home care and pain relief for cancer patients. She was eliminated as a suspect.

Ethan has a brother, Luke, who lives with his wife and two kids seven states away. Luke works for United. Twelve-hour night shifts, four days a week, sitting at a computer and managing plane routes. Again, eliminated as a suspect.

All four of Ava's grandparents are deceased.

I don't know everything about Ava and her family, but I know more than I should. I know Ava was a happy accident, conceived a week after Ethan Boone got a vasectomy. I know Natalie Boone took three months off work when Ava went missing, but now she's back to working part-time. I know Ava liked to dig in the dirt for red centipedes and go fishing with her dad, that she had her own tackle box with pretty, feathery bobbers. I know she dressed as a ninja for Halloween last year. I know Mason got three-days' suspension a few weeks ago for getting in a girl's face, screaming at her, and grabbing her shoulders. I know Ava had been begging for a puppy, and her dad used to take her to Pet Supplies Plus on Sundays after church. I know she occasionally wet the bed. I even know their address. Of course I've driven by their house. *Of course.*

How would I know all this unpublished, private information?

Teachers' lounge. The teachers' lounge of a preschool is a rich source of neighborhood gossip. So many mothers dishing dirt on their neighbors and friends to their child's teacher, trying to force a bond, show their value, win favor, earn private classroom details.

These are snippets that co-workers and parents have told me, with eyes wide and voices hushed, leaning in so close with pumpkin coffee breath or a smear of moist, cakey lipstick across their front teeth:

-My neighbor's daughter plays basketball with Ava's sister. She says Lila is kind of a bully. Not terrible, but that she's all elbows on the court.

-Did you know that Ava's brother can't stop crying? Isn't that odd? I mean, I guess it's not. It's survivor's guilt or something.

-One of Ethan Boone's students said he touched her shoulder inappropriately during class. But I'm sure it's nothing. Everyone else, students and teachers, gush about him.

-I wonder which one of them posted the video. Strange that no one knows, isn't it?

The first five days, officers and volunteers continuously raked nearby forests and prairies, wrapped in sweaters and mittens, armed with flashlights and water bottles. We had a lucky streak of warm April weather so it was possible the girl was lost somewhere nearby and not yet hypothermic. Divers trawled the two ponds in the Boones' neighborhood. Police used a heat-seeking drone.

Even when the warm spell broke and temperatures dropped dramatically, frost tipping the grass, search parties kept going out.

It was right around the one-month mark when people slipped into past tense when they mentioned Ava's name, and they stopped mentioning her every day. The PTA-organized call center was still running out of the local church, but there were only two or three working it; people had to go back to work, drive their kids to practice, shop for groceries.

After two months the search for Ava Boone had the

melancholic, deranged feel of Christmas decorations left out past April Fools' Day, pieces scattered, cracked, and forgotten. No one said it, but everyone knew: Ava Boone was dead. And if she was still alive, well, that notion had the same scraped-out feel of things shattered and lost.

9

HOUSE BURNED TO THE GROUND

Sweating, lungs stretching, I jog up my driveway in the darkness. Baby monitor and phone in hand, I type in the key code for the front door. Anxiety grips my spine as I take the stairs two at a time. *You shouldn't have gone for a jog. You shouldn't leave them, not even for eleven minutes.* I tell myself this every night, but every night the urge to flee is stronger.

Chloe and Wyatt are peaceful in sleep, and the house is cool and still. I shower and put on pajamas. With my hair wet and my calf muscles sore, I grab my laptop.

I get comfortable in the queen-size bed Nate and I used to share. When we were splitting things up, he said he didn't want it. Actually, he didn't want much, which implies generosity, but when I look around at our belongings—mountains of toys, second-hand furniture, boxes of old CDs and cassette tapes, an outdated TV—it's obvious he has scammed me yet again.

Our belongings are those of poor college students turned poor young marrieds turned child-safety-focused parents. In other words, everything we owned together is fairly shitty.

Last Christmas morning, at a time when he was no doubt fucking one of his co-workers, as we regarded the messy afterbirth of opened presents—sparkly red pieces of torn paper everywhere on the carpet, couch, and stuck to our feet by strands of tape; little doctor instruments and little Legos everywhere waiting to slice our soles—he'd said, "Wouldn't it be kind of nice if our house burned to the ground?"

Tired from wrapping into the early morning, I was too foggy to get his joke. "What?" I said.

"I mean, look at all our stuff. It's cheap and crummy. They have too many toys. If our house burned to the ground, we could start over and make it nice. Make better choices."

"I guess. As long as we all got out alive."

"Of course."

"And as long as we grabbed our visas and birth certificates because it would be a pain in the ass to get new ones."

"You're missing the point."

"As long as we grabbed the christening dress your grandma crocheted for you."

He smiled, softening and appreciating my joke. Every time he came across the hard, yellowed gown he frowned. He wanted to toss it but couldn't go through with it. She'd embroidered his name into the tag. "Yes, wouldn't want to lose my baby dress."

And so when he left, he didn't only unburden himself from screwing the same old, fidgety, dim preschool teacher, he unburdened himself from all our crappy stuff too. Probably bought himself an expensive lightweight TV, a nice La-Z-Boy, a classy set of dishes.

I search Ava's parents on social media. Ethan posted yesterday morning. *Not giving up hope. Anyone who knows anything, as unimportant as it may seem, please contact us.* But his words lack urgency. They are plain, uncompelling, impersonal. There's a phone number after his post, but it belongs to the police department. I've checked.

I yawn and check the time. 1:14am. I hope this isn't one of those days Chloe decides to start her day before sunrise.

I watch Ava's video. I've been watching it since she went missing, but this past week, my watching is compulsive.

I plug my laptop into a charger on the floor. I lie down and close my eyes, but my mind buzzes.

Ava's face behind Leland's window. Her brown curls. Her tiny palm. Her empty eyes. Her parted lips. What did she want to tell me?

You didn't see her. You know that, right?

It's been five months. She's dead. Everyone knows that.

I roll over and grab my phone. I open YouTube to watch Ava's video one more time.

10

TWIST THE HANDLE ON MY FRONT DOOR

It is her missing front tooth, the one on her right, and the fleshy gummy space remaining that gets you to smile at first. For a split second you wonder how she lost that tooth. Had she bitten into an apple, then pulled the apple away to see the fruit's white flesh stained by her own blood? Had she been horrified by the sight of her tooth, sticking out of the apple like a grotesque sculpture, small fibrous roots at the top like tiny worms? Had she cried out at her lost body part? Or had she yanked the loose tooth out herself and, gleeful and laughing, blood filling her mouth, held it up as if she'd discovered a treasure within her own body?

Then it is her side-to-side head bobbing, slow with Neil Young's folksy, timeless guitar strum. She's practically touching her ear to one shoulder and then the other. She's being silly, trying to hook a laugh from the cameraman.

Then it's her socks, striped pink and gray, pulled halfway up to her knees and mismatched with shimmery red ballet pumps, sequined Dorothy shoes that had once been fancy but were now scuffed and worn dull at the toes. She didn't just wear these shoes, she played *tag* in these shoes. Her white T-shirt has a cat's face on the front, and the cat's whiskers pop out stiffly from the shirt, making you worry about them getting caught in some crevice of the dryer. At the top of the shirt, there is a smeary, deep purple-blue stain, maybe from frozen blueberries, maybe from grape Kool-Aid. Her bright orange shorts have pink polka dots and they are short and snug.

She wears her syrup-brown wavy hair in two side pigtails, pulled together haphazardly, one landing higher than the other. This is a strong-willed child who can do her own hair, thank you very much.

The goofy outfit and the stain convey an impromptu video. No stage parent would dare dress their kid this shoddy while striving for YouTube fame. Unless their strategy was cleverly contrarian. Viewers hate an over-processed, over-coached child beauty queen. Maybe the parents were working off that script and had meticulously created a costume that appeared child-driven and authentic.

She is pretty in the way that most five-year-old girls are pretty. Flawless skin, chubby cheeks, and bright eyes. Brown hair that has a beachy, salt-wind sheen, both stringy and shiny. Old ladies who'd long ago tweezed their eyebrows, only to draw them back on when that was the trend, would comment on the girl's luscious eyebrows, full and expressive.

Then Ava Boone opens her mouth and sings the first line of Neil Young's wistful "Harvest Moon". Her voice takes you by surprise at first because it is hoarse and deep-toned for a small child. Then chills prickle along your scalp because, *wow, this little girl can sing*. She grasps melody and nuance, so unnatural for a five-year-old. And she isn't just a lovely singer, she is a *performer*. She holds her eyes wide and serious, then she breaks into a huge smile.

She is a beat behind on a few of her lines, and the man playing guitar, you assume it is her father, softly sings a few verses with her. Besides her slight lisp from the missing tooth and needing a little help with the lyrics, Ava Boone nails it. She makes you remember, *Oh,* this *song. I haven't heard this since my cousin's wedding. This is a great song.*

After the chorus, she decides she's done. To make her finale memorable, she strikes this surprising pose. All at once, she shoots her arms out to the sides like a tightrope walker, abducts one of her legs, and tilts her head sideways, sticking her tongue out. She holds the pose for a moment, as if a photographer has said, *OK, kids, now give me a silly pose.* It's right as she strikes this hyperactive pose that the video ends, and you're left staring at the frozen image of her laughing eyes, wide open mouth, and tongue skewed to the side. This static image haunts parents' minds everywhere.

Even though the video is gripping, it didn't go viral when it was first posted. Her video didn't get played on *Entertainment Tonight*, and she didn't get a call from *Ellen*. Her acoustic rendition of "Harvest Moon" went unnoticed for weeks.

But fame loves tragedy. Two days after she went missing, her one-minute nineteen-second video had over four million views. Some people posted offshoots of the video, dissecting, narrating their characterization over her singing, proselytizing the tragedy of child beauty queens and parents pushing their children toward the bright, luring yet dangerous flames of fame. *I bet they don't wish they drew attention to their beautiful child now.* They talked about her magnetic personality. In hushed, apologetic tones, they said, *You could see how someone would be drawn to her energy.*

People like you, like me, watch the video compulsively, yet secretly, hiding our Ava Boone viewing as if it were porn—*Oh, yes, I've heard of the video. No, no, I haven't seen it. Tell me about it.*

We watch it as a cautionary tale, as a reminder to not put our children on display, to resist the urge to brag-share our children's beauty, talent, intelligence, and wit. Keep our children's gifts secret. Bottle their personalities up and keep them for ourselves. The Boone family shared Ava with strangers, and then a stranger took Ava away.

We watch because she is enchanting. Most five-year-olds can't keep their eyes focused on the same location for ten seconds; this one stares right at us, bewitching us with her voice and demure while singing a memorized song. Here is a clever girl with a mind of her own who likes to dress herself and, as mismatched as she is, ends up appearing stylish. We like her, we want to be near her.

We watch because the video has an exclusive, private feel, and we are voyeurs at heart. Soft in the background is a man's gentle voice. He must be the one improvising on guitar. His chords are experienced, yet imperfect. This is a tender, spontaneous moment between father and daughter, and we, as mothers, cannot resist.

We watch the video to crack the case. We search for clues. What is her father doing off-stage? Is he relaxed and smiling, an old hippie strumming his guitar? Or is he pushy and menacing behind the camera, mouthing, *eye contact, eye contact!* The camera never wobbles. He must have propped it. Twice she scratches her neck under her hair. Is she a fidgety, sweaty, itchy child or is she trying to send a signal? There's a laminated world map behind her to the left. Is that red pushpin in Ontario, Canada? Why Ontario? That small fluff of white blanket to her far right, that's someone's bed, isn't it? Is this the parents' bedroom? The wall is painted pale gray, an unlikely color for a little girl's room. Did the father do it? They say he had no motive; they say he had an alibi—not a great one, but an alibi—but *did the father do it?*

We watch the video to mourn the child. We may be self-seeking and vitriolic, we may be hideous and insatiable, we may be grabby monsters, but we are not heartless.

And we watch the video because we forgot how beautiful that song is. With its nostalgic harmonics and legato, it has always been a lovely, haunting song. Now it is haunted.

"Harvest Moon", a cornerstone of weddings, is stained for years to come by the raspy voice of a little girl lost.

I'm dreaming. *I'm walking in flip-flops in the street because there's no sidewalks. I lift the lid of someone's garbage bin, toss a bag in, and keep walking.*

Nine houses later, I ditch my flip-flops to another garbage bin. Barefoot now, I weave my way back to my street, where there are sidewalks lit by street lamps.

Twist the handle on my front door…

Something flutters against my cheek and I smack it. My heart hammering, I open my eyes to darkness.

Everything feels wrong.

Air is too moist, too cool, and steeped in smoke. There's a rustling noise overhead. Movement, too, but everything is blurry. *Your contacts are out.* My feet are cold. *You're barefoot.* My bed feels hard and straw-like. Strappy stringy things against my calves. *Because you're on the lawn chair/recliner thing.*

What?

I'm outside. Terror grips me. I roll out of the recliner and onto the deck as quickly as I can, which is not that quick. Kitchen light is on, illuminating my cluttered countertops and revealing that the sliding door is open, but the screen is closed. Cold and sweaty, I hustle inside and slide the glass door behind me as if I'm shutting out monsters. I flip the lock.

Wow. Sleepwalking outside. That's fucking *new*.

My hair feels strange. I pull off a black winter beanie. Weird.

Yes, but not weirder than sleepwalking outside.

I drop the beanie on the floor and make my way upstairs, graceful as a drunk. Both kids are sleeping, safe and sound. I collapse into bed, checking the clock before my eyes fall shut. 3:18am. I can get a few more hours.

11

WE DON'T BITE

At 5:17am I give up on sweaty, restless sleep, my calves choked by sheets, and search "sleepwalking" on my phone. I squint one eye shut and read with my remaining eye as if I'm straining to see through a microscope. I feel both exhausted and anxious, so reading with one eye seems like I'm striking a balance.

According to Mayo Clinic, a person who sleepwalks doesn't typically have memories of the incident. Symptoms range from a person sitting up in bed and opening their eyes to more complex behaviors such as driving, urinating (closets are a popular target), screaming, and violent attacks on the person trying to awaken the sleepwalker.

This last symptom chills me. Chloe and Wyatt are the only people who might try to wake me. Should I have them lock their doors at night? That seems alarmist, even for me.

Sleepwalking is most commonly triggered by fatigue, febrile illness, or medications.

Well, there you go, shithead. Fatigue. You haven't slept in days; you deserve to wake up outside in the lawn chair, wearing a beanie.

I google "Can Adderall cause sleepwalking?"

It can, but it's rarely a direct cause. Neurostimulants commonly disrupt sleep. Once someone becomes sleep-deprived, they might end up sleepwalking.

I strip off my sweaty clothes and run a hot bath, squirting cheap apple-scented shampoo into the stream of water because I am out of soap. In a zombie-like, hunched stupor, I watch bubbles grow. I ease into sudsy, sickly-sweet scented water, my limbs a little shaky. When water envelops my thighs, I push the moldy faucet knob off with my foot. I tip my head back against the tub, careful to keep my bandages above water.

A doctor might say, "Looking at your chart, it shows that your psychiatrist upped your Adderall dose weeks ago. I think the neurostimulants are at the root of your sleepwalking. You should lower your dose or take a break altogether."

I argue with this make-believe doctor's logic: But I was fine until this week. It's my neighbor. I can't sleep because of my neighbor.

"He's dangerous," I whisper, my morning voice stuck and phlegmy. I picture Chloe on her belly on the swing, her hair airy like dandelion fluff, a Tootsie Roll in her mouth and three more clutched in her hand.

Besides, I can't function without drugs.

Wyatt's ladder creaks. Seconds later, pee splashes into the toilet down the hall. He flushes, and Chloe whines.

Here we go.

By the time I have my underwear on, they are both

screaming. I poke my head through my shirt, and Wyatt storms in, furious and with tears in his eyes. "She bit me. If she bites me again, I'm going to bite her back."

"You can't, Wyatt. You're too big and you know better." I teeter on one leg as I shove my foot into pants.

"If I don't bite her back, she'll never learn. She'll kill someone and end up in jail for life."

Three years old on a one-way train to murder. Come on, Wyatt.

He is angry at her and too dramatic, but also worried for her future. Sweet, I suppose.

"You don't know what you're talking about," I say, "and don't say 'kill'."

"I know more than you," he says, then slams my door against my wall, denting the drywall—damn doorstop is busted—and storms out of my room. I stare at the cracked crater. This house is falling apart on its own, it doesn't need help.

You can't let him get away with putting holes in walls.

You don't have time for a brawl. Set them up for a positive day. Punish later.

I find Chloe in her closet, ripping pages out of a book.

"Chloe, if we rip up books, we can't read them anymore and we'll have to throw them in the garbage."

"Don't throw my books away. You a nasty girl, Momma. If you throw the book away, you gonna be in big trouble."

Can everyone just fuck off a little?

"Don't talk to me like that," I say, barely holding onto calm. "Do you want to come down for breakfast?"

"I want juice," she says, holding tight to her tiny blanket and reaching up for me.

I pick her up and carry her on my hip to the kitchen. "Chloe, if you are mad at your brother, come tell me. Don't bite. We don't bite."

"Shut your mouth, Momma." She jams her blanket against my mouth, smothering me. She means to suffocate me.

Yesterday the pair of them had been icing-sweet.

Today they are spoiled yogurt, sour and bloated, full of poison.

Under pressure, people turn into monsters. Everyone has different pressure points. Wyatt cracks when Chloe gets violent. Chloe cracks when—well, she's three; looking at her the wrong way infuriates her.

"We don't stuff blankets in people's mouths," I say. "Naughty spot." I set her on the step stool in the corner.

Chloe screams, cries, and flops her body sideways onto the floor. I pretend to ignore her display, but I'm sweating. Needing to put some distance between my ears and her screams, I retreat to the closet-sized laundry room. Mildew. Like a punch in the nose. Crap. I forgot to switch the clothes into the dryer. No better time than the present. I open the lid.

All the wet, spun clothes and the inside walls of the washer are covered in super-absorbent diaper balls. *Wonderful*. I fish the diaper out and close the lid. No time for this type of infuriating project right now.

Wyatt is doing his homework at the table. The kid had all weekend, of course he waits until right before school. I keep my mouth shut. "Do you want eggs or cereal?"

Hulk whines at the back door. "Gimme a second, Hulk."

"Eggs," Wyatt says. I crack two eggs in a pan and pop bread in the toaster.

I go to let Hulk out. She is gone, but she left a puddle of pee. Wyatt is slurping cereal.

"I thought you said eggs."

"I said cereal." He stares into his bowl. *Shovel, slurp, chew.*

I open my mouth to argue, I'm positive he said eggs, but what's the point? I want him out the door as quickly as possible.

Minutes later, I watch Wyatt ride his bike down the driveway. I tell him I love him. He hears me, but says nothing as he pedals away. I step away from my house until I'm on the sidewalk, my eyes moving back and forth from Wyatt's meandering, wobbling bicycle to my creepy neighbor's front door. Wyatt turns the corner. Out of sight. I hope the fresh air, the act of pedaling, the chirping birds will melt his anger, and he will arrive at school bright-eyed and full of peace.

An alarming smell hits me when I walk back inside. Eggs are burning. I hustle to turn off the stove.

Chloe is missing. Upstairs, a door closes. At least she's not out in the yard.

With paper towels I soak up Hulk's puddle of piss. I scoop Wyatt's burnt eggs onto a spatula and walk to Hulk's bowl. "Stay, Hulk." She sits beside her bowl, legs trembling as she waits, bug eyes hanging on my every move. Drool clings to her bottom lip. I drop the eggs on top of her kibble.

"Go ahead, girl."

She goes to work on the eggs as if she hasn't eaten in weeks.

At least someone's grateful. I fill her water bowl and set it down beside her feeding frenzy. "Next time, try not to piss on the floor, how 'bout it?" She stops eating, gazes up at me with her big eyes and tilts her head. She's a good dog. "Or, hell, just piss on the floor. I'll clean it up. My bladder is pea-sized too." She goes back to wolfing down her food.

Finally, I step up the stairs and peek into Chloe's room.

She's wearing a feather boa around her neck, watching herself in the flimsy floor mirror. She does a quick, little tippy-tap dance with her chubby feet, then strikes a pose for herself, throwing her arms out like a scarecrow and sticking out her tongue.

I shudder, filmy with sweat. *Someone walked on your grave.*

That pose, it's eerily familiar.

Ava.

Ava strikes a similar pose in her YouTube video.

So what? It doesn't mean anything. Of course it doesn't. Little kids are silly and expressive. It's not even the same pose. Ava balanced on one foot, her body teetering, leaning to the side.

Still, the association is grotesque.

No one walked on my grave. It was more like Chloe tippy-tap-danced on Ava's grave. Or maybe it felt like they were dancing together.

12

PUSSY PUSS

I drive to my babysitter's house, park haphazardly and crooked in her driveway, and briskly gather Chloe and her daycare bag.

Walking into Jill's house, I immediately notice something new.

He is mid-twenties, attractive, and athletic. He sits on the ground, legs crossed like a kid, building Legos with Dawson and Mandy.

Chloe stiffens to throw my balance off and break free of my clutches. She wiggles and shimmies down my body and runs over to join them.

"Who's this?" I ask Jill.

"My son, Zach," Jill says, all delight and serendipity. "He's in town for the week, visiting for a friend's wedding."

From the floor, Zach smiles at me. Kind eyes. Killer smile. Only problem is, I have been incessantly reading about kidnappings and child predators. Every night after the kids fall asleep, I'm online four or five hours, chewing the wet doughy skin edging my fingernails.

Who are your child predators? I can tell you. They are family members, stepfathers and uncles. Women, too, but come on, let's face it: it's men who are more often fucked in the head. More geniuses, more psychos. Yin and yang.

Who should you worry about most? Men who enjoy the company of children. This seems harsh until you think about it. Who the hell really enjoys playing with kids? Parents do it only because they are obligated.

OK, that's not entirely true. It's occasionally entertaining. And parents love their kids. More than those reasons, they do it because they want their kids to end up emotionally stable, capable, and intelligent.

But if you're not the parent and no one's paying you, why would you want to hang out with a small child? It's exhausting. Like doing a comedy act in an insane asylum while you're frying eggs and vacuuming shattered glass.

I pull Jill aside. "So, he's here all day with you?"

"This whole week! Isn't it wonderful? He loves kids."

Phenomenal.

"Chloe, I forgot your muggle in the car." Muggle is our word for pacifier. I can't remember how that one happened. "Come here, baby."

I scoop Chloe up and out we go. I buckle Chloe in and, when she protests, I tell her I forgot it was a special day. I call my mom. When she says she has the day off and of course she'll watch Chloe, I cross myself, forehead to chest, left and right.

Chloe whines. "Take me back. I want to play with the big

kid. I want to build Legos. Take me back. You a nasty momma. I'm gonna teach you a lesson."

"Chloe, quit being a sour puss. You're acting like Oscar the Grouch." Negativity isn't a good parenting technique, but tell me she doesn't deserve it.

At a stop light, I call work and tell them I'm going to be late. I am worried about getting fired, but I also occasionally fantasize about it. I have a college degree and make ten fifty an hour.

From the backseat, Chloe yells, "Mom, you're like Oscar. You're being a pussy puss."

Don't engage. I bite my bottom lip.

Can I avoid calling Jill?

No.

Shit.

I put my earbuds back in and call.

Make up an excuse.

You're too old to waste energy on excuses.

She picks up on the first ring. "Grace, what happened?"

"Sorry, Jill. I didn't mean to walk out without explaining, I didn't mean to behave rudely, but I want a female, mom-run daycare environment."

"What?" she says, but knows what I'm insinuating because hostility edges her voice.

"I'm sure your son is an amazing human being, the best, he is probably going to cure disease and solve world hunger. I'm not joking. I'm sure he is a far better person than I am, but I'm just sticking to statistics here. I don't want my daughter spending all day with any adult males besides her father."

"I can't believe what I'm hearing. My son is a generous, compassionate person."

Of course this is what all mothers say about their sons before they get sentenced to prison. Hell, mothers say it when their sons are *in* prison.

"I have a son too, Jill. Wyatt is amazing and precious and brilliant with little kids, but if some mom doesn't want him babysitting their kid because he's a boy, as much as that breaks my heart and maybe his heart, I get it. Everyone is looking out for their own kid, you know?"

Silence for a beat, then her voice crackles loud with static, "You are the only mother who has ever, ever said anything like this to me."

"I'm sorry, I'm looking at statistics."

"You know what? I don't think I can watch Chloe anymore."

"She's my kid, Jill. She's three." I end the call and pull into my mom's driveway.

From the backseat, "You are a pussy, Mom."

I am so not a pussy. I want to tell her, but figure saying the word "pussy" might solidify it into her growing vocabulary. So I do the one thing that deflates conflict: I agree. "You're right. Keep it between me and you, okay, kiddo?"

I open Chloe's door. She's wearing a different face than the one she was wearing when I put her in. "What's all over your face?"

"I'm a tiger," she says and holds up a Sharpie.

I unbuckle Chloe, and she wiggles out of her seat. She hops

out of the minivan and runs toward my mom, who's waiting in the frame of her open door.

My mom squints her eyes to make out Chloe's face. "What happened?"

"She got hold of a Sharpie while being buckled tight into a five-way harness. She's a magician maybe."

"No," Chloe says. "I'm a tiger."

"That's what I thought!" my mom says. "You look exactly like a tiger," which earns my mother a big wrap-around-the-leg hug of appreciation.

"What would I do without you, Mom?"

"Without me, you wouldn't have been born."

"Succinct." I kiss her cheek and inhale her scent. Floral, stale coffee, a hint of sour cheese. When I was a teenager, her smell made me queasy. Now it loosens my back muscles and makes me sleepy.

"I want a lollipop, and Mom's a pussy," Chloe yells and runs down the hallway, her feet bare. Where are her shoes?

My mom's eyebrows go up.

I shrug. "I made the mistake of calling her a sour puss."

13

A FUCKING MARBLE IN THE MOUTH

For being late to work, I get condescending you-are-not-worthy-to-work-with-these-genius-three-year-olds glares from two female supervisors sipping from ceramic mugs and sitting behind the glass wall of the front office.

As I walk into my classroom, Liz smiles at me and says in her enthusiastic-teacher voice, "We got to do circle time together, Miss Grace!" The kids don't notice her sarcasm; they only hear sugar. "And we are getting ready to eat snack together, Miss Grace! All fifteen of us! We brought all of our chairs into your classroom. Can you imagine how fun that was?"

Liz's class is next door. Our rooms share a miniature bathroom with a miniature toilet and miniature sink. Bathroom doors leading to both classrooms are always kept open unless someone is using the toilet, and even then sometimes a door is left open. Our three-year-olds combine for music class and playground time, and Liz and I cover for each other. At sixty-five, Liz is the oldest teacher who works this insane asylum. She is the teacher most requested by parents because, according to her, she oozes wisdom and goodwill.

I once told her, "Nah. You just remind them of their granny. Everyone loves their grandma."

To which she replied, "If you need to tell yourself that to explain your glaring lack of requests, you go right ahead, hon."

"Hey, that kind of hurts."

"Shit looks worse on your own spoon than when you were dishing out."

"Wow. Patronizing and disgusting in the same sentence. And yet, I still want to hug you."

"That's because I'm fat, bitch."

In all honesty, I don't want to get fired. And I don't work here only for health benefits. I adore Liz. She is a dependable person in my life, a source of humor, a constant.

I even enjoy the view of her. She doesn't throw an outfit together; she is one of those women who wears *ensembles*. Today she's wearing sleek black pants, one-inch heels, and a black blouse with splashes of large white and red flowers. Her earrings and necklace are eye-catching, but not gaudy. Her eyes are playful. Her dark skin glows. She is a lovely sight.

I say, "Good morning, children, and thank you, Miss Liz, for being here on time." I drop my purse on the counter and wash my hands. "You're the best, Miss Liz."

"I am the best," she says, hands on hips, smile wide open.

Elsie marches up to Liz. "You *are* the best, Miss Lizzy."

Students giggle and declare who they think is the best, from their dads to Mickey Mouse to their baby sister's diaper.

Some three-year-olds are washing their hands, some are

already sitting in their miniature chairs at a long rectangular table, fidgeting and waiting for grub. The bathroom door is wide open, and Mateo sits on the toilet with his pants around his ankles and his left shoe untied, laces dangling. He's talking with Ivy, who sits on the floor inches outside the bathroom door, trying to get her foot back into her shoe.

I jump in, helping with hand-washing and shoelaces. "Abbie," I say, "you are doing a great job pouring today." Abbie pours water from a small plastic pitcher into kids' tiny Dixie Cups. Liz sets graham crackers onto paper plates.

The kids are noisy and wacky and sweet, and it makes me miss Chloe. I enjoy these children, but would rather spend my time with my own three-year-old. Hamilton Academy has a no-way-in-hell-will-we-let-you-teach-your-own-kid policy. I couldn't afford to have Chloe in this school anyway.

Abbie hands me the miniature pitcher, I thank her, and she sits next to Shamus to join the cracker feast.

Abbie has these eye-catching ponytail holders: a single shiny red marble attached to a black rubber band, which loosely holds a pigtail on each side of her head. So loosely I'll bet my day's salary those ponytail holders will be on the floor before craft time.

Shamus, eyeing Abbie's hair, discreetly slides her ponytail holder from her hair and puts it directly in his mouth.

"Shamus, take that out of your mouth right now," I say, calm yet firm.

He shakes his head: no.

Abbie's hand goes to her hair. She searches the ground around her chair for her ponytail holder, oblivious to it being inside Shamus's mouth.

I sympathize with Shamus. Girls get all the sparkly, interesting clothes and accessories. Nevertheless, I move quickly toward him. I know he doesn't actually think it is food, but social norms can be challenging for him. And, a marble in the mouth is still a fucking marble in the mouth.

"It's not food and it's not safe for mouths. Take it out now." I hold my open palm under his chin.

He pushes his tiny chair back to make a run for it, but trips onto all fours.

Please don't let him swallow it.

I run around to his chair. His eyes are wide-open, shocked. He's not coughing, not speaking, his lips are parted. His open-mouthed silence is terrifying.

"Liz! Call 911!" I say, my voice rising.

Her dress shoes quickly *tap tap tap* toward the landline mounted on the wall. Our policy is call first, ask later. With noise and activity abound, she might not even know what happened.

I already have my arms around Shamus, my hands between his belly and sternum. I clasp my fist with my other hand and I yank back and up.

Nothing happens.

I do it again, harder. Hard enough I worry about breaking a rib.

He throws up graham cracker mush. Something pings the linoleum, and I spot the marble. One long second of silence before he breaks into a coughing fit.

I crouch in front of him, and my kneecaps crash painfully onto the floor. I hold his shoulders and inspect his face. His

95

skin is splotchy and red. His coughing is tapering off, but his crying is gaining momentum.

"It's OK, kiddo." I pull him into a hug. Wet mushy vomit soaks into my shirt. He smells of graham crackers and snot and chicken nuggets. To my nose, all children faintly smell of breaded, processed chicken. I pull back to check his face again. I hold his sweaty-hair head. He's crying, but his crying isn't irritating, it's refreshing because he couldn't make all that goddamn noise if he wasn't breathing.

I say, "That was scary, wasn't it?"

He says something, but a sharp pain explodes deep inside my head. His mouth is moving, Liz's mouth is moving, but there's no sound. My pulse is pounding brilliantly behind my eyes.

I let Shamus go and carefully sit in his miniature chair. I close my eyes and lower my head—as if it were a fragile, flaking wasp nest—into the cradle of my arms.

Children. One way or another, they will be the death of me.

Liz's warm palm slides across my back. Her feminine, older scent bathes my senses. Powdery perfume and a hint of Vagisil. She smells like love.

My hearing comes back online abruptly, as if I had been underwater and I am now emerging. Some kids are crying. Several teachers are inside my classroom, talking in that hushed tone reserved for emergencies.

An ambulance siren blares at a steady, incredibly loud decibel. Its volume isn't getting louder or quieter. It must be parked outside the building. I lift my head as two paramedics walk briskly into the classroom.

14

OH, THAT KIND OF MONSTER

The paramedics spend more time with me than Shamus. My pulse and blood pressure are on the high end of normal. They ask me questions. I answer in the semi-truthful way a person does when they want to avoid a trip to the hospital. I do not mention bat scratches, rabies vaccines, neurostimulants, stress-induced insomnia, or sleepwalking. This information may be relevant, but seems like it could cost me my job.

The middle-aged paramedics, a woman and man, both have ponytails drooping down their backs like raccoon tails, fatty sacs under their eyes, and the puffy faces and bellies of alcoholics. They look like they've been on a hotdog-and-beer diet for years, but their professionalism, stamina, and alertness remind me that something about me isn't quite right. Either I inherited the worst possible combo of Mom and Dad's DNA or ate too much flaked lead paint as a toddler. There has to be some explanation for my subpar brain function.

My semi-truthful answers pass their litmus tests. They advise me to see an auditory specialist, then pack up an array of mostly unused supplies. In the classroom's miniature bathroom, with the doors closed, I throw away my vomit shirt (an outdated, crummy shirt not worthy of washing), clean myself up, and pull on a T-shirt.

The day proceeds at a calmer volume and pace than usual.

Hours later, after the children have been collected and taken home, I head to the front office. Incidents related to child safety must be documented.

Liz is already there, coffee in hand, telling the story of Shamus and the red marble ponytail holder to several wide-eyed teachers. Liz is not gossipy or calculating. They had probably asked; she was just answering their question.

Liz looks at me, deadpan. "You were a monster, Grace."

"What?" Maybe my hearing is still malfunctioning. Even so, I feel like a wounded animal, defensive and exposed.

"A damn superhero," she says.

Oh, that kind of monster.

She says, "Your reaction time was insane. You moved so fast. That Heimlich was the shit."

"Says no one ever." Melanie. Quick-witted, she always draws a laugh. She's fair-skinned with a powdering of freckles. Her hair is auburn and shaped with intent. Her makeup never smears or vanishes like mine.

Come to think of it, most of the women I work with seem to wear non-smearing makeup. I need to ask what they buy. As a group, my co-workers are well-manicured, professional, organized, friendly, and attractive. All of them. Even the ones that don't wear ensembles or polish their nails. I'm lucky to work with such pleasant, conscientious women. Or maybe they're lucky to work with me because I prop them up.

"We've been trained so many times," I say. "I guess it's a muscle memory thing."

Melanie says, "Grace, you look good. You've lost weight."

It's true, I'm down five pounds in less than a week. Not a healthy pace, I know.

A ball of nerves. That's what comes to mind. *You are a ball of nerves, Grace Wright.*

"What I'm losing is my mind," I say.

A few of them laugh because they think I'm joking. Liz gives me a quizzical look.

Jazmine says, "Liz told us you felt dizzy and had some issues with your hearing. Do you feel back to normal now?" Jazmine wears her dark hair in two immaculate French braids. Like her hair, she is a perfect balance of sugary sweet and stern.

"Tired, but fine. Once or twice a year I get vertigo. In the past my doctor said it's a virus in the inner ear. That's probably what I'm having."

They all nod knowingly. They understand tired and they understand vertigo. Most women I've talked to have experienced varying levels of vertigo after they've had children. Melanie used to love roller coasters. Since she had her first kid, she can't even ride the merry-go-round. Liz can't ride elevators.

How could the processes of pregnancy and delivery and lactation permanently affect the condition of the inner ear? The two conditions are so distant, so different. As seemingly unrelated as a person stubbing their toe causing their teeth to fall out.

99

My thoughts go to Ava's missing tooth, her smile, "Harvest Moon" strumming in the background, a male voice murmuring off camera.

The last rumor I heard about Ethan Boone was that he'd touched a student inappropriately. I'd heard it here, in the break room. That was three weeks ago.

"That fight or flight response uses up so much energy," Liz says and rubs my back. "I bet you'll sleep like the dead tonight. Call me if you need anything."

"Thanks, Liz."

Sleep sounds good. The dead part doesn't sit right.

"Has anyone heard anything recently about Ava Boone?" I say.

Everyone's eyes shift through emotions like a child's View-Master before all eyes settle on sadness. Nothing like child abduction to kill a conversation.

Jazmine unwraps a piece of gum and puts it in her mouth. "It's crazy how there's no news anymore, but my son Jack goes to school with Mason." Her eyes wide, she whispers, "Jack said Mason got pulled out of class by police twice since school started."

Melanie says, "But I heard Mason was taking her abduction as hard as his mom."

"Hm," Jazmine says. She doesn't want to say what she's thinking. Police suspect Mason.

Now that I've brought up an uncomfortable topic, I want to flee. I say, "I'd better go fill out my report." I pluck the correct document from a tray nailed to the wall and take it back to my classroom.

I've never done the Heimlich. I have never been a good "emergency response" person.

If Chloe screams, I typically run, frantic, heightening the frenzy, and yell too loudly on my way toward her, "*What* happened? What *happened*?"

Or, I freeze.

I am the person who is stunned when witnessing a car accident, my mind blanking out like the blue screen of death. Minutes after, I can't explain what happened. I truly have no idea who hit whom and which direction they were headed. Ask me the make and model of the car that sped away or, God forbid, the license plate, I am useless.

My steel reaction today in the classroom was unlike me. Calm and confident is not my forte, and these traits don't typically correlate with six consecutive sleepless nights. Or is it seven?

I take stock of the changes I've experienced since the bat attack. *It happened barely two days ago—of what is there to take stock?*

Sleepwalking.

My hearing going underwater for a few minutes today.

I add weight loss to the list, then take it off. I started dropping pounds when I found out about my neighbor.

The occasional mirage and the tilting of my surroundings go on the list and then off the list as well. Those started before my run-in with the bats. But they have gotten worse these past couple days.

Mirage? Tilt?

Hallucinations, Grace. When you see something that's not present, something that's not happening, it's called a fucking hallucination.

15

THE PSYCHIC PARTY

My mom's house is thirteen miles away. Smack dab in the middle of my route to my mom's is the Boone house. Well, it's not *smack dab* in the middle, but it's only a few minutes out of the way.

I park on the street across from their house.

Five minutes. That's all you get. Say what you have to say, then pick up Chloe.

I take the keys out of the ignition, but I don't have the nerve to open my car door. These people have gone through so much, how dare I invade their privacy? How dare I use teachers' lounge gossip to learn their address, stake them out, and catch them by surprise?

It's like rubbing a stranger's belly just because they look pregnant. No, the opposite. Pregnancy is typically a joyous occasion. Something hellish happened to these people. A monster stole their daughter in the night, and now I'm in their space, poking my fingers into their barren bellies. Rubbing cocoa butter in their puffy, bloodshot eyes.

I can't do it. I can't ring their doorbell.

But what if you can help them?

No. The advice I have is small. Something they've surely already been told.

There's a knock on my window, and I jump. My keys go airborne, landing with a thud down in the passenger's side footwell.

Ethan Boone is standing beside my window. His mouth is a hard line. His sclerae are pink, veiny, and watery, with a touch of jaundice. Serious wrinkles around his eyes, dark hollows underneath. He has gained weight in his belly. He didn't look this bad, this old, in the news story five months ago. I should have expected he'd look like shit, but it's startling.

He's just home from work. He's wearing tan pants and a short-sleeve cotton button-down: blue, green, and white plaid. His Honda Pilot is parked in the driveway.

He must have pulled in while you were spacing out.

I don't want to open my door because he's so close I'll hit him, but I can't roll down my window because nothing is manual anymore. I hold my finger up, *wait one sec*, and lean down to grab my keys from the floor. Time stretches. Keys in hand, I start my car, then power down my window.

His anger is simmering, ready to burst into a boil, but he restrains his voice. "I am so tired of you freaks watching my house. I never knew there were so many of you."

"I'm sorry. I just wanted—"

"You just want to hear every terrifying detail. You are all a bunch of fucking vultures, dying to eat up tragedy."

I'm chilled and my skin is tight. *You shouldn't have come here.
Idiot. How could you be so selfish?*

*No. It may be useless, but if it's the slightest bit helpful, it's worth it.
Say what you have to say.*

"No, no. I wanted, well, I wanted to help. I wanted to tell
you something."

His eyes change, becoming darker and smaller, and he
laughs. It's brittle. "We've seen enough psychics too. You're a
little late to the psychic party, you know. Listen, bitch." This
is the man described as humble and goofy? "My wife is home
right now. Here's a little morsel for your vulture appetite. She's
taking a bath and she's actually calm right now. Which is a
fucking rarity, as you can imagine. She can't handle pouring
tea for another psycho psychic."

"I'm not a psychic. I'm a preschool teacher."

"What?" He's confused.

"I live next door to a man suspected in your daughter's
case. Leland Ernest. I've been calling the police, the State's
Attorney's Office, trying to find out if this man is dangerous
and I can't find anything on him. I can't find out anything
about your case. I keep calling police, searching online—"

He cuts in, "How sad for you. Fuck you."

"I don't mean that. What I mean is, if you put information
out there, you might get tips. If people knew more about,
well, about that night, they might realize they saw something
suspicious. If we knew more about why people were suspected,
we might be able to offer information. There's been no
disclosed interviews. No details."

His eyes soften and he stares down the street as if an important piece of paper has blown away, something difficult to replace, but it's no use, it's too far. He's thinking. Then he gets close. If I were to power up my window, it might nick his nose. He says, "Our daughter has been gone for five months. *Five months.* Do you *know* what that *means*?" His spit hits my cheek. He is seething. He can't say it, won't say it. "We are trying to heal. We are trying to get over this. Leave. Us. Alone."

He turns and walks to his house, eyes down, shoulders dropped, back trembling. Because of me. His back is trembling because of me.

I don't mean to be a vulture, but I am. I gobble up tragedy, shove it into my mouth hastily, sloppily, with my hands. I feel it dripping, warm and sticky, down my chin.

Not because I'm bored. Not because it's shiny and startling and tragic like a car crash, but because it feeds my fear and it dictates the way I parent. It is my textbook.

I'm done crying by the time I pull into my mother's driveway. Chloe is packed and waiting on the front porch with my mom. Good. I can leave my sunglasses on.

16

EMPTYING A BOTTLE OF BLEACH ON THEM

Chloe and Wyatt appear to have forgotten what A-holes they were this morning.

We are eating microwaved lasagna. They are not complaining about their food, but actually eating it.

I keep expecting someone to ask me to get up and get something (more milk, another fork, a napkin, socks, a leotard), but they eat and chat quietly. Chloe informs us what her imaginary friends, Star Wars and Jessup, have been up to today: eating too many cookies with their grandmas, swinging on swings, cleaning pee-pee. Chloe's face is bright, excited, and marker-free. At pickup my mom said, "Acetone took that marker right off." I kept my mouth shut, but have been wondering about the possible side effects of scouring a toddler's face with acetone.

Wyatt says, "Kids at school were talking about this video on YouTube where this rabbit was growling at a big dog. They said it's not inappropriate. Can we watch it?"

"Let me check it out first. If it's OK, I'll show you tomorrow."

Wyatt considers bitching. Instead, he says, "Sorry I was complaining this morning." So he hasn't forgotten.

"It's OK. Everyone complains sometimes. It's what humans do."

"You don't complain much."

"Sweet of you to say, Wyatt." Tell your dad that, wouldja? He thought I was a real whiner.

Chloe climbs into my lap, wraps her arms around my neck, and stares into my eyes. Her nose grazes mine. "Momma, will you take off your shoes and socks and we can cuddle and put our feet under the blanket together and watch a show?"

I don't want to take off my shoes and socks. It's getting late, and I want to mow the lawn and start a load of laundry and wash the dishes.

"Sure, baby."

I turn on an episode of *Sesame Street*. I slip my shoes and socks off and lie beside her on the couch. I rub my bare foot against the underside of her pebbled toes and we snuggle. Wyatt joins us under the blanket. He rests his head at the opposite side of the couch, his knees pulled up and his toes brushing against ours. I hold my breath, waiting for him to bitch about baby shows. He doesn't complain, I relax, and the three of us laugh our way through Grover's ineptitude, Big Bird's dim-wittedness, Oscar's hoarding, Bert's OCD, and Cookie Monster's lack of self-control.

After this cloying indulgence, I put on another show and slither covertly out of this warm, cozy nest. As I tie my shoes, I say, "I'm going to mow the front lawn, Wyatt. Come outside if you guys need me."

Eyes on the TV, he gives me a thumbs up.

I get the lawn mower humming on my first try, a small victory. I occasionally have to knock on my other neighbor's door, the one who is not a suspected kidnapper, to ask him to yank the starter, which makes me feel like an inferior human.

His name is Blake Walner. He lives with his wife, Brooke, and two girls, Marian and Nora, in the biggest house on the block. Their lawn is mowed on a perfect diagonal and their yard is seamless with red mulch and flagstone and an inground pool in their privacy-fenced backyard. Their mailbox has a fresh coat of white. They are slender, well-dressed, and never put their garbage out a minute early or pull their bins back into their swept garage a moment too late. I have never heard them slander their children. They have their shit so together, it's baffling. I have stood at Wyatt's window, watching all four of them play together in their pool, wondering what is their secret? What do they know that I don't?

On the occasions I knock on their door for lawn-mower assistance, I'm sure Brooke curbs her giggle. I'm sure Blake rolls his eyes while he double-knots his clean shoes, gearing up to help me start my shoddy mower. I am their inside joke.

Now, as I mow my front yard, Brooke is walking back from her mailbox. She gives me a finger-waggling wave, but I pretend I don't see her. I'm wearing sunglasses so I can get away with it.

I met her the day I toured the house. I was walking toward

108

my minivan with my realtor. Chloe was still asleep on my shoulder, and my realtor was telling me in her secretive yet bubbly have-I-got-news-for-you voice that Tony Durtato was *very* flexible on price.

Brooke had been standing on her front porch, her cell to her ear when she walked quickly toward me in rhinestone sandals and linen pants. She slipped her phone into her pocket, introduced herself, and said with too much enthusiasm, "I have to tell you. This is one of the few neighborhoods in Kilkenny that has such a wide range of house layouts." She touched my arm, flashing her frosty-pink manicure. "Big and small and in between, there are actually fifteen different models. My husband's an architect, and he says fifteen models is pretty much unheard of."

She placed her hand on Chloe's back and peeked around to Chloe's face. I would have considered this rude if I hadn't been blinded by her shiny blond hair and images of her giving me Whole Foods bags filled with fashionable clothes and accessories of which she'd grown bored. She lowered her voice to a hush. "The elementary school is a short two-block walk, and there's a bike path that loops a pond a street over that way. What did your husband think of the house?"

Bitch. You could have told me.

As I push my mower, I sneer at her fully bloomed, manicured rose bushes. I picture myself emptying a bottle of bleach on them.

17

EXPLODING HEAD SYNDROME

Late at night, every night since I found out my neighbor is a suspect in the kidnapping of Ava Boone, I experience a disgusting metamorphosis.

After Chloe and Wyatt fall asleep and I sprint the block and shower and tuck myself into bed with my laptop, my clean, crisp outer shell crumbles and what emerges is filmy and compulsive.

Imagine a sweaty guy with sex-thirsty, glazed eyes, furiously jerking off to porn in bed in front of his laptop. That is me, minus porn and jerking off. Well, most nights.

Since I found out about my neighbor I have spent the majority of my designated sleeping time googling things like: *missing children* and *kidnappings* and *child predators* and more recently *rabies symptoms* and *bat bites* and *psychogenic hearing loss* and *panic attacks* or occasionally *images of great eyebrows* or *best sources of potassium* or *why are kids today so lonely* or *what is the difference between bipolar 1 and 2?*

You'd think I've read everything on missing children. You're wrong. There is always more.

Within an hour, my lingering fatigue has been replaced with energetic anxiety.

My browsing behavior is not helpful; I am not oblivious to my own recklessness. But when I skip my laptop routine, I still lie in bed with my heart racing, my mind concocting worse stories than what I'd find online. *Reading* tragic stories seems more productive than tossing and turning and *imagining* tragic stories.

My compulsion is not bound to missing children. My child-related worries spread far and wide like garbage dump hills.

The media tells me I am part of a generation of helicopter parents. I am too anxious. I manage my children's social interactions and schoolwork, bail them out of every small failure, and fill their time with safe, educational, monitored activities.

But how can I *not* hover after the media has fed me heaping spoonfuls of horror stories?

Their headlines, not mine.

Ten-year-old boy drowns seven hours after he leaves the pool.

What you eat during your pregnancy can cause cancer in your grandchildren.

If you praise your child, you may be raising her to be a sociopath.

Study shows breastfed infants have higher IQs.

Study shows breastfed infants are exposed to toxic chemicals.

1 in 5 children may experience exploding head syndrome.

If you love your kids, you are doing fine. Your kids will turn out fine.

OK, I made that last one up.

The media's stories are like parasites infecting my brain,

feeding on my love for my children, eating away at my common sense, bloating like worms inside me, and leaving me sick with paralyzing fear.

Then, the media shames me and calls me names. Helicopter Parent. Toxic Parent. Indulgent Parent. Narcissistic Parent.

They have force-fed me cotton candy twenty-four-seven for years and are now pissing and moaning about my rotting teeth.

They mean well. I know they mean well. Information overload is not their fault. I shouldn't seek their horror stories, their pop-science reports, their despairing warnings, their half-cocked, irresistible headlines, but I'm weak and I'm scared. Well-meaning media *terrorizes* my mind.

Even before I found out Leland was a suspect in Ava Boone's kidnapping—*murder*—I had trouble sleeping. Emails and scheduling and bills had buzzed in my mind like gnats until I got out of bed and addressed them. Horrifying news stories have always stuck to my brain, little fragments of iron from my cereal bowl to a magnet.

Since I found out about my neighbor, it's much worse.

The last time I was this sleep-deprived, I saw nurses climbing the walls.

Wyatt had been in the hospital as a newborn. Pneumonia. I was going on four days of no sleep. I would listen to his wispy, whistle-breathing while I sat beside his capsule or held him. My glazed, bloodshot eyes occasionally slipped closed, but something in the hallway would beep or whoosh, and my eyelids would fly open, my heart racing, and I'd wipe the drool from my mouth.

First it had been spiders. Out of the corner of my eye I

had seen spiders scurrying behind the curtains and under beds. Nate had raised an eyebrow and said, "If spiders are the nastiest thing in this hospital room, count yourself lucky."

Then I told him I saw one of the nurses sucking Wyatt's fingers and when I'd followed her into the hallway to confront her, she had scurried up the wall and perched herself in the corner, out of my reach.

Ten minutes later, Nate fed me applesauce out of a plastic container, the tin foil already pulled back. I'd thought he was being nurturing, but he'd crushed-up Silenor and Xanax and stirred them into the sauce. I slept for twenty-four hours.

When I woke, Wyatt's respirations were smooth and airy. No crackling. No rattling. The hospital room was free of spiders, and the nurses' shoes stayed on the ground.

18

EAT SOMEONE'S WHOLE HEAD

I wake to a quiet house. Open my eyes to catch the last moments of dawn and her mysterious bluish glow through the space where I can't get my curtain panels to properly touch.

Even through thick window glass, the birds' morning party is loud. Boisterously soliciting sex, hunting, and feasting: they are insatiable little Vikings.

My head feels heavy and sinking. My muscles are relaxed almost to the point of sleep paralysis. Even if I wanted to, I couldn't move. I love it.

I close my eyes again and lose myself to a perplexing, yet deliberate daydream.

I am dropping week-old pieces of chicken, slimy and stinky, onto the kitchen floor. I step out into the night. All the streets west of my backyard lack sidewalks and lampposts. That's where I go.

My daydream fast-forwards a few minutes.

I'm walking on asphalt, weaving through these dangerously dark roads. I glance down. I'm carrying a black plastic garbage bag. It's bulky and full but not heavy.

"Is this yours?" Wyatt says.

I open my eyes. A blurry Wyatt stands in my doorway. I grab my glasses from the bedside table and slip them on. Early morning's golden glow is coming on strong. Like a drunk after last call. "What?"

"There's a pillow in the hallway," he says. "Is it yours?"

"Huh?" I feel behind my head. My pillow is gone. "I must have gotten up to go to the bathroom and dropped it."

"Why would you bring your pillow to the bathroom?"

Sleepwalking again?

"Who knows. I'm tired." I stretch my arms and make the distasteful noises associated with a good stretch.

"Are you OK, Mom?"

"Yeah, I'm OK. I'm trying to wake up, that's all. Thanks, kiddo."

"Mom!" Chloe yells happily from behind him. "I'm *starving*. I could eat someone's whole head. I could eat Grandma!"

Wyatt says, "Ew. Don't talk like that, Chloe."

"Well!" she screams. "I could!"

I slap my feet onto the floor like they are monstrous slabs of meat and smack my cheeks with my palms. "Wake up, sister. Rock and roll."

19

A SHITTY ALTERNATE VERSION OF THE
VELVETEEN RABBIT

Thirty minutes later I'm standing on the deck, micromanaging Hulk's bladder and bowels—*Go potty. Go potty. Last call, Hulk. Last call. I got shit to do, dog*—when a kid runs across Leland's yard and disappears into his back door.

A girl. It was a girl. Her dark hair flowed behind her, fanning like feathers.

No. A bird flew through your peripheral vision. You saw movement. You're obsessed with Ava Boone, and your mind is indulging the holes in your vision. It was a damn bird.

Besides, if Leland kidnapped a girl, if he was *hiding* a girl in his house, there's no way he would let her out.

Maybe you did see a kid. Maybe his niece or nephew is visiting.

"Let's go, Hulk."

Finished with her business, she charges for me as if I'm covered in egg slops. She jumps onto my shins.

"Ow. Shit, Hulk. We've got to cut those nails." I'm wearing a skirt today, which is a rarity. Her scratches draw blood. "I guess you don't like when I wear skirts either."

I walk inside. Wyatt has gotten Chloe cereal, and she's sitting in her chair, eating. That's a rarity too.

"Look at you, sitting calmly and eating like a big girl."

"Yep."

"Hey, Chlo. Have you ever seen a little girl next door?"

"Nora?"

"Not Nora. The house on the other side. That way." I point toward Leland's house. "Did you ever see a little girl by that house?"

"Um, I think so." She's mesmerized by her cereal, and might not be listening to me. If that's the case, it's impressive. She can't make it to the toilet in time, but she can deliver a perfectly vague and easy-going answer to appease an adult and make them shut up.

"I'm serious, Chlo. There is no little girl who *lives* in that house, but I'm wondering if there's a visitor." Shit, I'm complicating things. *She's three; keep it simple.* "I thought I saw a little girl in the yard."

"She's outside now? Can I go play?"

"No, she went inside. Have you ever seen a little girl over there?"

"I'm pretty sure. I'm not sure what her name is though." Chloe tips her head to the side, thinking. Or pretending to think. "And she doesn't talk so maybe you could teach me sign language." She lowers the end of her spoon down into a small puddle of milk on the table and drags her spoon, making a sloppy milk star. "How do you say *play* in sign language?"

"I don't know. We should look it up. Chloe, when did you see a girl over there?"

"Hm," she says, soaking up my attention. "I think, was it, in my window? Maybe…" she pauses, thinking, "yesterday?" She looks at me for approval. She must not find it because she says, "Tomorrow?"

I'm pinching my leg, forcing myself to smile and wait patiently. *Give her your full attention, let her talk, and don't drill her. If you come on too strong, she'll clam up.*

She laughs, tipping her head forward. A strand of her hair gets caught in her mouth. "Hulk!" Pulling her hair out of her mouth, she says, "Hulk licked my toe."

"That's funny, Chloe. So you think you saw a little girl in the house next door through your window?"

"Maybe," she says, looking at her toes and scratching her calf. "Or was it when that man gave me Tootsie Rolls?"

My heart jumps into my throat. It's as if a stranger walked through my front door, holding an axe, and I'm paralyzed with blistering terror; I can't move, I can't speak.

I finally breathe. I find my voice, but it's trembling. "The, the neighbor? It was the neighbor who gave you those Tootsie Rolls?"

"That's what you said, Momma," she says thoughtfully. Then she gives me a teenager's snarky grin and cocks her head. "Them weren't poison. I'm not dead."

My blood is boiling. My head feels pressurized. I want to punch the glass door and shatter it. I want to throw all the glass dishes on the floor. I might actually need a paper bag. Inside my head, Lou's voice, then my own. *I will slit your throat.*

118

Focus on what's important right now. She's right. She's not poisoned. What's important is whether or not a little girl ran into his house.

Flu-like symptoms gripping me, I sit beside her and put my face inches away from hers. "Chloe. This is important," I try to keep my voice light, but I fail. I sound cross and shaky. "Are you playing make-believe or did you *really* see a girl?"

"Mommy's *mean*." She cries in the name of drama, then forces the fake cry into real tears. She runs away from the table and up the stairs, wailing. Believing something hard enough can occasionally make it real. Like a shitty alternate version of *The Velveteen Rabbit*.

You shouldn't be looking for a reality check from your three-year-old. Be The Parent. Be The fucking *Parent.*

Chloe didn't see a girl. She would have mentioned it before. You prompted her. You egged her on. Chloe didn't see a girl. And neither did you.

It was a stupid bird in your peripheral vision.

And Leland might not have given her candy. What had she said? That's what you said, Momma?

You seeded the idea. She's only three.

No, no. She said that on her own. Leland Ernest walked into your backyard while you were bringing in the groceries and gave Chloe a handful of Tootsie Rolls.

Fuck.

Fuck, fuck, fuck.

The whole world has gone silent, and all that remains is the ringing in my ears. The armpits of my shirt are damp with sweat. Sour panic and fear waft into my nose, but I don't have time to change.

Pretending Chloe didn't run into her room, bawling, I stand at the bottom of the stairs and shout happily, "Let's go, my peeps. Time for school."

You can convince yourself of anything.

20

HOLED UP IN A LOG CABIN OFF GRID

Thankfully, work is busy. I have no solitude and little opportunity to picture Leland Ernest walking toward my baby with a handful of Tootsie Rolls.

At the end of the work day, as I'm walking to my car, my cell rings. I recognize the number, and my pulse is already doing gymnastics as I answer.

"Hi, Mrs. Wright. This is Principal Wendy Shish from Flyview Elementary."

"Everything OK?"

"Yes, everything is fine. No one is hurt. I want to tell you about an incident that happened during recess today." Apparently there was an argument, and Wyatt called another boy a swear word.

I unlock my car, slide in, and close the door. Sun is beating on the seats and dashboard. Air inside my car is hot enough to kill a small dog. "What did he say?"

"Hang on," Principal Shish says, "let me close my door." Her chair cushion squeaks and a door closes. "Um, he called another boy a *fucking*."

My face burns with shame, but I need all the details. "A fucking what?"

"Apparently just a fucking."

"Fucking was the noun?"

"That's correct."

Sweat rolls between my breasts. I open my car door for circulation. "Wyatt doesn't swear at home, and I don't swear in front of him. Are you sure?"

Indeed she is. There are witnesses, including two teachers. Wyatt's punishment will be detention during recess for the rest of the week. Wyatt, she assures me, is not the only boy who will be serving detention. Others are in trouble as well.

I am in total agreement with his punishment. Phone to ear, nodding with eager eyes even though she can't see me, I am kissing her ass because:

1. I don't want to be categorized as a gullible parent who thinks their kid does no wrong.

2. I don't want to come across as an angry, accusatory parent who blames everyone but their kid.

3. I don't want to come across as apathetic toward bullying.

4. I don't want to come across as white trash.

I drive home on the fast side, my mind manic with questions, emotions, and the possible ramifications of this incident.

Is my child a dick? If so, how did I miss it? What mistakes have I made to lead him down this dick-path? I don't spank. Am I a pussified parent? Doesn't he understand that the school system has already discounted and depreciated us because we are low-income? Doesn't he know we need to be on our best behavior? I review a list of possible punishments and, worried I've been too easy on him, decide upon a harsh combo punishment.

Twenty minutes later he walks in the door. He usually calls, "Hi, Mom," while noisily and joyfully putting his coat and backpack in the closet. Today he is quiet.

I am sitting on the couch, but my calm is phony. I am nearing a rolling boil. "Wyatt. Please come in here and sit."

His face is drawn as he walks in. He's busted and he knows it. His eyes somber, he sits on a chair. Sweaty from his walk home, his forehead is shiny and his hair is sticking up at odd angles.

"Your principal called and said you called someone a swear word on the playground." I wait for him to speak. He doesn't, which pisses me off more. "I'm disappointed in you. Why did you do that? Why?"

He shakes his head, then stares at his shoes. Worn at the edges, the cloth is stretched and torn along the side, and a patch of his orange sock is visible. His shoes are expired by at least a month. Which pisses me off more. "Why didn't you tell me your shoes have holes?"

"They're fine."

"No, they're not." Principal Shish must think we're scum.

Hulk walks in and licks Wyatt's hand, comforting him.

"Hulk. Out of here." My voice is so harsh, Hulk takes me seriously. "No going to friends' houses, no TV, no video games for a month."

He lowers his chin even more. His back trembles as he sniffles.

"What do you have to say for yourself?"

"It's only a word."

"A bad word."

"Who even decided it was a bad word?" His words come slowly as his breathing hitches. A fat tear slips down his cheek. "It's a stupid word someone made up a long time ago. It's not like I punched anyone."

I inhale deeply, puff out my cheeks, and exhale as if I'm blowing bubbles. "True, but it's a trashy word so if people hear you say it, people might think you are trashy. Why did you do it?"

"Marty called Arjun *retarded*. I was trying to stick up for him."

Which slaps the bitchy know-it-all out of me.

Uh-oh.

I know both kids. Marty is a nasty eight-year-old. At the school carnival last year, I saw him kick his four-year-old sister in the ass. When she cried and tugged her mother's leg and told her what happened, the mother rolled her eyes at the woman she was talking with and shooed her crying daughter away. Marty is the kind of sly kid who gets away with crap because he's good-looking and athletically gifted. I've witnessed a number of parents covetously regard Marty, wishing their kids were as popular and agile.

Arjun is a quiet kid with a good sense of humor and a kind

smile, but he is also uncoordinated. One of the last boys picked for teams at recess.

"Tell me what happened," I say. *What you should have said when he first walked in the door.*

"I told you. We were all playing soccer, a bunch of the boys in my grade, and Marty kept calling Arjun *retarded*. So I called him a *fucking*." It's physically jarring to hear this abrasive word come out of his little-kid mouth, but his ineptitude with using the word softens the assault.

"Did you tell the principal you were sticking up for Arjun?"

"Yeah. Marty got recess detention too, but only for two days."

Recalling moments from the last thirty minutes of my life, shame swallows me. How did I get conned into a story to such an extent that I exaggerated the narrative? I am a public service announcement for how to *not* parent. I tried my damnedest to shame the young hero and convince him he was the villain. I am shit. *I* am a *fucking*.

I am off the couch and crouching before him, caressing his little-boy rough knees, staring up into his sad-dog eyes. I wipe his tears with my thumbs as tears slide down my face. "I am so sorry, Wyatt. I didn't know. You did the right thing, sticking up for Arjun. I'm so glad you did. That makes me so proud and I'm so sorry you can't go to recess this week; that sucks. Most of all, I'm sorry I yelled at you. I was wrong. So, so wrong. I'm so sorry."

I set my head on his lap and hug his waist. I am sweating now more than when I was nervously listening to Principal Shish in my hot car, more than when I was driving home and silently berating Wyatt.

You occasionally get these big-moment opportunities to

parent correctly, to demonstrate calm, to impart wisdom. This was one of them, and I blew it.

"Where's Chloe?" he says.

"She's with Grandma. I'm going to drop you off at Grandma's too because I need to go in for another vaccine."

"Oh. Do I still lose video games and TV?"

My eyes, pleading, meet his. "No. That was my mistake, my misunderstanding. I'll buy you a milkshake on the way to Grandma's. Let me make a quick phone call first."

"Thanks, Mom." He smiles and his eyes brighten, but the heavy sadness clouding them minutes ago when I assumed the worst of him and made his sweet, generous, innocent mind feel filthy is etched into my memory.

I wronged him. I didn't have his back. And he's already forgiven me. It breaks my heart.

Minutes later, I'm pacing in my bedroom with the door locked, scolding Principal Wendy Shish. Telling her I reamed my son *before* he told me what happened and why didn't *she* tell me what had really happened?

"None of the teachers heard Marty say anything." Of course they didn't. They're suckers for Marty's act too. "Two of the kids said Marty was teasing Arjun, but it doesn't excuse Wyatt's language."

I can't argue with that, but I'm furious that she missed the bigger picture.

I tell her I'm proud of Wyatt for standing up for the weaker kid. I may even mention she *knows* Marty is *a little asshole*. I end the call and sit on my bed, sweaty and exhausted.

The system is garbage. Even in elementary school. The system is doing the bare minimum. It makes sure the rules are followed in the name of liability, but has little concern with integrity and protecting the vulnerable. The system protects the wolves and tiptoes around the bullies. My mind is clouded with terrible stories and their trial outcomes.

Father rapes child for a decade. Child comes forward finally at the age of seventeen, the most difficult thing for a victim to do. Father gets only eighteen months in prison.

Woman gets court order against her abusive ex. She drives to the police station on two occasions because the ex is threatening to strangle her. Cops give the ex warnings, but say their hands are tied, and secretly think the victim (sleazy with her fat ass squeezed into short jean cutoffs, a low-cut shirt, and a groupie hairstyle leftover from the eighties) may be a lying vindictive bitch. How could the ex be so obsessive, so possessive of this ugly fat chick? Weeks later, her body is found in a quarry. The ex is long gone.

And this is the system protecting middle- to low-class criminals.

Nothing touches the wealthy. Their most heinous deeds are settled out of court because the most vulnerable chose money over dignity.

I am like a recently discharged soldier who has squeezed himself into threadbare fatigues that don't button over his newish beer belly, holed up in a log cabin off grid, black ink twitching on his muscled arms, furiously cursing the system through his dangling cigarette while he oils his gun.

I splash my face with cold water until my shirt is drenched.

21

CROSS-SPECIES LOVE

After I give my order at the Steak 'n Shake drive-through, I slip on my headphones to preview the "bunny versus dog" YouTube video. Wyatt waits silently in the back seat, statue-still, knowing one wrong move could crush his chances at having my smartphone in his clutches.

It's called "Heidi versus Peter Cottontail". In the video, a woman is recording her Golden Labrador mouthing a kickball. The woman is laughing and cajoling *Heidi (You want to get that whole thing in your mouth, don't you, Heidi?)* when a white bunny jumps out from the bushes and growls at the dog. This is a *bunny* in every sense of the word. Fluffy, cotton white, and clean. Someone's escaped pet maybe. This is not of the wild mangy rabbit-type that destroys my tulips and has me cursing, fist shaking in the air, on a bright spring morning.

Surprised, the Labrador drops the kickball and jumps back. The dog barks loudly, but most likely playfully; her tail is wagging. Her nose leading and sniffing, she takes a few cautious steps toward the bunny.

I expect the bunny to dart away, as they do, but this one makes a hissing, growling noise and stays put.

The dog, cautious but undeterred, moves forward, nosing the air, sniffing. The two animals are close enough to nuzzle, and that's what I'm expecting to happen because cross-species love is popular online. It's going to be one of those gorilla-takes-care-of-new-baby-kitten videos, I know it.

I'm wrong. It's more like those cruel stare-at-this-dot-for-sixty-seconds-and-something-remarkable-will-happen videos, but fifteen seconds in, a screaming devil face pops up and ruins your entire day and makes you question all of humanity.

The bunny growls again, jumps forward, and swipes its paw at the dog. Startling. Strangely upsetting. The Labrador flinches, darts back, then trots, tail down between her legs, toward the camera (and presumably her owner). End of video.

Rabies. Must be a bad year for rabies.

Like flitting butterflies, transient flu-like symptoms settle upon me for a moment—heat blows through me, my bowels waver, and I shake off a chill—before lifting away.

I tell Wyatt what's going to happen so he doesn't get spooked. I hand him my phone and lay my head back on the headrest.

A minute later, he says, "That was funny."

"Yeah, but in a super creepy way."

"But," Wyatt says as if we had a bet going, "it's *not* inappropriate."

"Agreed." My mind replays the rabbit's behavior. "I didn't know bunnies could swipe."

The car in front of me drives away, and I pull up to the

drive-through window. I pay, partly with a few soft and worn singles from my wallet and partly with the change I keep in the well of my door. I am tempted to steal a sip of Wyatt's shake from the fat red straw—cookie dough piled with whipped cream—but I pass it back, untouched, my hand left cold and wet. I still owe him. I shift into drive and pull away.

"Hey, Mom?" he says tentatively.

"Yeah?"

"Did you ever see that video of that girl who got kidnapped?" My tongue feels starchy. He adds, "She's singing some old boring song in the video."

I am tempted to say, "No." I am tempted to pretend I am above gaping at the car crash, I am above searching for the splash of blood on the splintered dashboard. But I owe him.

"I've seen it. Have you?" I glance in my rearview mirror, relieved that his eyes are not waiting to meet mine. He's gazing out his side window, watching everything rush by.

"Tanner showed me after school a few days ago. His mom was talking with another mom, and he showed me on her phone."

I wait for him to reveal his thoughts, keeping my eyes steady on the road.

"It's kind of weird when parents post stuff about their kids. Tanner said her parents deserved it." His tone is youthful and innocent, but the words hit like punches to my gut.

Keeping my voice even, I say, "Do you think her parents deserved for their child to be kidnapped?"

"Well, kind of," he says.

Anger clenches in me. Not at him, but at myself. I'm failing him. I am not talking to him enough about real life and tragedy. I am not guiding him toward empathy. He's only eight and he's victim-blaming. I take a deep breath.

"No one deserves to be kidnapped, Wyatt," I say firmly, irritation creeping in. "No one deserves for their kid to be kidnapped." I should be asking *him*, probing *him* to find the right answer for himself, that's what a good parent does, but I'm tense and impatient and want to make it clear.

Child stars and their parents are this well-defined, easily recognizable entity everyone feels comfortable ganging up on, but so many of us are only a wig and a forced smile and a smear of blue eyeshadow away from that. Tons of well-meaning, loving parents post proof of their child's beauty, intelligence, and talents on YouTube, Instagram, Facebook, Twitter.

I would. I have the most deliciously precious photos and videos on my phone that I would love to share-brag. The only reason I haven't is because I cannot properly time-manage my life.

To put photos and videos of our children out there feels justifiable. We lose our sleep, our food, our money, our beauty, and our youth to rearing children. It feels justifiable to show them off. *Look at my stunning child. Look at my artistic, intelligent child! I* made *this! It literally marinated in my amnion for nine months. It came from me. It is my accomplishment. I may be old and washed up, but look at this child! I did this.*

The parents who seek fame take it one itty bitty step further. *Look at my brilliant child. I deserve more than a nod of approvement for this. I deserve, my child deserves, money, an award, fame.*

"Yeah, you're right," he says, so easily swayed. "It's still a little bit weird, that video. It's like this fun video, and then she's," he pauses, "she's gone."

"I know what you mean." This conversation is a bit heavy. I feel an urge to flee from it. Which is exactly the problem. *If he's not getting empathetic cues from you, he's going to get his opinions from kids like Tanner.* "Hey, Wyatt? When we get to Grandma's, leave your cup in the front seat for me. I don't want Chloe to see it and start whining for sugar."

He laughs. "Why is she so obsessed with candy?"

"Most little kids like candy," I say, but that wasn't what he'd asked. He'd asked why his sister was *obsessed* with candy. When Wyatt was Chloe's age, he never whined or cried for candy. He would never sneak or lie or do anything, *absolutely anything*, for sugar. He would gladly take a cookie if you offered it, but he never ate from the sugar bowl or maple syrup bottle.

My cheeks flush and my eyes sting. I've managed to keep the image of Leland Ernest walking into my yard and giving Chloe Tootsie Rolls out of my mind the entire day. But now it's back, and I'm furious. How dare he?

You're not sure that's what happened. There are other explanations.

Oh, but I am sure.

I slip on my sunglasses so Wyatt won't see my tears.

I park in my mom's driveway. Wyatt leaves me with his empty cup and runs around to the backyard. Sun is shining, and he thinks Chloe will be on the swing set.

He's right. Chloe runs in for a hug, and he catches her. They settle on the swings, sitting side by side and talking quietly. He's probably telling her about the "bunny versus dog" video.

My mom sits on a lawn chair ten yards away from the swing set, which is made of metal poles and nails that protrude dangerously, waiting to snag clothing or flesh. It has a slide, two swings, and a carriage swing, all in a row. When Wyatt swings vigorously on the carriage, the anterior metal poles lift three inches off the ground, and my breath catches until the poles' bottoms touch back down. I have never said a word about my hatred for this rusty, serrated, tetanus-ridden swing set because she bought it for my kids, and they love it.

I hug my mom's head gently, taking in her shampoo. It's one of those color-resistant shampoos that smells like floral perfume spilled purposefully in a salon to mask the chemical stench of perm solution. I grab a resin chair stained with dirt and set it in the grass beside her chair. It's identical to hers, but mine has a crack along the back. It bows and splits a little as I lean into it.

"Valerie's nanny said she can watch Chloe," I say. "She's walking distance from my house."

"That sounds like a good setup. Nice and close. That little one has too much energy."

My mom isn't complaining. She loves taking care of Chloe, but she is also tired. She has used most of her vacation days to help me and can't afford to lose her job.

"It kills me because I want to be home with Chloe. I trust my friend's nanny as much as I can, but it's never enough trust.

Not like I trust you. And sixty percent of what I make will go to the stinking nanny I don't even want."

"Most people have to use daycare," she says, a stiff tone edging her voice.

My mom has had a tougher life than I have had. Her dad was hit by a truck while changing his Buick's flat tire on the side of an icy road. My mom was seven, sitting in the front seat of the Buick, when it happened. My mom's mother died of cervical cancer before my mom turned ten. An only child, she was handed off from aunt to aunt, not one of them enthusiastic to parent her, all of them hardened by their own troubled lives. Mom was cleaning houses before her fourteenth birthday.

She thinks my life has been too easy. She thinks I am spoiled. She thinks I liked the idea of marrying a doctor so I could ride the cash train.

Oh God, how I wish there were a cash train. I would ride it like a drunk twenty-something rides a mechanical bull at her bachelorette party.

"I know, Mom. I know. Most people have to work. It's pointless to complain. I'm tired and not thinking clearly."

"Are you eating? Every time I see you, you are thinner."

"I'm eating. Just anxious."

"Do you want to talk about it?"

I do. I want to talk. I want to tell her about Leland. I want to tell her I'm hallucinating and sleepwalking. I want to tell her everything.

But my mom has these bags under her watery eyes. She misses my dad. She worries about my divorce. She worries about my sister's marriage. She worries about getting old and deteriorating in some unbeknownst way that will burden me or my sister because she does not have enough money saved. She has too many worries already.

I want to tell Nate everything too. Nate loves me still. He loves the kids ferociously. But we aren't a team anymore. We are friendly enemies, nitpicking each other over petty kid-related decisions without any shared sex or humor to soften the blows.

Sex and humor, I realize now, are the glue of a marriage. Actually, sex is the glue. We are cavemen and cavewomen. Sex is so much more important than I imagined twenty years ago. Feelings of mind bliss and cosmic union during orgasm last for mere seconds, but the momentary high is surprisingly enough to outweigh the boredom and bitterness of incessant marriage.

If I told him everything, maybe Nate would comfort me and ask how he could help. But what if he tried to take them from me?

I can't take that risk.

"I'm fine, Mom. I don't need to talk. The kids are healthy. I'm so lucky."

Wyatt and Chloe play tag. She laughs hysterically as he pretend-chases her.

"After you get your rabies shot, go home and rest. I'll feed them and drive them to your house sometime after dinner."

"Thanks, Mom."

A little stress melts away. Alone time is golden. Maybe I'll jog. A jog might quiet this unhinged feeling. It's like a gear has slipped inside me and, with the strain of time—*all it takes is time*—the interconnecting mechanical parts are on the verge of springing outward and away from each other.

"Take my car. Tell me if you hear a clicking or if I'm going crazy." She says it casually, jokingly, but I hang on her words. Does she really think she's hearing things? Maybe the wobble is hardwired.

"You're not going crazy. If you hear clicking, I'm sure there's clicking."

Standing, she says, "I'll get my keys."

22

AND WHAT DID YOU DO?

Do you think he is a dangerous man?

That's what I want to ask Ethan Boone. That is what I need to know. Not the gritty, voyeuristic details of his daughter's disappearance. I need to know everything Ethan Boone knows about Leland Ernest.

I couldn't ask before. It felt too selfish. Too cruel. *Yes, your daughter has been kidnapped, has been missing for months, is obviously dead, but enough about you, Mr. Boone. Do you think my neighbor might be a danger to my happy, healthy children?*

Selfish? Clearly. Cruel? Hell, yes. But here's the thing. I can't go on like this. I am splitting into two separate people, and one of them scares me.

I'm in my mom's gray CRV. I'm wearing a Band-Aid on my upper arm from the rabies vaccine. The nurses got me in and out of St Joe's in fifteen minutes.

I turn onto Coppleton Drive. There's action in the Boones' driveway so I pull my car over to the curb three houses short of theirs.

Natalie Boone sits in the driver's seat of her SUV, checking her phone. Lila runs from the car, back into the house. An argument? Forty seconds later, Lila runs back out, a monstrous water bottle in her hand, the screen flapping behind her. No argument; she forgot her water bottle. She's probably heading to basketball practice. She slides into the passenger's seat, and Natalie carefully backs out and drives away.

Should I ring the bell?

Maybe Ethan Boone is home, watching television, a beer in his hand, enjoying a little quiet time. Is that possible? If your kid gets kidnapped, do you ever enjoy a little quiet time again? Kick back and enjoy a beer again? Do you ever truly enjoy *anything* again? How long must go by before you can flip through television channels and stop on a comedy? How long before you can sit down with your other kids and watch the movie *Elf*? Five months? Five years?

You start out hoping with every ounce of your being that your kid isn't dead, but at some point, you start hoping they *are* dead because the alternative, that they are alive and suffering, is too much to bear. At some point, all you want is for someone to find the body. All you want is closure. For your child, foremost. Then, for yourself.

My hand is trembling as I open my car door.

The Boones' garage opens, and an old Saturn backs out. I get a glimpse of their garage—pristine, organized—before it closes.

I shut my door, put my keys back in the ignition, and follow the Saturn. This car is crappy. Dent in the rusted bumper. The driver wears a baseball cap. Mason. I'm following the sixteen-year-old.

He probably worked all last summer and this summer to save up for this car. Maybe his parents pitched in. It seems like good parenting: helping your teenage son buy a used car, teaching them financial responsibility. I'd like to do something similar with Wyatt.

Mason doesn't drive far. I follow him into a crowded Walmart parking lot. He parks far from the entrance. I park far from the entrance as well, but four rows down from him.

He doesn't get out of his car. *He's meeting someone.*

Ten minutes go by before another shitty car pulls up beside his driver door. This one, *real* shitty. Tinted windows. A cracked back window reinforced with cardboard and duct tape. I'm not excellent at identifying car models, but I'm thinking along the lines of an early 2000s Pontiac Grand Am.

Mason's hand goes out his window. A hand reaches from the passenger side of the other car. There is a trade.

Mason drives away.

Drugs.

Hm. Mason could be a normal teenager experimenting with relatively safe drugs like LSD, weed, or shrooms. Then again, normal, relatively harmless teenage drug use usually involves friends and parties. He's flying solo.

Could be he's selling. Could be serious, maybe heroin. Could be he's intertwined himself so tightly with shady characters and criminals that it has something to do with his little sister's disappearance.

Did you know Ava's brother can't stop crying? It's survivor's guilt or something.

Maybe it's just guilt.

Thirty minutes later I am jogging on the street against traffic. My sunglasses shield me from eye contact.

Smells of smoking wood and charring chicken shift with the breeze. Half a dozen people grill in their backyard and another half dozen burn branches so they won't have to pay for yard-waste stickers.

Basketballs *boing*, metal rims *clang*, dogs bark, and cicadas shriek, their calls rising and falling regular as ocean waves.

Early evening is glorious. Wide blue sky, sunny and warm, but not uncomfortable. Cool breeze blows intermittently and casually from the east, an unusual direction for us. *Mary Poppins weather.*

A woman in a floppy hat clips her rose bushes. An old dude watches a baseball game in his zipped-screen garage, the muted roar of thousands of fans flowing to the street. Women and men of all ethnicities and ages walk dogs and babies, sometimes both.

I notice a tick emanating from deep inside my head, keeping rhythm with my left sneaker hitting pavement. I've heard it before, usually when I run. It's got to be sinus-related; it has that moist crunching quality I connect with mucus, sinuses, and ears, but still. Could the ticking be a red flag, a symptom of something more nefarious? I imagine my brain, all its folded nooks and buried crannies, overheating, and counting down, tick by warning tick, the approaching meltdown.

A bare-chested, pot-bellied man lies on a plastic lounger in his driveway. An arm's length away from his lounger, his little Smokey Joe wafts beefy hamburger smoke toward the street. The Steve Miller Band plays at a modest volume from an unseen stereo in his dark garage. He has a bandage on his hand.

This is Lou, the man who told me Leland Ernest is a suspect in the kidnapping of Ava Boone. The man who told me Leland was following his daughter, Rachel, home from school years ago. The man who told Leland, *If you talk to my daughter again, I'll slit your throat.*

I still haven't seen the seventeen-year-old or the wife. It makes sense that I haven't seen the teen; often they're on their bed or couch, sleepy, bored with schoolwork and consumed by their phones. But what about his wife? Doesn't she work or help with the yard? Get the mail? Either he killed her, made her up, or she is a shut-in. Imagining her as a TV-addict shut-in elevates my spirit. Someone more messed up than me.

Lou has no inkling that since he told me my neighbor might be dangerous, I have barely slept.

I imagine stopping on his sidewalk and saying, "Hey there, Lou. Get a load of this. While I was bringing in the groceries the other day, Leland had the nerve to give my three-year-old a handful of Tootsie Rolls."

"And what did you do?" he would say, his voice flat, his basalt eyes unblinking. "What did you say?"

Yes, Grace. What did you do? What did you say?

141

Nothing, you did nothing.

Well, I'm not—

You're not what?

Well, I'm not entirely sure—

Pathetic. Weak.

There's a dead robin inches off the curb. Its wings are flattened, it is sunbaked, and two flies hover above it. I leap over the bird, grateful I noticed it in time to avoid bringing death home on the bottom of my sneaker. My mind is still ticking, keeping time with my left foot.

I pass Lou's house without saying a word.

A teenager on his skateboard passes me, the wheels of his board grinding loudly against the cracked asphalt. For a split second, he tilts 45 degrees to the right. I blink and he is standing erect again, his right foot touching the street, propelling him faster. A half-block ahead, he turns the corner, gone.

Sweating hard, breathing harder, I pound out the last sixty seconds of my sprint. A small burst of endorphins gushes inside my head. I force a smile (*smiling makes you happy*).

Three houses away from my house, I transition sloppily from sprinting to walking. The ticking inside my head stops abruptly, reaffirming its association with the business of inner ears or sinuses.

My beautiful next-door neighbor Brooke and two of her beautiful friends sit in lawn chairs on her driveway, laughing and drinking out of red solo cups, a wine bottle on the ground between their chairs. Their small children doodle on the driveway with chalk. None of these women or children appear distressed or distracted by the suspected child kidnapper living one house away. Maybe it's a distance thing, and Brooke truly feels unthreatened by Leland because he's not *her* next-door neighbor. My kids are the default bait, the sacrificial offering keeping her children safe.

I consider stopping to talk, but I'm still pissed that she didn't tell me about our freaky neighbor and she didn't tell me not to buy this house. Also, my accommodating, considerate side knows that joining their impromptu driveway soiree would bring discordance to the affair. I wear turmoil like perfume. People smell it.

By and large I belong indoors, holed up with the other self-doubting, wobbly, anxious, financially distressed people. As a group, we generally do not go outside and mingle. We are ghosts. Behind closed curtains, we fret over unpayable lawyer bills and debt and loneliness or our ex-spouses' cruel or threatening texts. We rush through grocery stores, rarely making eye contact because we aren't sure if, when spoken to, we will lose our shit.

I give my neighbor and her friends a wave and head for my mailbox, perpetual puker of bad news, useless crap, and environmental burdens.

Leland Ernest's garage door opens. His black Dodge Charger, rust along the back bumper, slowly backs out. Mid-driveway, it stops. He steps out of his car, leaving his engine running and his car door open, and walks back into his house. Forgot something. Happens to me all the time.

I wait by my mailbox, pretending to leaf through my mail.

143

Behind my sunglasses, my eyes are trained on his garage.

Seconds later, he comes out carrying work gloves in one hand. The outline of his body is so crisp, so bold, it seems he is the only person in the world. He wears a brown short-sleeve button-down shirt with an oval-enclosed logo above the breast pocket. One of the letters in the oval may be "F". He is going to work.

Where he works is a question that's been burning a hole in my mind.

If you think too hard, you will miss your chance.

I walk briskly up my driveway and type my code into the garage door keypad. I note his direction, duck under my lifting garage door, and dash inside. In a frenzy, I grab my mom's car keys from the kitchen table. I notice Wyatt's little league cap on the floor. I grab that too. His head is smaller than mine, but I'll resize it as I drive.

I have my mom's CRV started before I close the car door. I back out of my driveway in jerky fits. I'm not used to the CRV's overly responsive brakes, but I don't have time to coddle the brake pedal. I speed down Cherry Lane.

Damn. My garage door. I'm pretty sure I forgot to close it. *It'll be fine.*

Leland turns left onto a two-way street that only gets busy during the peak of rush hour. I follow. His Dodge Charger is far ahead, waiting at the light in the left-turn lane, but no other car separates us.

My mom's CRV is gray, the most mundane of colors. I wear sunglasses and Wyatt's baseball cap. *No way he'll recognize you.*

I am sweat-slick and flooded with adrenaline. Trees, cars, bikers, and clouds appear crisp and solid. No hint of wobble.

Second car you've followed in two hours.

So this is what you do when you have the evening off?

23

A STARCHY, SCRATCHY GRAVE

I'm driving down a two-way road pinched by mature cornfields. I've been following him for fifteen minutes. He's known it's me from the start. Lured me here so he could hide my dead body among the corn husks.

Quit it. He's driving to work. He's a normal guy who didn't give Chloe candy. He's a normal guy who had a misunderstanding with Lou's daughter. He's a normal guy who coincidentally gave Ava a Happy Meal toy shortly before she disappeared.

Disappeared. As if it were a magic trick.

Besides, a corn field is a terrible hiding place for a dead body this time of year. Any day now they'll cut these stalks to the ground. He knows that.

My hands slip along the steering wheel, and my sour-sweat stink fills the car. The corn stalks closing in the road are so tall and thick, it feels like I'm already suffocating in a starchy, scratchy grave.

Leland Ernest's brake lights flash, and I step on my brake. He slows and swerves left, revealing a bicyclist on the road.

Black spandex leggings. Hot pink spandex tank top. Blond hair spilling from her helmet.

Leland comes to a full stop beside the bicycle. Even though I'm sixty feet behind, I stop too. I don't want to be sitting on his bumper.

The bicyclist flails her arm at him and loses her balance. She puts her sneaker on the ground to stop her fall, and ends their brief exchange with her middle finger.

His tires squeal and smoke as he guns it.

What the hell? What did he say to her?

I ease onto the gas, allowing more distance between our cars.

I am not a calm investigator. I am like an eighth-grade girl who has snuck out in the middle of the night, walking through dewy grass and sweating though the night is cool, to meet a high school boy. Wise enough to know she's walking toward danger, green enough that she can't articulate or imagine the details of what that danger might be.

Corn gives way to a scattering of townhomes. We cross train tracks, then pass an industrial park where the road leading in winds around squat, mostly unlabeled buildings. The only labels in sight are for *Jake's RV Rental* and *CR's Boat Repair*. We are clear of Whisper County and moving deeper into rural Niles County.

This is ridiculous. Abandon your pathetic investigation.

I decide to turn around at the stoplight ahead, at the intersection of a shopping center, when his turn signal comes on.

He turns into the Farm and Fleet parking lot.

I follow.

He stops near the front of the lot, waiting as a minivan slowly backs out. An old Mazda Protegé the color of stale blood turns the wrong way down his aisle and weasels into the minivan's spot.

Bad idea, Protegé.

Leland slowly drives past the wrongdoer and turns into the next aisle. No slamming his door and picking a fight. No honking. No giving the menstrual-red car the finger. I park two aisles away.

Leland sits in his car for two or three long minutes. I sweat and pretend to talk on my phone. He steps out, holding a plastic bag in one hand, keys in the other. Instead of heading toward Farm and Fleet, he walks through the half-full lot toward the Mazda.

Oh no, he's going to smash the Mazda's window, isn't he?

He doesn't. Only walks alongside the Mazda before he disappears into Farm and Fleet.

I back out of my spot and drive slowly past the Mazda. Empty. The driver must have walked into Farm and Fleet as I parked.

The car is shabby, a few small dents, a dusty windshield. A fresh silver scratch splits the paint from front tire to rear tire.

It's nothing. Just a scratch. Hell, Chloe dragged a rock across my mom's CRV weeks ago. My mouth gaping at her handiwork, I was about to dole out punishment when my mom patted my shoulder and said, "No worries. That's what kids are for."

Just a scratch.

Except my stomach feels oily because here is an angry

person, a temperamental person, who feels he has nothing to lose. To top it off, this Mazda is old, a real piece of crap. The owner might not even notice the new scratch, which somehow makes the offense more disturbing.

I close my eyes and see Ava Boone. Her small palm pressed against the glass of Leland's second-story window. Her blank stare floating above her palm. Her brown curls. Her lips slightly parted, ready to speak.

I see Chloe's tiny, open palm holding three Tootsie Rolls.

And what did you do, Grace?

What did you do?

24

OCCASIONALLY I HAVE A
HULA HOOP AROUND MY NECK

I am bent at my kitchen sink, my lips under the running faucet, gulping lukewarm water like a kid as water splashes onto my cheeks and shirt and into the grimy sink cluttered with dirty dishes.

Don't think too hard.

You sure about that? Maybe you should think a little harder. Seems like you're on a rampage here, indulging every one of your neurotic impulses.

I slip on a pair of disposable nitrile gloves. I keep my hair up in Wyatt's baseball hat.

My yard backs up to a house inhabited by a young couple who work long, driven hours. Leland's property butts up to a house occupied by two teenage boys. Their adults may or may not be home from work yet, but it's likely the boys are home. Leland's yard ends in a bundle of saplings, a miniature forest, and the foliage mostly obstructs the house directly behind his.

If caught, I will claim Concerned Neighbor. *Oh my gosh, I was on my back deck shaking out the rug and heard glass shatter next door. I wasn't thinking; I ran over and walked in.*

The houses kitty-corner and adjacent to our yards are blotted out by bushes so mature and overgrown, they are essentially trees. The west sky is a lovely swirl of fiery pink and purple sunset clouds, but sunlight still reigns. Early September. Darkness won't conceal a thing for an hour or two.

I drop a small throw rug on my back deck and walk casually through the grass to my neighbor's house.

His back porch is a ten-by-ten slab of cement possessing one plastic chair and one plastic pot of marigolds, which seem well-cared for and lovely.

This isn't going to happen.

I am not willing to shatter glass. I am not willing to break a door or window. He wouldn't leave his house unlocked.

This is not going to happen.

When the sliding door eases open, I freeze, stunned and uncertain of my next move. Out of fear that his backyard neighbors might see me through the foliage, I get over my fear quickly and step inside.

The distinct, stagnant odor of his house hits me first. A male odor: hot dogs, dirty sneakers, and the last fumes of an evergreen air freshener. His kitchen counters are clean. Bare. Plain.

This house was built in the eighties, and no owner has had enough money to update the laminate cabinets and countertops. My kitchen is the same, but my laminate counters are cluttered with dirty plates, too many forgotten cups, and half-baked art projects: cotton balls and paint brushes cemented to dried paint on paper plates and Play-Doh glued and taped to toys.

Treasured heirlooms and sentimental Christmas decorations

get socked away in cold, musty basements. People hide prisoners in basements too. At least that's what my internet searches have revealed. That's where I go first.

I step down unfinished stairs into the dark, guiding myself by the wooden railing, bracing myself for anything from jars of floating body parts to a caged human. I Braille-read the bumpy cement wall, find a switch, and flip on the light.

Leland's basement looks exactly like mine, except his is tidy and mostly empty.

I breathe in. Wet stone and a hint of animal. Cement walls and floors are bare except for stacked cardboard storage boxes.

The boxes are labeled. *Boy Scout magazines. Smithsonian magazines. Grandpa's tools. Leland's baseball cards. Old cell phones/electronics. Piano books. Non-fiction. Fiction. Dad's photo albums.*

Suspecting his labels are decoys, I lift a few lids. Sure enough, the contents match the labels.

I clear my throat. "Ava?" I say, my voice sounding unused, rusty. "Are you down here?" I can't believe the words are coming out of my mouth. *You don't seriously believe she's in this house, do you?* "Ava?"

Silence, except for the buzz of a fly trying to escape a tiny window that doesn't open. *Good luck, fly.*

I walk the periphery of the basement, making sure I'm not missing a secret, horrific room. The first closed door I come upon looks like it opens to a closet. It does. Inside the three-by-three-foot room are a few rusty barbell weights and a hole in the ground housing the sump pump. I continue walking the perimeter of the basement, careful not to disturb small spider webs where the floor and wall meet.

Around the corner is a second door. Cheap standard hollow door, cheap gold-painted handle. From the layout, I expect this room to be larger than a closet. This space probably houses the furnace. I open the door and my heart does a quick triple step. I'm correct about the furnace. And there's a utility sink too, the faucet corroded.

But also. Right in front of me. A dog cage big enough for a German Shepherd. Empty, but still, a *fucking* cage. Leland doesn't have a dog, why would he need a large metal crate? The bars are sturdy, and there are hinges on the front of the cage for a padlock.

I inspect the cage for some clue, a swatch of torn clothing, a shred of shoelace, a long human hair, but there's nothing. It's clean and bare. I clear my throat again. "Ava? Are you in here? My name is Grace. I'm here to help get you back to your parents?"

Silence, except for the fly. Of course. Because she's not here. *It's been five months. Regardless of who took her, she's dead.*

Sweat breaks along my cool skin and I shiver. *It's just a dog cage. He had a dog, it died, and he kept the cage because he's planning on getting another dog. You are the crazy one. You are the criminal. You.*

I close the door, flip the light off, and run up the basement stairs. I wrap my fingers around the handle of the sliding back door, ready to flee, when a nagging voice inside my head calls me a pussy.

The ones who are really crazy, the ones who know they are crazy, those are the ones who are careful. Those are the ones who meticulously organize

153

their shit. Those are the ones who wouldn't keep a child in plain sight in their basement. Those are the ones who scrub their cages with an oxy cleaner and toothbrush.

Upstairs, the carpet is pale blue. First bedroom possesses a roller shade, an old dresser, and a single bed. I open each dresser drawer quickly. Empty, all of them. This is his guest room. Maybe a grandparent or cousin visits once or twice a year.

A computer on a desk occupies the next bedroom. His computer is turned on, and the screen is waiting for a password.

I don't bother. I can't manage to figure out how I run out of storage on my smartphone and what is using all my data, or even what it means to have my data used up; trying to bypass someone's password is out of the question.

Jammed in the crevices of the desk, two photos stand upright. One is of an old man. Grandpa?

Something creaks downstairs. My heart thumps and my pulse quickens. I wait, listening. Air sighs in and out of my lungs. His air conditioning is on, but barely. It's stuffy up here.

Old wood expanding in the heat, that's all it was.

The other photo is of a young boy holding a fishing pole, a small bluegill dead on the hook. Solid and big-boned, the boy is holding onto his baby belly. Leland. He has shiny white-blond hair and a slight tan. He stands on a dock below a stale sunset, slate water behind him.

Last bedroom. Heat is oppressive in here. Leland left his roller shade up, and the sun has been cooking the air all afternoon. Birds chirp loudly. His window is cracked open. Warm air has been leaking in.

I have transcended frightened and criminal. My body's receptors couldn't sustain the adrenaline jolts and they burnt out. I am strangely calm, a little sleepy even.

I take in his bedroom. Queen-size bed. Pale blue bedspread. He's made his bed, not obsessively, but neat. Beside his bed is a nightstand holding a pair of nice headphones and a mason jar of pencils. In the corner of the room, an old Casio keyboard. His drawers are filled with neatly folded clothes. Nothing hidden underneath the clothes. Closet is open, revealing clothes on hangers, shoes, and shoe boxes on the floor.

Maybe I should hire this guy to help me organize.

I rummage behind hanging clothes, I open shoe boxes. A sewing kit, a collection of bobbleheads, some chewed dog toys. I don't squeeze the toys, but they have that cheap, rubbery, flimsy shape to them indicating they might squeak. Mementos of a dog he had. Which might explain the cage.

I open the small drawer in his nightstand, and I scream. It's pathetic and wispy, but it's a horrified scream.

In his drawer is a scattering of Jolly Ranchers, Starbursts, and Tootsie Rolls.

Heat blooms in my head. My jaw is clenched.

I close the drawer, stand beside his bed, and gaze out his window at the candied sky.

You still don't know for sure that he gave Chloe candy. But let's say he did. Even if he did, it doesn't make him a child predator; it only makes him a person that doesn't comprehend proper adult-to-child behavior. It makes him socially off kilter, not a criminal.

Like you.

It's not him. It's you. Go home and go to sleep. All you need is sleep.

Somewhere outside, a dog barks furiously, startling me. My hand jerks, yanking the cord of the headphones on his nightstand, which catches the mason jar and knocks it off the edge. Pencils scatter on the rug.

The dog barks like mad.

Damn it, Hulk.

I'm pretty sure it's Hulk. Could be a squirrel is mocking Hulk. Could be my mom pulled into my driveway with the kids. Could be anything.

I get down on my knees and gather the pencils, getting whiffs of my fresh fear-stink and stale jogging-stink. Thank God for this blue carpet. I'm lucky the mason jar didn't shatter.

Hulk abruptly stops barking, and, my ears primed, I listen. Dusk's birds sing with vigor. Cicadas shriek. A baby cries houses away. A lawn mower drones down the street.

Pencils and jar back in place, I quickly peek under his bed (bare, not even a stray sock) and grab hold of his bed to heave myself up.

My fingers slide between his mattress and box spring and connect with something hard and small, something with irregular edges. I move my fingers around the object, knowing what it is before I pull it out.

A Shopkin. A plastic stalk of broccoli with small hands, eye-lashed eyes closed in delight. I lift the mattress and find a small white sock and a plastic yellow shovel.

Is that Chloe's shovel?

We've had a number of tiny plastic shovels, a variety of colors.

They crack and usually don't last longer than a few weeks.

I inspect the sock. It's unwashed; the sole is dusty gray and stippled with rubber dashes to prevent small feet from slipping on bare floors. It could fit a two-year-old foot or a six-year-old foot. Socks stretch. We have these socks. Everyone has these socks.

Fuck.

These items could belong to Ava Boone.

These items could belong to Chloe. He could have found them in his yard while he was mowing and jammed them in his pocket. Happens to me all the time. After I mow, my pockets are busting with Legos and marbles and tiny notepads and occasionally I have a hula hoop around my neck. Toys lay forgotten all over my yard. Leland Ernest could be a kind neighbor, stowing them away instead of tossing them in the garbage. He's been waiting to drop them off at my house, but he's shy and socially awkward.

BUT!

Why would he hide them under his mattress? Hiding the neighbor kid's belongings under your mattress is not fucking normal.

Oh God. What if they do belong to Ava Boone?

I feel like I am hanging one-handed from a bowing branch on a tree dangling over the edge of a cliff with a knife skewering my neck. I can't breathe. I am waiting to fall.

I can't move.

Something creaks in the hallway, *loud*. I jerk and hit my head on the corner of the nightstand. *Ow. Fuck.*

A pair of eyes watch me from the doorframe.

His cat.

With white fur on its face and a streak of white between its eyes, and black fur around its yellow-brown eyes and the top of its head, the cat looks like a burglar wearing a black mask. Belly white, back black, it's also wearing a cape. Maybe a superhero instead of a burglar. The cat is fat, mangy, and ghoulish.

It slinks over to me and brushes against my leg. Leland probably lets this cat out at night to eat mice and roll in rabbit turds. Still, I instinctively run my fingers through its fur.

Your senses are on overdrive. You need to get out of here.

I notice the bedspread isn't awash in sunlight anymore. Shadows and shade dominate the room. I haven't been here more than fifteen minutes, right? Twenty, max. I glance at my watch, but it doesn't matter. I never checked the time.

Get. Up.

I jam the Shopkin, sock, and yellow shovel under the mattress. I can't remember exactly where they were before, how they were positioned.

I rush downstairs and close the sliding glass door behind me. I glance west and am stunned by the sky. Sunset pinks and oranges sweep the horizon, appearing too vibrant. Photoshopped. Feels like a dream.

Snapping out of it, I peel off my nitrile gloves and shove them in my pocket. My hands glisten and drip with sweat. I feel more confused, more conflicted than ever. My worries for Ava Boone, my worries for Chloe, have ballooned. I didn't find incriminating evidence, but I found circumstantial evidence. *Suggestive* evidence. I feel twenty years older.

25

THIS WON'T HURT A BIT

I approach the back of my house. Chloe and my mother chat sweetly in the kitchen, their voices playful and sing-song like morning birds. The pair sit at the kitchen table, smashing globs of Play-Doh into plastic waffle presses. My mom is smiling, getting a kick out of whatever comes out of her granddaughter's mouth.

I slide open the clunky screen, which is on the verge of derailing once again. "There's my two favorite girls," I say, slipping out of my breaking-and-entering criminal mindset and into the role of mother with such ease, even I am amazed.

"Mommy!" Chloe shouts and stands up on her chair, opening her arms for me. I scoop her up and feel the strength in her skinny arms and legs as she wraps around my neck and back. I squeeze my eyes shut for a moment while we hug, but all I see is the wire cage on the cold cement floor of Leland's basement furnace room. "Mommy, I'm *so* glad you're home. I missed you so much."

"We were wondering where you were," my mom says without sarcasm. She is happy to play Play-Doh and, strangely, matches Chloe in enthusiasm and attention to detail.

I've had quite an evening, let me tell you!

Chloe squirms out of my arms. Back to Play-Doh.

I aim for semi-cheerful. "I was in the shed."

"Wyatt looked there, I thought."

"I was also talking with the neighbor."

"You left your garage door open. You shouldn't do that. For safety, you know?"

"I forgot. Thanks for the reminder. Where's Wyatt?"

"He went up. Said something about Legos. Are you alright?"

"Sure, why?"

"You look sweaty and, I don't know, *something*. You don't look good." My mom stands and walks to the sink. "Sit. Let me get you some water."

"Thanks, Mom." I sit heavily. Like my pockets are jammed with rocks.

"Grandma bought me shoes," Chloe says, sliding off her chair and hopping toward me.

Red ballet shoes, pebbled with sparkles.

Weight bears down on my chest, wringing the air from my lungs.

Ava's shoes. Those are Ava's shoes.

But they're not Ava's. They are brand new, the tag still hanging from one.

I push my face into a smile for Chloe, and she hops down the hall.

"You are getting too thin," my mom says, setting a glass of water on the table in front of me. "Would you like me to make you a sandwich?"

I can breathe, but I am unsteady. Like I'm both hungover and recovering from surgery. "Oh, OK. Thanks."

"Well, what kind of sandwich do you want?" She sighs, suddenly irritated. She doesn't want more work; she was only trying to be polite.

"You know what, there's leftover spaghetti in the fridge. I'll heat up the spaghetti."

"No sandwich?"

"I'd rather have the spaghetti. Go home, Mom."

"Are you sure?" She puts her hand on my shoulder.

I pat her hand. "Yes. Punch out."

"Did you hear the clicking?"

"I heard it. I once had a loose heat shield that sounded similar. It was rattling and needed to be screwed in tighter. Cost me seventy bucks maybe."

Wow, you sound so incredibly pragmatic and knowledgeable.

She kisses me on the back of my head and grabs her purse and the bottle of water she's been refilling for a month now. I'm about to grab her a new water bottle, but fuck it, I'm exhausted. It's only a dirty water bottle, she'll live.

"Clean up in the bathroom," she says, humor in her voice, after she passes the bathroom and before she walks out the front door. It's the last thing I want to do, but I force myself to stand.

Toilet paper overflows from the bowl, like perky colorful

tissue paper bursting from a gift bag. The empty roll lies, discarded, on the floor.

Chloe couldn't have been in here more than thirty seconds.

"Doesn't it look pretty?" Chloe says from halfway up the staircase.

"Maybe if I didn't have to clean it up. Please don't throw things in the toilet. It gives me more work." As she runs up the stairs, I add, "If you want to use toilet paper, you have to start peeing on the potty."

I plunge the toilet, pumping and sloshing, wet toilet paper sticking to the top of the rubber plunger. It's the cottony plush paper, the kind with faux stitching. How did this even get into my house? I have a policy against luxurious toilet-clogging paper. Someone smuggled it in. My mom?

Toilet unplugged, I transfer the plunger to the corner behind the toilet where it always waits. As if it needs to find its way back to the toilet, it leaves a trail of toilet water along my scarred, water-damaged, uneven wooden floor.

The plunger disgusts me, truly disturbs me, and, if I think about it too long, is a genuine source of worry. The person who redesigns the plunger so the inside rim doesn't slosh with shit water and drip life-threatening bacteria onto the floor will be a billionaire. Have we been using the same plunger design for over a hundred years?

I walk upstairs and stop at Chloe's door. She is sitting on the floor, checking diligently between her toes. Her new sparkly red shoes are nowhere in sight. Thank God. Her dress is up to her waist, and she's wearing no diaper.

"Where's your diaper?"

"Mom," she says, "can you pretend to be a nice mommy?"

Don't get sensitive. She's three.

"I thought I was a nice mommy," I say, trying to be silly, but my voice is flat.

"A nice mommy that takes care of babies?" she says, her voice like spun sugar, like cotton candy.

"I *am* a nice mommy. I took care of you when you were a baby."

"Can you pretend to use a nice voice?"

Oh, for fuck's sake.

She brings me a baby doll. "Take it."

My bones feel brittle, my chest flutters. A gust of wind could knock me to pieces. I sit and do as I'm told.

The dolly is naked. Red crayon scribbled on its forehead. One eye stuck open, one eye shut. Disquieting.

This baby has been mistreated. Wyatt used to undress this baby and whip it down the basement stairs. When Wyatt was six, he carved a hole into this baby's butt crack with my letter opener. That same night in bed Nate and I dissected and analyzed the incident as if it were a billion-dollar merger. We made lists of pros and cons, created spreadsheets and slides. I'm kidding about the spreadsheets, but it was an intense conversation. In the end, we agreed Wyatt's decision to surgically give the baby an anus for the reason of proper digestion made sense; he'd been playing realistic make-believe, and his father was a gastro surgeon. Case closed, Nate and I had sex and laughed about the poor dolly before drifting off to sleep.

I miss Nate. I miss his lack of anxiety, lack of planning, lack of actual *thinking*. His lacks would piss me off to extreme, but right now I miss them. His lacks balanced my excesses.

I hug the mutilated doll. "Chloe, the man next door might be a bad guy. If he talks to you, I want you to run inside our house and tell me right away, OK?"

"OK, Momma." Like it's no big deal.

"If anyone besides me or Grandma or Wyatt offers you candy, come tell me right away. I promise I'll give you a treat, OK?" She might start lying to me, telling me strangers everywhere are giving her candy, and demanding treats from me. I don't care.

"OK," she says. "What's wrong, Momma?"

"Nothing. I'm fine," but my voice is fickle.

"Don't worry, Momma. I'll take care of everything. Do you need me to change your diaper?" Her eyes are expressive and concerned. Her voice is downy; a gentle breeze could carry it away.

"No, thanks. I wear big girl underpants."

Chloe slaps both my cheeks and squishes them together and tugs them up and down in a manner of which I'm sure dermatologists wouldn't approve. I feel the collagen under my cheeks tear.

"Mommy, you will be OK. Let me get you a Band-Aid." She grabs her doctor kit. "Don't worry, this won't hurt a bit." She pushes a plastic shot against my arm, puckering my skin.

"Ow, that hurts."

"Don't worry. You will feel all better."

"Thanks. Do I get the Band-Aid now?"

"Not yet. You need another shot."

Wyatt laughs in his room.

"I'll be right back, Chloe."

Leaving the ugly doll on the floor, I stand and peek into Wyatt's room. "What's so funny?"

"Everything. More shots. Big girl underpants." He has made a little nest of blankets on his floor. Hulk lies in the nest, on her back, paws in the air. Wyatt rubs her hairless belly.

A boy and his dog.

I sit beside him and join in with rubbing Hulk's belly, waiting for Wyatt to say whatever amazing thing will come to him.

"Did you know birds die of light pollution?" he says.

"No."

"During nighttime, they are drawn to lit-up cities. The lights kind of hypnotize the birds and confuse them. Birds circle the lit-up billboards and lit-up buildings until they tire out. When they're exhausted from circling, they crash and die."

"I had no idea, Wyatt. That's sad."

I stop petting Hulk. In an effort to win my attention back, she wraps her front paws around my arm and scratches me.

"Ow. Hulk, that hurt." Tiny blood bubbles emerge along the scratch.

"Are you OK, Mom?"

"I'm fine. It's a good reminder that I've let her nails get too long."

On my way to the bathroom to wash my arm, I peek in on Chloe.

She is naked, standing on her tippy toes on the edge of an open and wobbling dresser drawer, reaching for a glass music box I placed on a high shelf because I didn't want her to play with it.

She loses her balance, and her body tips backward. In three wide strides, I am there to catch her small baby body as she falls. I throw my weight to the right, and we land on the single mattress instead of my momentum throwing us at the window.

In her mind the world is cushiony and safe, and she is quickly squirming away from my grasp, already making the next joke, thinking up the next task for me. I lie on her bed, heart jackhammering, my spirit buckling.

Leland Ernest and the items hidden under his mattress are steel scraping flint in my volatile mind.

26

MY VAGINA WAS MADE IN CHINA

Here's something I haven't mentioned. Chloe resembles Marilyn Monroe. I sound delusional, I know, but bear with me.

Her hair is airy and voluminous and white-blond. She has arched eyebrows and a widow's peak (dominant trait on Nate's side). More poignant than physical traits, her voice is breathy and high, and she does this flirty thing where she tilts her chin down and smiles while she's saying something taunting like *You can't get me* or *Of course I didn't eat it, silly.*

She's like a gorgeous woman with cherub cheeks and a toddler's body. She'll be grotesque by the time she's thirty, I'm sure. Bad timing runs on my side of the family.

Enhancing her allure is her dark sense of humor.

She'll run away in the wretched maze that is the public library or down a sidewalk littered with brilliant red leaves or into the fucking street. I'll chase her, scolding her in a stern voice, and she'll laugh deliriously until the moment I catch her and she feels anger in my rough grip.

She'll put dog food pebbles in Hulk's water bowl and coo,

Hulk, see if you can find it.

To get my attention she'll say, *Hey*, slap my cheek, and ask me when lunch is as if she didn't slap me.

She likes television shows with a dark edge. She's enraptured watching the mean old grandfather yell at Heidi and send her to bed without supper.

She talks about her vagina with an evocative, incomprehensible maturity. We'll be dancing to pop music and she'll stop suddenly, turning to me as if a genius notion has dawned on her, and say, *Is this song about my vagina?* when it actually is. She has jumped on her bed, laughing and singing, *My vagina wants to go to Disney World. My vagina was made in China.*

This is a child I need to protect from the world outside my house.

This is a child I need to protect from herself.

My worries are not exclusive to my child. I am not one of those parents who blindly believes her own daughter outranks other children in beauty and intelligence.

I see these girls *everywhere*. Little girls with minds that seem to be more mature, more provocative, than the actual child can possibly be. Little girls with velvety skin and long limbs and stunning highlights in their wind-tangled hair. They quietly regard the world with doe eyes or they run at it with brash smiles. Their innocent minds and little bodies are too heavenly and mysteriously irresistible for a deranged mind.

Boys get stolen too, I know. I worry about Wyatt, but my concern for him doesn't wrench the air out of my lungs. Maybe because of his age. Maybe because of statistics.

Unfortunately, I understand an obsessive, predator mind. All too well.

The Predator Mind considers a specific fantasy with such frequency, with such detail, the fantasy becomes familiar and natural. Doable.

I lie on my bed in the dark, shoes on, and strain to grasp barely audible sounds of life in my house. Hulk's moist crotch-licking from outside my door. Down the hall, Wyatt's nasal snore on the intake. Chloe sucking her pacifier. *Three sucks, rest. Three sucks, rest.*

It is 10:08pm when I take off my shoes and open my laptop. I wildly roam the vast wireless space. I cast my anxious net wide, searching everything from snow globes to light pollution to rabies-infected bats to YouTube toilet repair to YouTube survival tutorials. *How to escape a car sinking in water. How to survive a nuclear fallout.* Note to self: *buy potassium iodide pills.*

I come across a story titled *Top Ten Character Traits to Teach Your Child* and dive in because I worry that if I were to skip it, I might miss some key insight that could have improved my kids' lives. The psychologist author tells me, if I want to be a good parent, the first trait to instill in my child is: *Live in the present. Enjoy the moment.*

The psychologist author tells me I need to model this behavior to my child; I need to show my child how to be present, enjoy nature, be mindful, and pay attention to her feelings and the feelings of people around her. If I teach my kid to live in the moment, my kid will learn empathy, kindness, and conscientiousness.

I resolve to not take the bait. *Fucking media terrorists.* I will not let this article play upon my parenting insecurities. Why?

Because *I live in the present.* Let me tell you, it's not all it's cracked up to be.

I live so much in the moment, I am *trapped* in the moment, heart hammering, palms sweating, bombarded by my own observations and self-interrogation. I live so much in the present, I am incapable of imagining the future. I can't plan well. Can't foresee that the intensity of each moment will fade with time. Can't sense that tomorrow or maybe next week, what I am worrying about right now will no longer be a worry.

Just for shits and giggles (and partly because I ceaselessly doubt even my strongest opinions), I glance at the next trait I need to teach my kid.

Be adaptable, the psychologist tells me.

Adaptable? Really? You know who excels at being adaptable? Hoarders. They adapt seamlessly and silently to sharing a small living space with cockroaches, Ziplocs containing their own feces, mounds of black-speckled, molding laundry, and fuzzy green bread.

Homeless people, there's an impressively adaptable group. A person's got to be flexible to eat from a dumpster or sleep on a sidewalk busy with gawking, homefull pedestrians.

Murderers, too. Who's more adaptable than a person who ends another human's life, then washes bloody tissue scraps off their skin, has a cup of coffee, and maybe heads to work?

I'm adaptable. I shake my head and close my laptop.

It is 11:48pm when I pull up my covers. 12:16am hits. 12:57am.

I have tried to distract myself. I have tried to drown my worries about Leland Ernest and the items I found under his mattress, but they keep buoying to the surface of my mind.

Not items. Charms. Trophies.

And the large dog cage. He has no dog. Maybe he had a dog, but maybe it was a small lap dog.

Leland Ernest is a cloud of weed killer, pregnant and moist and spreading, poisoning my every budding thought. The odor of his house is a slimy residue on my tongue. His proximity is the chest pain of an impending heart attack.

27

A CROWBAR, A CREDIT CARD, AND A HAMMER

Another dream.

Instead of putting a coffee pod into my machine, I'm stuffing it with a little girl's dirty sock. When coffee doesn't drip into my mug, I'm baffled. Why is this machine not making coffee? What am I doing wrong?

The old-fashioned coffee maker. Dig that up. I still have some coffee filters and expired grounds. As I descend the basement stairs, it hits me. I gave the old coffee maker to my sister.

I sit on a basement stair, confused and fatalistically modern. I have become reliant upon my complicated, expensive coffee machine, and now that it won't make coffee with a little girl's dirty sock, what the hell do I have?

Make coffee the way Grandma did, on the goddamn stove.

My dream fast-forwards ten or twenty minutes. *I am sitting at the kitchen table, my mug in front of me, sipping my coffee from a plastic shovel. My tongue probes stray coffee grit along the side of my cheek.*

A gang of fruit flies hovers over a bunch of bananas on the counter. One of them roams over and lingers in front of my left eye.

I slap my hands together vengefully and put him out. His small carcass drops to the table and I blow him onto the floor.

I would never smash an insect so violently and enthusiastically when the kids are watching. The pressure of setting a good example—being a helper, a problem-solver, a deep-breath taker, a non-complainer, a life-valuer, a bright-side-looker—weighs on my neck perpetually. No wonder my neck aches and has lost flexibility.

I sip nasty coffee, swallow a few grinds. I like the quiet, but also dislike it. The void of my children is gaping.

Out the sliding glass door, the sky is bubblegum pink.

On the table in front of me are: two pairs of pants with deep pockets, two long-sleeve shirts, blue nitrile gloves, a large Ziploc full of plastic grocery bags, a Ziploc of shredded leftover chicken, brand new pairs of male sneakers and flip-flops (each pair is three sizes too big for me and has never been worn), a crowbar, a credit card, and a hammer.

Chloe's sleepy calls of "Momma, Momma" rouse me. I blink my eyes open. I'm sitting in a chair at the kitchen table. The room is dark except for the glow from a floor-level nightlight. My watch reads 3:17am. *Sleepwalking again.*

As I stand, my fingers meet something unexpected. Cold, sweaty metal.

The business end of a hammer. It's one of our older ones. The wooden handle is riddled with scratches. I'm pretty sure it belonged to my dad.

In a sleepy haze, I slip the hammer into our kitchen junk drawer, which is already jammed with crumpled receipts, marbles, coins, batteries, gum, screwdrivers, a stethoscope, and a full strand of Christmas lights. Glancing at that open junk drawer is like gazing into a mirror. The disarray of the stupid junk drawer pulls me away from sleepiness toward bright white neurosis. I resist, clinging to mind-numbing sleep as I bump my way upstairs.

In her dark room, Chloe's sitting in her bed, statue-still, listlessly staring at her open door. Neither of us says a word. We are both half-asleep. I lie down in her bed, and, feeling the weight and warmth of my body beside her, she easily falls back asleep.

28

LEAD GLASS, CHIPPED BONE, AND A SPLASH OF ANTIFREEZE

I call my realtor at 6:05am with the intention of being directed to voice mail. I can't afford to move, but I need to make this call. What choice do I have?

I close my bedroom door gently and say, "Hi, Jane, this is Grace Wright. I just moved in here so you're going to think I'm nuts, but I've decided to put my house back on the market. Can you schedule me in for some photos? Nate has the kids this weekend so I can clean the heck out of this place. I should be good to go Saturday afternoon. I will buy flowers! Or you could use the former owner's photos. Whatever you think! Thanks."

Do I want to change my message or accept it?

Good to go? I will buy flowers? Do I sound insane? My hands tremble.

Accept.

I open my door. Wyatt's standing there.

"Good morning, Wy." I smile and pull him in for a hug. He does his usual: head turned away, body turned away, barely tolerating my hug. I am repulsive. "I'm wearing deodorant, perfume, *and* I brushed my teeth," I say.

"Who were you talking to?"

"It's not important. You want eggs or cereal?"

"Eggs."

"Lunch—you want ham and cheese or P and J?"

"P and J."

"I'm on it." I could ask Wyatt to make his own lunch. He's capable, and it would help me, but morning is an especially fragile time. I may pretend to be in charge, making the rules, barking out the rules, but it's a façade. I'm at their mercy. If they lose their temper, if they melt down, if they refuse, then I will be late for work. So I tiptoe around them, cleaning up their messes, putting their shoes where they can find them, and averting disasters they don't see coming. In the morning, when we need to be *on time*, I'm their bitch.

Also, because I divorced their father, I always feel like they have *less than*. Guilt is not a good compass, I know that, but it is my compass.

"Thanks, Mom."

I rub his fluffy hair and head to Chloe's room.

She's wearing only her diaper and she's sitting with her legs in the W position, her toes pointed back. Media terrorists have conveyed to me several times that the W position is bad for her knees, *very bad*, but she's so quiet and pleasant as she puts small things—doll shoes, paper clips, marbles she should not have, stickers—in a Tupperware container, there's no way I'm going to reposition her legs.

"Morning, Chloe. Thanks for playing on your own like a big

girl. I'm going to make eggs. Come down when you're ready."

"I want raisins and blueberries," she says buoyantly.

"Sure thing."

"I want to wear a dress," she says slowly, testing me.

"OK, bring it down and I'll help you put it on."

"I want tights and orange juice," she says, knowing she has the upper hand.

I grind my teeth and suggest, "May I *please* have orange juice."

She repeats what I said and adds sweetly, sincerely, "Thanks, Momma."

I take in her precious pebbled toes, her bare chest, her small, flat nipples. Dizziness settles upon me. I'm standing on the top stair so I reach for the railing. I slide my hand along it as I carefully make my way down.

My foot on the bottom step, last night's dream jolts me like a tuning fork touching dendrites in my brain. Warning me. Beckoning me.

Me stuffing a little girl's sock into the coffee maker. Me drinking coffee with a child's shovel.

A child's sock. A child's shovel. *You found those things under his mattress.* There is something *wrong* with him.

I open the junk drawer and touch my fingertips to my dad's old hammer. That I'm accessing dangerous tools *while* I'm sleepwalking is worrisome. I don't have time to dwell on this new, bothersome behavior, so I compartmentalize and move on.

My eggs turn out perfectly, but freeing the miniature boxes of raisins from their shrink-wrap is challenging for me this morning. I grab what's closest: a pen. I only need to make one small tear to liberate the cluster of miniature boxes.

But like most decisions made under stress or fatigue, the pen is a bad choice. Damn thing explodes onto my shirt, Jackson Pollock-style.

"Ooh," Wyatt says. "That's not good."

I bite my bottom lip and force a long breath. "On the contrary. This shirt is twice your age." I toss my ink-splattered shirt in the garbage. One less ugly shirt to wash. If these minor, messy catastrophes continue, my wardrobe will get a minimalist's makeover. I'm going topless until we're ready to walk out the door. Who knows what else I'll end up covered with?

"You're not going to wear just that to work, are you?" Wyatt says, his expression nervous as he glances at my bra.

I should find his question funny. Instead, my heart aches. I'm that unpredictable, that temperamental, he actually thinks I might head to work topless? Dang.

I smile. "No, I will wear a shirt to work."

My cell phone rings. I am setting plates and food on the table.

"Aren't you going to answer your phone?"

"Nope." It's probably my realtor. The less communication, the better.

Chloe hands me a pale pink cotton dress, and I pull it over her head. "Pink pigtails, please," she says. I follow her into the bathroom. She stands on the step stool in front of the mirror. While I brush her hair, she points to different freckles and bruises on her body and asks about each one. "When can I get them gone?"

Already she's focusing on her imperfections. Where has she learned to criticize her body?

"I like those freckles, Chlo. They're cute. They're my little friends."

Tilting her chin down, she glares at me in the mirror. "I don't like them. Them are *not* your friends."

"They'll go away on their own." I'm too tired for the truth.

"Even that one?" She points to a big freckle on her neck.

"Maybe. We'll see."

"Mom!" she fake-screams, eyes wide, regarding me in the mirror. "I see your *breasts*. Where is your shirt?"

I tell her about the pen. She puckers her lips and furrows her brows. "Will I get them breasts?"

"Yep. When you're twelve."

She clasps her hands together as if she's auditioning for a commercial. "I can't wait!"

I sure as hell can.

"It's dad's night so he'll pick you guys up this afternoon," I remind her. My hands tremble as I twist pink rubber bands around ghostly wisps of toddler hair.

"I will miss you at work," Chloe says. "I will put this in your hair so you don't get lonely. Come closer, please." It's some sort of barrette, and she snaps it in underneath my hair. She does this all the time. I'm always pulling surprise barrettes out of my hair. Half the time, when I'm yanking one out, I'm wondering when she snuck it in.

"I will miss you too, Chlo."

She cradles my face in her hands and looks back and forth

179

at my eyes. "You have lightning bolts in your eyes."

My heart flutters, which is silly. She means nothing by it. I'm sure the awful yellow bathroom lights are reflecting off my eyes. Still, I probe. "Does Dad have lightning bolts too?"

"I don't think. You look pretty, Momma."

"Thanks."

"Just don't smile because your teeth are brown."

I smile extra wide, and she giggles. "We've got to get moving, Chlo. Go have a few quick bites of eggs, raisins, and blueberries."

Ten minutes later, I slide into the driver's seat. I'm the last one in. Wyatt managed to buckle Chloe into her car seat. I glance at both of them in the rearview. There is a smear of deep violet near the top of Chloe's pale pink dress. I feel the tug of déjà vu, and my squishy insides quiver.

Ava.

The blotchy stain consumes me. It's like my vision has singed to gray, and this blueberry stain is the only color, vivid and cool, in the whole world.

Ava had a blueberry stain near the collar of her shirt.

It's stupid, it's only a stain, children on every street are literally wiping their sticky, moist hands across their shirts right now, smudging their clothes, but still, I can't shake this eerie familiarity.

Get control of yourself, Grace.

In my rearview mirror, Chloe gives me one of those forced, squinty-eyed, smiling-hard smiles. Her teeth are washed in blue. Her lips are a chilly, plump violet.

180

I smile back at her, then at Wyatt. "You are both wonderful people. I love you guys."

I put it in reverse and roll down the driveway.

In the periphery of my vision—a man stands inside my garage beside the door to my house. I blink once, twice, three times, and he's gone.

It's a trick of the light. Dark garage to outside brightness plays with your retinas.

The shitfaced toddler shakes my mind, the snow globe, trying to concuss me. Flakes shudder, and the turbulence is a desperate, raw type of irritating I associate with being stuck in the purgatory of plateau before orgasm.

Last night I read that snow globes used to be made of lead glass, chipped bone, and a splash of antifreeze. The latter, mixed in with water, would slow the chipped bone flakes' fall. All these things macabre and poisonous, it seems fitting they'd be a metaphor for my mind.

29

FUCK LYNYRYD SKYNYRD AND THEIR "FREE BIRD" NONSENSE

It's garbage night.

When I get home from work, I roll the garbage and recycling bins to the curb, one at a time, creating baritone rumbles which match the tall, bloated clouds set against a gray sky. Storms on their way.

As I walk up my driveway, a breeze ripples the fabric under the arm of my shirt. I stop and take in the breeze, slowing down and enjoying it as if I were licking ice cream. One of my neighbors is playing Lynyrd Skynyrd's "Free Bird". I imagine me and the kids in the minivan, driving down a bare strip of highway surrounded by pastoral land. Driving fast, sky everywhere, tall grass bending to the wind for miles.

You are not stuck. Take the little cash you have and blow out of here. Go somewhere rural, start over. Let the kids live dirt poor and eat and sleep and read. You don't need any of this crap you think they need. Friends. Award-winning schools. None of it matters. You love them. That's all that matters. Take them and go. Before it's too late.

But you never know what school you'll get.

You will have no money, no job, no childcare, no connections, no help.

Most of all, Nate will find you and wring you out in court. You will lose everything.

Fuck the breeze. Fuck Lynyrd Skynyrd and their "Free Bird" nonsense.

You are stuck. So fucking stuck. So deal with it.

30

HIS FINGERNAILS DUG IN

Thirty minutes later I park directly in front of the Boone house. My window is open, and my elbow hangs out. I glance in my rearview. My hair is windblown and wild.

Gray sky is tinted fiery orange, streaked with yellow, and blotted with overflowing clouds. Birds shriek, panicking over the coming storm. Dogs bark and squirrels work their extreme sporting events, slingshotting branches and ruffling leaves.

You are going to walk right up. You are not selfish. You are trying to help them. You are trying to help their daughter.

They haven't given up hope. Of course they haven't. It's their child. How could they? Ethan Boone posted days ago on Facebook.

The Boones' garage door opens. Ethan Boone rolls his recycling bin down his driveway. Leaving my purse in the minivan but palming my keys, I walk up.

His face changes when he sees me. His disgust takes my breath away. He keeps rolling his bin. He's trying to ignore me.

Don't let it bother you. He is hurting.

"I found something," I say. "It's important."

He lets the bin drop. His mouth remains an angry line, but his eyebrows raise in interest. His eyes are vacant and afraid. His expression is like a child's discordant collage.

"I found a Shopkin under Leland Ernest's mattress."

Ethan closes his eyes, says nothing.

"He also had a little girl's sock and a small plastic shovel. It's yellow. Leland gave your daughter a Shopkin, didn't he? Was it the broccoli Shopkin?"

He opens his eyes, and they're wet. He clenches his fists, then splays his fingers. "How did you know that?"

"Someone told me." I definitely can't rat out the State's Attorney's Office rep.

His eyes are bleary, desperate. The corners of his mouth twitch. "Did you tell the police?"

"No. I broke into his house. I can't tell them."

His eyes flicker with shock. He pushes his palm through his messy, graying hair. He's grappling with his thoughts. "Why? Why would you do that?"

Where to start? How to be concise? How to be *gentle*?

You're past gentle. Just tell him. "I've been seeing things. I'm not sleeping. I thought I saw your daughter in his window, but wasn't sure if it was real," I say. Ethan winces at this. His shoulders droop. His eyes are like house windows, and no one's home. "Leland's back door was open. I searched his house. She wasn't there, but I found the broccoli toy and a girl's sock and a toy shovel." The skin under one of Ethan's eyebrows is twitching. Maybe he's overcaffeinated or sleep-deprived.

Just like you.

"They were hidden under his mattress," I say.

Tell him about the dog cage. I can't. It's too cruel. Too horrific.

He covers his face with both hands, stands like a statue for a few seconds. "Oh my God." He wipes his tears away. His eyes are red from crying, bloodshot. He has aged so much since his photo in the paper.

"I have kids too," I offer, gazing up at the gray A-bomb clouds. "I couldn't stop worrying about this guy Leland. I wanted to know if you thought he was dangerous. Then I found those *things*. A little girl's things. I'm out of my mind."

He grabs my arms, gripping me tightly, his scraggly fingernails digging into the back of my triceps. It hurts, but I ignore the pain. This man is struggling. He's angry, but he won't hurt me. *He won't hurt you. He won't hurt you.*

Please don't hurt me.

His eyes are angry and bulging and veiny and jaundiced. He's got this weird black-red dot on his sclera, maybe an artifact of a burst blood vessel. From crying or vomiting. He gets in my face, stinking of alcohol and body odor. "Leave us alone," he growls.

"What do you mean?" Was I unclear? "Is it your daughter's Shopkin?"

He speaks slowly, squeezing my arms tighter, pinching my skin. "We can't stand it anymore. We can barely breathe. Don't come back here. Don't fucking come back."

"But you posted on Facebook the other day. Anyone who knows anything, contact you."

I pull my right arm away, but he's gripping me too tight.

"Let go of me." My voice sounds paper-thin.

He lets go.

"You think he's dangerous, right? He's a dangerous man?"

The fury in Ethan's eyes vanishes and is replaced with a dementia-like confusion. As if he's not sure how he ended up outside. As if he's not sure he belongs in this universe. Abandoning his garbage bin in the middle of the driveway, he walks into his house.

I run to my minivan, my skin stinging where his fingernails dug in.

31

THE SHITFACED TODDLER HAS FALLEN ASLEEP ON A PILE OF STUFFED ANIMALS

I found an answer to Wyatt's bird-formation question. I'm slow, but not apathetic.

Turns out, birds take turns being Point Bird. They are perpetually and seamlessly shifting their position in the V formation as they fly because leading the V quickly fatigues the Point Bird.

Other birds in the V cruise easily along the downdraft of the bird in front of them, getting free lift and saving their energy for when it's their turn to step up.

Each one of them bears the burden of being Point Bird, briefly. Each bird spends less than a minute, often mere seconds, at the vertex of the V before switching places with another bird. Each takes a hit for the good of the team regardless of whether they are related and regardless of social hierarchy. It's called reciprocal altruism.

It's my turn to be Point Bird. I will not *drop it*. I will keep pushing and prying.

Ten years from now I don't want to find out that Leland

Ernest kidnapped and murdered a few kids. I don't want to have to soothe myself with complacency and blatant lies. *Oh well, what could I have done?* I don't want to be a gaper, a gossiper, a part of the inactive herd.

I vow to be Point Bird.

I vow to live for my kids.

The media terrorists have tried to shame me for this. They have told me, *Put your career*—your empty, unfulfilling career where you may have to jump through hoops and surround yourself with people you dislike and obey policies you don't morally agree with—*first*. They have told me, *Put your marriage*—to another adult who might decide they don't want to stay married because you don't give enough oral or you are not as attractive and peppy as you used to be—*first*.

But what is more noble than to live for my children? To eat and breathe for my kids? To nourish their souls with stories, advice, encouragement, and confidence-building, intelligence-provoking games and toys? To love them so much I occasionally hover, eating up every precious giggle and discovery? To offer them all my time and energy so that they may look to me for guidance instead of looking to their binge-drinking, hormone-addled peers? To ultimately offer them, kind, capable, and free-thinking, to the world?

The media terrorists would label me a Helicopter Parent.

So fucking be it.

It is 7:23pm when I lie down on the couch and close my eyes.

Rain pounds the roof like falling nails, and its belligerence soothes me.

My mind, the snow globe, is serene and lucid. The shitfaced toddler has fallen asleep on a pile of stuffed animals, and the snow globe sits on the floor, clear and still. Crystal.

I wake up, horrified and shivering, my heart pummeling. I'm in my bathtub, steeped in frigid water. My nipples protrude like volcanic islands surrounded by murky seas. It's dark, but there's a faint, soft glow from the bathroom nightlight.

Sleeping in the fucking bathtub? You're going to drown yourself, dummy.

My nightmare is still with me and, even though I'm shivering, it is fresh and hot and pungent as the trickling blood of a shot-gunned deer. I see the whole thing in sequence.

Me breaking into Leland Ernest's back door with a crowbar and a junk-mail credit card. It's as easy as the bearded man decked in camo on YouTube promised me.

I leave the crowbar on the cement porch and enter his house, my nitrile-gloved fingers gripping and regripping my hammer, my hands sweaty inside the gloves.

My heart bangs loud and full against my ribcage. Sweat slips down my neck. Time slows.

The lights are off in Leland's house, and it has that after-lunch, deli-meat, elementary-school smell. A half-eaten hotdog in a bun sits on a paper plate on the counter. A supersize plastic mustard bottle beside it. He left the mustard out. *I hate when I do that.*

My clothes are damp from the rain, but not heavy. I am careful in my strides, almost shuffling, so I don't trip on his cat. I climb the stairs swiftly, drawing creaks, but for some strange reason, I'm not worrying about it. Dreams are weird like that.

Doors to the office and spare bedroom are closed. Bathroom door is cracked. Leland's door is wide open. An open door leading to darkness. Beckoning me.

His lumpy shape tents the blanket on his bed. His drapes are closed, but parted ever so slightly, and the barest sliver of blue moonlight casts a thin rhombus on the wall beside me. Rain patters and pings on the shingles. He left his window wide open. Why?

I take a silent breath, tighten my clammy, nitrile-gloved hand around the wooden handle of my rain-moist hammer, and in one quick movement pull back the blanket.

My heart drops into my uterus.

Empty. *His bed is empty. But he was just here?*

Are you sure?

I saw the outline of his body.

Did you?

Then where is he? Bastard turned the tables on me. How did he know I was coming?

He didn't. He couldn't.

I'm blinking hard, staring at the empty bed, out of breath and grasping for explanations. He's in the basement. He's working the night shift. He's out drinking. He sleeps in the guest room. He's in the bathroom. He's in the fucking closet.

I shake my head, trying to loosen the cobwebs. But why did I see him in the bed?

You wanted to see him there.

I turn fast, my back to the wall in case he's in the closet.

There he is, blocking the doorway of his room. He is a dark silhouette, without eyes, without a mouth. Sparse moonlight casts a faint plank of light on the wall inches to his left. His silhouette is gorilla-like, slouched, jutting chin, thick arms. The bat he holds in his hand hangs down, brushing the carpet. A caveman carrying a club.

I am out-weighed, out-muscled, and out-weaponed.

I have screwed up, made a phlegmy string of bad choices that is suddenly, grotesquely obvious to me.

Leland Ernest stole six or seven nights of sleep from me, molding me into a jumpy, irritable, unpredictable soldier, my jittery finger stiff and sore against my machine gun trigger, my elbows in the mud, blinking my eyes over and over to keep the sweat out and because I'm seeing ghosts of friends I know aren't there.

My pants are soaked through, but it's not piss; my crotch and ass sweat profusely. My hands are sweaty and freezing inside the nitrile gloves. I have the adrenaline shakes. I am in the throes of fight or flight.

No one knows I am here. Leland Ernest is going to kill me. My children will be motherless.

Stop. You have already thought this through. He took Ava, but he will not take Chloe.

Leland's cat slinks behind him, brushes against his leg, and creeps toward me.

"What do you want? Who are you?" Fear and threat meld in his words. His voice is husky with sleep.

I say nothing.

"You broke into my house." His tone is wet with fury and accusation, but his voice rises into a question with a hint of bewilderment and awe.

I say nothing.

"Who are you?" he spits.

192

I say nothing.

I wear a black winter beanie and dark clothes. My only advantage right now, if you could even call it that, is to say nothing. I'm not sure I am capable of speech anyway.

Standing here, as far away from him as possible, seems to be my best option.

Halfway to me, the cat pauses near the bed and sniffs at the mattress.

Above the gentle sound of rainfall, sirens rise in the distance.

I am not a religious gal and, even if I were, even in my exhausted, frenetic state of lunacy, I am still not crazy enough to believe some deity would help me out with murdering my neighbor, heinous as Leland Ernest is. Nevertheless, I am thrown a bone. I would be stupid if I didn't try to catch it.

"Before I came over, I called the police," I say. "They're on their way."

He doesn't flinch at my voice, the revelation of my womanhood. It's as if he knew. "You lie."

The sirens, still blocks away, stop, leaving the room silent but for the soft rainfall outside and my pulse banging against the backs of my eyeballs.

He laughs but the cadence is off and he sounds slightly girlish. Like an adolescent boy, his voice occasionally losing its masculinity and fluttering away.

He was flirting with Ava. *My adrenaline-flooded arteries, my tremoring bones, my thumping pulse cannot sustain this intensity.* You found a little girl's sock under his mattress. *The cat brushes against my pant leg and skulks under the bed.* He was trying to teach Ava to whistle. He gave Chloe candy. *My skin is hyper-sensitive, and bile lurches up my throat. He gave Ava candy. He was trying to teach Chloe to whistle.* You need to protect Chloe. *With my free hand, I grab the mason jar full of pencils from his nightstand, and throw it at him. Pencils go flying.*

He raises his hand to block the jar. He deflects it, and the jar hits the wall behind him, shattering spectacularly. I charge, lifting my hammer and swinging it down, aiming for his temple. Bone cracks, thunderous and awful. Before his back hits the doorframe, I strike him again in the same spot.

He stumbles sideways, putting a hand out to break his fall. Another cracking sound. Maybe his wrist. His cheek hits the carpet anyway, and his face is exposed by the faint blue moonlight. Thick dark blood runs into his open eyes, into his open mouth.

His leg goes out and trips me. I'm not sure if it is accidental or intentional, but I go down. I scramble back, out of his reach, and get back on my feet.

He has managed to push himself up and he's sitting with his back against the wall as if he were relaxing, except his face is veined in blood. Half his face falls within the beam of moonlight, the other half blends into darkness. He moans, whimpers, and coughs. It's the wet cough of a pneumonia patient. A string of bloody phlegm dangles, wiggling, on his meaty lower lip. He opens his eyes, then closes them.

I don't want to do this. It's disgusting. Regret swells inside my belly like menstrual blood. I stand over him, breathing loudly and open-mouthed, winded. I have rolled up my sleeves for numerous disgusting jobs without complaint, but this, this is beyond anything I could have imagined.

I struggle for an alternative. Too late. There is no alternative.

This is the way you protect your children. This is for Chloe. This is for Ava.

I swing my hammer at him again. His blood hits my tongue. Oh, God!

Disgusted, I want to spit, but can't leave my spit in his house. I close my mouth around his blood, tasting metal and salt and meat.

His body is entirely on the carpet, but his head is contorted, kinked awkwardly against the wall. He says, "I know—"

"What? You know what?"

Moments ago, standing in the doorway, he looked like an angry troll. Now he is childlike and sleepy. His eyes flutter open, but they are too heavy, too much of a burden, and they close. He is drifting.

As if he is going to whisper some valuable insight or secret or forgiveness, I plead, "What is it? What?"

There is no mystical secret. No penance. Nothing. End this. Get out of here.

I am sobbing without tears. I don't want to, but I hit him three more times in the same spot. This time with my mouth shut tight and my eyes squinted. Clots of tissue splatter my cheeks and forehead. Two or three bone shards bite my skin.

I back away, chest heaving.

My mind breaks from the gravity of the situation and leans toward absurdity and facetiousness. Exercise gurus never speak to the physical benefits of violent, gunless murder! Good thing I've been sprinting a mile. This is the hardest damn workout I've ever had.

From under the bed, the cat's glowing marble eyes mark me.

Now shivering in cold bathwater, I'm staring at black specks of moldy grout between my bathroom tiles. Nightlight's glow is faint. *Go to bed. Forget about Leland. Forget about your violent nightmares.*

I grab a crumpled towel from the bathroom floor. It's damp and mildewy, but I use it to dry off anyway. My clothes are in a pile near the tub. They're damp too. *You must have sloshed water.*

You're as bad as the kids. I catch a faint whiff of bleach. Glance at my watch. 3:53am. *You can still get a few hours.* I pull the plug, and water glugs down the drain.

My nightmare is fading. My heavy exhaustion burns away at the vivid details, leaving the edges black, singed, and hazy with smoke. Dialogue, gone. Internal thoughts, gone. I only remember the plot. That, and the supersize mustard.

My skin still damp, I pull on my warmest fleece pajamas—polar bears riding sleds—and collapse into bed.

32

BRAND NEW TATTOO ENGRAVED IN MY SKIN, JUST BEGINNING TO BLEED

My alarm wakes me at 6:30am, the latest I can get my ass out of bed and make it to work on time. I am the type of tired reserved for the heavily medicated, my limbs filled with liquid metal. My body got its first taste of deep sleep in over a week and, with the decadent taste on its tongue, it is ravenous and gnawing for more.

Hulk is tip-tapping her nails on my floor because she is excited I'm awake and also because her bladder is full. I really should get those nails trimmed.

My hair is damp. *Oh, that's right. You woke in the tub*. Dull aches in my forearms and the backs of my knees urge me to stretch, so I take a minute to do so, reminding myself nagging aches are good; they suggest I am a hard worker and I am lucky to be able to move.

As I slip into my clothes, the doorbell rings. Hulk bolts and slides down the stairs, barking like mad.

Nate and the kids stand on the porch. Sidewalks and driveways are tinged dark from rain, but the early sun is bright.

Wet grass shimmers in the morning light.

Nate gives me a kind smile, then hustles back to his idling car. The kids take off way too many clothes in the foyer while telling me random stuff. The deluge of their questions, their chatting, plays on my brain like a small child pounding on a piano.

I pull Chloe up into my arms. "Did you eat breakfast, Chlo?"

"No!" She laughs, amazed she hasn't had breakfast yet.

"No breakfast! Oh boy, we'd better fix that." I squirm my mouth into her neck and kiss the soft skin there smelling of lollipops. She laughs and tries to close her neck, but my mouth is already wedged in and I'm enjoying her boisterous laughing too much.

I remember we're running late.

I get them cereal and pull Wyatt in for a hug. I squeeze him too hard. He lets me, and hugs me back for a change. And here I didn't even put on deodorant.

With Chloe and Wyatt fed and packed in the car, I look both ways before I back out of the driveway. I am alert and calm. Rain has cleaned and refreshed the earth. The morning is sunny and breezy. I roll down everyone's windows. Wind rattles the trees' leaves, freeing small rain droplets to sprinkle the sidewalks and grass.

There's no avoiding seeing Leland's house. And once I see it, I can't pull my gaze away. Nothing appears outwardly unusual, yet his house stands out. The butter-yellow vinyl siding that was previously faded and mildew-speckled is now sharper, in technicolor, against a dull neighborhood backdrop of monotonous houses and trees. His house is striking. His house is like a brand-new tattoo engraved in my skin, just beginning to bleed and swell.

Clouds pass overhead, dimming the bright morning and casting a moving shadow across my dashboard. Alarm sinks teeth into my skin. I can't breathe.

Sock. Shopkin. Plastic shovel. I am back in Leland's room two days ago, finding a little girl's items under his mattress.

You should have called the police.

Sock. Shopkin. Plastic shovel.

You couldn't call the police. You broke into his house.

The tired, overweight engine of a garbage truck sighs. The familiar sound eases my panic. I breathe in. Out. The truck turns the corner onto my street.

33

RIPPED OPEN THIS DIMENSION TO OOZE BLOOD INTO MY CAR

Work is work. Bad pay. Good people. Cute, impressionable children. A time-suck. A pleasant distraction. A few laughs. Constant cleaning, which, today, includes: spilled paint, a hard macaroni project, juice puddles, tiny beads springing free from a torn necklace and rolling in every possible direction, and a broken coffee cup in the breakroom, the last one being completely my fault. It didn't crack simply; it shattered, and small shards struck my skin.

After work, I pick up Chloe, then Hulk, and we head to PetSmart.

A pet store is as good as any playground. As Hulk gets her nails cut, Chloe has a blast. We talk to the cats. We gaze at the fish. We keep our eyes glued to the trembling hill of hamster bedding, waiting for a tiny pink nose to emerge.

"What are they doing under there, Momma?" Chloe is delighted.

I am even feeling calm enough to play hide-and-seek. I hide behind the aisle-end section of feather toys for cats. I wait a few seconds before peeking my head into the aisle. When Chloe sees me, she scream-laughs with joy and rushes my leg like a twenty-five-pound linebacker.

"Momma! I thought you were gone but then I saw your brown teeth and smelled your smell and I knew it was you." Kids, the ultimate ego-deflators.

"What do I smell like?"

"A plant."

"A good plant or a stinky plant?"

"Good plant."

At least there's that.

When it's time, we open the door to the Grooming Room. Perfumed air blasts us, sweet oatmeal and chocolate wash, but underneath are the buried scents of dog urine and freshly squeezed anal glands. Drowning out the foul stink of excretions with the aroma of delicious desserts? Cruel deception.

Chloe, Hulk, and I walk out, careful to dodge the random piles of shit in the parking lot.

I am happy when all three of us make it to the car with feces-free shoes and paws. I let Hulk loose in the backseat and I buckle Chloe.

"That was fun, wasn't it?" I say, seeking props, as I do.

"I want to do it again," Chloe says, wanting more, as she does.

I drive away from PetSmart and I'm in the midst of a sketchy four-lane left-hand turn when Chloe screams, "There's blood everywhere! Blood! It's on my blanket, Momma!"

I'm not the type of driver to whom you yell "Boo." I'm a driver on edge, over-caffeinated, and, OK, taking speed.

Her scream panics me and I dart into the middle of the intersection. I get a trail of angry honks, and a few cars swerve around me, but no one crashes on account of my stupidity. In my near miss, I solemnly swear I will never make a risky left-hand turn again. I will drive an extra twenty minutes out of my way if need be.

You made the same solemn swear last month.

Chloe is bawling. I can no longer decipher what she's saying, but I definitely heard the "blood" part. I swerve onto a side street, put the minivan in park, unbuckle, and turn to face her. There *is* blood on her blanket! More brownish than red. I frantically scan her screaming face and clenched fists for an injury, but her tear-wet skin is perfect and intact. A smear of snot crosses her cheek. Where did the blood come from?

The seats are dotted and smeared with blood, all of them. There's blood splattered on the carpet. Reddish-brown blood, stale menstrual blood, is everywhere.

For a full second, I'm certain some demon has ripped open this dimension to ooze blood into my car. Even Hulk senses the dimension invasion; she's berserk, jumping from seat to floor and back again.

A moment before diving headfirst into my own insanity, I glance at Hulk. Her front paw is matted in blood.

PetSmart motherfuckers.

I've heard dogs bleed fast and plentiful, but I thought it was wild exaggeration.

Chloe is still sobbing. I climb into the back seat, unbuckle her, and pull her into a hug. I explain what happened, tell her

Hulk will be fine, and we will wash her blanket. None of these things help. My sleeves are wet with her tears and smudged with her boogers.

I fish around in my purse for a lollipop. The lollipop does the trick. She settles down to focus on sucking and sugar.

I wrap Hulk's bleeding paw in the crumpled tissues I find under the seats of the minivan. Tissues, which may contain gum or boogers, that Chloe and Wyatt have cast carelessly onto the floor of this neglected vehicle.

Ha! Just when I think I should criticize myself for not cleaning more often or my children for being so sloppy, our trash comes in handy! More fuel for my slovenly ways.

I pop in a silly songs CD. Chloe blinks and smiles.

I drive home, wondering why the groomer didn't simply tell me she cut the nail too low? She could have wrapped Hulk's paw before we left. It wouldn't have been a problem. The groomer *saw* me. She saw me talking and laughing with Chloe. She had to know I wasn't one of those people who obsesses over their dog or threatens lawsuits. She had to notice how easy-going and normal I look.

Maybe not as normal as you think.

Or maybe it had nothing to do with me. Maybe the groomer didn't want to say she'd made a mistake. No one likes to admit their incompetence.

I turn onto my street.

There are four cars parked in front of Leland Ernest's house, two of them police cars.

34

A WOMAN'S VOICE SAYS TO MY ASS

Police cars make me nervous.

Of course they do. Police cars make everyone nervous.

I park in my driveway.

Normal. Be normal.

I carry Chloe inside, and Hulk follows at my feet.

I don't want the police to come to my door. With everything I've been meddling in, I'm feeling guilty. Detectives have rung enough doorbells to spot a guilty person as she answers her door.

Stay calm. What would you do right now if the cops weren't next door?

Easy. Clean up Hulk's blood.

I throw Chloe's blanket into the washing machine and turn on the brainless Barbie show she loves and I hate. I change into shorts and, barefoot, head outside with a bucket of soapy water and a dish rag.

I plop my bucket on the driveway, then roll my empty recycling and garbage bins into the garage.

Hulk's blood has already browned and become one with

the fabric and carpet. I scrub. It smears, then lightens. I'm pretty sure I can get this car back to its baseline nasty, moldy-smelling self.

The sun beats on the vinyl dashboard, and inside the car it's hot. I'm sweating, but I enjoy the physical labor. The uncomplicated essence of it, the type of slender, strong body it builds, the type of black-and-white thinking it lends itself to.

Hulk barks like mad from inside the house.

"Excuse me," a woman's voice says to my ass.

I back out of the minivan, dropping my towel on the car floor.

A man and woman dressed in plain clothes stand in the grass a few feet away from me. *Detectives.*

The woman is young. Her hair is pulled back into a messy ponytail. Her face is angular, yet soft. Her skin is olive-toned and flawless. Puerto Rican, I think. Her beauty stuns me like a slap in the cold. I have met women like her on occasion. Stunning women who work regular jobs: teachers, nurses, and police officers. Each time I run into these women, I wonder, Why are you working this ordinary job? Why isn't some dude paying you ridiculous amounts of money to be eye-candy on his yacht? Don't you look in the mirror in the morning and say, Pshaw! I do not have to go to work today. Look at this face. I can do whatever I want!

The man is attractive too, but far less exotic than his partner. His skin is fair with a slight summer tan. His body is slender, but his bones are solid. His hair is dark, his jaw is smooth, and his familiar blue eyes are kind and non-judgmental, which probably helps him solve cases. He looks older than me, but he is my age exactly. His name is James. I haven't seen him in over twenty years.

The woman says, "I'm Detective Acosta. This is Detective Mahoney. You are?"

"Grace Wright."

"Nice to meet you, Grace," he says, nodding, keeping his hands at his sides.

Oh, we are playing that game. Interesting.

Hulk is still barking madly, the little watchdog.

"What happened?" I say, blocking the sun from my eyes and squinting so they can't read my eyes clearly.

"When is the last time you've seen Leland Ernest?"

"Oh, um, I guess a few days ago. I saw him on his patio."

Drinking a juice box. Disgust wells up inside me.

"Did you hear anything unusual last night?" Detective Mahoney says.

"I don't think." I consider it, then shake my head. "No."

"So, Grace, you were home last night?" Detective Acosta says, scratching her neck, trying to seem casual. Her fingernails are short, unpainted, but somehow perfectly pretty and petite. No earrings or rings on her, just a simple digital watch. A boy's watch.

"Yes. I was home. Went to bed kind of early actually." Acosta's skin looks airbrushed. Even her eyelids, her eyebrows, are stunning. "My husband, well, ex-husband, had the kids last night. I leave the bathroom fan on for noise and keep the windows closed because of my allergies. If there was anything to hear, I probably wouldn't hear it." I'm rambling. Her beauty is distracting. *Try not to look at her.* "Did something happen? What happened?"

Mahoney says, "Has there been anything related to your neighbor or his house that struck you as unusual lately? More visitors? More activity in front of the house? Arguments?"

Come to think of it, I did break into his house a couple days ago.

Oh, and also, yesterday I told Ethan Boone that Leland had a few little girl's items hidden under his mattress.

"Oh my God," I whisper. "Did you find Ava?"

The detectives glance at each other and shift stances.

Detective Mahoney says, "Grace, why would you think we stopped by about Ava?"

"I heard Leland was a suspect in her case. Did they find her?"

Detective Acosta bites her lip, then releases it. Both of them are superb at milking silence. *Don't fall for it. Wait them out.* She finally says, "Grace, where did you hear Leland was a suspect in Ava Boone's case?"

It annoys me that they keep saying my name. It's a sales technique. They are trying to lull me into familiarity. I feel uncomfortable, sweaty-sticky. I wish I were wearing shoes. I feel exposed, sloppy. Strands of hair have fallen against my cheeks. I push my hair back and sigh.

"The guy down the street, near the end of the block. His name is Lou; he told me. I'm pretty sure most of the neighbors know. What's going on?"

"How often do you talk to your neighbor Leland?" Detective Acosta says, glancing briefly inside my minivan.

"Pretty much never. He always struck me as…" I search

for a neutral word, something besides *stalker, predator, kidnapper.* "He struck me as odd. What happened?" *How many times do I have to ask?*

Detective Mahoney tips his chin down a bit, his light blue eyes somber. "Your neighbor was murdered."

Good thing they didn't catch me at my door in my air-conditioned house. Good thing I was scrubbing my hot van a minute ago. My face already heat-flushed and pebbled in sweat, my clothes already stained, they can't gauge my anxiety.

"What? Jesus," I whisper. Chills prickle along my cold stomach, and I steady myself against the minivan. I search for what I'm supposed to say; there are no convenient words when someone is *murdered.* "I'm sorry. That's crazy. Isn't that information private? I mean, are you supposed to tell people?"

She smiles as if I gave something away. Detective Mahoney, the more humble of the two, says, "If someone has a medical emergency, we don't discuss that with neighbors. If we are uncertain about how someone died, we don't jump to conclusions. In this case, a neighbor found him this morning, and the coroner has already filed cause of death so now we are trying to collect information from anyone who might be able to help."

"Where is the ambulance or, or, the coroner's van?"

Detective Acosta says, "Many of the vehicles that were on your street earlier today have left."

"How did he… I mean, was it a gun?"

"We can't discuss that," she says and looks at my neck with assertive eyes.

"Oh." I touch my bandage, ready to tell her about my bat scratches.

"So, Grace," Detective Acosta says, "if you could help us out and tell us anything you have noticed, like, have you noticed any cars parked in front of his house recently?"

"Um, no. I don't think. I'm busy though. Single mom, two kids, full-time job. I'm not paying attention to the neighborhood, you could say."

"How old are your kids?" Detective Acosta says.

I know where she's headed. I pointed her in that direction, after all, by mentioning Ava. *You shouldn't have mentioned Ava. No, it's fine that you mentioned Ava. It's normal that you mentioned Ava.* "My boy is eight. My little girl is three."

"Must have been disturbing to hear your neighbor was a suspect in the kidnapping of a little girl," Detective Acosta says, getting straight to the point and playing me for an idiot.

You are an idiot. You put yourself in their crosshairs.

Acosta plays sympathetic, her eyes sorrowful. "I can't imagine being a mother, a *single* mother, and finding out something so upsetting."

"Yeah, it pissed me off. It worried me. It worried all of us in the neighborhood, I'm sure. But what are you gonna do? You have to let the police figure it out. And, well, have you?" I say, playing the same game she's playing with me. "Figured anything out, I mean. Do you have any idea what happened to Ava Boone?"

"It's not our case," Mahoney says. "Detectives are still working it."

209

"It's been a long time though. If they haven't figured it out by now…" I say, letting my unspoken words hang, my tone turning accusatory. I'm pissed they haven't found her or solved her case. I should be pissed.

They might find out you've been probing.

That's OK. I should be probing. Everyone should be probing.

"How long have you lived here?" she says, not taking my bait.

"Three months."

"When did you find out your neighbor was a suspect in the case of a missing child?"

Not missing. Kidnapped. Murdered.

"Maybe two weeks ago," I say, pretending I don't know exactly how many days it's been. "Like I said, a neighbor down the street, Lou, told me. Most of the neighbors know, he said."

Detective Mahoney smiles and nods. He is the listener, the gentle cop. I bet they switch roles when interviewing a male.

"Is there anyone else besides you who has been angry with Leland?" Acosta says. I see what she's doing, trying to put me on the defense, trying to raise my hackles, trying to get me to point a finger somewhere else.

As a matter of fact, yesterday I told Ethan Boone that Leland might have his daughter's sock under his mattress.

Oh, and Lou down the street. That crazy dude threatened to slit Leland's throat. You believe that shit?

"Not that I know of," I lie, not entirely certain of my motives.

"What happened to your neck?" Detective Acosta says.

"What? Oh, I keep forgetting." I touch the gauze taped to my neck. "I got attacked by bats."

210

"You're kidding," Detective Mahoney says, a genuine smile widening on his face.

"No. It happened several nights ago. I was going for a late-night jog, and they ran into me, the bats. I went to the hospital for post-rabies exposure shots. It's on record, if you want to check," I add. I pull the gauze back to show them. "It's already scabbed over and the doctor is almost positive I didn't get exposed to rabies, but to be on the safe side, they're giving me the series of shots and I keep it covered. My daughter is always wrapping her arms around my neck."

"That's wild," Mahoney says. "Seems like the summer for strange animal stories. My daughter showed me this YouTube video the other day. This bunny growling at a Labrador." He touches his partner's arm and says to her, "Did you see it?"

My eyes linger on the touch. I'm curious how close they are.

"No, you'll have to show me," she says, but she's uninterested. She's glancing around at houses, deciding which neighbor to attack next.

"My son and I watched the same video. Peter versus Heidi," I say, realizing I appear too enthusiastic.

He points at the toddler seat in my minivan and laughs, "I remember all the cleanup when my daughter was that age. Juice, smashed crackers, broken crayons. It was always something. What'd she spill?" His eyes settle upon my towel, which is stained brown.

"Blood, actually. Not my daughter's, my dog's. I got her nails clipped today and they cut too low. It's splattered all over the backseat."

"I didn't know clipping a nail could draw so much blood," Detective Acosta says, interested, peeking in.

"I'll show you." I walk to my front door and open it. Hulk comes barreling out, wagging her tail so hard, her ass wiggles. She brushes against their shins, licks their hands, and sniffs their crotches. Hell of a watchdog.

Tissues gone from her injured paw, dried blood mats her fur.

Detective Mahoney bends down, scratches Hulk's ear, and lifts the injured paw. "They did an awful job. You could get a Dremel for thirty bucks, grind her nails yourself."

I smile. "I was thinking the same thing. You have a dog?"

Detective Mahoney nods. "I grind her nails. Shave her myself too." He is not playing a role, he's not acting. He's reacting, real time. He laughs, "I used to shave words into the dog's fur to make my daughter crack up."

"Words?"

"Hug me. Happy Birthday." Memory fading, his smile fades. "Well, we appreciate your time, Ms. Wright. Grace. We will let you get back to work. If you remember anything that seemed off or seemed funny even, please give me a call. The smallest, most random details can turn out to be useful." He hands me his card, and I'm stuck holding it because I have no pockets.

Detective Acosta looks at Mahoney. "That's probably the first time someone's told us they're cleaning blood out of their car." She's trying to get under my skin. Pin me as guilty of something. Make me feel awkward.

Mahoney smiles at me. "First time someone told us they were attacked by bats too. Seems like you have your hands full."

You have no idea.

They walk back to Leland's house.

He didn't remember you. Or was he faking?

I drop his card in my cup holder and go back to scrubbing fabric.

How would they describe me?

Chatty. Unforgettable because of my bloody minivan and bat attack. Unsympathetic to my neighbor's murder. All these things are normal enough.

35

A MIDDLE-AGED MONSTER

Ethan Boone murdered Leland. Had to be him. Had to be. Had to.

I picture Ethan's reaction when I told him I found a little girl's items under Leland's mattress. *Covering his face with both hands, he said, "Oh my God." Wiping his tears away, his despair abruptly shifted to rage.* I can almost feel his ragged nails, his grip, rife with fury, digging into my arms. He had the craziest look in his eyes.

And, holy shit, it's *my* fault. Ethan suspected Leland, but I confirmed his suspicion. That poor Boone family. Lost their daughter, now they're going to lose their father.

You will keep his secret.

You put that poor man in this situation, you will protect him.

You need to let him know his secret is safe. Soon. So he doesn't point the finger in your direction.

My guilt and my conversation with the detectives have left my body and mind fatigued and useless. Hulk detailing my car's interior with blood didn't help.

After dinner I leave dirty dishes and uneaten food on the

table and collapse on the couch beside Chloe.

Walking back from the bathroom, Wyatt says, "Hey, Mom, why are there police cars down the street?"

I don't have the energy or level-headedness needed to answer this question. "I don't know, Wyatt. I'll ask the neighbors about it later. Let's watch *Wheel of Fortune*."

He drops it and plops down on the couch beside me.

I love watching *Wheel of Fortune* with my kids. Scratch that, it's the only adult program I'll watch with my kids. I gave *Family Feud* a try once, but had forgotten how trashy it was. Lots of, "Survey Says, Lap Dance."

I get a kick out of how much effort Wyatt expends trying to solve *Wheel of Fortune* puzzles. He averages one out of ten and, in my opinion, one out of ten is a perfect effort–reward ratio for learning persistence. Chloe shouts out letters while laughing and running back and forth along the couch, hopping over Wyatt and me.

The Wheel is also good for teaching empathy since contestants are constantly landing on Bankrupt. Wyatt is convinced the Wheel has been meddled with and, after six or seven Bankrupt spins, he hypothesizes in technical detail how they've rigged the game.

The only thing that bugs me about the show? The glowing-yet-humdrum family intros... My wonderful husband works at Xerox and sings in a barbershop quartet. My beautiful daughter plays soccer and is on the honor roll. I am a sales associate at JCPenney and enjoy scrapbooking and sea-shelling.

I want something meatier. I want real.

Mine would go like this…

Pat, my ex is a surgeon skilled at fixing shitty intestines. He is known for his late-night, compulsive online-shopping habit—everything from batteries to birdseed—and he can't turn down free pussy.

My eight-year-old son is a lover of dogs and fart jokes, notorious for making his sister giggle as well as punching holes in drywall—though not at the same time!—and can occasionally be found studying his butthole in the mirror.

My toddler enjoys jumping off slides, furniture, and into deep bodies of water, no regard for consequences. She is a genius at apologies, whispers love in my ear with lollipop-sweet breath, but refuses to keep her socks on.

And me, Pat?

I might just be a middle-aged monster.

36

DEMONS SENT FROM UNDERGROUND HELL-CAVES

It is officially *The summer of bats*.

Not only according to me. Hadley Stykes, reporter for the *Kilkenny Sun*, has come to the same conclusion.

She wrote, "The rabies-infected bat count in Whisper County is up to twenty-one, which is the highest count since they've been recording it (1987). Keep in mind, twenty-one makes for a low percentage overall since thousands of bats live in Whisper County. There have been only three human cases of rabies in Whisper County in thirty years and no human cases of rabies in the county for eight consecutive years."

Here's hoping I don't break the streak.

I'm not sure why I keep reading about bats. If I trust all the literature, and I do, as long as post-exposure prophylaxis is given within six days of exposure, victims survive in every case. I suppose it's the manner of the bat attack that bothers me. I haven't come across a single story of someone being attacked by a *cluster* of bats.

And the more I read about bats, the more I worry. Bats carry at least sixty viruses capable of infecting humans. We're talking serious shit like Ebola, Marburg, SARS, and, *a-hem*, rabies.

Bats don't die from these viruses because when they take flight, their internal body temperature rises to 106 degrees, which initiates some badass immune response that allows them to harbor viruses safely, but pass those viruses on through their feces and piss and saliva so humans die painfully, excessively salivating and hallucinating while partially paralyzed and unable to swallow.

If you believe every living thing was put on this planet for humans, bats are certainly demons sent from underground hell-caves to spread disease, fear, and chaos.

I worry about the unknown. Why did a gang of them attack me? Were they sick with a new disease yet to be identified? No doubt there are countless subtle viral infections that have yet to be catalogued and understood.

The summer of bats.

Funny how so many of us label time by music, disasters, and pests. Maybe it's because as we get older and lose memory and wit, there is too much to mentally juggle, so we simplify.

The year of Hurricane Katrina.

The summer the Cubs won the World Series.

The winter we got twelve feet of snow and couldn't get out of the house.

The summer of the Seventeen-Year Cicada. That was a fun one. Wyatt had been three and in little-boy bliss. Usually he had to search for bugs. That summer, he would take one step outside and they would crash into him. He'd find them on the porch, their wings moist, unable to fly, because minutes ago they'd squeezed themselves out of a molt, their crisp empty translucent shells still clinging to the porch.

The spring Ava Boone went missing.

The summer my neighbor was murdered.

After Wyatt and Chloe are sleeping, I lace my sneakers tight, giddy at the idea of jogging now that Leland is dead. This is wrong, I know, which makes me even more giddy. My cheek muscles ache.

37

THE BOY-DOPED SILLINESS I SMOKED

I skip the sidewalk and hit the asphalt, playing my 90s playlist because Detective James Mahoney has been standing quietly, hands in pockets, shoulders shrugged, faint smirk on his face, sweet blue eyes, in the back of my mind all evening, waiting for me to give him proper consideration.

The moon is full and glowing, backed by lit clouds.

I'm pounding the asphalt, approaching the furthest point from my house, approaching the place where bats blindsided me, and anxiety smacks me in the chest like a wet-towel slap in the locker room. Painful. Burning. Breathtaking.

I worry for the Boone family. I worry about my role in Leland's murder. I tipped off Ethan, and now a man is dead. I worry about being a terrible mother. I worry for my health—something is happening to me, I know it. I worry for my children's future; I desperately want them to have peaceful lives. I worry about growing old alone. I worry about my house falling apart.

A dark cloud has drifted in front of the bright moon, taking a small bite out of it.

There's a car to my right, behind me. *No, it's keeping pace with you.* My pulse triples. Goosebumps break along my cool skin. *Be ready for anything.* I yank out my earbuds.

"Bush," a voice says.

"What!" I scream. *Perv.*

"You were singing. 'Chemicals Between Us' by Bush?"

Detective Mahoney. His elbow rests on his open window. Street lamps cast a yellow glow, and I can make out his eyes and smile.

I slow to a walk. I relax a little, but my heart is still fluttering. "Yeah, I guess I was singing." I'm the perv.

"You're living in the past." His car is crawling beside me. Chevy Impala.

"Oh fuck off," I say.

He laughs. "I was kidding. Wait," he says softly, "are you crying?"

"I'm fine."

"What happened?"

"It's nothing. I cry when I run. It's just something I do. Like brushing my teeth."

He says nothing.

OK, I'm not making the best impression. My pulse drums. His engine idles.

I stop and face him. "Why did you act like you didn't know me?"

His car stops. He puts it in park right in the middle of the street, looks to his steering wheel for an answer, and turns to me. "I don't know. I was caught off guard." He smiles sheepishly.

"I had a crush on you in high school."

"Me?" I laugh, but it's not flirty, it's loud and accusatory.

I was not the crush type. Not one of the beautiful ones. Not of the popular crowd. Not a party animal. I smoked and drank, but kept myself under control. No sexy clothes or heavy makeup. I had bad hair.

I ran track. Hurdles. God, how I loved hurdles. In my wide-open and probing teenage mind, I believed I wasn't entirely human. Running hurdles, the avian leap and lift, solidified the thought.

I loved the all-weather track rounding the football field. Vulcanized rubber baking in the sun, a faint sulfur odor, the warm scent of grass, and the brassy smell of the wire fence enclosing the stadium. Chalk white lines painted on smooth yet textured track. I didn't even mind the stench of Lakewood High's basement track surrounding the weight room. Sweat, corroded metal, cement, and mildew under shitty lighting.

When I wasn't running, I had my nose in a book. I had a few friends, none of them forever or lifelong. I had a few boyfriends.

James Mahoney was my high school opposite. Star baseball player, but not your stereotypical asshole athlete. He was reserved. When he smiled, a hint of mischievousness slid up one smooth cheek.

I say, "I could have used the confidence boost decades ago."

A horn startles me, and a car swerves to pass James's car. Driver sticks his arm out the window, gives James the finger.

Does Detective Mahoney have a cop ego? Will he chase the

222

Finger Giver down, humiliate him, and write a ticket?

James smiles at me, unruffled, unfazed. He rakes his hand through his hair. "Yeah, well, I was a self-conscious teenager myself. And, to be fair and honest, I had a crush on half of the girls in school. At sixteen, sweaty hands were a turn-on."

"Sweaty hands?"

"When I recognized you this morning, I reverted to that hormone-charged boy for a few seconds."

"Huh."

"What?"

"You're a detective. You're not supposed to get easily flustered."

He bites his lip, sexy, and says casually, "Who's watching your kids?"

His question obliterates the sexy lip-biting thing. I roll my eyes. *Jesus. Once a parent, you can never escape judgement.* "I do one lap. I'm gone for ten minutes. So if you would let me do my thing." I turn away from him and run.

I expect his Impala to creep into my peripheral vision or maybe pass me, but it doesn't. Where'd he go? Is he still in park back there? There's no way I'm turning around to check. I continue to run home, sprinting as fast as I can. Why? In case he's watching, I want to convey the full extent of my athletic ability, of course.

Butterflies still dancing in my stomach, I am kicking myself for ditching our conversation. For being too defensive.

Stop. Please. Idiot. You are out of your mind. You can't get weak-kneed over the detective who's investigating your neighbor's murder case, you boy-crazy, horny dumbshit.

I'm two driveways from my house when I lurch into my cool-down walk. I'm panting hard and sweating hard, but my mind is back to cold-hearted and steady.

Gone is the boy-doped silliness I smoked minutes ago.

Headlights flip on between my house and my dead neighbor's house.

I'm pretty sure it's his Impala. Door opens, and he gets out. He shuts the door and leans against it.

He's not done with you. Careful, Grace.

As I walk toward him, cool and resolute, he lights a cigarette.

"You're a smoker? Who's living in the past? My kids think smoking is like robbing a bank."

He laughs, letting it trail off to silence. "What I said before? I didn't mean, well, I wasn't judging." He sighs and rakes his fingers through his hair again. "What I meant was, you're divorced?"

"Yes."

"Me too. For a while now. How long for you?"

"Five months."

"Maybe after this investigation is over, I could take you to dinner?"

More to the point: Maybe after I'm done investigating you for homicide, we could go on a date?

Nate never smoked, but I've dated smokers and I do miss the taste of a smoker's nicotine-and-raisin kiss. It tastes a little like home, a little like strange.

Careful.

I want to say, Hell yes! But dating him would be a bad idea.

Especially when I have information he wants. Information I need to keep bottled.

I smile politely. "I don't date divorced men." *You haven't dated at all.*

He laughs. "But *you're* divorced."

"I didn't want to be. He cheated five times. Actually, he admitted to five, so it was probably fifteen."

"I didn't cheat."

"Let me guess. When the baby came, she *changed*."

I've heard "she changed" so many times, said so sincerely and believed so intently. These words make my scalp prickle.

What, she didn't give you enough attention anymore? You poor baby, she's got your child on her tit every two hours, she's wearing diapers for underwear to soak up blood, and she hasn't slept for months, *she's changed all right*. How about sticking it out for a year before you jump ship? Or lightening her load by taking care of your child?

If "When the baby came, she changed" is the most frequent line, the best line I've heard from a divorced man was that his ex-wife didn't share his spiritual beliefs so he couldn't stay married to her. In other words: bitch wouldn't go to church and let God in so I divorced her ass.

James flicks his cigarette into the street. "You shouldn't make assumptions, and why my marriage failed is none of your business. So who do you date? Twenty-year-olds?" His smirk is back. He is not put off. How is he still interested? Even I find myself irritating. Oh God, I have to look disgusting. My clothes cling to my skin and I stink.

"I haven't dated anyone. If I did, I guess it would be guys my age, widowed."

His eyes widen and he laughs like a free-spirited kid. "But they could have *killed* their wives."

In my peripheral vision, I sense movement. I search the darkness. Three houses away, a pair of glowing nocturnal eyes hover near the ground. Raccoon, skunk, or cat.

"Good point," I say. "I will investigate the dead wife's cause of death thoroughly. Good night." I walk to my door without glancing back.

My knees are weak, and the butterflies in my stomach are frantic. I haven't had sex in so long and the possibility of it makes me irrational. When sex was available, endlessly lingering in the corner like a pile of clean laundry waiting to be smoothed and folded, I took it for granted. Now that it's gone, it's like water.

Pathetic, Grace. He is pursuing you only because he is investigating your neighbor's murder. He is only trying to use you for information. You are by no means beautiful, you are not particularly kind or warm, and you have done nothing to peg yourself as intelligent or accomplished.

Still.

I lock my front door and hustle upstairs. For the first time in years, I take a cold shower on purpose. This must be how it feels to be a sixteen-year-old boy. My skin is crawling. I want to pull my hair out. What's wrong with me?

Which reminds me that there might be something actually wrong with me.

38

YOU BROKE MY NOSE

I wake to the irritating commotion of Wyatt and Chloe arguing. I pee as fast as I can, skip glasses or contacts, and jump in as a blind referee.

Yellow flag usually goes to Chloe because she's unreasonable, fickle, unpredictable, and melodramatic, but this morning the foul goes to Wyatt. He is explaining to her the variety of punishments she will incur if she does not clean up her act. He mentions detention, suspension, juvie, and maximum security before I get my blurry-visioned body on the scene.

"She is three, Wyatt. Three. Her behavior will evolve so much before she even gets to kindergarten."

"She needs to learn how to be a normal human."

Chloe sobs louder.

I get in Wyatt's face. "When you were three you broke my nose at the public swimming pool." *Remember, asshole?*

Of course he doesn't remember, but I've told him the story. He was so stubbornly independent, he kept telling me to go away, he could swim on his own. Dumb little fuckers, these children. I wouldn't let go of his writhing, intent-on-drowning body, so he head-butted me in the nose. Broke it right at the top. Only when I run my finger down the slope can I perceive a tiny inconsistency.

He is typically patient with her, but he, like his mother, has a mean streak.

"You know not to punch now, Wyatt, but you punched when you were three. Now, go take a break in your room." *And get out of my sight.*

I pick up Chloe, rub her wet cheek against my own. Through her tears, she says, "Why isn't anyone want to be my friend?"

"Wyatt loves you, he's just grumpy this morning. We all get grumpy and say grumpy things."

"But nobody wants to play with me."

"Wyatt likes to play with you." As if to counter my statement, banging noises rise from Wyatt's room. I have no idea what he's up to, but it doesn't sound like anything is breaking, so I let it go. "And I like to play with you too," I say.

"Can we play Play-Doh right now?"

She pinned me in a corner. Already the con artist.

"Let Mommy get dressed, and then we can play Play-Doh as I make breakfast."

As I make eggs and butter toast and pour orange juice, I make pit stops at the table to squeeze Play-Doh hair out of the little plastic guy's perforated head. She cuts his hair with a plastic knife.

Trying to prop up the kids, make them feel peaceful, make them feel whole in this soulless world, it wears on me. Like doing the dishes. There's always more because everyone eats all the fucking time.

I am glad for work this morning. As Wyatt walks out the door, I feel lighter. When I drop Chloe off, I feel energized.

During our combined music class with Miss Jenny, the energetic, barefoot music teacher, Liz pulls me aside. Her eyes wide and serious, she says, "How *are* you?"

"Same old."

"Grace. Your neighbor," she whispers, giving me a harsh parental look. "I saw on the local news this morning your neighbor was murdered. *Murdered.* Were you going to mention it?"

"No. It's actually too overwhelming to think about. I can't consider it and pay attention to the kids at the same time. I need to compartmentalize."

Her eyes soften. "OK, I understand that. Later, though. We'll talk later. *Seriously.* I mean, what did you—" she says, then stops herself. "Forget it, I won't ask you about it now. Not now. How is your hearing, by the way?"

"What?"

She smiles and swats my arm flab.

"My hearing has been totally normal." I don't want to talk about my state of health. "How's it going in your household?"

"Well, Sonya is wetting the bed and it's not cute because she's nine, and Camden smells like weed when he comes home after school, but they are on their own too much, so what do you expect?"

Liz's daughter, Tanya, is a single parent of two, and they live with Liz. Tanya has a patchwork of scars courtesy of both her ex and past drug abuse, and she's barely holding onto her night job as a dispatcher.

Liz's four other children seem to have their shit together. One of her kids is a high school teacher, one is a lawyer, two are military. Three of them are happily married with kids. Four out of five ain't bad. Honestly, it's damn impressive.

But that's not how you look at it when they're *your* offspring.

"I'm sorry, Liz. It's not easy. For any of you. But kids go through phases. They will come out of this. Tanya loves them and you love them, so they will turn out just fine." I don't think I actually believe this, but it is something I would like to believe.

"True, true," she says indifferently. She probably doesn't believe this platitude either. "Hey, besides your hearing, you seem to be a little up and down. And you've lost weight." Her eyebrows go up, her chin tilts down.

Miss Jenny is handing out maracas and singing a jazzy version of "Mary, Mary, Quite Contrary". When Wyatt was born, I googled all the nursery rhymes because I have a terrible ear for lyrics. Turns out, most nursery rhymes have a dark side. Silver bells and cockleshells all in a row are metaphors for the queen's torture devices, or so they say. I can't remember which queen.

Lucas and Ryan are getting wild with their maracas and paving a pathway to trouble for the rest of the students. I rush in with feigned calm and high-energy compliments and redirect them. They are back on track, blissfully unaware of my manipulation.

Note to self: If Detective Mahoney comes back snooping, I need to redirect his energy.

"I've had a bad stretch of shitty sleep, but I'm coming out of it now," I say.

"OK, hon. If you need to talk, I'm here, and I've heard it all." Not only does she have five kids, but she has six siblings.

"Yes, I believe you, which scares me."

She laughs, deep and rich.

I'm about to let the conversation end there, keeping it light and glossy, but some part of me needs to dig deeper. "Liz, how did you ever manage five kids and not lose your head?"

She raises her eyebrows. "Who says I didn't lose my head? When I struggled—let me rephrase that—when I wanted to strangle one of my own children, I told myself my mother had seven of us. Mostly on her own." Liz's dad died when she was little.

"I've tried the 'other people have it harder' thing; it doesn't work for me."

"Then break your day into dangling carrots," she says. "Wake up looking forward to coffee. When you've had enough coffee, look forward to wine."

"Good idea," I say to end the conversation. There's no point to it. Liz is a stronger person than I am.

As much as I adore my kids, as much as I live for them and would die for them in the blink of an eye, I was not built to be a mother. For me, mothering is like trying to loosen a stripped screw from a plastic toy.

39

LOSE A FEW TOES

I need to talk to the Boones and I can't wait.

After work, I park outside their house. Natalie's car is in the driveway.

Today is her day off. I called her employer, faked that my teen needed a counselor, requested Natalie, and found out her schedule.

You are Point Bird. You will not let things drop. Go ring her bell.

I sit in my car. Two minutes tick by. *Five minutes, that's all you get. Five minutes, then you will ring her bell.* Another minute ticks by.

The front door opens and Natalie Boone hobbles out of her house. Hobbles because her right foot is casted. She's wearing a boot. What the hell happened to her?

And why is the Boone house so active? My fourth time here this week, and someone has always been coming or going. *Because you come right after work.* That's Lila's after-school activity time, Ethan's get-home-from-work or take-out-the-garbage time, and Mason's drug-dealing time. What will Natalie do?

It takes an extraordinary amount of effort for her to get in

232

her car. I backwards-calculate how much time I have before I have to pick up Wyatt and Chloe. Forty-five, fifty minutes.

I follow Natalie like I followed her son, Mason.

She turns into the Walmart parking lot. Maybe Natalie and Mason are a mother and son drug-dealing duo.

Unlike Mason, she tries for a spot as close as she can get to a set of doors. She doesn't have a handicap placard, but she manages a good parking spot anyway, then wobbles into the store.

I hope this is only a quick run for milk and bananas and not her stock-up-the-garage-fridge, $300, once-a-week blowout. I don't have that kind of time.

I only have to wait twenty minutes.

With that boot, she's easy to spot. Natalie hobbles out with her cart quarter full. It was maybe a forty-dollar trip, a run to make tonight's dinner plus a few extra items. She's got three plastic bags in her cart and a rectangular box of canned sodas on the bottom rack. Someone in her house likes diet root beer.

I meet her as she approaches her car. I make it seem accidental.

"You look like you could use a hand."

She's surprised and worried, but when she sees I don't have a salesperson's slippery smile or a thief's hard eyes, that I'm a middle-aged lady like herself, she relaxes.

"I'm OK, really," she says.

"I'm the same way. I hate when people are trying to help. I'll grab the soda. No need to tip me," I joke.

"Oh, OK, thanks."

I maneuver the case of soda from the bottom rack into her tidy, vacuumed trunk. Folded blanket and flashlight in there. How a trunk should look. Mine has toys, candy wrappers, half-empty crushed bottles of water, and bags of clothes the kids have outgrown that I still need to drop at the Salvation Army. "That looks like it was painful," I say. "What happened?"

"I ran over my foot with the car. Can you believe it?" From the wonder in her cadence, she still can't believe it. She's loosening up. "I thought I put it in park, but I had it in reverse. Stepped out of my car in the driveway and the car rolled back and ran right over my gym shoe. Worse pain I've ever felt. They thought I would lose a few toes, but now it looks like I'll keep them so there's that. Stupidest thing you've ever heard, right?"

I imagine her pulling into her driveway, her mind somewhere far away, with Ava, and not paying attention to her dashboard. Her muscle memory, her years of training herself to shift the car into park, failed her when she needed it most. Poor woman.

I say, "I was at a stop light once when my older kid was two. He wouldn't stop screaming about his seatbelt. I was so flustered, I stepped out of my car to help him and forgot I was still in drive. Hit the car in front of me. Everyone was fine. My car was only going a half-mile per hour, but I felt like a lunatic. The guy I hit couldn't understand what happened. So embarrassing, but, so, no, not the stupidest thing I've heard."

She half smiles and almost laughs, which comes out sounding like, "Hm." She drops a bag into her trunk and sucks air through her teeth. Pain. She must have moved a toe or stretched the wrong way in that boot.

"Time for your pain meds, maybe."

"Oh, no. I don't take those." Her reaction is exaggerated, her eyes horrified by the thought of pain meds. Maybe she's a holistic gal. Tea tree oil and elderberry. Brewing her own tinctures with cheesecloth and mason jars. Or maybe she realizes she's spent too much time talking to a stranger and she's panicking.

"The way they talk about pain meds these days, it does seem like a good idea to avoid them," I say. "They have their uses though. My father took loads of pain meds, Fentanyl patches and Oxy pills, when he was terminally ill and under hospice care at home."

She wants to say something, but holds back. Bites her lip. Eyes watery, she decides to go ahead and says, "My sister works as a hospice nurse."

That's right. Sarah.

Natalie reaches into her cart for her last bag.

"I'll get your cart for you," I say.

"Oh. Thank you." She tosses her last bag into the trunk, lets it drop, and there's a crinkling sound. Something papery in there, maybe a bag of bakery bread. I say, "Seems like a tough job, hospice. She must be a gentle woman, your sister."

Her smile bends naturally. "She's a saint. Single mom. Two kids. Going to people's houses in the middle of the night, comforting them. A damn saint. Bends over backwards for people." Worry washes over her face as if she's said too much.

"Well, thanks again." *Walk away. Just walk away.*

No. You have to tell her she can trust you. It's your fault, after all. Your. Fault.

"I'm so sorry," I say, shaking my head, irritated with myself. "I should have told you who I was. Who I am. My neighbor is Leland Ernest."

"Who?" She's only vaguely interested.

"Leland Ernest."

"I'm sorry," she says, smiling, feeling self-conscious, "I'm bad with names. Am I supposed to know who that is?"

She is telling the truth. Or she is a brilliant liar.

"He was a suspect in your daughter's case."

As if I slapped her face, she wobbles backward and catches herself on the car beside hers. A Caribbean-blue Prius. Flustered, she searches her purse, grabs her keys, then drops them on the ground. Mumbles something that sounds like *pretty pickles.*

I pick up her keys before she can, but don't offer them. It's cruel, especially considering her temporary handicap, but she needs to listen. "I found some things in Leland's house. A little girl's sock. A Shopkin. A little plastic shovel." As each of my words land, her eyes widen further. She covers her mouth with her hand. "Yellow," I say. "The shovel was yellow. I told your husband yesterday, and now today Leland is dead."

She shudders at "dead".

I find it hard to believe she doesn't know Leland is dead. I find it hard to believe the detectives haven't contacted the Boones yet. I would think Ethan and Natalie were the primary

236

suspects in his murder. Also, it seems Ethan didn't tell her about me. But that makes sense. Why would he want to upset her?

I hold her keys tight in my sweaty fist and try to force a connection with my eyes. "I wanted to make sure you know: I didn't tell the detectives about your husband. I won't tell them anything."

"What? My husband?" Her eyes are wide with fear. "Give me my keys. Please." I feel terrible, like I've assaulted her, but I need her to know we are on the same side. Same team.

Quietly, I say, "I'm relieved Leland's dead. I'm so glad he's dead. I won't tell the detectives anything. I won't even tell them I talked to you or your husband. You have my word."

She furtively glances at people passing, considering if she should ask for help. It's getting close to dinnertime, and the parking lot is busy. Dozens of people have walked by in the past few minutes; she could easily flag one down. Deciding to keep it between us, she pleads, her voice a whisper, "Please give me my keys."

"I'll protect your family. Your husband."

"My husband doesn't need protecting," she says, her voice cracking in panic. "Leave my family alone or I will call the police."

"Don't you need to know if it's Ava's Shopkin?" I say frantically, accusation in my voice. "What if Leland had your daughter? What if she's alive?"

She takes a step toward me, leans into my space. Her mushy fear hardens and her face is like a stone wall. "It has been five months. Exactly one hundred forty-eight days. Do you have any idea, any idea, how long that is? Do you?" Her growl softens to a mere whisper. "My daughter is gone." Her cheeks shine with fast-falling tears. "Give me my fucking keys."

I offer her keys in my open palm. She grabs for them so frantically, her ragged, unpolished nails scratch my hand. She recoils as if I were sewage and struggles to get in her car. I pull her cart away so she doesn't bang into it and send it rolling.

Holding the cart, I stand beside her car and wait. In case she wants to say something. In case she wants to ask about the Shopkin.

She backs up recklessly, nearly running over my toes.

40

PLAY, PAUSE, REWIND, PLAY

Twenty minutes later I am driving Chloe and Wyatt home, but my mind is still with Natalie Boone in the parking lot. Her reactions, her lack of reactions, bother me like a single strand of hair caught in my mouth, woven through a bolus of food while I'm chewing.

There's something I need to check at home. We are only a few minutes away, but I need to be there *now*. I'm drumming my fingers against the steering wheel to the beat of my throbbing headache.

Chloe is strapped into her car seat, playing puzzles on my phone, when a call comes through. She doesn't bother asking me, she answers it.

"I can't hear you, Daddy."

I glance at her in my rearview while I'm waiting to make a left. "Chloe, you have to press the speaker button. Do you see all those curved lines? Wyatt, can you reach over and help her press the speaker button?"

Wyatt reaches over.

Nate's voice chimes in loudly. He's mid-sentence, talking about taking her swimming.

She cuts him off, telling him all about how she's going to build a swimming pool in the backyard, and it's going to take a lot of work to dig a hole, and she's going to need a lot of workers. I tune her out, I tune their conversation out.

I am picturing the dazed, barely interested expression on Natalie Boone's face when she said, "I'm sorry, I'm bad with names. Am I supposed to know who that is?" She had no reaction when I said Leland Ernest's name. None.

Through my phone's speaker, Nate says, "Tell Mommy I need to talk to her. Ask her if we can meet at Burger King for dinner in thirty minutes."

Which is irritating because:

1. I want to go home and take off my pants.

2. I despise all fast-food restaurants with kiddie hamster tubes. They are juicy and sticky with snot, and one of the kids always ends up sick exactly one to three days later.

3. If I shoot him down, Chloe will throw a tantrum. Her love for indoor playgrounds is fierce, and I have denied her a trip to Burger King for nearly a year. It's hard to believe she even remembers the last time we went, but abstinence has made her BK memories stronger and deliriously magical.

4. The mental effort I'm expending to keep my shit together right now is massive. The right side of my head is pulsing, and the back of my shirt is soaked in sweat. I don't think I can handle/manage/juggle one more thing.

How dare he ask in Chloe's earshot? What can he possibly need to tell me that he can't tell me when he picks up the kids tomorrow morning?

He heard about the murder. Fuck. That's got to be it.

"I haven't been to Burger King in a zillion years!" Chloe says. "And I'm starving!"

"Can we, Mom?" Wyatt says.

"OK, we can go," I say, turning onto our street. "I need to stop at home for ten minutes first."

"Yes," Wyatt says, his fist pumping the air, as if he made his first three-point shot.

Chloe says, "You are the best mommy in the whole world." Which makes me feel like crap on several levels.

I turn into our driveway. "Chloe, please say goodbye and hand me the phone." I reach back with an open hand, and surprisingly, she gives me my phone. I expected a fight for a show or game. I sigh and turn off the engine. "Wyatt, please unbuckle Chloe and put your backpack away."

"Did you ever find out about the police cars on the street?" Wyatt says.

"Not yet. I'll tell you when I know."

"What police cars?" Chloe says.

241

"It's nothing to worry about, Chlo. Please try to go potty, and then we'll go to Burger King."

They bounce out of the car, their happy minds contemplating Burger King's playland.

Sweaty and chilled, I head straight for the kitchen and open my junk drawer.

No hammer. I stare accusingly at the open drawer, as if it betrayed me. My lower lip trembles.

No hammer.

I swear I placed it here. Was it two nights ago when I woke up to find a hammer on the table? Seems like two. Or three. Could be four.

Other mundane things strike me as monumental.

On garbage night, you fell asleep on the couch, but woke in the tub. Why were you in the tub?

To wash away his blood.

Why were your clothes wet and crumpled on the floor?

You were out in the rain.

I give myself ten minutes to ransack the house and garage.

Where is that fucking hammer? Why can't you remember where you put anything? Why are you so fucking lazy that you can't put anything back in its place?

It's not here. You got rid of it on garbage night.

No. No, I don't believe it. That was a dream.

I try to tune out Chloe and Wyatt's bickering and requests, but they gnaw at my nerves: *He said. I need. I need. He took. She is. He called me a. She is.*

I find two hammers in the garage, but neither is the one I'm

242

looking for.

If only I knew how Leland died.

I search the basement, opening boxes, drawers, and cabinets, knocking over piles of papers and old bills I should have thrown away, but didn't because I worry about identity theft and don't own a shredder.

Something is off about the Boone family, I'm sure of it, but Ethan Boone didn't kill Leland Ernest. Which makes me wonder if I did.

No. No, that was a dream. Of course it wasn't you. Come on. Ethan did it. His wife is a great actor. She's a psychologist. She knows how innocent people are supposed *to respond.*

True. But Natalie said if I hassle her family again, she is going to call the police on me. Which would put both of us under a microscope.

Or maybe Ethan killed Leland, his wife knows about it, and now he's planning on killing me so she's trying to keep me from going to the police.

That's shit, and you know it.

You know what happened on garbage night. You've been thinking it over, pressing play, pause, rewind, play, for days. You said it yourself...

The Predator Mind considers a specific fantasy with such frequency, with such detail, the fantasy becomes familiar and natural. Doable.

I picture Leland. Bits of brain tissue on his cheek, neck bent wrong, dented skull.

Just a dream, wasn't it?

Tasting his salty blood upon my lips.

It seemed like a dream.

Everything seems that way lately though, doesn't it?

I give up on the hammer and lock myself in the bathroom.

You woke in the tub. Your clothes: wet in a pile on the floor. Your hammer: missing.

From the other side of the door, Chloe is barking demands, and Wyatt is yelling at me because she's giving him a headache and I let her get away with too much.

You reviewed your plans over and over and over. Meticulously. Waited until garbage night.

I put my hands over my ears and close my eyes. When the kids do this, I scold them. *It is not acceptable to cover your ears.*

His voice muffled, Wyatt yells, "You say, no locking doors."

I feign calm. "Uh, I'm going to the bathroom."

"No, you're not. You make all these stupid rules for everybody else, but you don't follow them."

I say nothing. *Disengage. Disengage.*

"Momma!" Chloe screams, banging on the door, "I command you to open this door!"

"Pee! I'm going pee!"

At the top of her soprano, glass-shattering range, she screams, "Let me in right now!"

"You should answer your phone," Wyatt says. "It's ringing."

This is crazy. It was a dream. You know it was only a dream. Get it together. You were supposed to meet Nate five minutes ago. Compartmentalize.

I flush the toilet and wash my hands and open the door.

Chloe's face is red and streaked. Wyatt is gone.

"I had to go pee, Chloe. It's OK. I needed privacy. You

244

want to go to Burger King?"

"Yes!" Even as tears are rolling down her chubby cheeks, she is delighted.

"We are going out for dinner right now," I yell at the empty space above the stairs, which is the most slothful, pathetic mode of communication. I hate when the kids yell questions or commands at me from a different room, but I'm tired.

From his room, he yells, "I'm coming," his tone buoyant, his resentment and irritation forgotten.

I grab my keys and phone. Missed call from Liz. Message from Liz.

-Call me when you have a chance. You should talk to someone.

I text back.

-You are so sweet, but I'm OK. Too busy right now to talk. Love you.

As I buckle Chloe into her car seat, I make the mistake of telling them I have to go to the bathroom.

"I thought you *just* went," Wyatt says, skeptical.

41

COPPER AND IRON AND ANIMAL

"I don't think this is going to go well," Nate says.

"Wow. In that case, I'm so glad we're here. It makes the stomach flu the kids will have tomorrow night so worth it."

He smiles because he likes my sarcasm, then hides his smile away because he's gearing up to tell me something.

Please don't let it be that he wants full custody temporarily because my neighborhood is not safe, because he heard about the murder. And also. Please don't let it be that a girlfriend is moving in with him. I don't think I can take Chloe and Wyatt having a second mom. Literally. I think my body would say, *Fuck it, I give up*, and heart attack out of this life.

Chloe and Wyatt are sitting separately from us. I ordered their food, set their tray on a table sandwiched in a booth to avoid one of them falling off a chair. Falling or tipping is usually inevitable. I told them they have to eat their chicken nuggets before they go play.

Chloe shouts, "Hi, Momma! Hi, Dadda! I'll be right here if

you need me. Me and Wyatt are eating like big kids."

Nate gives her a thumbs up and an earnest smile, then turns to me with his beautiful, mischievous eyes. "This isn't going to seem fair but I need to say a few things."

"Fire away. I can't wait."

"I'm sorry," he says quietly, his eyes cast down, but he forces them up to meet mine. "I'm so sorry. I know I've said it before, but I haven't said it for a while. Looking back, I can't believe I betrayed you. I love you and I can't believe I wronged you so horribly. I'm so ashamed. But—"

I knew there was a *but* coming my way. I bite my lip, force myself not to interrupt.

"But I was lonely," he says sadly. "You can be withdrawn. Secretive."

Relieved that he hasn't heard about Leland's murder, I tune him out and gaze over at the kids' booth.

Chloe has a French fry in her hand, but she is entranced by Wyatt's talking. He's teaching her something. He's using his hands, and his tone is patient and warm. If caught in the right mood, the kid is a fucking All Star.

Back to Nate. I'm not sure what I missed, but I get the gist. He continues, "You are so busy worrying about the kids, which is great, but you had nothing left for me. You can be a little cold."

So glad I hauled my ass to BK.

"Men are supposed to be tough, non-emotional. I can't be that way. I need attention."

I roll my eyes.

He catches my eye roll and says, "Not *physical* attention, Grace. I needed you to let me in."

Without anger, without emotion, I whisper, "So it's my fault you fucked other people."

He flinches as if his ears are delicate. As if *I* am vulgar. "No. It's my fault," he says. "Completely my fault. I wish I hadn't. I'm explaining that I was lonely. And now, the loneliness is worse. It's so hard being without you guys. And then when I have them, it's even harder."

Chloe is still cracking up. Wyatt deserves extra video-game time.

"So," I say coldly, "it's hard being lonely and it's hard managing the kids so you'd like to go back to us being a family."

"That's not what I mean," he says, trying to ignore my sarcasm. "It feels like," he says, tilting his head back and letting his eyes fall closed. He's trying to find some inner strength, so I brace myself. He opens his eyes, says, "It feels like you make up these secret reasons to hate me and then you let those reasons grow. If you had talked to me—"

"You fucking other people, did I make that up?"

He flinches again. "No, you didn't."

"How could I trust you again? Honesty is the foundation of a relationship," I say, but it feels like I'm regurgitating a greeting card.

Is it? I mean, really? It's supposed to be honesty, but maybe that's not the most important thing to me. I was happy enough when he was cheating on me and I had no idea.

"You *can* trust me, Grace. I would never hurt you on

purpose. I was immature. A midlife crisis, whatever. I'm done with it. I'll change jobs. Whatever you want. I want another chance." His dark, serious eyes are pleading. "I miss you. I miss us talking. Remember how much we used to laugh?"

He looks so sad, he is so sad, but I'm drained. I've got nothing left. I actually feel bad for him, I do, but my perspective is clinical. Impersonal. Like he's a third cousin or something.

"We're done, Mommy," Chloe yells. "We're going to go play hide and seek—don't worry, we won't touch our mouths and throw up tomorrow!" They're taking off their shoes and then they disappear into a tube. I survey the doors. There are two, they have alarms. I spot a camera mounted high in the corner.

I scrutinize the families. There's a man and woman with four kids. I notice one is coughing. It sounds moist. Another is technically too tall to enter the structure, a solid four inches above the cut-off line. I will have to keep an eye on him. There are two women with two little girls. There's a grandma with a preschooler built like a pro wrestler. He's eating a sundae and has two toys in front of him. Got to watch that kid the most.

"I can't do this right now. I'm tired. I don't feel that great. I can't think. I don't have anything to say right now because I'm that tired."

He looks at me, then watches the kids for a long minute, savoring them, then looks at me again. "OK, Grace. I want to let you know one last thing. I'm seeing a therapist."

Dating a therapist. Probably a massage therapist. I'd like to drop my head onto the table and sleep.

"Dating a therapist?"

He smiles and it's a good smile. "Talking to a therapist. She's helpful. If you're interested, you could come with me. Or even go by yourself. No pressure." Nate is not the type of person who sees a therapist. He has said, on more than one occasion, therapists are for weak people. If I wasn't so tired, I'd be impressed.

He opens his mouth, then shuts it.

"What? What else?" I say, exhausted, annoyed.

He hesitates, considering what he wants to say. "Thanks for meeting me." He moves his hand towards mine, but stops himself. He taps his hand three times on the table, stands up, hunts the kids down, gives them big hugs, and walks out of the playground.

I'm stuck here a good hour. Great. *Thanks again, Nate.*

While Chloe and Wyatt play tag in giant hamster tunnels with strange kids, I rest my chin in my open palm and allow my eyelids to fall.

I picture myself swinging my hammer at his skull. I've replayed this dream so many times, I know it by heart…

His blood hits my tongue. Oh God, why is your mouth open? *I need to spit.* You can't. You can't leave your spit in his house. *I close my mouth, tasting his blood, copper and iron and animal. I think of pigs. His body is flat on the carpet, but his head is tilted awkwardly against the wall.*

He says, "I know—"

"What?" I say. "You know what?"

His eyes close, his throat gurgles, and blood slips down his chin.

I dry heave, covering my mouth with the crook of my arm. I don't want to, but I hit him again. Tissue splashes my cheeks. Splinters of bone pierce my neck.

Pale blue moonlight highlights the horror. His forehead is caved in like a sinkhole. His eyelids are closed, bulging and black. Stink is coming off him. Blood, sweat, and piss.

My heart is throbbing, panicky, expecting him to spring to life like an actor in a haunted house. I back away, gasping and gagging. What did he know?

Maybe he was going to say: I know you. You are exactly like me. Batshit crazy. You don't belong in this world.

Or maybe, deep down, he loathed his impulses. Maybe he was going to say: I know I am heinous. I am a monster. Thank you. Finally. Thank you.

Or maybe he was going to tell me where he dumped Ava Boone's body, in which case, I've fucked up.

Remember, it was just a dream.

Resting my chin on my open palm has irritated the loose skin under my jaw. It feels as if I had a sliver there and now I've pushed it in deeper. I brush my fingertip over my skin and feel the slightest irregularity. It's probably a stiff, defiant hair. I've never gotten one on the soft skin under my jaw, but the body gets more haywire every year.

I scan the play area for Chloe and Wyatt, and spy them up high on a rope net. Chloe is smiling, which is all I need to see.

I grab my purse and hustle into the play-area bathroom. I'll be quick, and Chloe and Wyatt are up high, out of a potential kidnapper's reach for at least a minute.

Under the harsh light in the bathroom, I move my face close to the large mirror over the sink. There is definitely something there, just below my jaw. I brush it with the pad of my thumb again and feel it move under my thumb like a hair, stiff and plastic. I drop my purse onto the counter and dig in my makeup bag for tweezers.

On my fourth try with the tweezers, the splinter comes out. I place it on my open palm. The sliver is opaque, white, and fine. It could be anything. The tiniest shard from the ceramic coffee mug I dropped in the breakroom this morning, a fragment from a plastic toy the lawn mower chewed up and spit out, an aberrant hair, *anything.*

My heart feels like it's bursting. Sweat breaks on my upper lip.

Bone. It looks like a shard of bone. Is that even possible? What does this mean?

I run my hands under the water, washing the splinter away, down the drain, and then I dab my wet hands across my forehead and neck.

It means you better be really fucking careful.

42

ARE MY SOCKS WET?

After an hour of hamster-cage play with only minor injuries—a scraped knee for Chloe and a raspberry elbow for Wyatt—they are actually ready to put their shoes on and get in the car.

It is Friday night, which is *Cherish Night.*

I've never called it Cherish Night out loud as it would cheapen the affair.

Every other weekend Nate gets the kids. He picks them up Saturday morning and brings them back Sunday night. So, I've made it a tradition to show them a good time on Friday. Typically, we play board games, eat ice cream, and read books: all the things I want them to remember me by should I never see them again.

I know all of this is backwards, starting with trying to impress them and outdo their dad, but Nate is tough competition. He takes them for chocolate-chip pancakes in the morning, whipped cream on top, and hot chocolate, whipped cream as well, and off to the store for a just-because toy, followed by McDonald's Happy Meals at lunch, and Cici's pizza buffet for dinner. I'm not sure how a GI surgeon justifies feeding his own kids a highly processed diet, but there it is.

He is a bag of air-spun, melt-on-their-tongues, blue and pink cotton candy. I am bitter broccoli and peas. Nate wants them to be happy *right now*. I am trying to protect their future. He wants them to smile and giggle. I want them to avoid heart disease and diabetic amputations. He gives piggyback rides and throws them in the air. I give them haircuts and baths. Being with Nate is like being in Times Square on New Year's Eve. Being with me is occasionally like being in China, working in a shoe factory.

I should want to savor every moment with them before Nate whisks them away in the morning, but on this Cherish Night I am preoccupied.

You need to be careful. Careful as a criminal.

I let them watch a movie with no moral message while I bleach every square inch of my bathroom. I let them eat Pop-Tarts for dinner while I rewash my laundry. I put them to bed without baths or teeth-brushing while I check my face, neck, and hands for small cuts or slivers of Leland's splintered bones. I find nothing definitive; I have small nicks in my skin everywhere, at any given time. I don't read a single book. I don't do or say anything to make them feel special, let alone *cherished*.

When they are snoring softly in their rooms, I sneak out of the house and run one mile. The night air is warm and humid and smells like rain. I shower and, with wet hair, lie naked in my bed and close my eyes.

I've left his sliding door open and dropped slimy, week-old pieces of chicken on the floor inside his door.

254

Walking in darkness and rain, I zigzag up and down the roads west of my house, walking on the street. I'm taking a long route home, meandering away from his house and circling back to mine.

I stop beside a plastic grocery bag trapped under a rock. I take a pair of flip-flops that are three sizes too large for me and several black garbage bags out of the grocery bag. Peel off my extra layer of clothes and my too-large sneakers. I stuff all of it into one of the garbage bags, then slip my cold, pruney feet into the flip-flops.

As I lift the lid of someone's garbage bin, the odor of rotting meat wafts out. I gag, briefly. I toss one of my bags in and walk fifteen houses. Wiser this time, I hold my breath before I open the lid of another garbage bin. In goes another bag. This one has my father's wooden-handled hammer.

I expect one or two passing vehicles, headlights cutting through mist. I don't encounter a single car or person.

I open my eyes and stare at my bedroom ceiling. I don't want to relive Garbage Night.

Keep your eyes open all night if you have to.

Thunder wakes Chloe at 1am. When she cries, I jump out of bed swiftly because I haven't fallen asleep yet. Cold and naked, I pull on yoga pants and a T-shirt and socks. I gracefully sweep her limp, sleep-warm body into my arms and tell her the rain is giving the trees a drink. They are happy because they were thirsty. And, doesn't the rain sound like beautiful music? Doesn't the thunder sound like the squirrels are juggling nuts?

She says nothing and easily falls back asleep.

Chloe wakes again at 2:30am. I go to her promptly, hyper-awake and jittery, because I was falling asleep when the thunder woke me too.

"I hear monsters, Momma." Sitting in her bed, her lids blink slowly, heavily.

"It's the thunder, baby. It's raining. Remember, the trees were thirsty and now they're so happy."

We go back and forth about monsters and rain for a few minutes before she lies her head down on her pillow and closes her eyes.

The night is getting away from me. I am running out of time to sleep. I read for a half hour and drift off.

Chloe wakes me at 4:30am. She is screaming.

I fight through a wave of deep, heavy, limb-paralyzing sleep. I emerge from it, groggy and not in control of my body. Heavy pressure in my belly urges me to the bathroom even as she's crying and yelling. I trip on the floor and bang my elbow into the doorframe. I maneuver the hallway and kids' bathroom in the dark and I'm a foot away from the toilet when my sock lands in a cold puddle. Gooseflesh pops along my neck and arms. I *detest* wet socks. And, no one even took a bath. Why is the floor wet?

Chloe is yelling for me.

You never let me sleep.

I lower my ass onto the toilet, but the toilet seat my ass was expecting never meets me. I fall in. Cold toilet water washes over the region of my body I work *so hard* to protect from filth.

Fury clenches my insides. Violence hums like static electricity along my skin. My hands ball into hard fists. Under my breath, "Motherfuckers."

"Momma! Momma! Where are you?"

I hold my pee, pull my yoga pants up over my wet ass, and stumble into Chloe's room. I step on what is undoubtedly a Lego and feel the soft skin of my foot split open. *Motherfuckers.*

I am a tightly coiled spring, ready to brusquely unfurl.

"Momma, I was calling you. Where were you?"

My chest tight, my skin hot, my pulse thumping hard and fast, my bladder pressing, I reach down for her. I pull her into my arms and press her moist cheek to mine. Through clenched teeth, I say, "I'm sorry, baby. I was in the bathroom."

"Is the thunder going to get me?"

"No. You're OK, baby. You can sleep in my bed." I carry her into my bed and lay her head on my pillow and tuck my down-alternative comforter under her chin. "I have to take a quick shower because I got dirty, but I'll be right back."

"Don't leave me."

"I'm not leaving. I have to pee and take a quick shower. It will only take a minute."

"OK. I'll wait for you."

Warm shower water pelts my skin, uncoiling my muscles, dissolving my fury. Tinged pink from my bleeding foot, water pools at my feet.

My behavior, *my anger*, is dependent on frivolous variables. How much sleep did I get? During what stage of sleep am I interrupted? Are my socks wet? Does my foot ache? Is my pussy wet with toilet piss-water?

They say your true character reveals itself during hardship, which worries me. When the going gets tough, I tend to morph into a raging monster.

I walk naked, skin moist, cold and goose-bumped, into my room. Chloe sleeps, her lips like ribbons, her cheeks full and tender, her hair feathery upon my pillow, her small body cradled by the cushiony hills of my bedspread. I watch her chest rise and fall, over and over, while I drip water onto the wood floor.

43

SOME SORT OF EXPLOSIVE DEVICE

Today I am going to get shit *done*. Today I am going to pretend I can Start Over. Today I will pretend there has never been a murder on my street. Today I will pretend my hammer is not missing. Today I will pretend I've never met the Boones, and I've never heard of their daughter. Today I will pretend I have nothing to hide.

I am putting last night behind me. I don't even mention the toilet seat to Wyatt. I smile a lot. Fake it till you make it.

Nate whisks the kids away at 8am. Not a word about yesterday's conversation at Burger King. I'm going to pretend that never happened either. I'm giving my mind the Day Off.

My ADD medication takes the reins. I boost the effect with a strong cup of tea and I am buzzing. I scrape forgotten, faded stickers off the kitchen floor with a knife while I sing "All Star" by Smash Mouth.

By 11:30am the dishes are clean, the kitchen sink is scoured, the toilets are disinfected, the floors are washed, and the kids' clothes are clean and tossed, *unfolded*, into their drawers.

I make myself eggs and toast and a second cup of tea. I text my realtor.

-Please disregard my previous voice mail, Jane. We are staying. Thanks!

With Hulk curled at my feet, I pay bills as I eat breakfast. After the fat cats get paid, I walk outside.

The outside of my house is like a scrotum housing two testicles, meaning, my mind considers it the male domain, not fully knowable and involving an array of equipment and procedures that will never feel natural to me.

It is *knowable.* I walk around the house, making a mental list of chores.

Grass is getting long, luring ticks and mosquitoes to the party in my backyard. Shed is falling apart and infested with bees. Swing set is splintering and rusted. Vinyl siding on the north side of the house is moldy. Garage is brimming with toys that have either become tripping hazards or homes for small rodents. Hoses need to be detangled. Hulk's turds need to be hunted and bagged. Weeds are spiky and treacherous on the south side of the house. Their posture, cocky and shameless, indicates they won't succumb easily.

The chores seem towering and endless. In a moment of profound laziness, I look forward to death.

On the bright side, the asshole who sold me this house, binding me to the creep next door and moving his wife and three girls far far away, rigged his garage with an impressive stereo system. He mounted six speakers throughout the garage and wired them to a stereo shelved in the back of the garage.

The outdoor chores will kick my ass, but I'll get my ass kicked while listening to good tunes. *Thank you, Tony Durtato.*

The classic rock station comes in crisp and without a trace of static—a wonder and an enigma. As I roll the lawn mower into the yard, the DJ tells me that after commercials, he's playing an hour of David Bowie. I haven't listened to David Bowie in years. If I get the mowing done quickly, I'll get to enjoy the music. I'm already looking forward to it.

I toil, sweat, and troubleshoot for fifteen minutes, but can't get the mower's engine to do anything more enduring than cough and gurgle.

Feeling incompetent sucks.

Which is the lesser evil: knocking on Blake's door or calling Nate?

I sit on the driveway and squint at the sun.

Kids whiz by on their electric scooters, graciously oblivious of me. An old couple walks by with their kind-faced dog on a leash. The man asks me if I need help.

"I'm good, thank you." I wave.

The woman says something to me, something about the business of mowing lawns, I'm not sure. Another couple is headed my way. They are younger, walking a dog and a child, and will no doubt try to interact with me out of sheer courtesy.

I lie on my back, close my eyes, and make myself invisible.

Gritty cement warms my arms and legs and reminds me of being a kid. *No need to get up. Relax. No need to work so hard to try to be normal.*

Through my garage speakers, David Bowie sings "Life on Mars?"

"You dead?" A man's voice startles me. He gently kicks my sneaker.

Alarm running through my veins, my eyes fly open but aren't adjusted to the sun. A fuzzy figure stands above me. There's bursting white light where the figure should have a head.

It takes a few seconds for my brain to recognize his voice.

"God?" I say.

James Mahoney laughs. *Detective Mahoney.*

"I was playing dead. Waiting to see if some kind human would come help me. I wasn't expecting to be kicked."

"That wasn't a kick. It was a nudge. What are you doing?"

My eyes adjust, and his figure comes into focus. He wears worn khakis, a gray T-shirt, and casual dress shoes that have been scratched and faded to such an extent, they now qualify as outdoor work shoes. He's wearing a baseball cap, like he's a kid. His light eyes sparkle.

His allure reminds me: I must look disgusting. There is a fine layer of dirt on my sweat-filmed body. Although I can't smell myself, I don't think there's any way I don't stink. I'm guessing my face is puffy and blotchy.

I sit and lean back on my hands. "My mower doesn't like me. I figured if I cuddled and cajoled it, I might convince it to give me a second shot."

"How did that work?"

"It's been around the block, heard too many lines."

"You want me to give it a go?" His mischievous tone gives my stomach a twirl.

"You would be my hero."

He yanks the cord, but can't get anything going. Muscles strain and shift up his arms. A breeze of his remnant pine-and-soap deodorant blows my way. He tries again. Nothing.

Silence drawing out my insecurities, I say, "The oil and gas aren't empty."

He carefully tips the mower on its side and tinkers with it. "You can tip the lawn mower over, but tip it this way. Otherwise, oil will spill where it shouldn't."

I open my mouth, but close it. When someone's trying to troubleshoot, they don't need a chatterbox. And I'm a little worried I might shout *hammer*.

He turns it upright, pulls the cord, and it purrs.

"You're a genius." Dumbfounded, I stand.

"Your spark plug was loose. It needed to be reseated."

If he only knew how badly my spark plug needs to be reseated.

"Are your kids inside?"

"With their dad."

"Your oil is a little low. Let's fill it."

"In the shed." I head around back. He turns off the mower and follows me. My nerves sizzle. Would he attack me? No, he's a cop. Doesn't always mean much, I guess, but I do know him. *Do you?*

"That's some stereo system," he says. "I still hear Bowie."

The DJ plays "Rebel Rebel".

"Six speakers in the garage, courtesy of the guy who lived here before. Tony Durtato, the roofer."

When I open the shed door, hot air comes at me like it's starving for flesh. I step inside and let the door fall free behind me, but it catches on a raised mound of grass, as usual, and keeps itself propped open a quarter of the way. The stink of ammonia and decomposing grass is thick, but doesn't make me gag like I did when I opened the shed thirty minutes ago.

He follows me into this tight space, which cranks my pulse.

Why did he follow me in? Is he one of those violent cops with a God complex who rapes women and beats teenage boys?

Chill. He came in here to help you. He fixed your lawn mower.

You sure about that? He's investigating Leland's murder.

He lets go of the door, but it catches again and remains ajar. A tall, thin slice of light falls into the dark shed. It's not enough light to read by, but it's enough for me to locate the oil on the shelf.

"You should put a few motion-sensor lights in here," he says. "You can get small ones for a few bucks at the hardware store."

"Good idea."

I grab a container in each hand. "Here's the oil and the gas." Turning toward the door, I bump into him. I didn't know he was so close. "Sorry."

He doesn't move.

Uh oh.

His thumb slides along the bare skin of my inner arm. It's the most erotic touch I've felt inside this decade. Blood rushes to my sweet spots. I am not entirely certain as to what's going

264

on. I have a good guess, but this scenario, being touched by a man other than my husband, ex-husband, is so foreign to me I can't be sure.

My muscles are clenched, my nerves are buzzing with anticipation. I stand still, uncertain.

"Can I?" he says.

I'm waiting for him to finish his question, but he doesn't. My skin is slick and burning for him to do *something* so I say, "Yes."

He eases the containers away from my fingers and sets them on the rotting plywood floor. He stands in front of me, his clothes barely brushing mine, his chin in front of my nose. Leaning in, he grazes my bare inner thigh with his fingers.

Inhaling sharply, I nearly orgasm. Only thing stopping me is sheer will.

Something inside me breaks. I have been so completely focused on my children, I had secured and stowed away my desire. Now, like a giant warm water balloon, it bursts inside me with heavy liquid warmth.

My tongue quickly finds his mouth and my hands go for the front of his pants. I have never appreciated the male organ as much as I do in this moment. My whole life, it has been there, waiting, vying for attention, desperately yearning for gratitude. I unbutton and unzip his khakis and slide my hand around his warm skin.

"I want this."

His breath catches. "Are you sure?"

"Yes. Right now."

"You're sure?" he says again.

"Lay down."

He does, pushing away a Home Depot bucket full of small shovels and dangerously sharp, rusty metal rods. A plastic snow sled slips toward him and he shoves it back to its teetering location. I step out of my shorts and underwear and grab hold of his dick. I straddle him and rub it back and forth on my skin, approaching orgasm. The cheap sled slips loose again from whatever it was balancing on and hits me in the side of the neck. I throw it to the back of the shed and shove him inside me.

I am *gone*. One with the universe. My head floats away into space. Deep gratitude for his existence, for his muscles and skin, swells inside me.

Don't say hammer.

He laughs gently. "Whoa, that was quick. Let me catch up."

"Make sure you pull out."

He holds my hips, lifting and pulling me. He works hard for a minute or so before he abruptly stops. He cranes his neck, lifting his head off the floor, a move which appears awkward and painful.

"What is it?" I say.

"Is that buzzing?"

I listen. Humming. Very soft and quiet. Coming from where I threw the sled.

"I think there are bees living in the far corner, but they haven't bothered me yet."

"I have an EpiPen in my glove compartment."

"What? Why? Are you allergic to bees?"

"Deathly."

"Let's go inside." I pull away, but he grabs my hips tightly. His fingernails dig into my skin. "Ow."

"Sorry."

"We can finish inside my house."

"No," he says and moves under me. "No way am I stopping. If I get stung, call 911 and shoot me with the EpiPen."

"Is your car unlocked?"

"Yes, unlocked."

"You leave your police car unlocked? Don't you have a gun in there?"

"Locked in the trunk."

"Can't you unlock the trunk from inside the car?"

"No. Be quiet."

I can't hold back my smile.

A basketball bounces on a driveway nearby, the sound methodical and easy, the slightest echo of vibrating rubber adding an interesting complexity. Blake's lawn mower revs, then settles into an unyielding growl. The shed door is a good six inches ajar, but I don't care. I don't care if Blake comes over to give me lawn care advice and peeks into my shed and sees my bare ass bouncing. I am simply having too much fun.

Within two minutes I have another orgasm. Sixty seconds later, he is pulsing and emptying himself inside me.

I say, "No, you didn't just do that."

Breathy, he stammers, "I'm sorry. I couldn't help it. I had to."

I roll off him and lie on my back beside him. Deep in my brain, one of my neurons waves a red flag and shouts, "Uh, he *might* be selfish," but this neuron is so far buried, it's practically invisible; it's the neuron the others pshaw and ignore. I'm not mad, not right now. I feel too good for that. I laugh, "You've got some incredible fucking nerve."

Still breathing heavy, he says, "I had a vasectomy."

Strangely, this makes me sad. I don't want to have more children, I'm too old for it and not that great as a parent, so my sadness shocks me. The desire to make more babies is not my own, so where is it coming from? Maybe it's hardwired.

Still, shooting a load into me? Kind of pushy. I'm elated now, but I'm positive two hours from now, when his juice is leaking out onto my underwear, making my clothes wet and sticky, I'm gonna be annoyed.

"I guess it doesn't matter. And I have an IUD."

"An explosive device?"

"IUD, not IED. It's a birth control device they implant in the uterus."

"Sounds scary. Did it hurt?"

I find his consideration, or maybe it's curiosity, charming. Considering he carelessly filled me with seminal fluid a minute ago, it's got to be the remnant oxytocin blast from my orgasm making him *appear* charming. "Only when they put it in. I can't feel it now."

He inhales deeply and lets his breath out meditatively. "I feel like I'm sixteen. You are incredible."

"Of course I'm incredible. I let you fuck me."

He laughs.

After orgasm, my flexibility and sensuality don't stick

around. I hoist my stiff body carefully and arthritically. Splinters and dirt stick to my back, ass, and knees. Instead of brushing them off, I step into my underwear and shorts. "I have to pee. I can't believe you're still lying there, a beehive five feet from your naked body."

"You'd get my EpiPen and save me."

I consider making a joke. Instead I respond honestly. "I would save you."

He calmly gathers his clothes. Funny, my deep gratitude and yearning for his dick have vanished. His flaccid penis is mildly interesting, at best. My mind is dusting its hands, ready to be rid of him, ready to go back to my outdoor chores.

"Do you want to come inside for a glass of water or something or are you heading to your car?"

He laughs. "Well, I can't leave yet. I was going to fill up your mower."

"That's right. I guess you did warn me you were going to fill it up."

I step out of the shed into the blinding light, into the warm sun, into the world of chirping birds and people trying to connect and make things work, and it feels like being born.

44

THE PORN COP

Minutes later I walk from the bathroom to the kitchen.

James Mahoney stares out the window over the sink, a plastic cup of water in his hand. That he chose a plastic kid's cup instead of glass is endearing. His damp hair curls a little, and short hairs escape down the back of his neck. Sweat stains his gray T-shirt in the shape of wings. His triceps are tanned and hard. On my body these same muscles betrayed me long ago.

James and I were not friends in high school, we haven't seen each other in twenty years, yet he is familiar. Our language and humor are strangely in sync. I don't believe in soul mates, so this synchronized rhythm must be a vestigial effect of suffering adolescence at the same time in the same location. We shared the same neighborhood, same teachers, same hangouts. It makes me trust him. But it shouldn't.

"You found a cup," I say.

He eyes the cup in his hand, then he eyes me over his shoulder. "I *am* a trained detective, and they weren't doing a great job of hiding. What's so funny?"

"Nothing."

"You're smiling."

I sigh with my whole body. I want to touch his triceps. Instead I lean against the counter. "I remember sex always did this for me, made me feel normal, but I forgot the actual feeling. It's nice." It's true. I feel like a balloon lifting playfully against a peaceful blue sky. Blissful.

"Wow, it's been that long?"

"Six months."

He puts his cup in the sink and closes the distance between us. He hooks his finger in the elastic waistband of my pathetic, fifteen-year-old workout shorts—Why haven't I thrown these shorts away? They deserve to die. And how have they not disintegrated?—then snaps it against my skin. My heart flutters and I'm pretty sure I bat my eyelids.

"I'd be happy to make you feel normal again tonight. Tomorrow, too. I have dedicated my life to community service, you know."

It obviously hasn't been quite as long for him. Otherwise he would have mentioned it so I wouldn't feel like such a prude. I want details, but it doesn't seem like the right time to probe.

Also, get a chlamydia test.

"Do you have sex with potential witnesses on each new case?"

His blue eyes twinkle. "Are you saying you witnessed something?"

"No, sir."

"I don't usually have sex with witnesses."

"What about your partner?"

271

"What about her?"

I roll my eyes. "She looks airbrushed."

"She's only a few years older than my daughter."

"You're skirting the question, Detective."

He faces me square, loses the smile, and stares into my eyes. "I didn't hear a question, but no, I have never had sex with my partner. Ariana is a kid. A beautiful, intelligent, tough kid who has worked hard to make detective at a young age. We are close. She's like a daughter. Occasionally she hangs out *with* my eighteen-year-old daughter." He tilts his head, guessing I'm doing the math. "I had her young. I was twenty-one."

His answer is perfect. Too perfect. As if he were so incredibly genuine and trustworthy, his boss assigned him to partner with Ariana, the porn cop, because he was the only man who could be trusted with her.

"Hmm," I say.

He smooths back a strand of my hair, moves his hand down my head, and tugs my ponytail. "Can I take you to dinner tonight?"

I breathe in his cologne-scented sweat. "Don't you have to work?" I say, breaking from this foolish flirting. "Aren't the first forty-eight hours the most crucial or something?"

"It's been nearly sixty hours, but the most crucial period is the time between the murder and when we arrive on the scene. I put in too much time Thursday and Friday. I was told to take the day off. Even when it's day three of an investigation, time off is important. Mental health and all that." He smiles and leans in. His chest brushes mine. He gazes down at me with a blend of playfulness and desire. "Go to dinner with me."

"You aren't trying to frame me for my neighbor's murder, are you?"

His eyes lose their playfulness and turn stony. Scrutinizing my expression, he says, "Why, did you do it?"

I step in closer and whisper in his ear, "I'm not the type."

45

FILTHY, LAZY CRYBABIES

This is a terrible idea. James Mahoney will be my downfall.

Yet he is also my savior. I can't get over how normal I feel. Still. Hours after orgasm. Connected. Capable. Mentally healthy.

Plus, serendipity is cheering me on. I have a sample of his seminal fluid on a piece of toilet paper inside a Ziploc bag in my refrigerator. If he ever accuses me of any crime in front of a judge, I'm pretty sure having sex with a suspect would take the air out of his case. The sample may lack sperm because he's had a vasectomy, but I'm guessing they could link it to him. My bag of his jizz relaxes me. I no longer worry I'll blurt *hammer* or *I can still taste his blood*.

We go to dinner. He takes me to a cozy Mexican restaurant, easy Latin music, dim lighting. My margarita arrives and I drink quickly. My palms are sweaty and my cheeks hurt because I'm smiling hard. Tequila's warmth sluices through me and I say, "It's hard to believe we were in high school over twenty years ago."

"Half our lifetime ago. Everything is different now."

"Tell me about it," I say, my mind feeling velvety, a nice

place to lounge. No sharp edges in there.

"It's hard to put my finger on exactly how things have changed."

"No it's not," I say. "One, the internet. Two, smartphones. Three, *Annie*."

"Annie who?"

"The movie. Did you see the remake?"

"Strangely, yes."

"What can those remake *Annie* girls do? Sing a little? But, holy cow, those 1980s *Annie* girls were Olympic material. Backflipping across rows of rusty mattresses, hanging from fire escapes, sliding down wooden staircases on their stomachs, fracturing their ribs, all while singing and smiling. Thirty years later, what kid backflips across rows of rusty mattresses? The collective attitude toward children used to be more careless," I say, my lips syrup-sticky and salty. Tequila loosens springs, levers, and gears inside me, opening me up like I'm electronic, and a cool breeze blasts my copper insides.

He's laughing, and it hits me.

He is Nate's opposite.

Nate's eyes are dark, mischievous, intelligent, and blazing with secrets. James's blue eyes are bright, transparent, and slightly weary.

Nate has the blond, breezy hair of a surfer. James's hair is dark, starting to gray, and failing at order.

Nate has the slim runner's physique of a self-preserving, calculating academic. James's body has a rugged strength I associate with physical labor. He is the type of guy whose knees will "go bad".

My comparison is pathetically superficial, but in this moment, the shallow contrast of their features strikes me as mathematically true as a physical law describing the universe. Which could be the margarita.

I hold my chin in my palm, eyes wide as an overachieving student while James gets me up to date on gossip. He tells me about Jason Ricks, the quiet science nerd in our class who opened a death-scene cleanup business and is now profanely rich and hip—the kind of guy who wears T-shirts printed with Zen philosophy. He tells me about Robbie Hartash, the gentle, big-hearted dopehead who ended up in prison. He tells me who owns pet pigs and pet alligators, who moved to Singapore and Bali, and who lives in their car and showers at the Y. Through his cop glasses, the world is as black and white as our waitress's uniform. I enjoy seeing the world in this simple, confident hue.

Buzzed on gossip I had no idea I was interested in, I say, "I have not run into a single person from high school in twenty years."

"I run into people from high school all the time."

"It's your job. My out-and-about routine consists of going to my preschool job, carting my kids to daycare and activities, visiting my mom's house, and the grocery store. There's six or seven places I go, and it rarely changes."

"Your kids are little. You'll be out more when they get older."

I can't imagine my kids physically being older and no longer needing me. I can't imagine myself older. I can't imagine venturing out socially and partaking in more small talk. I don't see the appeal.

"I don't think so. I think I'll sleep more and catch up on all the good TV I've been hearing about for the past decade." I rub my upper arm. I got another rabies vaccine today, and it aches a little bit. "I never would have guessed you'd be a cop."

He raises an eyebrow. "Detective."

"Whatever."

He laughs. "I never would have guessed you'd be a preschool teacher."

"Me neither. Once I had kids, it was convenient." I don't want to talk about my career choices and the various areas in my life where I aimed lowish or settled. "Why join the police force?" I sip my drink, but shouldn't. My stomach is souring.

"You never heard about my brother?"

"I never knew you had a brother."

"Five. I'm Irish. Anyway, it's a crummy story. My older brother, Colin. Awesome kid. The peacemaker in our family. And the musician. Guitar, harmonica, mandolin. Creative. Good heart. Didn't have a manipulative bone in his body."

This story isn't going to end well. I bite my lip to dampen my uncontrollable smile.

"Colin was going to school in Chicago," he says and gulps from his beer, giving me a moment to admire the motion of his Adam's apple and the skin along his jaw, which is aged and thick, but still taut and smooth. His razor missed a small patch of stubble. He wipes his mouth with the inside of his wrist. "He lived in a cheap apartment in a shady neighborhood, as poor college students do. Guy broke into his apartment in the middle of the night. Colin maybe tried to fight the intruder, more likely he offered him breakfast. I'm not sure how it played out, but the guy shot him, and he died." His voice softens, his pale eyes are swimming and vulnerable. He's a cop, but he hasn't been hardened or burnt out.

"I'm sorry," I say, and drop my hands into my lap, squeezing them tightly together.

"It messed me up," James says, "that arrogance and lack of regard. The idea that one person can have such a narrow scope of another person's life. I was eighteen. I hadn't decided my path yet so Colin's death decided it for me."

If he only knew how filthy my marrow is with righteousness. If he only knew I am the quintessence of his hatred. I bite my lip. *Don't say hammer.*

Fifteen minutes later we stumble into my house, tipsy, sex-crazed, and frantic as teenagers. We make out on the stairs as we tug at each other's clothes. We pant our way to my bedroom and have sex on my desk chair, his tongue flicking my nipples. I orgasm as quickly as a teenage boy. He follows shortly after.

He rests his forehead between my bare, slick breasts and whispers, "I like you."

My insides still vibrating, I hover in that shaky climatic state where I could laugh or cry. A kaleidoscope of emotions—sad, needy, joyful, confident, callous—fight for the title.

"Why? Why do you like me?" I say. I'm not seeking affirmation, I'm desperately curious. His attractiveness surpasses mine. His goodness surpasses mine.

He tips his eyes up to meet my gaze and bites his swollen lip thoughtfully. "First time I met you, you were on your hands and knees in your minivan, ass in the air, your fingers in blood."

"You're drawn to sex, violence, and grit. Makes sense. You're a cop."

He smiles. "Second time I met you, you were jogging and singing and crying. You told me you only dated widows."

"I see." I dismount him and stretch out on my bed, hand propping my head. "You like sensitive, confusing girls."

"Third time, you were on your back on your driveway like a kid who doesn't care what anyone thinks."

"Filthy, lazy crybabies are also your thing. Interesting mix."

He laughs and walks into the bathroom, leaving the door open. He pees, and I watch. Few things in life are more intimate.

Poor James Mahoney. He has no idea how imperceptive he is. He's mistaking my self-exposure for honesty when it's driven by my poor judgement and lack of self-control. He is sweet and trusting. A naïve cop, he's an oxymoron.

I want to protect him from myself. If only I had self-control.

He's a big boy. It's not your honesty he likes, it's your volatility.

He says, "You want to watch a movie and have a sleepover?"

I'm satisfied, tired, and slightly bored of him. I'd rather be alone. "Not really, but I can do favors."

Thinking I'm joking, he laughs.

I shower, repeating the mantra *Be careful* so many times it loses its meaning.

46

THEY FED ON HIM

Hair wet, he pulls his shirt on and says, "It must be fate we're on the same visitation weekend schedule with our kids."

"I don't believe in fate," I say, placing two sodas on my nightstand and a big plastic bowl full of popcorn on my comforter. "Also, I don't want you to meet my kids."

"OK," he says slowly, withdrawing.

"That came out wrong." I settle my hand across the front of my neck, holding it there. I wait until he looks at me. "My kids are my whole world. I want to make sure they never doubt it. I don't want it to ever cross their minds that they have competition. It's hard enough that their mom and dad have split. I'm guessing you know what I mean."

He smiles. "Yes. Believe me, I get it."

We settle upon a Bill Murray movie. Though we don't psychoanalyze our pick, Bill Murray conveys an apt blend of nostalgia, maturity, irreverence, and foolishness: a decent metaphor for this brand-new relationship. I turn off the lights, slip into bed beside him, the popcorn bowl between us, and press play.

"Tell me something about Leland," he says.

My pulse triples. I brush imaginary crumbs off the comforter.

Idiot. He's using you. How was that not obvious from the start?

"I don't know. I never knew him. Barely ever talked to him. I told you this. At first I thought he was odd, but I tried not to hold it against him. I waved hello, that's about it. I once helped him move a dresser up his stairs, but even when I helped him, when I was in his house, we barely talked." I speak slowly, pretending the words are coming to me now, unplanned, unrehearsed. "Once Lou told me Leland was a suspect in Ava Boone's kidnapping, I was wary of him. Tried not to look in his direction. I didn't feel at ease. Days before the murder, I actually decided to move. It wasn't worth the worry to stay." Does he know I called my real estate agent?

"I guess you don't have to worry about moving now."

"I guess not," I say, watching the opening credits. "One less thing to juggle. It sounds awful, but I'm relieved."

"Is that all you feel? Relieved?" He sounds considerate, yet methodical.

That's because this, right here, is an interrogation. "I don't know. All I know about him is that he might have kidnapped a girl months ago. If that happened, he's killed her by now. How should I feel?"

Silence. "When did the guy down the street tell you Leland was a suspect?"

"Recently. A week ago. Maybe two. You already asked me that when you and Ariana stopped by."

"Sorry, bad habit."

My palms are sweaty, and I'm hoping he doesn't reach over to hold my hand because then he'll know. I grab a handful of popcorn and hold it. I keep the remote in my other hand.

"Do you know what happened to Ava?" I say, trying to focus on the police department's shortcoming.

"It's not my case."

"I know, but do you?"

"No."

"Do you think she's dead?"

He's quiet. "Yeah."

"If it were my kid, I would never stop looking. What if it were your daughter? Would you stop looking?"

"I don't know," he says, shaking his head thoughtfully. "I don't think I would stop, but it's a real mess what the families go through." He grabs a handful of popcorn, acting nonchalant when he says, "Tell me about Lou."

Opening credits done, the movie begins. I hit pause. Bill Murray's mouth hangs open. Looks like he's going to be sick. "Haven't you already questioned him?"

"Yeah, but I'm interested to hear your thoughts. What did Lou think of Leland?" he says, his voice monotone and subtle, trying to slip into the shadows.

Skin tightens and prickles along my skull. Here is a chance to direct the investigation. Here is a chance to point the finger. *Lou told Leland if he so much as spoke to his daughter again, he'd slit his throat.*

But here's the thing. I like Lou. I like that he had the nerve to get in Leland's face and threaten him. Lou was the only person on my street bold enough to warn me about Leland. Like me, Lou is a guy who doesn't shirk burden; he's willing to jump in as Point Bird.

And here's another thing about Lou. He's a poor male who isn't cautious with his words. He is gruff and wears his potential for violence like a merit badge on a sash. These qualities make him vulnerable to the justice system.

But maybe, maybe Lou actually did it. Maybe Lou killed Leland. Maybe your dream was just a dream.

I picture the fine white sliver I tweezed from my neck. A fragment of Leland's shattered bone. I picture myself waking at my kitchen table, holding my dad's hammer. Which is now missing.

Lou didn't do it. Lou threatening Leland, that happened years ago.

I turn to James, making eye contact. "I don't know Lou. I just moved here and I'm busy. I don't really know anyone on the street. Lou seems calm. Normal. Nice guy." *You should have never hit pause on Bill Murray.* "How is the case going?"

"Piss poor. I have a feeling this one's going cold."

"What do you mean?"

He angles his body towards me. "Our clearance rate is seventy-one percent for homicide, which is pretty damn good. That's still twenty-nine percent going unsolved. *Witnesses* help us solve cases." Even under the covers, such a vulnerable position, he projects confidence and good posture. His eyes are clear, honest, and energetic. "We have no witnesses, no one offering home security videos, and I don't blame them. Who wants to go out of their way to vindicate a suspect in a child kidnapping case?"

Thank God. My toes go cold. Giddiness grabs hold. I bite my lip so I can't smile. I turn my gaze upon Bill Murray's open mouth.

"Plus," he says, "Leland's got no family, no advocates. And you got the crime scene, which was a total clusterfuck."

"Why?"

"It rained the night of Leland's murder, and the back door was left open."

Yes, it was. My head feels airy. It's a good thing I'm sitting.

"So you can imagine," he says, "it was a mess. We had to call a trapper to catch a raccoon hissing under the bed. We had tracks and piss from a raccoon, cats, squirrels, maybe a fox. So many damn cats. Our DNA evidence should be processed in the next twenty-four hours, and I'm not expecting it to be extremely helpful. There are people in your neighborhood who let their cats roam. With house cats going in there," he says, "we could have whole families' DNA at the crime scene."

I can only hope. Cheers to roaming house cats and their freewheeling owners.

His voice drops. "Animals didn't only walk the scene, they fed on him." His soft, somber voice gets to me.

I close my eyes.

A string of bloody phlegm dangles, wiggling, on his meaty lower lip. He opens his eyes, closes them.

The murder feels more real than it has so far. Opening my eyes, I shiver to escape the coldness coming from within.

284

They fed on him.

"Was it a gunshot or a stabbing?" I venture, clinging to a chance at innocence.

He hesitates. He's not supposed to say. "Blunt force trauma to the head."

It's like I've jumped into an icy pond. My hypothermic body can't remember how to breathe. I squeeze the bedspread so tightly, my muscles cramp.

"Plus, it was garbage night," he says.

I know.

"Your yards back up to houses on a street that has no lampposts. Once the sun goes down, it's pitch black on that street. No one would see a thing. I can see the guy dumping incriminating evidence in various garbage cans."

"I know."

"What do you mean *you know?*"

"I mean, I can imagine." I stare at the television. "I'm sorry, but I don't want to hear about it. Forget I asked. I'm not cut out for homicide details." I unpause the movie and stuff a handful of popcorn into my mouth.

47

I'VE BEEN HIDING MY PENIS

I jolt awake not because I am well-rested, not because of the warm and gentle sunlight creeping over my bedspread, but because someone's fingers are inside my underwear.

I hated this when I was married to Nate. I hate it now. Anger spikes inside me, and I want to smash James's head between my hands and say, *Do you know how few times I have woken up naturally in the past eight years?*

But last night's conversation—interrogation—regarding Leland's investigation lingers in my head like the stink of broccoli left out overnight, and I welcome the chance to clear the rotting fumes. I roll toward him, stick my hand down his pants, and smile. "I can't believe you slept over."

"Same here," he says, a smile spreading, sleepy and wholesome, across his face.

"I just met you," I say.

"Twenty-five years ago."

Even though I'd rather be sleeping, my body is warming to his fingers. "I should brush my teeth."

"You are not getting out of bed. We'll skip kissing."

"Slow down. I'm getting too excited."

He doesn't slow down. One of his fingers moves inside me in perfect time. I orgasm around his hand, clutching him, trapping his arm.

"You want it so bad, don't you?" He wraps his arm around my back and flips me onto my stomach. From behind he wiggles into me slowly and gently, but once he's in, he's rough. Too rough. But he's also quick, which mostly cancels out his roughness.

He flops beside me onto his back. I roll out of bed because my morning bladder is threatening to burst. While I'm in the bathroom I take a dangerously hot bath. Heat sucks the life from me and clears my mind. I am numb, nearly lobotomized, worry-free. I wrap myself in a towel and open the door, steam rushing past me into the bedroom. I flop onto the bed, face down.

"Do you feel normal?" His words tumble around a smile. "You want to go to breakfast?"

"That sounds nice, but what I've been wanting to ask you since you walked into my house yesterday is, can you fix my hallway closet? The hinge is busted."

He laughs. "You've been making a list for me?"

"You have no idea. I can't turn my brain off."

"Can I borrow your toothbrush first?"

I walk to the bathroom, put the toothpaste on my toothbrush for him. He lifts an eyebrow. "Did you think I was going to use too much?"

"Sorry, it's habit."

In the mirror, he watches himself brush his teeth. I open

my medicine cabinet, open a prescription bottle, and pop a capsule in my mouth.

"What do you take?" he says, his mouth foamy, his voice garbled.

"Adderall." I put my mouth under the faucet and drink. In the mirror, his mouth is still foamy, but he is palming his forehead, eyes closed, shaking his head. As if he knew this was too good to be true. As if he realized I've been hiding my penis. "What?" I say.

He spits. Meeting my eyes in the mirror, toothpaste coating the sides of his mouth, he says, "You take speed?"

"Screw you. I'm forty." I say "I'm forty" as if by forty a person is done screwing up.

"Drug abuse doesn't discriminate by age."

"Thank you, Public Service Announcement." God, he really is a boy scout. I would laugh if I weren't so insecure. Feeling defensive, I say, "I'm not some college kid trying to stay awake for days."

"Do you know what meth does to you?"

"Come on. It's not meth. It's the extended release capsule version. I'm not snorting it."

"Amphetamines can cause heart attacks and induce paranoia and psychosis."

Psychosis? No shit. I knew the cardio risk, obviously. I can feel my heartbeat quicken. Never heard about psychosis.

"Well," I say, "every medication has risks."

"Incredibly addictive stuff and classified as a Schedule Two controlled substance."

I laugh. "Words only a cop says."

He sighs, almost smiles. "How long have you been on them?"

"Since Wyatt was two."

"Hm."

Do not let him shame you. Do not hold his ignorance against him.

He has no idea this drug helps me keep my job, my kids fed, and to drive safely.

Also, I've tried everything else. After Wyatt was born, I tried rigorous exercise, no meat, no dairy, lots of coffee, no coffee, meditation, self-help books, cold showers, and hot baths. None of these alleviated the feeling of tar running through my veins and gumming up my brain.

The phone would ring and as I would run to get it, I would repeat, *Wyatt is in the bathtub Wyatt is in the bathtub.* I would hang up on the telemarketer inside ten seconds and head to the sink to wash dishes, already forgetting Wyatt was in the tub.

I frequently left the oven on overnight. Even though I would tell myself, *Don't forget about the oven. Don't forget.*

I kept a Post-It note on the dashboard: *Don't forget the baby carrier.* As in, *Don't leave the baby strapped in the carrier on the garage floor, inside the house, or inside the car.*

I fought postpartum exhaustion, depression, and guilt for two years before I turned to drugs.

Like cowboys in a draw, James and I stare at each other in my bathroom mirror. It's grimy with oily-finger smears and spit flecks. He sighs with his whole body. "How many times have you needed to hike your dose?"

"Five times." Dr. Nasir upped my dose last month.

He hesitates, nods, then walks out of the bathroom.

"So, what, you're leaving now?"

He turns toward me and gives a tired, but calm smile. "No. I'm going to fix the closet."

I wasn't expecting that.

"We're good?" I say.

He steps forward and kisses me on the forehead. "We're good."

"What a relief, because I have been waiting for one of these sex-in-exchange-for-handyman-work relationships to fall in my lap for months."

He laughs and runs his fingers through his hair.

48

RIPPED FROM MY MOTHER'S WOMB

James fixes the bathroom faucet handle and fiddles with the broken garbage disposal. Says he'll pick up a new disposal over the next couple days.

Gratitude bubbles like geysers up and down my limbs. I make him an omelet. I follow him around my house in a daze as he tightens screws, many of which have remained three turns from being fully tightened since I moved in. Nate took our beloved cordless drill and its breathtaking array of adapters.

I make James coffee and we sit at the kitchen table, talking like old friends.

My phone buzzes with a text. Nate.

-Work called me in on an emergency. Can I bring the kids now?

I want them back in my arms, I'm greedy for them, but I'm also annoyed. When he texts like this, he's assuming I can—*I should*—drop everything for his job.

-Sure, bring them now.

I hurry James to the front door. We make out like teenagers

in the foyer for a minute, then I shove him out. He trips on the outdoor mat, and we're both laughing as he jogs to his car.

After his unmarked car drives away, I sit on the couch and gaze out the window, butterflies flitting in my stomach. I fantasize about marrying James. I fantasize about being on his healthcare plan. I fantasize about two incomes. I fantasize about him repairing loose hinges and gurgly appliances and having sex whenever I feel out of sorts.

Shallow, I know.

I like James. But liking him is secondary. His attractiveness and kindness are also secondary. Having money to buy milk or pay my electric bill or fill a cavity so it doesn't turn into a more expensive, painful root canal: these are the big things. The big things occasionally bring people to the edge of insanity or make them homeless.

Nate's car rolls into my driveway, and the kids pop out of the doors. They actually *pop* like solid bubbles of energy, their springy momentum nearly causing them to tumble and fall onto the driveway.

Nate remains in the driver's seat. He waves and backs out of the driveway.

Huh. I am feeling something new toward him. An absence of anger.

Wow. Revenge sex is grossly underrated.

Chloe and Wyatt burst into the house, noisy and energetic, talking simultaneously about all the random moments of the weekend that crowd their minds.

"We saw two grownups *climb* a *tree*," Wyatt says as if he

saw a dog grow wings, then fly away. "*Grown* men. They were geocaching."

"Dad says he'll take us," Chloe says.

"We went to Dairy Queen," Wyatt says.

"I got a cone with sprinkles," Chloe says, "and I stepped in gum!"

"Did Daddy clean it off your shoe?"

"Nope. Still there." Her voice lifts in joyful, sing-song sarcasm. As if she were my middle-aged, divorced girlfriend rolling her eyes at my ex's contemptible deed.

Of course he didn't. Why would he clean the gum off her shoe? He wasn't taking her back to his place.

She lifts her shoe to show me the gum, but loses her balance and tips back. Her head is a half-inch from banging into the doorknob when I catch her. "Mommy, I missed you so much." She bear-hugs me and her teeth grind near my ear.

"It smells weird in here," Wyatt says. "Like Dad's cologne or something."

"I was cleaning. I found one of Dad's old coats. You guys hungry?"

"Starving," he says, dropping his bag at the front door and heading for the kitchen.

Chloe says, "What did you do while we were gone, Momma?"

"Missed you," I say.

We have a calm afternoon of reading books, cuddling, and cleaning. We eat mac and cheese and carrot sticks for dinner while we watch *Wheel of Fortune*.

Chloe is sleepy. I give her dozens of kisses, in her neck, on her soft cheeks, on the inner corners of her eyes, on the bottoms of her feet. She falls asleep before I tuck her blanket under her neck.

I climb the ladder to Wyatt's bed and heave my body over the rail. He keeps his body still and quiet while I scratch his back. He is enjoying my physical touch. He missed me.

After a few minutes he breaks the silence. "If I scratch your back, can we do riddles on your phone?"

"Scratch *my* back? This must be my lucky day."

We both flip over. He scratches under my bra, the most generous of gestures, and I open my Riddles app.

"The man who made it didn't need it. The man who bought it didn't use it. The man who used it didn't want it."

We both give up immediately and I check the answer. "Coffin."

He says, "That's a good one."

"It is. Here's the next. Ripped from my mother's womb. Beaten and burned. I become a bloodthirsty killer."

"What's womb?"

"Uterus. Where a baby grows. These riddles are so morbid."

"What's morbid mean?"

"Disturbing. Gruesome. Death-related."

"Read it again."

I do. The last sentence echoes in my cavernous mind.

I become a bloodthirsty killer.

I don't feel like a killer and I am the opposite of bloodthirsty. I didn't *want* to do it. I don't even feel criminal. I feel like a middle-aged, weary, scarred wolf trying her best to protect her pups. My memory of that night is both vivid and blurry, but most of all, distant.

"I give up," he says.

"Me too." I click for the answer. "Iron."

"I don't get it. Why is it iron?"

I read the riddle again. "Oh, that's clever. Ripped from womb means pulled out of the earth. You get iron from rock and soil. You can heat it and beat it into a weapon like a sword."

Or a hammer.

"Mom?"

"Yeah?"

His hand drops away from my back. "Tanner said our neighbor got murdered."

Hot and cold flashes race through me. *Of course he's going to hear at school. It was a fucking murder, you idiot. He should have heard it from you. You weren't going to let Tanner be his life teacher, remember? You had your chance. He asked you about the police cars on the street. You blew your chance.*

"That's true, and I should have told you." I'm relieved to have my back to him, to not meet his gaze. *Coward.* "I'm sorry, I didn't want to worry you." My skin is hot, early menopause sweaty. Good thing he's not touching my back anymore. "The police said we shouldn't worry. Our neighbor was mixed up in bad stuff, he was a bad guy, but they're close to catching the guy who did it."

"What bad stuff?"

"I don't know. When I find out, I'll tell you." *For someone who wishes he heard it from you first, that was shit.*

I'll do better, I promise. Just, not *now.*

"OK," he says, his voice easy, trusting.

"Last riddle," I say, mustering a bit of enthusiasm. I don't want his last thoughts before he falls asleep to be imagining his neighbor's murder. Or wondering why his mom keeps secrets. "I go in hard and dry. I come out soft and sticky. You can blow me."

My cheeks burn. I don't think he knows what *perverted* means, so I don't mention it.

Behind me, he laughs. "That sounds weird."

"It does. The suspense is killing me. Let's get a clue. First letter is G."

We both sit quietly. He scratches my back again. I lie still, enjoying scratches, not bothering to use my brain. I am the dog in this relationship. I happily take what I get.

"Is it gum?" he says.

I type in GUM. "Bravo, you got it. I would have never got that one."

I flip toward him. "How did you get so smart?"

He shrugs.

"I love you, kiddo." I touch his cheek with the back of my fingers and descend his ladder.

As I walk to my bedroom, my phone buzzes in my hand. A text from Valerie.

-Grace! I heard about a murder on cherry lane? Your cherry lane?? I heard the dead guy was the suspect in Ava's kidnapping. Your neighbor????!!!

-Yes. crazy, huh?

By the time I've brushed my teeth, she's already texted back.

-OhMyGod. Are you terrified? How was he murdered? Did they break in and shoot him? Oh my God. What are you going to do? Security system?

296

I'm so sorry. What can i do to help? I'd offer to have wyatt over, but adam has strep throat. Can i bring dinner? Buy you a gun?

I remember something James said last night. *Relieved? Is that all you feel?*

Shit.

How did I miss it?

Scared. I'm supposed to be *scared.* Some psycho broke into my neighbor's house and bludgeoned him to death with a hammer. *Thank you, Valerie.* How do I get so wrapped up sometimes, I miss big things? Crucial things.

49

TRAP THE WARM, STRUGGLING BODY INSIDE A PLASTIC STORAGE BIN AND FASTEN THE LID

I wake up to a quiet house, elated to find I'm the earliest riser. My bladder urges me to get out of bed, but my bed's cushiony warmth coaxes me to stay. *Just another minute. Two. Five, max.*

I replay my conversation with Natalie Boone in the Walmart parking lot. She mentioned her sister works in hospice care, which brings back memories of my dad.

I remember the night he died. Mom called around 4am to tell me he was gone. She'd gotten up to pee, checked on him, and found no pulse. I quickly drove over.

The hospice nurse had beaten me there.

Angie. Her name was Angie. She said a prayer over my dad, then corralled us back into the kitchen. My teeth still chattering from the strangeness and sadness of death, I made Mom tea while Angie talked and talked, her voice like warm water, telling us pleasantries about Dad, about what came next, about her family, as she opened all the remaining pain patches and stuck them to a disposable, absorbent, blue bedding pad. She pushed the plunger on the syringe filled with morphine, squirting the medicine onto the pad while filling the new and awful void with her melodious voice.

Your five minutes is up. Ass out of bed.

I walk into the hallway. Chloe is clapping as she wakes up. Wyatt walks out of his room, rubbing his eyes. He stops in the hallway to listen to Chloe clap.

"Yay, yay," she says, in her bed, her eyes still closed. "Yay, dog bones."

"Good morning, Chlo," Wyatt says in a sweet, parental voice. "What were you dreaming about?"

"Dog bones and flying and cotton candy."

He smiles and whispers to me, "That makes no sense."

We migrate downstairs.

While I fill their cups with water, I gaze out the window over the sink. The tree edging my property catches my eye because an animal moves among the branches. It does not move neurotically like a squirrel. It doesn't shudder, bob, or flee like a bird. It isn't native to trees. It is slower, more meticulous.

Yellowish eyes glare at my house beneath a black fur mask.

Leland's cat.

My heart flutters, and I break into a cold sweat.

Of course cats can't talk, but could forensics scrape damning evidence off my dead neighbor's cat? Maybe an animal-whisperer-forensic-psychologist could communicate with the cat and abstract tension and accusation from the cat in my presence. Or maybe they could hook the cat to some futuristic telepathic apparatus to decode its brain waves.

What is Leland's cat doing in my tree? Did it come to stalk

me? Is it stuck? Do cats get stuck in trees or is that a myth pervasive in storybooks for the purpose of portraying the many talents of firemen?

Cold water overflows onto my hand.

"What are you looking at, Momma?" Chloe says.

"Nothing. I'm sleepy."

I set their cups on the table and pour Cheerios into their bowls. *You are not to look outside for thirty minutes.* If the kids notice it, that cat will undoubtedly become the central talking point in our household for weeks.

If, in thirty minutes, the cat is still in the tree, I will coax it with lunchmeat. Trap the warm, struggling body inside a plastic storage bin and fasten the lid (which I've already drilled with air holes to prevent suffocation in case one of the kids were to close the lid on another), place the bin in my trunk, drive ten or twenty miles away, and set the cat free in a patch of forest preserve.

I am making Wyatt's peanut butter and jelly sandwich for school when the doorbell rings. Hulk goes mad, barking, dashing, and sliding to the door.

"Wyatt, can you see who's at the door? If it's a friend, you don't have time to play before school."

Wyatt walks down the hallway, stops, then runs back into the kitchen. "I don't know who it is. Two grownups."

"Good job not opening the door for strangers. Stay here."

I walk to the door, irritated. Some know-it-all is ready to sell me new siding, new windows, or a new religion.

I peek out the door's side windows. Sadly, I would have preferred a religious cult salesman.

James and Ariana stand on my porch. They wear plain clothes, plain expressions. Their plain car is parked next to the curb in front of my house.

Asshole played you. Hate boils up, but I also want to congratulate him. God, he's good. Sociopathic good. He may have played me, but it doesn't mean he can connect me to a crime, it doesn't mean he knows anything. *What could he know?*

My heart is adding extra beats as I open the door. *Don't say hammer. Don't say hammer.*

Hulk is still barking, which is comforting and a good excuse for not opening the screen.

Ariana says, "Hello, Miss Wright. I'm Detective Acosta and this is Detective Mahoney. We met a few days ago."

He hasn't told her. Of course he hasn't. I'm no police expert, but fucking someone you've interviewed as part of a murder investigation is likely against the rules. Which makes me wonder why he fucked me. That could ruin his case against me.

I can't bear to meet his eyes. Looking at Ariana, I say, "I remember. Hulk, quiet." Thankfully, Hulk never listens to this command. She continues barking.

"We had a few follow-up questions for you," she says.

"Mom," Wyatt yells, laughing and sounding amazed. "There's a cat in our tree."

"Hang on one second," I tell the detectives. I close the door halfway to block their view into my house and head for the kitchen, hands trembling. "I need you two to be quiet. I'm putting on a TV show."

"But there's a cat in the tree."

"OK, I'll look later. I have to talk to these people." I skip *Mister Rogers' Neighborhood* and *Sesame Street* and go for the sparsely seen and revered Disney Shows. *Mickey Mouse Clubhouse* should do it.

Opportunity. Make this an opportunity.

Hulk is still standing at the screen, barking like mad, so I doubt they heard the word *cat*. I walk back to the door, remaining behind the screen with Hulk.

I say to Ariana, "Sorry about that. Have you caught the guy yet?"

Ariana says, "Not yet, but—"

"Because I'm feeling scared and worried about my kids, worried about our safety." Even though the kids can't hear, I lower my voice. "It's strange because I didn't feel scared before and now it's sinking in. He was murdered in there. Right. Next. Door."

Hulk's barking hasn't let up.

Ariana holds her hands together in front of her waist. It is a solemn, church-like, patient gesture. She says, "I understand your concerns. We do have more cars patrolling this area. Usually, with something like this, it's an isolated occurrence." She clears her throat to indicate sympathy-time is over. "We came by this morning because we have a few follow-up questions."

My heart races. I place one hand on the doorframe to keep steady.

Don't say hammer.

James adds, "You haven't been singled out for any reason."

Huh. His tone strikes me as accommodating and sheepish. It's missing the boastful *gotcha*.

I keep my eyes trained on Detective Acosta. Perfect posture, modest breasts. She is stunning. Her face is made of perfect shapes, her olive skin is flawless, glowing actually, and her eyelashes are thick, elegant spider legs. *Wait.* She's not even wearing makeup. How is that fair? I bet she has the best track record in her department for ensnaring male suspects and revealing the inconsistencies in their alibis.

She says, "You've lived here about three months, is that correct?"

"About that, yes."

"During the time you lived here, how many times have you been inside Leland Ernest's house?"

Hulk is still barking, but she's taking small breaks now.

"Um, only once. Maybe five or six weeks ago, he was struggling to move a dresser. He'd rented a van and was working on getting the dresser out of the van by himself. I was outside with my kids and offered to help. I would have felt like a jerk if I hadn't." All true.

You told James about the dresser the other day. Did he tell her?

I feel chilled and shamed.

James used you. He was in your bed a night ago, squeezing you for information, and now he has the nerve to stand on your porch like he did nothing wrong.

"How come you didn't mention this when we spoke before?" she says.

"I don't know. You didn't ask, and it didn't feel relevant. I was also a bit shocked."

"What room did the dresser go in?" she says.

"His bedroom. Well, I'm assuming it was his bedroom.

There was another room with a bed in it."

"So, you walked the dresser into his bedroom?"

"No, I kind of stopped at his door. Once the dresser was in his room, he told me that was good enough." This is true. I bite the inside of my cheek hard enough to draw blood. *You should have said you walked into his room. If they found your DNA inside his room, there would have been a reason for it. This could be a big fuck-up, Grace.*

If I wasn't feeling conned and pitiful, if Hulk wasn't barking, if it wasn't a busy weekday morning, I would have chosen my words more carefully. I would have remained cool and vague.

It's OK. It's going to be OK. If they find your DNA in his bedroom, well, you'll come up with a reason for that. You might have taken a few steps into his room, it's such a stupid, petty detail, it's difficult to remember stuff like that. I swallow down the taste of copper and my sour saliva.

"How did you see there was another room with a bed in it?"

"Well, the doors were open so I saw what anyone would see when they pass an open door."

"Did you see anything strange at the time or did he say anything odd?"

"I don't think so, but he did strike me as awkward."

"In what way?"

"I don't know. Antisocial, I guess. Avoiding eye contact. Unorganized because, well, if you're going to be carrying a dresser up the stairs, you should probably call someone, have some help, have a plan. He seemed like a middle-aged guy who didn't connect with people. I mean, honestly, I thought he was odd even before I talked to him. Why move into a single-family home two blocks from an elementary school when you're single? It never made sense to me. People pay these property taxes for the schools."

Detective Acosta nods, emotionless. I bet she doesn't even bother with trying to make emotional connections. Her efforts would be pointless. Suspects could never see her as common, as one of them, as someone who has ever faced a single obstacle, even if she claimed she had four kids, raging dandruff, rank athlete's foot, and was so hairy, not only did she have to shave her beard, but also her hands, arms, and chest.

And if she doesn't need to *relate*, she must have other tricks in her bag. It pains me, but she's probably incredibly clever and intelligent.

"Would you be willing to volunteer a DNA sample? Just a quick cheek swab. Fast and simple."

Get ready. This is the moment where your home, your life, crumbles.

"Why?" I say.

"Our forensics team came across female DNA so it would eliminate you as a suspect."

James adds, "You aren't required by law to give us a sample. We're asking if you're willing to volunteer it." Again, he sounds apologetic. *Huh. Maybe he didn't play you.*

"I'm a suspect?" I ask Ariana.

"We're widening our range to anyone the victim knew."

The word *victim* agitates me like a shirt tag itching my neck. *Leland Ernest was suspected in the kidnapping of a five-year-old girl. He had a little girl's sock and toys tucked under his mattress. A fucking cage in the basement.*

"Um, I don't know. I don't want to get involved unless I

305

absolutely have to. Legally, I mean. If there's more questions, can we do this later? I'm going to be late for work."

"Sure, we will be in touch with you," James says. "Thanks for your time."

Detective Acosta hesitates, confused by her partner's consideration and apologetic tone. On most cases, he must be colder.

As if perfectly cued, Chloe screams one of her high-pitched, I-am-being-tortured screams. She is most likely fine, Wyatt probably looked at her the wrong way, but the scream lends the opportunity to end this nightmare.

"I'm sorry, I have to go."

I close the door gently and check on the kids. Chloe and Wyatt are fine, mesmerized by the television. Who the hell knows why she screamed?

I fall into a chair at the kitchen table. My heart is pounding. Sweat has beaded between my breasts. I'm feverish. I'm baffled. Is James a player, a traitor, or a screw-up now pinned in a tight spot?

My eyes search the backyard, scrutinizing the tree where my dead neighbor's cat perched minutes ago. No sign of it.

50

A SHADOW DATABASE

I have a mini nervous breakdown in the shower. I sob quietly and make it quick. To get myself out of the shower, I turn the faucet as cold as it will go.

I pull on an outfit I don't have to think twice about. "You guys ready?" I call to my open bedroom door.

No answer.

"Chloe?" I say.

"I'm not doing nothing," she says, her soft voice coming from her room.

I find her behind the rocking chair. Her lips, along with the skin around her mouth, are blood-red. On the floor: two uncapped peppermint-flavored ChapSticks gouged by bite marks; pink baby lotion poured into teacups; and chunks of my deodorant resting in a plastic bowl.

Maybe this kid has vitamin-deficiency-caused pica.

"Which ones did you eat?"

She holds up the ChapStick.

Call poison control to be sure. Not now, but on the way to work.

After I drop them where they need to go, I make the call.

Poison control tells me that even if Chloe ate ten ChapSticks, a quarter cup of lotion, and half a stick of deodorant, she will be alright.

Next call goes to Chuck. He answers.

"Hi, Chuck, this is Grace Wright. I have a quick question for you."

He says nothing. It's been a while. Since my neighbor's dead, I haven't had a reason to harass him.

"Chuck?"

"Yes, I'm here, Grace. I'm not sure if I can answer, but go ahead." He is hesitant, nervous.

He thinks you killed your neighbor. He knows you killed your neighbor.

"Two detectives stopped by this morning and told me they are asking all Leland's neighbors to volunteer a cheek swab for DNA samples. I was late for work and I didn't volunteer. I'm wondering if I should have."

"Grace, I don't give legal counsel. I don't know anything about the homicide case."

Stop being such a pussy, Chuck.

"Chuck, I am not looking for legal counsel. I am not going to sue you. I am asking, like, ignorant person to knowledgeable person. If I was your cousin or your niece or your sister or your neighbor. What would *you* do?"

"Uh, I wouldn't *volunteer* my DNA for anything. Once your DNA is in a police database, it's in there or in a shadow database *forever*." Chuck's got a little paranoia in him after all. "Grace, I would wait for a compulsion order. If they don't have that court

308

order, they have no evidence against you." He sounds exhausted. Is this how he sounds all day or is his exhaustion reserved for me?

"Chuck, I didn't do anything. I'm just trying to get a feel."

"Of course you didn't." It's not clear if this is what he truly believes. His tone might be cut with sarcasm or maybe he's burnt out on legal details and senseless crime. "I'm saying, if they have evidence, they get a court order."

"Do most people volunteer their DNA?"

"I don't think so."

"Does it look suspicious if I don't volunteer?"

"Yes and no."

Good enough.

"Thanks, Chuck. For returning my calls. For answering your phone. For seeming like a decent human being."

"You're welcome. Call anytime." He's warming up, getting energized. Who isn't a sucker for gratitude?

"I'm pulling into work," I say. "I've got to go."

My phone vibrates with a new text.

-Call me. We need to talk.

James.

I turn off my phone. My head feels faint and weightless. I can't remember if I ate breakfast.

51

WHEN THE STOVETOP IS FLAMING

After work and after I pick up Chloe from daycare, I put *Mister Rogers' Neighborhood* on the TV.

"No *Rogers'*," she says.

"It's *Rogers'* or the highway."

"I want the highway."

"OK, I'll look to see if we have *the highway* in a minute. I have to get the noodles going."

I put on *Mister Rogers' Neighborhood* nonchalantly, non-confrontationally. I fill a pot with water, set it on the stovetop, and while I'm igniting the burner, the doorbell rings. Hulk darts to the front door, barking like she's never heard the doorbell.

It's James, I know it. I ignored his text.

My stomach sinks. I stare into my pot of calm water, unsure if I should answer the door. Is he going to arrest me? Will he show me a court order and demand a cheek swab?

"I'll get it," Chloe yells and runs for the door.

I intercept her with a big scoop-hug and tickle. "You're

so helpful, but it's a grownup for Mommy so I'll get it, sweet angel." I burrow into her neck, worried they might take me away, worried this crumbling house, this lovely, gorgeous crumbling house and our chaotic but perfect life may be over.

She is giggling from my tickling when I set her on the couch.

"Again, again," she begs.

"In a minute, Chlo. Let me answer the door before Hulk wears herself out." I choke a little on my words.

Make it quick. Leave the burner on as an excuse. He can't arrest you when the stovetop is flaming.

Walking down the hallway to the front door feels psychedelic or like a horror scene: the hallway goes on and on.

Hulk barking beside my calf, I open the door.

"I'm so so sorry," he says quickly, before I even meet his eyes. "I couldn't give you warning because I wasn't alone all morning and I was so worried you would think I planned this and didn't tell you on purpose, but it came up only this morning. Cross my heart. I'm so sorry. Please forgive me."

I wasn't expecting this gushing apology. My fingers are ice-cold and I'm sweaty. I gaze into his eyes. Pale blue, gentle waters, sad and longing.

He says, "I need to know we're OK."

"We're not OK." It's not just that I thought he was going to arrest me or betray me. It's so much more complicated. I told him I didn't want him to meet my kids. Now he's on my porch. He messed with my head all day. I have so little clarity left. I can't allow him to steal my attention away from my kids. My kids deserve my full attention and energy.

311

"Grace. I can't stop thinking about you. Can I come in for a minute?"

Mister Rogers is singing a pleasant song. I should have put on something more catchy than Rogers. She's going to run to the front door any second.

I put my forehead against the screen. "This, us, it's not a good idea," I say, but I'm not committed to the argument. I want it both ways. "I can't fall for you."

He opens the screen and steps close to me. "You're not falling for me. You're going to fuck me, and I'll be on my way."

I love the smile curving around his voice, but I'm still caught in the fight. I'm righteous in the fight. "I don't want you to meet my kids, I told you. I don't need a man confusing things."

"I can't help it."

"That is such a *guy* thing to say. You should fucking help it. Women help it all the time."

Except he drops his hand and cups me between my thighs. Brain signals overload and sizzle, and my focus is gone. I can't form a single coherent thought. My legs are weak. I let him back me into the bathroom.

He pushes my skirt up around my waist and gets down on his knees. Uses his finger to hook my underwear to the side.

Oh God. When was the last time?

My toes are tingling. *You're floating away.* My head drops back as if my neck has been slit and bumps the knob on the medicine cabinet behind me. The cabinet pops open, and a number of hair accessories that had balanced on narrow, water-warped, toothpaste-crusted shelves inside the cabinet spill onto the counter and floor. *Later. Clean it up later.* I reach both hands behind me and brace my fingertips against the cool laminate sink so I don't collapse. My legs are going numb.

I explode into a blackhole of thoughtlessness and pleasure. He turns me around, and eases into me slowly, my orgasm still shuddering through me.

I open my eyes. Eyes beholding me, he bites my shoulder and moves his hands underneath my shirt. He moves my bra up, which is the absolute wrong way—he's going to stretch it out and I only have *two* (good bras are expensive)—and tugs my nipples and gets rougher inside me.

I am cooling, wanting my personal space back, but I fake enthusiasm for the sake of good manners.

"Mom!" Chloe's bare feet are padding down the hallway. "Where are you, Mom?"

"In the bathroom. I'll be there in a second." He pumps faster, rougher, staring at me through the mirror. Will he hurry up already?

"I thought you screamed, Momma."

"I'm fine, baby."

"I don't like Rogey." Her body fall-leans against the door. Her mouth is five inches from me. "Can you put on another show?"

"Yes. I'll put one on if you go sit on the couch. You want *Octonauts*?"

"Yes!" Delighted and chatting to herself, she runs down the hallway.

I pull away from his stare and assess the countertop. Wyatt's toothpaste, toothbrush, and an air freshener are in the sink.

Chloe's barrettes and rubber bands are scattered on the counter.

He moves faster.

I feel both relaxed and anxious. I adore him, hate him. I vowed I'd never bring a guy in the house when my kids are home. And why is he taking so long? Wyatt will be home from soccer any minute. How did this happen?

James stares at my eyes in the mirror while he fills me up. I stare back at him for the sake of politeness. Orgasm is such a private act, it's odd that he prefers eye contact. In his vulnerable state, I *see* him. Not a player. Not a traitor. Not a user. This morning was unforeseen, a mistake. He rests his forehead on my shoulder like Chloe does when she's tired. Puffs his cheeks, then exhales. "I like you."

"I bet you do."

He lifts his eyes up to look at me in the mirror. "I'm sorry about this morning."

"Did any of my neighbors give you a cheek swab?"

"Three out of ten." Thank God. I don't stand out. My neighbors appear to be a cynical, paranoid bunch. My respect for this neighborhood jumps.

"Why are you asking random people for DNA samples?"

He zips up his pants. "We ran the crime scene DNA against our previous arrest database and came up with no matches. Asking for voluntary samples is one of the next steps."

"Have you ever volunteered *your* DNA sample?"

"Hell no. Once they have your DNA, it stays in the databases forever."

I turn and I poke him in the chest, *jokingly*. "Hypocrite."

His detective pop-in wrecked my morning and had my adrenal glands working overtime. I swallow a small but hard seed of resentment.

He gives me a mischievous, self-satisfied smile. Notion striking him, he tilts his head, one of Hulk's moves. "So," he says, "you're feeling scared now?"

"Yes. I was out with Hulk late last night and started thinking about the scene. Blood. Violence. Imagining what it looked like and what type of person could do that. You said blunt force trauma to the head. What was the murder weapon? I never asked." *Well played.*

He hesitates; it's against the rules to tell, but he owes me. "Forensics is working on narrowing it. For blunt force trauma, the typical suspects are pipe wrench, golf club, Kel-Lite, Maglite, crowbar, or hammer. Looks like it's probably a pipe wrench or a hammer."

I let my mouth drop open, surprised even though I shouldn't be. "Oh God."

"It's probably better you don't volunteer DNA," he says, a touch of schoolboy nervousness creeping into his eyes. He shifts his weight. "It will give you a break from Ariana." He hesitates. "She thinks you did it."

"What?" I mean to sound appalled, insulted, but my voice barely cracks a whisper. I want space, I want to turn away from him so he can't see my throat reddening, but this bathroom is so small. I back against the door. He's still so close.

"I told her she was way off," he says, his eyes guilty. Probably realizing he should have told me this before he

315

fucked me. "Ari said, 'That's because you're screwing her.'"
He smiles, he can't help it.

"What? You told her?" Now my anger settles in, which is good. It will explain away the red blotches probably creeping up my neck and cheeks.

"No, no, no," he says. "I wasn't acting myself when we asked you to volunteer DNA. She said it was a dead giveaway. She's no idiot."

"Is she going to tell on you, get you fired?"

"No, we're like family," he says, sure of himself, sure of her.

"Why would she think it was me?"

He shrugs and takes a step closer. "She thinks it's one of the neighbors. Blood splatter puts the killer between five six and five nine, so she's leaning toward a woman. She thinks you're strong enough. She wonders if he threatened one of your kids or said something about one of your kids to make you lose your shit."

Worry slithers in my gut like snakes. James is too close. And these bathroom lights, with their yellow cast, make everything ugly.

Is he really blowing off Ariana's suspicion of me? Or is he trying to trip me up?

He wouldn't. You saw the vulnerability on his face. No one's that good at faking.

When you're screwing him, you're not faking it either. Yet, you have his semen in your crisper.

"Are we actually discussing whether or not I am a killer? I was going to sell my house, you know. I told my realtor to come take pictures."

"Unless you called your realtor and told her you were selling as part of your premeditated plan to kill your neighbor." With the back of his hand, he brushes my cheek.

"You think I'm that strong?" I force a smile.

"Have you ever heard of a mom lifting a car when her child was underneath?"

"I thought that was urban legend."

Blood pumps through my arteries in frantic spurts. I have to redirect this conversation, and by redirect I mean pull out the floor so he free-falls. Dirty talk and shoving my hand down his pants are my best distraction, but we *just* had sex. Did he plan it this way?

"Stay here," I say, pulling my skirt down to cover my ass. My thighs are slippery and sticky. I pull my bra down over my breasts, irritated because it's a clawing sensation—why didn't he unhook my bra?—and close him into the bathroom. I'm only halfway to the TV room when the splash and sizzle of water boiling over the top of the pot jars me.

Idiot. How could you forget so quickly? God knows what could have happened to Chloe!

I turn off the flame, put *Octonauts* on for Chloe, then peer out the front door.

No sign of Wyatt.

I open the bathroom door. James is meticulously placing toothbrushes and barrettes back onto the cabinet shelves.

Endearing. Intrusive. Annoying.

"You need to go. My son will be home any minute. I'll clean up later. Leave it."

He stops tidying and comes close, sniffing behind my ear. "Can I come over tomorrow night?" he whispers.

"No."

"When?"

"I don't know." *Never. Be careful, Grace.*

He kisses my neck. "When?" His breath is warm and moist in my ear, and sends chills down my back.

"Wednesday."

"Can I ask you one more question?" He steps back, his eyes playful, his chin down.

I am walking a fucking tightwire. "What?" I hold my breath, waiting for his tricky murder-trapping question.

"Do you do anal?"

I cough and laugh, my spittle pegging his cheek. Dropping my smile, I stare at him, deadpan. "Not with that thing. If you were the size of my pinky, sure."

He closes his eyes and tips his head back like he's conversing with God.

52

THEY KNOW WHO DID IT

After Wyatt and Chloe are sleeping, I am back to shaken snow globe. The shitfaced toddler has risen, zombie-like, from the dead and is stumbling around, bumping into doorknobs, woolly and hungry.

Ariana suspects you.

I am back online with a vengeance, gorging myself on information and anecdotes. Amphetamine-induced psychosis. Anxiety. OCD. Heart attacks. Hallucinations. Emerging viruses. What to write in a letter to your kids in case you die unexpectedly. I circle back to amphetamine-induced psychosis. I should quit my meds. I'm not feeling well.

The thing is, I'm not willing to quit my meds. At this point, I need them to stay awake.

It's 10:45pm when my phone rings. I startle too easily.

Liz.

I don't want to answer, but I need to. I've blown her off and I don't want her to get worried enough that she starts sharing her worries with others—my mom, Nate, our co-workers. And also, she is a good friend. Strange that I have to remind myself of that.

"Hey, Liz."

"*Grace*. Tell me *everything*."

"I'm OK. Really. Police said it's a targeted murder, you know, because Leland was a suspect in the Boone case, so they don't think anyone else is in danger."

"Did you ever talk to Chuck?" Her neighbor. It appears he didn't mention what a nasty dick I was.

"Yes. He told me, off the record, that Leland was a sicko. Flirting with Ava, giving her presents when he was painting the Boone house."

"Hell, I had no idea. You must be relieved. Creeper child molester living next door is dead. Good fucking riddance."

I laugh. I have felt bad about feeling *relieved*. It makes me feel a little sturdier, steadier, more at ease, that Liz, a woman who has her shit together, is validating my relief.

"Yes, I *am* relieved. You know he gave Chloe candy when she was on the swing set and I was bringing groceries in."

"Shit, I would have killed him myself."

Yes. Yes, me too.

"What did Nate say?" Liz says.

"I haven't told him, and he doesn't look at the news. I'm afraid to tell him."

"Fuck it then. Don't. You don't read the news, you lose."

I laugh again. I might be able to sleep after all.

She's right. Don't tell Nate. Maybe you'll get lucky and Wyatt won't mention it. It's possible. The mind of an eight-year-old is fluttery.

"I heard they know who did it, and they're getting their ducks in a row for an arrest."

"What? I didn't hear that," I say, my voice a cracked whisper. "When did you hear?"

"Thirty minutes ago. Susan texted me. Her brother's a detective."

"But I've met the detectives on the case. Susan's brother isn't one of them."

"Who knows? Maybe they're sending out that rumor on purpose to see who squirms."

"Can they do that?"

Her voice distant, the phone away from her mouth, Liz says, "Oh, hey, babes, you need anything?" Then, to me, she says, "OK, Grace, Sonya doesn't feel so hot. See you tomorrow."

They know who did it.

If they are close, why wouldn't James say so?

Ariana suspects you.

And I'm back online, gnawing the wet skin along my fingernails, my mind buzzing.

Chloe calls for me at 5:58am, minutes before my alarm goes off.

I catch my laptop before it falls off the edge of the bed. I hobble, blurry-eyed, sweaty, and reeking of body odor to tell the kids Good Morning. If I can start their day with a cheery, positive attitude, sometimes it sticks.

They both politely respond with cheery salutations of

their own, which rarely happens. I pat myself on the back for dragging my ass out of bed.

Ariana suspects you.

It hits me like a heart attack, wringing the air from my lungs. An impending feeling of doom. I read that symptom last night somewhere. My fingers tingle. My legs feel weak.

They know who did it. They're getting their ducks in a row for an arrest.

I am the first one downstairs. As I head toward the kitchen, my stomach drops.

Leland Ernest's cat is standing on my back deck, right outside my sliding glass door, staring at me. I charge down the hallway toward the cat. Go away, you tell-tale heart!

It darts away before I reach the glass door. I unlock and slide the door open and search my backyard for the cat, my head twitching this way and that like a caffeinated dog searching for a squirrel. Nothing but grass and crisp morning air and the whistling of birds.

Maybe they're sending out that rumor on purpose to see who squirms.

Did I imagine the cat? My skin flashes hot. It's possible.

"What is it, Mom?" Wyatt says.

I realize I look crazy. *No, you* are *crazy.* I slide the door shut and lock it.

"Nothing, sweetie. Eggs or Cheerios?"

53

FISHBOWL GLASS GEMS GO FLYING

Next afternoon, it's Nate's turn with the kids.

I feel better than yesterday. Warm, faint, and a little weak. Like I nursed two shots of vodka. Not great, but not bad. I schedule an appointment three days from now with my gynecologist.

I am sitting at the kitchen table, paying bills. *Mail. Forgot to get the mail today.* I walk out my front door and into the heat and harsh sun, the screen door flapping behind me, and Ethan Boone is marching diagonally across my lawn.

Just a hallucination, Grace. Relax. It's only a hallucination. Sun is blinding. Your eyes will adjust.

But my reflexes take over and I back up slowly toward my garage. Garage door's open. Why is my garage door open? Oh, that's right. Chloe was playing with glass gems, the round, flat turquoise ones people put in fishbowls. You can buy them at the dollar store or you can pay ten times more at the pet store.

Ethan is coming at me and he looks *so* real, right down to the coffee stain on his plaid short-sleeve button-down, the wrinkles in his khakis, and his jaundiced eyes. *Just a hallucination. Breathe.*

"Grace Wright," he says, his teeth clenched, my name coming off his tongue like a curse.

Not a hallucination.

Panicking, I scan the street, left and right. No one's out. No one's walking their dog. No kids are riding bikes. Where is everyone? I can't make it to my front door; he's blocking my way. If I run through the garage, he'll catch me. It's better to stay in the open. Besides, my muscles are stiff with terror. I'm not sure I could run if I tried.

He growls, "I know you, *Grace Wright.* I know where you *live.* I know where you *work.* I know where your *kids* go to *school.* You fucking bitch. How do *you* like it?" He is close. The pores on his nose are large. His tongue is yeasty white. His stale breath stinks of beer. Does he drink on the way home from work? Maybe he stopped at a bar.

He pokes my chest hard.

I stumble on the uneven border between my driveway and garage. I lose my footing and fall back. There's a certain age where falling becomes terrifying. I'm definitely at that age. My butt hits the cement, and pain shoots up my spine. My arms stop me from rolling. *Ow. Ow. Fuck.* I'm on the ground in my shaded garage.

He's still coming at me. Leaning down awkwardly. He's too old to be in this back-straining position, too out of shape, yet his hands grab my shoulders and he's squeezing.

Oh my God, he's going to strangle me. I can't believe this is how it's going to end.

In my maple tree, the birds are chirping. They sound so damn happy. Sun is brilliant. The atmosphere is all wrong for murder.

"You crazy bitch. You harassed my wife. Told her I *killed* someone? How dare you? Do you even know what you've done?" Up close, in the shaded garage, he is monstrous. Despair has infected his face like a virus. His skin is gray-toned, his nose is oily and blotchy, and his eyes are bloodshot.

His grip slides toward my neck. I try to pry his hands off, but I'm in such a weak position. I have no leverage. My words tumble out in a rush, hoarse and pathetic. "Sorry. I'm so sorry. I'm sorry. I know you didn't kill him. I know that now. I thought I saw Ava, but I was hallucinating. Seeing things. It was my medication. It was the drugs."

His grip eases and falls away clumsily. My vision adjusts to the shade in the garage. He stumbles back a few steps until he's standing in the sun-soaked driveway, his shoulders slouched. Like a gorilla. Like Leland stood. Tears slide down his thick cheeks, his face scrunches in fury, and he kicks Chloe's little bucket. Dozens of fishbowl glass gems go flying. Turquoise pebbles sparkle and shine as they sail across the driveway and into the garage. *So beautiful.* They fall, plinking like a million raindrops on the cement.

That's gonna be a bitch to clean up.

"Fuck," he yells, strangely yelling louder at the *end* of the word. He must have stubbed his toe on my driveway. It's pitted and terribly uneven.

His body falls in that slow, frozen manner men fall when they get hit in the balls. Controlled, stiff, trying not to move too much. He catches himself and rolls into an awkward sitting position near me. Curling up, he wraps his arms around his knees and lowers his head. Like a kid. He's crying so hard. "Fucking *drugs*. Stupid *fucking* drugs." His clothes reek of yeasty beer and body odor.

"I'm sure you can help him," I say. "He's not in too deep."

"Huh?" He's lost.

"Mason," I say. "He's so young. He can get clean, I'm sure of it. Kids, their brains are still so flexible and healthy. They're so different from us."

"Mason?" he says again, his eyes wet. "You saw Mason doing drugs?"

"I'm sorry. I saw him dealing in the parking lot. Walmart."

The corners of his mouth tremble, jerking downwards. He clears his throat. "You're sure?"

"Yes," I say, pressure building in my forehead and behind my eyes. I'm so sad for him. "Wait, you didn't know?"

He doesn't answer. He blinks and stares ahead at the driveway. His back is shaded in the garage, his legs are in the sun. A carpenter ant is making its way towards his shoe. He squishes it.

"It's all my fault," I say, tears slipping away from me, down my cheeks. "Everything. Please tell your wife I'm sorry. I won't ever drive by your house again. Ever. I'm going to fix my medication dose."

Am I?

Yes. Yes, you are. You have to. You thought Ethan Boone was a hallucination. You can't go on having hallucinations, dumbass.

"Mason," he says, shaking his head. He's staring at the ant

326

carcass, half smooshed, half smeared, but its round head and fine antlers are still intact. "Ava loved Mason so much. She used to sit on the floor in his room and listen to him play his guitar. She loved when he'd let her sing along. She'd make the silliest faces, trying to get him to laugh." Ethan laughs. It's breathy and he chokes up. "He thinks it's his fault. He feels so much guilt. He thinks him posting that video lured some creep. Even though she was always begging him to record her. Even though she begged him to post it. She's such a pushy one, Ava."

He stares at me, tears dried on his cheeks, his lower lip swollen and quivering. "He thinks it's his fault and that makes me want to cut my heart right out of my chest and stomp on it." His face tenses, angry. "What am I supposed to tell him?" he asks me.

I shake my head. I don't know.

He buries his face in his elbow, crying again, his back vibrating, and says, his voice squeaking, "What can I fucking tell him?" He sucks back his tears and wipes his face on his sleeve. He nods and looks at the ant carcass again. "We have to learn to live with our mistakes," he says. "We have to hold it together. We have kids to raise, family to take care of."

He stands up slowly. Like a man who's gained weight quickly and isn't familiar with the heavier version of himself. He stares down the street, his face long and empty. His voice hoarse, he says, "That toy you found? It's not Ava's."

He turns and walks down my driveway. I want to ask what he means by that, but I promised him I would leave him alone. He digs in both pockets for his keys. He drives away fast, ignoring my neighbor's *Slow Down, Kids Playing* sign.

On my hands and knees, I pick up little blue gems. I don't find all of them—I'm sure some of them are under Wyatt's pile of Nerf bullets or Chloe's small mountain of chalk—but I get the ones I can see.

I grab my mail, drop it on the kitchen table, and put my mouth under the faucet.

I have the saddest, most awful feeling I know what happened to Ava. I'm also pretty sure I killed an innocent man.

There's no such thing as an innocent man. We're all guilty of something.

Yeah, but some of us much more guilty than others.

Leland had a child's sock under his mattress. He followed Lou's daughter home from school. There's nothing innocent about that.

I'm still at the faucet, splashing my face with water, when James calls from the porch, "Hello."

"Come on in," I call.

Snap out of it.

He walks in and looks at me. My eyes red and puffy, my face pebbled with water, my shirt soaked at the neck from drinking at the faucet. "You OK?" he says.

"Yeah, just hot. I was pulling weeds. Allergies."

"I thought I saw some guy leave your house."

"Huh?"

"Five minutes ago. I was parked down your street, taking a call. I saw a guy leave."

Huh. Could he be spying on me?

"Oh. Delivery. Something I ordered." I point to a padded envelope on the table in my pile of mail.

He looks at it and nods slowly at the coincidence that I

would drop a delivery in the same pile as I dropped my mailbox mail. Dating a detective: impossible.

Snap out of your funk. Compartmentalize. I smile. "Do you think I'm cheating on you?"

Eyes uncertain, he shrugs.

Ariana suspects you.

"Let me tell you something, Detective Mahoney." I raise my eyebrows, force a playful tone, and walk toward him, putting my body between him and the padded envelope. "I never once cheated on my ex and I can barely handle you. I simply could not manage two relationships." I stop a foot away, close enough to breathe in his scent.

His face and body loosen.

"Why do you always wear a gray T-shirt?" I say playfully.

"I'm a uniform guy. I don't get sick of things. I can wear the same thing over and over and over." His face cracks into a smile and he laughs.

"Yeah, me too."

He brushes a finger down the slope of my nose. "I stopped at the hardware store and got the parts to fix your disposal. Let me grab my toolbox."

If they were getting ready to make an arrest, he wouldn't be here fixing your disposal. Must have been a rumor.

I say, "Sweetest words I've ever heard."

54

WIGGLING HIS FINGERS INTO LATEX GLOVES

The high-powered, gravel-whisking, and water-glugging noises direct warmth and blood to my crotch, which is unexpected. Thunderous, mechanical, hazardous rotating blades have never aroused me before. It appears as if the pleasure centers in my brain shorted out and have been rewired by an electrician with a sense of humor.

James turns off the garbage disposal and faucet, and returns his tools to his toolbox.

Sweaty, weak, and horny, I turn the faucet and garbage disposal on again and watch the water disappear into the black hole. The rubbery, Venus-flytrap teeth are crusted with food. From now on, I will keep you clean. I am going to take good care of you.

Refrigerator suction pops open behind me. Uh-oh. I have two sealed sandwich bags of toilet paper laced with seminal fluid stashed in the crisper.

James and I turn to face each other simultaneously. He's holding a sandwich bag of slick toilet paper. "What's this?"

For a moment, I'm struck speechless.

Best way to explain this?

"Put it back. *Believe me.* I'll tell you later."

At my warning, he makes a disgusted face and puts it back like he's holding a bag of dog shit.

"Hungry?" I say. My arousal has gone cold.

"Thirsty."

"Water bottles are on the top shelf in the back."

He maneuvers around the sour cream and yogurt and comes out of the refrigerator fisting a bottle of water. He puts it to his forehead. A pinched, focused expression creeps into his face, and I worry he's going to bring up another reason Ariana has me pinned as the prime suspect.

He looks past me, his expression becoming urgent, intense, and says, "Is that your neighbor's cat?"

He steps past me and grips the edge of the counter. He's staring out the small window over the sink.

"What?" I say, following his gaze. Leland's cat is in the same tree as before. It looks like it's staring at us. "I'm not sure. I'm not sure I even knew he had a cat. Lots of people let their cats out in this neighborhood." *You're talking too much. Guilty, dumb people talk too much.* I close my mouth.

He is pulling latex gloves out of his pocket and moving out the sliding glass door.

"Do you always carry those around?" I say, following him out into the yard.

"Mostly," he says, wiggling his fingers into the gloves and slowly approaching the tree.

How much evidence can they pull off a cat anyway, especially a cat that's been living outside for days? Then again, I'm no forensic scientist. Sweat pops along my forehead.

"You should leave it alone," I say, trying to steady my trembling voice. "What if it has rabies?"

He ignores me. He stands at the base of the tree and sweet-talks the cat. The cat wears a collar. *Stupid of you to mention rabies.* Owners who bother with collars also typically vaccinate. The small tag twitches and jingles, seeming to wag at me. *Shame on you, you rotten woman.* The cat turns away, climbs higher, jumps to the neighbor's maple tree. James tracks the cat, moving slowly, trying to cajole it. The cat maneuvers swiftly through the tree, leaps to the ground, and flees.

James doesn't bother running after it. He walks toward me, peeling off his gloves.

This relationship will never work. The thought strikes me quickly and painfully. The heart-palpitating uncertainty of getting caught will be incessant. I am not disillusioned enough to convince myself I have nothing to hide.

55

HIJACKING OUR BEHAVIOR

James has been sleeping three hours when he wakes up and, squinting against the eerie blue glow of my laptop, mumbles with confusion and contempt, "What are you doing?"

"I can't sleep."

He squints in the direction of the clock, but can't make anything of it. "What are you doing with your laptop? What time is it?"

"2:17."

"What? Why?"

"Did you know an infection with the toxoplasmosis parasite can cause aggression and risk-taking and schizophrenia in adulthood?"

"What?" He's uncoordinated and mostly asleep, but trying to sit and open his eyes.

"It's a parasite you can be exposed to from undercooked meat, unwashed vegetables, cat feces, and just digging in the soil. It lives *in* the soil," I say, annoyed with his inability to catch up, as if he were plagued with a shameful IQ. "If you get infected with it, it forms these cysts in your body and your brain and, well, you're fine, you don't know you're sick, but you end up with an increased risk of schizophrenia, aggression, and risk-taking." I can almost feel the weight of the hammer pulling my hand, feel my palm sweaty inside my nitrile glove against the hammer's wooden handle. "I remember *eating* dirt as a kid. I literally ate dirt all the time. And it was my job to change my cat's litter box." My voice cracks. "Fruity Pebbles. I loved that cat."

He smacks his cheeks with his palms and rubs his face like he's washing it. He looks like a raccoon cleaning itself. "So you're OCD," he says like he knew I seemed too good to be true. He used the same tone when he found out I take amphetamines.

"Frankly, I don't think I could have OCD with my house looking as shitty as it does." I angle my body slightly toward his. With his large, slouched shoulders and his thick hands resting on my comforter, James looks too big for my bed. My laptop screen bathes the room in a dreamy, eerie glow. I say, "Just because you haven't heard about something doesn't mean it isn't real."

"I don't understand what we're arguing about? I'm waking up." He turns toward me and sighs. He has decided to work with me. "I believe you. I believe whatever news you read, but think of how many people have schizophrenia. Maybe one percent? Less than that. And *think*, Grace, think. *Every* kid eats dirt. This, it's not a," he hesitates and says, "logical concern."

"It's not about eating dirt," I say, trying to pinpoint the root of my worries, reaching into my dark, fractal mind, fingering sharp, crooked, yet fragile branches, and probing for the base of the trunk, "it's the *unknown*." My hand goes to where the bats scratched me. Thin lines of scabs have flaked off, and the skin is smooth. "How many other parasites and viruses we don't know about are hijacking our behavior? Could be dozens."

He is wide awake, his posture upright and stiff, but now he's staring straight ahead toward the bathroom. "Aren't you tired?"

"My body is tired, incredibly tired, it wants to fall away, but my brain is something entirely different."

"Well," he sighs again, "you're too old to develop schizophrenia."

He's right. It usually sets in during adolescence. "Thank you."

"And even if you've had these cysts in your brain since you were a kid," he says calmly, sleepily, "and the cysts changed your behavior from what it would have been, you've never known what you're missing so who cares?" He turns toward me, his face lit blue from my open laptop. "I like you. Maybe the cysts gave you a more interesting life."

Maybe a little too interesting.

My heart is still fluttering, but I am thankful for his responses because he isn't writing me off. "You are a good person, James Mahoney."

He closes my laptop, sets it on the floor, and pulls my backside into the curve of his body. His groin pushes against me.

"Not up for it," I say.

"Me neither," he says, so incredibly full of shit. Males. Always primed, rain or shine, awake or half-asleep, in sickness and in health, outside or inside, half-dead, whenever. After a few minutes of moderate humping, his body stills around me. My mind continues to reel. I'm also having mild abdominal pain.

Five minutes go by. He whispers, "You awake?"

"Yes."

"What are you thinking?"

"You don't want to know."

I'm thinking about Heidi versus Peter Cottontail. That bunny, fluffy and clean, had to be someone's escaped pet. That bunny's aggressive behavior was shockingly unnatural. *Just like your aggression.* Maybe that bunny had been infected by an unknown virus. The same virus I caught from the bats.

Quit it, Grace. You're off the deep end.

OK, maybe there was no virus, and the bunny was simply sick of being the victim.

"Have you thought about taking anti-anxiety meds?"

"I tried those. They make me too sleepy to manage work and life."

"Goodnight," he says, his breath warming my hair, and pulls me in tight. I expect his groin to kick into a rhythm again, but it doesn't.

"You aren't going to lecture me? You aren't going to say, *Maybe you can't sleep because you take speed, meth head?*"

"I tried that with my ex-wife."

"She was a meth head?" I say, laughing.

"You know what I mean. The lecturing. Go to sleep."

He slips his warm, rough hand up the back of my shirt and caresses my back with the same nonchalant, yet generous strokes I have laid upon Wyatt's back. The anxious flutter in my chest settles. Even before James started rubbing my back, he eased me away from fatalistic neurosis and toward calm sanity. How did he do that?

"Goodnight," he says again. I may actually be able to fall asleep soon. He is such a good man, this might go somewhere if I don't mess it up. If my neighbor's murder case goes cold soon.

But you don't deserve him.

Shh, I tell myself.

But you promised you'd never let a man into their lives because you would always put them first and you are not naïve enough to trust a man utterly and fully and completely with the kids.

Shh, I tell myself.

But you killed a man. With a hammer.

Shh, I tell myself.

I say, "You have to leave by seven because the kids will be home at seven-thirty."

"I have to leave by six-thirty," he says. "Work."

56

PUT ON A DIAPER AND HEAD TO THE O.R.

Next morning, Liz and I sit on a bench, watching our kids on the playground, when Nate texts me.

-Call me as soon as you can.

My heart puts in a few extra beats. *Oh no. The kids.*

Why didn't I get a call? I'm listed as the kids' first emergency contact. Nate is second.

I check my phone to see if I missed a call earlier.

I didn't.

"Emergency text," I say to Liz, trying to remain calm, but I'm already sweaty and frantic. I call him as I walk toward the six-foot chain-linked fence that keeps the children caged and safely away from the parking lot and strangers. A minute ago, the warm sunshine and gentle breeze were soothing. Now the sun cuts too sharp, too harsh. My skin is burning. I shield my eyes.

"Grace?" Nate says.

"Yes, yes, what is it?" I expect the worst. One of them is dead. Choked to death on a grape. A pretzel. A ham sandwich.

Chloe wandered away from daycare and was found dead against the curb.

"My mom broke her arm," he says.

I laugh with relief, and cover my laugh with a cough. "She's alright?"

"She's fine, but she fell and she's shaken up. You know my mom."

I do. Snotty, country-club, golfing, thin, bejeweled, and perfectly coiffed Harriet. She excels at etiquette, party planning, and getting drunk on wine. Gushes over her two cats more than her only grandchildren.

"I'm sorry to hear about your mom. I'm working. Can I call you later?"

"Well, I was calling because she asked if I could bring Wyatt and Chlo to visit tonight and we'd spend the night," he says, tentatively, because my mother-in-law has always been cold to me and isn't much warmer toward my kids. I want to deny her to spite the bitch. I want him to beg and apologize for his mother's character flaws.

I say, "Sure. Why not?"

Silence. He assumed he would have to beg. He clears his throat. "Are you sure? Wyatt would miss a half-day of school."

"Actually, we don't have school tomorrow. District day off. Even if he were to miss a day, it's third grade. When do you want them ready?"

"Does five work?"

"Sure. See you then."

I end the call and text James.

-Nate is taking the kids tonight. 5pm. Unexpected. Come over when you get off work.

I sit next to Liz and set my phone on the bench.

"Your people safe?" she says.

"I thought someone died, but my ex-mom-in-law broke her arm."

"You only wish she died."

"You're evil."

"Yeah, and I'm right."

Izzy is climbing the slide and Mateo's at the top, ready to blast her with his Buzz Lightyear gym shoes. I rush over while telling Mateo to wait. He doesn't, of course. He's three and he's got a wisp of a mean streak in him that, over the next five years, will either be easily snuffed or stoked. I pick up Izzy as Mateo's sneakers come whooshing down.

"Izzy, we only go down slides. Not up. We slide *down*. Mateo, when someone asks you to wait, you wait nicely. Like a statue, remember, hon?" I say hon for my benefit, to solicit sweet feelings. They say smiling makes you happy. Talking sweetly has to do something.

When I sit beside Liz again, she says, "It's not cocaine then."

"Huh?"

She points to the text waiting on the screen of my phone. James.

-My lucky day. See you at 6pm. I'll wear my gray T-shirt.

I smile.

"I can't believe you didn't tell me," she says, her voice silky as usual, but the jagged edges of irritation lie just under

340

the smooth surface. "I've been worried about you. The crazy situation with your neighbor. I mean, murder? Fuck. Seriously? And you were avoiding talking to me. Shit. I can't believe you didn't tell me."

"Just happened."

"Just happened, my ass," she says, a smile sliding into her voice. She's already forgiven me. "Tell me about the gray T-shirt. Tell me how good he is."

"No."

"Let me live vicariously, you stingy bitch," she laughs. "This old vagina is retired, but it can still dream."

"Good God, for the sake of the children. You know Tabby will go home and tell her mom Miss Liz's vagina is retired, and we will both get fired. Besides, no one is making your body retire. Go get some of your own."

"Sex isn't worth the hassle of having a man hanging around. I don't need another one to feed and pamper, I got grandchildren coming out of my ears," she says. Liz's second husband died a decade ago. Heart attack. "Well, at least that gray T-shirt explains you having your head in the clouds and losing weight. I thought you were lit on drugs."

"You didn't."

"You've been weird, Grace. Even before the murder."

"You think?"

"Beaming and excited one day, quiet and spacey the next. And you've been blinking a lot. Almost like a tic. I figured you had allergies, but then I figured it was your lack of sleep. You said you had insomnia. Then I thought you might be losing it over your neighbor's murder. Mostly I figured it was drugs."

"Why didn't you try to put me in rehab?"

She turns her upper body toward me stiffly and raises her eyebrows. "What?"

"I can't believe you thought I was abusing and you didn't intervene." I'm joking, but I mean it.

"Seriously? Don't be so damn needy." She's joking, but she means it too.

My eyes check the playground, searching for signs of stressful body language. The goal is to perceive the slightest suggestions of friction and intercept the conflict before it lands. Slide to sandbox to tricycles, these small bodies and minds appear free and light-hearted. Still I keep my eyes vigilant because children are unpredictable as wolverines: territorial, clumsy, and always hungry.

"You're right," I say. "I'm needy." I scoot closer to her and weave my arm under hers, take her hand in mine, and lay my head on her shoulder.

She squeezes my hand. "I still love you."

Did Nate think I was too needy?

No. He thought you cold and secretive.

Well, can't argue with secretive.

Please. Five times.

How many times have you had sex with James?

It's different. Nate and I are divorced.

Yeah, but it feels the same, doesn't it? Feels kind of even, *don't you think?*

"Have you talked to Susan today?" I say. "I thought the police were getting ready to make an arrest."

"No, I haven't seen her today. Who knows? Maybe she's full of shit."

Hours later Wyatt and I sit on the front porch, waiting. I run my fingers through his hair. "You need a haircut, brother."

He pulls away a little. "I like it long."

"OK." I rub his back. I love his sleek shirt under my fingers.

Late afternoon is warm and golden, but storm clouds are approaching from the south. Air is thick with ragweed and fatty burgers smoking on the grill. Flowers and weeds are late-summer wild and straggly because most people have forfeited the fight. I never started fighting. No point to it now. Autumnal equinox is days away. Cool fall air lurks, waiting to descend. The plummeting of temperature, the yellowing of leaves, always feels so sudden.

"I love summer," I say.

"I can't wait for snow," Wyatt says.

"That's because you're nuts."

Chloe, five feet away, on all fours on the driveway, has spotted an ant. She tries smashing it with her finger. Reminds me of Ethan Boone squashing that ant with his shoe. *Poor Ethan Boone. Poor Ava.*

"Chloe, we don't kill bugs outside. This is where the ant lives. You're a guest in his house."

Wyatt, blurts, "Of course she kills bugs. She's Chloe. She's a murderer. That's what she does."

"Wyatt. Don't use the M word. You used to kill ants too. Little kids don't know better."

No one ever called me a "murderer" my entire life. At three, Chloe has heard her brother label her "murderer" a half-dozen times.

When she's grown, will she remember that her only sibling, someone who knew her well, occasionally characterized her as a murderer? Will the words slowly sharpen and harden until, at some point in her teens or twenties, they splinter her self-perceived sense of goodness and she begins to doubt she is worthy and deserving of love?

Don't blow up. Bring them back to calm. I rub Wyatt's back again, but he shrugs me away.

"Why not kill it?" she says lightly, offhand, as if she is justifying every convicted killer locked away by the courts.

Calmly, I say, "He's alive like you and me."

She gives the ants a break and looks directly at me. "But he's *not* like you and me." She's not being snotty, she's being philosophical.

"He's not hurting anyone," I say. "He's hunting for food or going for a nice walk."

"But maybe he's *going* to hurt someone," she says. That she's making a case to kill a dangerous entity before it can harm leaves me breathless.

Wyatt giggles. "Yeah, Mom, he might be planning an attack on a pill bug. He might be a mean ant." At least he's back to calm.

"Thanks, Wyatt."

Shade descends upon the driveway, and I gaze upward. A row of stacked storm clouds cuts fast through the blue sky. Whoever's grilling burgers better wrap it up.

"Squashed him," she says. "Two points."

The random, aimless, and heartless slaughter of countless bugs at the hands of toddlers has always bothered me. Irritation is popping under my skin.

Nate's car pulls up. I sigh and say, "How about a kiss for an old lady."

Chloe charges me with open arms and wraps me tight. She gives me a kiss on the lips, makes a kissing sound effect, and licks my cheek. She lets me go and runs to Nate. In the wake of her love attack, my nose, right breast, and neck twinge in pain.

Wyatt laughs and gives me one of his reluctant, disgusted, pulling-away, this-is-torture-for-him hugs, but then licks me on the cheek too.

"You're both worse than Hulk."

Wyatt runs to Nate's car.

Once the kids are buckled, Nate walks up the driveway. "Thanks again." He throws me a shy smile, and it hits like a baseball. Fast, and it stings. He's so clean cut, so handsome. It's no wonder nurses pull down their ugly scrub pants for him. Standing four feet away, gazing at me, he says, "Are you seeing someone?"

"No," I answer quickly, and regret I answered at all. I don't owe him an answer. I wish I were standing.

He takes a deep breath. As if anything is difficult for him. "You can say no, but I was wondering—"

I want to fall into his arms in a heap, in one big exhale, and say, *Yes*. Whatever you are willing to give, the answer is *yes*. I want his arms around me. I want him to pay my bills. I want a partner, someone to balance my crazy with his own crazy, someone to talk me down. I want the father of my children to take care of us, the yard, and the ratty house. I want him to brush away my tears and to love me when I look like shit because I gave him children.

"No," I say simply.

He half-laughs, lifts his shoulders, and lets them fall. "I miss you. I miss us. All four of us. I guess I already told you that."

I bite my lip. I am trembling with a toxic mix of desire, guilt, and rage.

Speak carefully. Don't let him drag the worst out of you.

The worst of me *wants* to be dragged out. *Craves it.* It is filthy and gnarly and oozing with nasty, panting anticipation. It is waiting for me to weaken and slip the key into its cage so it can free itself.

He's only missing me because he thinks I might be dating. I quickly granted him the kids this evening, and he hadn't expected that. He thinks someone else might actually want me, and I might be worth more than he figured. He has probably noticed I'm thinner, I have an after-sex glow about me, and he's being drawn in superficially. He's probably not even aware of why he's drawn to me.

I want to shred his ego. I want to tell him that a hot cop is fucking me, that he can't keep away.

Are you sure you're not making shit up about Nate? He said he missed you at Burger King, and he didn't say it because he thought you were dating. He's a good guy, you know.

"I was so happy with plain," I say and find I can't say anymore. Maybe because it's all that needs to be said. I breathe deep. Air is moist and loamy. Rain is coming.

"I know. I know. I was too, but," he sighs, "God, I wish I

346

didn't fuck up." His eyes shift and lose their confident doctor veneer. "I'm working through some medical school stuff with my therapist, and, well, I think it's helping."

I'm surprised at his mention of medical school, but I guess I shouldn't be. Nate once told me doctors commit suicide twice as often as non-doctors. Most medical students start out young and burning with a desire to help, but school and residency bully and torture them with sleep and food deprivation and other cruel devices.

When Nate was a first-year intern, the stomach flu hit him hard when he was at the hospital. During a brief intermission from his uncontrollable diarrhea, he sought out the resident surgeon and asked to go home. The resident chewed him out for taking holiday in the bathroom and told him to "put on a diaper and head to the O.R."

Nate didn't, of course. Too confident for intimidation. That's probably how he made it through med school and emerged intact.

Good doctors also worry about misdiagnosing their patients. Intellectual doctors often question their own utility. Combine that deep worry and abuse with access to medication and the uncanny knowledge about how to kill themselves in a tidy, efficient manner: bam, they are suicides waiting to happen.

"I was hard on you," he says. "Judgmental. Like my parents. I'm working on that. Grace?" His gaze drops to the grass, the weeds sprouting everywhere, and the dead branches that need picking up. "Do you think people can change? Do you think people can make terrible mistakes, but then decide to change, and then never make those mistakes again?"

How can I say no? Saying no would be giving up on myself.

"I hope so, but I'm not sure."

Chloe yells from the car, "Daddy! What's taking you? We've waited hours. This is too long to be true!"

"I'd better go," he says, his eyes liquid and warm. "I will have them back tomorrow morning by ten." He turns away and takes a few steps toward his car, but turns back. "Possibly by eight." This he says in case I *am* dating someone, to keep me on my toes.

Asshole.

Or maybe he is possessive because he loves you.

Or maybe he means "possibly by eight".

A fat raindrop bursts on my arm and another hits my cheek. Slow, meaty, warning drops. As if the clouds all split, rain comes fast. I scurry into the house, but my arms are already shower-damp. Safe behind the screen door, I watch Nate back out with my precious cargo.

Chloe calls out her open car window, her voice casual and upbeat, "Don't get hit by lightning and get dead, Mommy."

"I won't," I yell.

Wyatt stands and leans over to roll up her window as Nate's back tires drop onto the street.

Worry pokes tiny holes in my heart. I always worry when they are not with me. Chloe is afraid of thunderstorms. Will Nate say the right words to calm her, make her laugh, and make her forget about the scary storm? Will Nate remind Wyatt to buckle back up? Wyatt always forgets to buckle up. It is raining—no, pouring—they have an hour drive on the highway, and Wyatt will forget his seatbelt. Dread tightens its fist in my gut.

Relax. Wyatt will buckle up. Chloe will remind him. She is a tiny, bossy Mother Goose.

The rushing rain sounds like wind. Drops smash against leaves and pavement and cars, each with a different nuance and tone. Thunder rumbles, deep and ripe.

I let my forehead drop against the metal screen, bowing it ever so slightly.

If we got back together, could it be different? Could he resist strange sex?

He had been bored with me, though, hadn't he? I had not been intellectual enough, not impressive enough, not beautified and manicured enough, not shiny enough. He wanted to be adored. He wanted passion and desire.

Is that true or are you making that up to justify your anger and your flaws?

I already regret what I said to him. It lacked a punchline, it lacked teeth. What I said was so uninteresting. Forgettable. So *me*.

No. He understood.

I *had* been happy with plain. Plain routine. Plain conversation. Plain weekly meals. Plain sex. Oh God, how I loved plain sex! Knowing I could count on a plain and reliable orgasm. I knew every move he was going to make and I could accept it without uncertainty. I was happy with Nate, extensive work hours and all. I believed in the integrity of his work.

How could he keep his cheating secrets and come home to me and look me in the eye when he told me a joke, when he kissed me, when he fucked me? How could he do that?

You have a secret too. A monstrous and disgusting and violent secret. But you still look the kids in the eye and pretend you're a good person. It's only

349

one teeny tiny monstrous part of you, but so many of the other parts are good.

Maybe Nate and I are more alike than I thought.

Do I want him back? Damn him for confusing me.

The rain is pounding the cement, making a racket like a boat's motor. Late afternoon sky is gray with a dangerous yellow tone which turns my mind to tornados. Lightning flickers, barely detectable against the light sky. Thunder groans.

A pain grips my lower abdomen and I bend, my cheek, my mouth, pressing against the screen, the taste of cold rolled steel upon my lips. The pain feels menstrual. It feels like a fucking force to be reckoned with is what it feels like.

I hope Wyatt is wearing his seat belt.

Pain lets go, and my spine straightens.

In front of my house a car slows and turns into my driveway, its headlights sweeping and lighting the mist. Rain blurs the shape and color of his car. Headlights wink off. He slams his car door and, as if to spite him, the rain intensifies. He is probably racing to get out of the driving rain, but I imagine he can't wait to put his cool hands on my hot skin.

His gray shirt clings to his frame. He opens my screen door, and the springs creak. A raindrop clings to his eyelash, another to his cheek. He smells of worms and water from a sunbaked hose. His hands grip my shoulders, but he says nothing.

My hands are on him. My body, my heart, aches with a need more primal than sexual desire. I need to feel normal. I need to feel connected. If I don't get his clothes off quick, I will burst into tears.

57

A HYSTERICAL BITCH WHO HAD NO FAITH

Shower-moist, wrapped in a towel, and chilled, I walk into my bedroom. I need to adjust the thermostat. This house is too cold for me. I'm tired and my thighs are shaky-weak. I have gone from slutty middle-aged seductress to feeble old lady within the span of a shower.

My bedroom is dark, but the diffuse light from my tiny bathroom behind me is sufficient. Curtains are drawn open, and James stands at the window, fully dressed and peering out at darkness. The thunderstorm passed and, in its wake, left a soothing, trickling rain.

"You ever see that cat again?" he says.

"No." I shiver and go for underwear. A mild wave of nausea moves through me. I'm glad I skipped washing my hair. Wet hair would have made my chills worse.

I hang my wet towel on a doorknob and pull my pajamas on quickly.

Hulk's nails click on the wood floor. She's under my bed, circling and resettling, still anxious from the storm.

"We should do something," he says. "Go to the zoo."

"Zoo's closed. Unless you're talking about breaking in?" Is James one of those cops who speeds through intersections with his lights and sirens blazing just because he can? Even people who join the police force for the right reasons can fall in love with breaking rules.

"No, I mean next weekend, when you don't have the kids. We could go on a bike ride. Or a hot air balloon ride. I've always wanted to go up in a balloon."

I half grunt so he knows I am listening but simultaneously have no opinion. I dig in my sock drawer for my coziest pair. I sit on my bed and pull them on.

"Well, we should do something together besides sex and fixing your house." His tone hints that he's joking, but there's an underlying truth there. He may be starting to suspect this relationship might not work without the sex. He isn't the cop who loves breaking rules. He's the cop who is a nice guy. He's the cop who gives people a chance to explain, who pulls over to help an old guy change his flat tire.

I step beside him and stare out into the darkness. With the light from the bathroom behind me, the yard is fully black. Not even a tree branch reveals itself.

"We can do something besides sex, but I should tell you something about myself: I enjoy boring." I expressed this same sentiment to Nate hours ago, but used the word *plain*. I've gone from plain to boring surprisingly quick.

Do I really enjoy *boring*?

Yes. Yes, I do.

Life is a constant string of fast balls. I am content when the pitcher takes a break to talk with the coach, and I get to stand there and do nothing. Chomp on my wad of gum. Scratch my balls. Sniff the air.

I'm baffled when pregnant couples say they don't want to find out the sex of their unborn baby because *there are so few surprises in life.*

So few surprises in life?!

Every moment is a surprise. I don't know if I will wake up in bed to Chloe snuggling beside me, all smiles and candy breath, or if she'll accidentally give me a titty twister with her foot or scream in my face that I ruined her day. If Wyatt will offer to help with the dishes or punch a hole in the drywall. If the person driving in the lane next to me will wave me ahead or if they'll be high on crack and will ram into my car for the hell of it, maiming me or my children.

I don't even know what I will do. I am random, inconsistent, and unpredictable. *Unknowable.*

It's as if colossal power lines hum in the humidity one hundred feet over my head, and the buzzing static, the discord, saturates my skin. Something's about to happen, some surprise, maybe good, more likely bad, and I will be stunned by it. A fish drowning in air.

So few surprises in life?

Really?

"I enjoy boring too," he says. "But I'd also like to go on a hot air balloon ride."

Dull pain radiates in the center of my abdomen. I hunch a

little and it fades. "OK, next weekend we'll do something. But I'm not ready to go on a hot air balloon ride until Chloe is eighteen. If we were to hit an electric wire and die, and Chloe had to navigate high school without a mom, I would never forgive myself."

He turns to me with wide eyes. "I have to wait fifteen years for a hot air balloon ride?"

"Of course not. Just take someone else. Take your daughter. Then you can take me in fifteen years and you'll be a pro and you can act all brave and chivalrous."

He looks out the window. "I guess."

"Listen, you shouldn't stay tonight. I don't feel great."

Which is true, but I'd also like to put distance between us and conversation. I don't want him returning to entertaining the idea that I killed my neighbor. I'm also feeling sluggish and careless with my words.

"I can't anyway. I'm working the case. I should have already left," he says, glancing at his watch. "Sorry if I upset you the other day. You know, when I was talking about Ariana and the case?" His eyes probe mine.

To see who squirms.

"Upset me? Nah," I joke. "Your partner, who you've said is like a daughter, suspects me in a violent crime. No big deal."

He smiles, but it's strange. The smile of a car salesman. "You weren't the only one she suspected. She was thinking of neighbors. She's smart. Because of her thinking, we have a lead."

"Why didn't you tell me?"

"You're always distracting me." His car salesman smile is making me sweat.

354

"What a relief," I say. "It will be nice to be off the hook." The sarcasm in my voice is razor sharp. I'm struck by my viciousness. I am going out of my way to make him feel guilty because his partner suspects me of a murder I committed. Nate did the same thing when I first accused him of cheating. He acted like the notion was absurd, and that I was a hysterical bitch who had no faith.

Not only are Nate and I more alike than I thought, I share his twisted cruelty.

I'm dying to know about their lead. *Who* do they suspect? Could he be playing me? But diving into conversation is a bad idea. Like diving into the ocean, the water hides so many hazards. Better to stay dry.

"Can you lock the door on your way out?"

"Sure."

I slip underneath my covers and lie on my back. Instead of taking the hint, he lies beside me on top of the covers. He is on his back as well, staring at the ceiling. "It's strange, though," he says. "We're closing in with Leland's murder, but it's one of those cases that I kind of don't want to solve."

My cold palms sweat. "Why?"

He hesitates. "Leland was a real creep. He harassed a few girls and women. He assaulted his grandfather's nurse."

My pulse quickens. "I looked him up. I didn't see any charges."

"None of his victims pressed charges. Most times, victims just want it to go away."

"Did you find anything in his house that belonged to a little girl?" Like, say, a broccoli Shopkin under his mattress?

"No. I don't think he took Ava."

If police searched Leland's room and didn't find anything under the mattress, then where did Leland put the sock, shovel, and Shopkin?

It's not possible you imagined those items, is it?

No, no. I touched them. Held them. Those were real.

"Bottom line," James says, "he was an asshole who harassed girls and women. His behavior would have escalated to violence. So, you know, part of me wants to congratulate his killer. Thank the killer," he says, his voice dimming, slowing. He's measuring his words. "I don't want to put this killer in prison. I think they were just trying to protect their kid."

No shit. Well, hey, you're welcome!

But, also. Panic presses down on my chest. *He knows. He must know.* I pull my comforter under my chin and shiver. "Please turn the thermostat to seventy-two before you leave."

His hand rests on my forehead. His skin is cool. "You're sweating. You want some Tylenol?"

I do want Tylenol, but more than that, I want him to go. If he brings me medicine, he might think up another excruciating, cryptic detail about my dead neighbor's killer. I adore James, I do, but this whole thing is getting to be too much work. Our relationship is a slippery amalgam of compassion, ruinous secrets, and sex.

"No thanks," I say, panic still squeezing my chest, my lungs, my greasy heart.

"Call if you need anything."

"Thank you." Hulk's metal tag clinks on the floor as she sprawls beside my bed. "James?" I say.

"Yeah?"

"Who is your lead?"

He hesitates, then says quietly, "A neighbor." My bed creaks, and James's footsteps retreat softly. "Oh, and, Grace," he says, his voice at the top of the stairs, "If police ever interview your kids? All questions stop if a kid asks to stay silent."

Downstairs, the front door closes gently, securely.

He's got to know. Why else would he say that? Maybe he's just providing handy law enforcement tips! He can't think you killed your neighbor. If he did, he wouldn't keep stopping by, fucking you.

Is Lou the neighbor they suspect?

Lou is vulnerable, an easy target. I worry for him.

Don't worry. They won't find anything linking him because he didn't do it.

58

JUDGE, JURY, AND EXECUTIONER

It's a hot, sunny day. Maybe our last hot day. Nate drops off the kids, and I turn on the sprinkler. Within minutes, Wyatt and Chloe are in their suits, giggling as they run in the slick, wet grass, through a screen of falling water.

I set a picnic, and the kids eat lunch at the table on the deck, bright beach towels wrapped around them and slipping off their dewy shoulders. Their eyelashes are moist and clumped together, their hair drips onto their backs; their eyes shine with ideas. They eat only for fuel, then they are back to the real work of childhood.

I skip clean-up and sit on a lawn chair on the deck, my bare feet resting on the table. When I keep still, I have no pain at all.

Half-eaten watermelon slices and cherry pits remain on plastic plates. A late summer wasp lands on a watermelon rind. With the buffet of sweetness, I doubt it'll bother me.

Chloe bends over and aims her butt toward the sprinkler, laughing hysterically, then running away. Wyatt is all over this butt-centric joke. He does the same thing and springs away.

I consider turning on music, then veto it. The hush of water hitting grass, the kids' ringing laughter and quiet chatter, along with the rising tick of cicadas in the trees, are a perfect symphony.

Hulk lies on the deck in a wash of sun, half on her back, as if she has been working three shifts a day for weeks and is utterly exhausted. Her bare pink belly rises and falls in a slow, relaxed pattern. Couple of moles on her belly. *Get those checked out. When you have a spare three hundred dollars.*

My phone buzzes with a text. Nate.

-I'm sorry. No "buts" this time. I'm an asshole and I'm sorry. I'm not going to move on. I'm going to wait for you.

I should respond, but my thoughts drift, unfocused. *Later. Text him later.* I breathe in the earthy scent of water from the hose and turn off my phone.

The doorbell rings, and Hulk scurries to the screen. She barks frantically as she stares into the house toward the front door, which I left wide open to create a breeze within the house.

James. He's standing with his hands in his back pockets, a childish posture.

I should scold him—I don't want my kids to see him—but I am sun-sleepy. I stand, which sends an ache into my lower back. I grimace against it, slide the screen, walk the dark hall as my eyes adjust to the indoor lack of light, and open the front screen for him.

"Come on in," I say, smiling. "You want a glass of sun tea? I just made some."

His mouth is a hard line as he walks past me, headed to the kitchen. He is antsy and giving off a break-up vibe.

Peace slips away from me, and anxiety checks in, chin high, back stiff, with a salute. Why does he want to break up?

I shouldn't have told him he has to wait fifteen years for a hot air balloon ride. I shouldn't have exposed myself as sickly and old. I should have treated him like a shiny new boyfriend. Worn prettier underwear, more makeup. Made him a pie. *Men need to feel appreciated, damn it.*

Pain stabs my lower back and I reach out to the wall. *Stay still, like a statue; it will pass.*

My doctor's office is closed today so it's either the walk-in clinic or the emergency room. Every time I go to the walk-in clinic, I get sub-par, sleepy pseudo doctors who like to chat. Going to the ER for back pain that comes and goes seems pathetic. I don't want to spoil the peace of this day with nagging the kids to get in the car, yelling at them to be still while we sit in the waiting room, having to give Chloe electronics so she doesn't put her fingers on every germy thing.

Monday. Call the doctor Monday. First thing.

I limp down the hall toward the kitchen. Fuck it, I'll go on the stupid hot air balloon. If we hit a power line and I die, Nate will step up.

"About that hot air balloon ride," I say.

James sets something on my kitchen counter, but what's trapped under his palm is hidden. "You dropped Chloe's barrette," he says.

"Oh, thanks. Let me peek on the kids."

I peer out the back screen. The kids are giggling. They moved the sprinkler near the swings, and when they swing

360

forward, their toes and legs get wet.

Alarms are ringing up and down my spine before my mind catches up. I'm off-balance. My ears warm and tingle as if I said something off-color at a funeral.

Oh no. Chloe's barrette? I've never been in James's house. That means he found it—

"Under the bedside table in Leland's room," he finishes my thought, accusation sharp in his voice. "A few strands of your hair are trapped in it."

I spin toward him and stare at what he placed on my countertop. Beside his meaty hand is a photograph of a hot pink barrette inside a plastic baggie. Beside the bagged barrette is a piece of tape, the number 4 written in Sharpie. *Evidence. This is a photograph of evidence collected from Leland's house.*

My expression of surprise and guilt must confirm any lingering suspicion he had because he says, stone-faced and cold, "I was thinking it was something he picked up at a grocery store. Some child dropped her barrette, and he picked it up, brought it home as a souvenir. I didn't think much of it until we were in your bathroom and a bunch of these same barrettes fell out of your medicine cabinet."

While you were fucking me.

His mouth opens again, but then he chews his bottom lip. He wants to say more. Instead he eyes my kitchen suspiciously, scrutinizing random junk on the countertops (chunks of Play-Doh, rotting bananas, broken crayons, a dirty sock), then he paces. Only four feet in either direction before he's forced to turn; he's a lion in a cage. His muscles are rigid, he keeps his arms at his sides, simultaneously intimidating and adolescent.

Panicked, I'm on the verge of tears, on the verge of fury, on the verge of violence. I consider denial. *What are you* talking *about, James? I bought those generic barrettes at Walmart. Leland could have gotten that barrette anywhere.* Denying adamantly until the day I die. Except he didn't come here to ask. He's sure of himself. Why is that? Did he run his own covert DNA test equivalent to the Ziplocs of spooge stored in my refrigerator?

As if he can read my mind, he mumbles, looking at the floor, "I have a good friend in the city. Forensics, he works forensics. He says it's your hair." He covers his eyes with one palm, squeezes both his temples. "You told me and Ariana you didn't step foot inside his room."

Wow. So James is not the paragon of goodness you thought he was. I picture him in my bathroom with the door closed behind him, plucking a few of my hairs from my matted hairbrush and bagging them.

James and I, we're done. And, I have his seminal fluid in my crisper. I'm insulated.

"James," I say, attempting pragmatic, but my words betray me and come out rushing, like a flash-flooded river sweeping up cars and knocking down trees, "I swear I saw Ava Boone *in his house*. When he was at work, I had to check. Police wouldn't tell me *anything*. No one would tell me *why* he was a suspect. I found a girl's sock and a toy under his mattress and a big cage in his basement. It tore me apart. I couldn't sleep. He had already given Chloe candy, and I needed to protect her. I don't even remember how it happened. It's like it was a dream. I woke up after garbage night and I was in the tub and my clothes were wet from the rain and my hammer was missing. I—"

"Your *hammer* was missing?" he says. "What are you talking about, Grace?"

"I thought Ethan Boone killed Leland, but the more I questioned Natalie and Ethan, I realized Ethan didn't do it. And then I found a splinter of what I think was Leland's bone under my jaw." My words are still a torrent, wildly pulling everything in, topsoil and twigs and rotten leaves and plastic of all sorts, mixing everything up, making everything turbid.

His head trembles. As if it is going to come apart, he grabs it in his hands. "A splinter of Leland's bone? What are you talking about? Oh my God, Grace. You *questioned* the Boones?"

I stop and take a moment to let regret fill me up. It appears I have read the situation wrong. James came here knowing only that I'd been in Leland's room, nothing more. He hadn't jumped to the conclusions I thought he had. Maybe James walked into my house stone-eyed and cold because he thought I'd fucked Leland or something.

The thing is, I've been aching to confess. I've been aching to share my thoughts, my theories.

I exhale, trying to keep the quiver out of my voice, trying to slow down. "I followed the son. He deals drugs in the Walmart parking lot. I talked to Ethan. I talked to Natalie. I don't want to get them in trouble, they've suffered so much, but I'm pretty sure they accidentally killed their daughter."

"Grace! You need to stop."

My forehead is burning up as my words pour out, "Because

if my daughter was missing, I would *never* stop looking for her. I would *never* say she was dead. And they kept saying, 'Leave us alone. She's dead.' I think there's a drug connection because Natalie is freaked out by drugs, and her sister works hospice and has access to drugs, and the son sells them in the Walmart parking lot. One of them killed the little girl—it was an accident, she overdosed by accident, I think—and then they had to cover it up because they are family. They are good people trying to protect one another. The sister, Sarah, she means well and her heart is big and she's overwhelmed," I say, pleading for them.

James squeezes and opens his fists. *Squeeze. Open.* "You should have given that information to the police. All of it. Oh my God. Leland? You *broke* into his house? Why didn't you tell the police what you found? Why didn't you tell *me*?" He drags his palm down his face, then shoves it into his eye and wipes his tears.

Even in the midst of this grotesquely surreal conversation, he is sensitive. It makes me want to keep him.

"Because I broke into his *house*, James. You know how the system works. It protects the wolves. It protects the wolves until they kill. I was trapped." My abdomen seizes when I move, so I'm standing still, fingers splayed on the kitchen counter. If I felt stronger, I'd be touching him, trying to humanize myself. "You came into my life one day too late," I say quietly, more to myself. "Had I known you, I would have asked you for help. I wouldn't have killed him," I whisper, and it feels so good to let those words out of me. Like a cold soapy shower over soiled, bug-bitten, itchy skin.

You shouldn't have said that.

I know. I know. But it feels so good.

Confusion and disgust flare in his eyes.

"Killed him," he repeats quietly, introspectively. "Grace, you need to get help. You're sick." Anxiety flashes in his eyes, as if he's worried I'm hiding a weapon.

"Fuck you and your arrogance. You people who don't even know yourselves because you've never been put in a spot. You've never felt desperate." *You've never experienced a psychotic break.* "You've never had to make a choice, a real choice, a dire choice. You can say you're lawful and you're moral, but that's only because you're coasting. If he lived next to you and he was after your child, you would do the same."

He bites his lip and works the muscles in his jaw and cheeks. He's fighting to keep his mouth shut tight. He gazes out my back screen at something. My grass, my kids, the watermelon on the table, I don't know. "You live in a bubble," he says.

I erupt into laughter. I wasn't expecting the laughter and neither was my lower abdomen. Pain blacks out my vision for a split second. "*Of course* I live in a bubble. I have no time to step out of my bubble. This bubble is *so* demanding, I am sweating when I wake in the morning. I pee with the door open. I open new credit cards every month for the zero-interest period. I never——"

Sharp pain explodes brilliantly inside my lower left side. *Appendix?* Did my appendix burst? What side is my appendix on? I can never remember what's where. I steady myself against the counter. My T-shirt's short sleeve, damp, grazes my arm.

"I'm divorced too, you know," he says. He's staring at my counter, maybe at the hardened chunk of oatmeal cemented to the laminate or the tea-stained dish, the tea bag hanging off the edge, sad and limp like a used tampon. Seems like he hasn't noticed my physical pain. Fine. I wouldn't want him to think I'm playing him.

I don't want to compete, I don't want pity, but *come on*. Divorce isn't a one-way ticket to madness. Every divorce is different. His is easier than mine; mine is easier than the one involving threatening texts that close with *you cunt*; and that divorce is easier than those entailing chronically busted lips and broken ribs.

Breathing through the pain, I say, viciously, "What was it that you said? Oh, that's right. I remember. You wanted to *thank* the killer."

He opens his mouth, closes it. He shakes his head and walks toward my front door.

The pain is gone. It was on like a faucet. Now it's turned off. "Get back here," I growl.

"You need help, Grace. Get yourself a lawyer while you're at it."

"I have your seminal fluid in a Ziploc."

He turns slowly and stares at me. "*That's* what was in it?"

"You heard me. And don't pretend to be high and mighty because you fucking snuck my hair to your buddy in forensics."

He stares at me, dumbfounded, then he looks up at the ceiling. He bobs his head as if he hears a rhythm. "Wow." He shakes his head again. "Wow. You know, I think you actually love that you're divorced."

"I hate it."

He turns away and speaks to the screen. "You love it

because you get to be judge, jury, and executioner, and no one will tell you otherwise. Kids can be easily brainwashed and abused and they rarely question adults." He is out the door, strolling through my grass toward his car.

Hating him, I linger at the screen. I am already over him. "You were never on my team. I was just someone you were fucking."

He hears me, but doesn't stop. He's in the street, opening his car door.

Oh my God, the Boones! Why did you tell him about the Boones? You were supposed to protect the Boones. What have you done? Worry rolls in fast, smothering my anger. I imagine Ariana, wrath in her movie-star eyes, snapping cuffs on my wrists in front of my confused children. Snapping cuffs on Natalie and Ethan.

"Wait! James," I say, my tone clipped and anxious.

I am running barefoot in the grass.

The clouds above are downy and moving too fast across the swirling blue sky. Sun shines too yellow-white, and my vision dims. The mailbox slides in and out and in of my field of vision, like I'm standing in the middle of an earthquake. Grass grazes and pokes my ankles. Does it need cutting again? How does it grow wild so fast? Pain splits my back and bursts in my skull so specifically. Did a vessel burst?

Vertigo. You are experiencing vertigo.

I'm running to his car but can't get my voice to call his name. Beyond a circle of stones showcasing hostas, the chrome passenger door handle of his car reflects the sunlight, blinding me. The engine hums. Old car exhaust is thick in my throat. My surroundings sway and skate and, because I am still ambling forward, my fall is inevitable. I extend my hands to break it.

Don't hit your head on a stone.

They need you.

The bright sky is darkening.

Call me what you want, I adore my children. Everything I do is for them. I love my children with a hardness like iron and bone. I love them so much I want to crush them and consume them and meld with them. *Die for them.*

59

Citrus perfume fills my nose. The blurry shape of a woman in a loose blue shirt hovers over me. *You're not wearing contacts.* Her blond ponytail swings as she busies herself with something.

Behind my head, something mechanical beeps three times. Hospital!

I'm lying in a hospital bed. This woman in blue is a nurse. I lift my arm. An IV traps my wrist. Anxiety blooms in my chest like octopus ink in seawater.

Hospitals are sex warehouses of orgies and lawlessness. Teeming with antibiotic-resistant microbes. Mazes of corridors and closets and nooks where employees without boundaries lurk, whispering, giggling, and conspiring. If someone turns on a black light, this room is gonna light up. Spooge everywhere.

I can't suck in a good breath, a real breath.

This is the place, these are the people, who steam-rolled my marriage and family and stole our peaceful, normal life.

I know my fears aren't logical. This hospital is a place where people are healed and saved. Doesn't matter, my heart rate monitor is ringing, and I can't breathe.

Where are Chloe and Wyatt? I try to ask, but my throat is like baked, cracked clay.

The nurse rubs my arm, "It's OK. Try to relax." But her cold hand on my skin makes it worse. Another nurse comes in, this one in pink, and she messes with my IV.

My chest loosens. My body lightens. It's floating away from me.

They drugged you. They are going to take off all my clothes and make fun of me and rub their genitals all over me. *Stay Awake. Do. Not. Fall. Asleep.*

60

HER VERTEBRAE WERE YANKED BY A HOOK

My throat is dry, my eyes are dry. As if someone blew sawdust at my face.

You fell asleep.

Do I feel violated?

Actually, dear God, yes! My lower abdomen is tender. I am sore inside.

Tears well and my bottom lip quivers, but I stomp out emotion.

Stay calm or they will knock you out again.

Fuzzy bursts of yellow and pink blot out the corner of the room. Flowers. Pink balloons sway above. Someone sits in the corner, smiling. His lips are red. Maybe it's a woman; everything is still blurry.

"Mom?"

Nothing.

"Who are you?" I say. "I can't see well. I don't have my contacts or glasses."

He says nothing.

I try to draw out details from the blur. His body is flesh-colored; he's wearing no clothes. Like I said, *hospitals*. Maybe he's wearing a tan shirt and tan pants.

"Go away, please."

He sits, tree-trunk still.

I worry I'm not in any old hospital. Maybe they know I'm a criminal and they've put me in a prison hospital. This is my guard, who has been instructed not to speak to me. Maybe the bats that attacked me were carriers of a barely known virus, and I'm in a secret research hospital. The gravity of both scenarios sends me over the threshold of panic and anger.

"I said go away!"

On the table beside me is a teddy bear. I throw the furry bear at the man across the room, and pain tears through my abdomen. The bear strikes him square in the nose, and the man slides down the chair and onto the ground, smoothly and quietly, emitting the slightest squeak.

Oh. Blow-up doll. My co-workers probably brought him. There's no way a prison hospital would allow me to have a blow-up doll.

Still, I worry. How long have I been here? Who has Chloe and Wyatt? Has James turned me in?

James didn't tell them. If everyone knew you killed Leland, they wouldn't send you flowers and a blow-up doll.

A woman wearing patterned scrubs walks in. "Ah, you're awake," she says, thrilled. "Welcome back. You are doing fine. I'm Kathy."

"How long have I been here?" My voice is raspy, and I force a painful swallow. "Where are my kids?"

372

"Your children are perfect and eating all their vegetables and brushing their teeth. I was instructed by your husband to tell you that." *Ex-husband*, but I'm not going to correct her. I want her to think I have people on my team. I want her to worry about making a medical mistake. "You have been our guest for two days. From the looks of your room, I would say you have a lot of people who care about you."

My bottom lip quivers. *Don't you dare cry. Don't you dare let this charlatan manipulate your emotions.*

"What happened? Do I have rabies?"

"I haven't heard anything about rabies. Did you get bit by a dog?" she says, her tone hinting that her brow is knitted.

"Bats. Scratched by bats."

"Really? Sounds like quite a story." The worry is gone from her voice, replaced by disinterest. "Dr. Birnbaum will be by soon enough. You can talk to her about bats. You're here because you had to have emergency surgery. Your IUD got lodged where it had no business and you were bleeding internally. You are very lucky you got here in time. Let's sit you up so you can drink. Your throat is sore, I bet." She presses the remote, and the top of my bed lifts.

So it was the IUD.

I worried my guilt was eating me from the inside, like acid corroding my soft organs and pulling me apart painfully, cell by cell. *Psychosomatic Abdominal Torture.*

The hormone-emitting chicken bone springing free from my uterus and planting itself elsewhere was responsible for my pain, but it probably couldn't explain away my sleepwalking, my hallucinations, my *violence*.

An awful memory hits me so hard, I flinch.

You sold out the Boone family. How could you be so reckless?

Like a spoon, shame scrapes me out, leaving me hollow as a clinging cicada husk. I picture Ethan Boone, alone in some remote location, digging. It had to be him who buried the body because while, yes, it's the mother who flits and pecks like a bird—constantly busy fetching strings and wet grass and newspaper to make the nest—and it's the mother who is tirelessly feeding her babies, grooming them, comforting them, when something this monstrous happens and it rips the backbone right out of the mother as if her vertebrae were yanked by a hook on a line, and she can't move, she just *can't* move, *just can't*, it's the father who is left to do the foul, immeasurable task of burying.

I picture him in the forest on that rainy night, his body shuddering, tears racing down his cheeks. I picture Ava's red shoes on the forest floor. These shoes, *Dorothy's shoes*, are her trademark, so my mind incorporates them. *There's no place like home.*

"There you go," the nurse says. "Now you're up. Look at your beautiful flowers."

"I couldn't see a million dollars if it were on my lap," I say, my voice sounding rough, like crinkled newspaper. "Do you see my contacts or glasses lying around?"

"Let me check the bathroom, hon."

She comes out quickly and hands me my glasses case.

"Thank you. I hate being blind." As the words leave my mouth, I want them back. She probably has patients who are *literally* blind.

I can't think of anything to say that will fix my tactlessness.

Cheery, she says, "Now you can see your beautiful flowers. You want to know who they're from?"

"Sure."

She plucks four tiny envelopes from four bouquets, lays them in my palm, and closes my fingers around them. Thoughtful. Her skin is cold and smooth. "I'm going to get you water. I'll be back in a minute."

My name is written on the front of all four. One is from my mom; her fat loopy cursive gives her away. Liz's tight, tidy cursive marks the next envelope. The third is from Nate. He can't write in cursive, claims he missed that month of school. On the last envelope, my name is printed in an unfamiliar style, lean and broken.

My stomach flutters as I open it and pull out the small card.

I hope you get better.

-James

I'm not sure how to interpret his words. Is his statement simple and sincere or is it a jab? Like, *You're fucking mental, pathetic, and repulsive. I hope you get better.*

61

A TWISTED SCAVENGER HUNT

Wyatt. It was Wyatt who borrowed my dad's hammer. I found it in the back of his closet while I was panic-hunting for money to pay the pizza guy. Wyatt came across the hammer in our junk drawer and made off with it, as kids do. He used it to hammer a few nails into the wall in his closet. From the nails, he hung soccer ribbons and rubber band bracelets. If only I'd asked him earlier.

I didn't kill Leland Ernest. I daydreamed and nightdreamed of killing him, but I didn't. The killer and me though, there was *a lot* of overlap in our logic. Carrying out the crime on garbage night. Leaving Leland's sliding back door open and dropping meat by the door so cats and skunks could ransack the crime scene. I favored slimy chicken; he used ground beef. *Insane minds think alike.* Same method, too. Blunt force trauma. We both had the rage of protective parents.

The barrette James found in Leland's house? I'm not sure about that. I don't remember wearing one the day I broke into his house, but Chloe could have snuck it in my hair that day. It's equally possible the barrette fell out of my hair while I was working in the yard, and Leland picked it up from the grass.

What I thought was a sliver of Leland's bone in my skin must have been a tiny fragment of the coffee cup I shattered at work. Or perhaps a freakish rogue hair.

I have been out of the hospital ten days now. My abdomen is still achy, but I'm stronger.

Also, I completed the full series of rabies vaccines, so that slow and painful death is off the table.

James stands barefoot behind his screen door with a cigarette in his mouth and a beer bottle in his hand. No gray T-shirt today. Uniform in the washing machine? He's wearing jeans and a black T-shirt with a scattering of tiny holes at the crewneck from cigarette ash. Or maybe he bites his T-shirts. His posture and expression are both intimidating and troubled. The small foyer and hallway behind him are shadowed, and I can't make out a single plant, coat rack, or coffee table. Strange, I have never been in his house.

I always made him for a boy scout, a do-gooder who would have been horrified by the monsters lurking in the dark corners of my mind. Of course I could be the source of his unhinged air, I'm *undoubtedly* the source, but maybe he's always been troubled. If he's a house-smoker, he's knowingly exposing his daughter to secondhand smoke. Not very puritan.

What I'm trying to say here is, *Man, he looks good*. I was dating up. I can't do better than James.

"What?" he says, bored, no intimation of opening the screen.

Since the porch I'm standing on is a step lower than his house, I have to aim my gaze higher than usual to find his eyes.

"I wanted to tell you, thank you. For taking care of me. Calling an ambulance. Calling my mom. She said you stayed with my kids until she got there."

"Anyone would do the same."

"That's not true, but OK."

He takes a drag from his cigarette, turns his head, and blows smoke. "I didn't tell anyone you broke into your neighbor's house. I didn't tell anyone you thought you killed Leland." His voice shrinks and he gazes down because he can't meet my eyes. He's embarrassed for me, or for himself. "And the Boones, they never mentioned your name either. You're in the clear if that's what you're worried about."

"Oh. OK." I want to tell him I'm a good person. Most of me is good at least.

If I had met James one week earlier than I did, I would not have harassed Natalie and Ethan, I would not have broken into my neighbor's house, I would not have considered murdering my neighbor or convinced myself I did. I truly believe that. Which is alarming and breathtaking. Some of us are that adaptable or weak; our potential for violence hinges upon one or two seemingly inconsequential variables.

I want to explain to him how lonely and terrified I felt. I want to describe my level of sleep deprivation. I want him to know that under normal circumstances, I am *normal*.

None of these explanations will excuse my actions, not in his opinion. He cannot comprehend that I was *certain* I killed Leland, yet went on with my day-to-day activities, sex, joking. Even if he could forgive my delusions, he could never get past me storing his spooge in my fridge. That one's a sticking point. So why bother?

He takes another drag and drops the butt into his beer bottle. "So you're feeling better?" He is only going through the motions. He wants me gone.

"Yes. I'm better. It was my IUD. My explosive device," I joke. His mouth remains a hard, unforgiving line, and my joke withers. "They tell me it could have caused a number of my symptoms. It messed with my hormones, which messed with my brain and body in all sorts of interesting ways. They're also convinced that my sleep deprivation combined with my meds induced psychosis. Like you said."

"You were right about the Boones," he says. "You heard?"

I did. Preschool teachers' lounge gossip.

It was opioids. My god, it's always opioids these days. After her back injury years ago, Natalie got addicted. When her doctor stopped supplying, she convinced her dear sister to be her supplier. Ethan found out and gave Natalie an ultimatum. She quit the pain meds, went through one week of vomiting, shaking, and mind-rattling pain. Her withdrawal scared the hell out of him; he wasn't sure he could go through with it. Instead of flushing the meds down the toilet like she instructed him, he hid the pills in their one-year-old's room. Ava's room. Ava wasn't walking yet, and Ethan hid them up high in the closet. No way could she get to them.

Natalie stayed clean for years, Ethan forgot about the bottle of pills, and in the meantime, Ava grew.

She loved playing make-believe, that little girl. Unicorns and super puppies and princess cats and tea parties with sea creatures. She was excitable and loud and talked a mile a minute and loved to dance on the couch and sing in the bathroom, but it also wasn't uncommon that she'd play quietly in her room for two or three hours at a time.

When her parents found her cold, lifeless body that evening, the empty prescription bottle bearing a stranger's name on the floor, and a couple pills set out like candy on her tea party plates, they knew someone in their family would go to prison. Natalie worried it would be her sister, Sarah, a single mother who worked the night shift as a hospice nurse, consoling families. Sarah, whom Natalie had coerced to be her drug supplier.

Late that night Ethan Boone buried Ava in the Springhill Valley Forest Preserve a few hours south. No cairn. No cross. No flowers. No trace.

Every time I brought up the possibility Ava was alive, it must have torn them apart.

"I heard about it," I say.

"I didn't tell anyone you solved it. I figured you didn't want the credit or attention," he says, his head cocked, his eyes drifting up. He's sour. Huh. James is competitive. An alpha. He likes to be the smart one. Hindsight, that explains his attraction to me, at least partially. I came across as unremarkable, pathetic, and overly emotional. I made him feel like he had his shit together.

"That's right. Thanks," I say, humbly, because even though he likes having the upper hand, I feel sorry for him. No one in his department could solve the case, he couldn't solve the case, but an unhinged single mother of two nailed it pretty quick from the outside.

380

But how could he compete? One unhinged, desperate parent can spot another unhinged, desperate parent. It's like looking in the mirror.

"Will they go to prison?" I say.

"Too soon to tell. I think they're charging Ethan with involuntary manslaughter and concealment of homicidal death. Very likely he'll serve time."

I lay my hand against the cool siding to counter dizziness. *It's not your fault. Police would have figured it out eventually.* But I don't believe that.

"Natalie will probably avoid prison," he says. "They're both claiming she didn't know the meds were in the house, she thought he'd flushed them, and that he threatened her to stay quiet about the burial."

Thank God. Being responsible for her smallest child's death will torture her ceaselessly; at least she will be around to parent the other two.

"The sister. Sarah?" I say. Single mom with a heart of gold and no backbone, always trying to make everyone else's life easier.

"She'll lose her nursing license and her job, but she might avoid prison," he says.

My greatest fear, the fear that steered my actions—losing my kids—has become a real possibility for these people.

He rubs his jaw, and his eyes burn with thought. He's trying to figure out the clues he missed with me. "Please don't come by my house again." If it hasn't already, it is dawning on him now. He dated down.

I walk to my car, worried I may have ruined his life. He will never be a confident detective. He will second-guess his ability to read people. He might end up working as a patrolman or maybe a high school cafeteria security guard.

What's worse is, I didn't only kill his career. He might never trust another woman again.

He is a good guy who deserves to be happy. Despite his competitive alpha nature, he is calm, generous, and willing to compromise.

I was right though about just being someone he was fucking. James *really liked* me, sure, but if he had been my kids' father, if he'd been in it for keeps, he would have stayed. My psychosis, my stalking, my perceived violent moment, my stash of his seminal fluid, wouldn't have been deal breakers. He would have stayed for our kids, and, over time, he would have forgiven me and loved me again. Eventually.

Hell, in a year or two, we would be joking about my semen stash in the crisper. Something like, "Can you grab the carrots? They're in the crisper next to the slick toilet paper."

The eroders of a marriage's vitality are also the eroders of abhorrence: sex, routine, shared experiences, shared jokes, and time. Like water and wind weakening jagged, angular rocks, they smooth intense emotions and they desensitize. For better or worse.

I'm on a twisted scavenger hunt, and my list is simple and cruel:

1. Visit one of your victims.

2. Visit another of your victims.

I park several houses away from the Boone house.

A man is scrubbing spray paint off their garage door. Red words on a white garage.

Child Killer.

A bucket at his feet, he's scrubbing the letter K, but it's no use, the shadow of smudged letters bleeds through. Whatever he's using isn't going to cut it. That garage is going to need primer and paint. Several coats.

The man is not Ethan Boone. I don't know who he is, but I'm guessing he's a neighbor. The low sun berates his back. With the inside of his forearm, he wipes his eyes. Maybe he's crying. Maybe he's sweating. Maybe a little of both.

The Boones have been tagged, marked as the worst type of people in something semi-permanent and glossy and lipstick-red from the hardware store. Their mailbox is in the grass, tipped on its side, the post standing bare. Grass needs cutting. Egg yolk clings to their front window, thick as dried phlegm.

But they aren't here to see it.

They are gone. Word from the preschool teachers' lounge is that they've fled, are living in a rental while Ethan sits in a jail cell, awaiting trial.

The community might have been able to forgive the child's accidental overdose, depending on how the story was pitched, but the community could not forgive the Boones' lying, their pleas for help, their playing the role of desperate parents begging for the return of their child.

The Boones' betrayal stung. *How dare you let us lose sleep, let us ruin our shoes to wade through muck for hours on end, our fingers cold and stiff? How dare you let us waste our time answering phones, making casseroles? How dare you let us worry ourselves sick about our own children?*

My betrayal of the Boone family is a deeper pain, lasting and gnawing, like a surgery screw twisted into bone that aches with the changing barometer. It will be inside my bones, a part of me, and will endure even as my body ages and deteriorates.

62

BRING ON THE DRUGS AND DRAG RACING

Tony Durtato murdered Leland Ernest.

Leland had been harassing Tony's seventeen-year-old daughter, Emma. He had sent Emma aggressive love notes and texts when the Durtato family lived in this house, *my house*. When Emma didn't reciprocate his interest, dead animals showed up on the Durtatos' back deck. Mice. Bunnies. Parakeets. Goldfish. That stain on the back deck Tony was eyeing as we talked about why he was moving? I'm planning to give it a serious scrubbing.

Tony Durtato never bothered filing police reports. Maybe he'd considered violence as a possible resolution from the start, daydreaming about it like I had. He put his house up for sale and bought a house thirty miles away. Tony and his wife had solid jobs near their first house, *my house*, so they didn't want to move much farther.

Thirty miles wasn't far enough. A month ago, Leland found Emma. He left notes *in* her car and trapped under her wiper blades, and showed up at the Olive Garden where she worked. Third time he showed up, Emma was fired. Even her sleazy, cocaine-jazzed manager was not willing to expose his staff and customers to that type of risk.

Tony, who sold me this house to escape, could not get his family away, could not keep his daughter safe. Somehow it escalated into a confrontation in Leland's house with a pipe wrench. I don't know the full story, and I don't want to know.

My mind is unable to process the homicide. Strange, but I can only consider it superficially, as if it's a tidbit from the board game Clue.

Tony Durtato killed Leland Ernest with a pipe wrench in the bedroom.

Lou's daughter, Rachel, directed detectives to the Durtato family. Rachel and Emma were friends; they stayed connected on Snapchat. When detectives started circling her dad, swooping down to peck and rip him apart, Rachel spoke up. Told them she wasn't the only girl Leland had harassed. Told them Leland had cost Emma her waitressing job only weeks ago.

James and Ariana cornered a fragile, traumatized Emma, and she couldn't stop crying.

I think back to that last night James and I were together for just a few hours. He was upset about the case. He mentioned that a kid could refuse to talk to police. He had probably spoken to Emma that same day.

Desperate to spare his daughter from further interrogation, Tony stepped forward and admitted guilt.

One parent protects child; another child protects parent— the family preservation instinct can be savage.

But to know your parent violently killed another person— what an anchor on that child's mind.

The thought stops my heart. What if Wyatt and Chloe knew I was capable of that violence?

Like Ethan Boone, Tony is awaiting trial. Taking Leland's harassment into account, he will probably get a light prison sentence. But still. *Prison.*

And that yellow shovel, that sock, that Shopkin? I don't know. Probably Chloe's. Probably left in our yard like so much of her other crap, then gathered and tucked away by Leland Ernest.

I kind of regret that it wasn't me who killed Leland. I know that makes no sense. Tony will go to prison; I am free to enjoy my children. But I want to be Point Bird. I want to be a fearless protector of my children and other people's children. The type of person who walks into an escalating argument instead of shuffling to their car and pretending the injustice happening around them is none of their business.

Whatever you want to call my neurological condition, it has passed. Call it bat-attack PTSD. Call it Sleep Deficit Syndrome. Call it Sleep Deficit via Media Terrorists and Finding a Child's Totems Under Suspect's Mattress COMBO Syndrome. Call it amphetamine-induced paranoia and psychosis. Call it Major IUD Hormone Fail. Regardless of label, it's gone. I still worry and I may be tired until the day I die, but I am no longer hallucinating.

I try to keep my distance from my laptop, taking a break from the heavy worries of Third World starvation, sex slavery, and horrific war deeds. I don't watch Ava's video. The Boones' tragedy is a maelstrom, a strong whirling force capable of pulling me down and drowning me. Instead, I read romance novels before I fall asleep.

My new neighbors are moving in today.

Everyone wants to know who bought *the murder house*. The whole neighborhood is crossing their fingers for someone good. Living near *the murder house* carries stigma. It's bad for home prices. It carries a reckless vibe, like hey, there's already murder in this neighborhood, bring on the drugs and drag racing.

I don't fear the vibe. I'm optimistic.

Peeking from behind my window curtains, I yearn for a starter family.

Professional movers—men with horrifically heavy items strapped to their back—walk with their chests at right angles to their legs.

Whoever is moving in has enough cash to hire movers. A good sign. I'd rather be surrounded by people making better decisions and more money than me. It's humbling, maybe humiliating, but makes for a safer environment for my kids.

63

UNDER MY SKIN

Brownies are done, cooling in a pan on the stovetop. The house is warm. Chocolate is rich in the air. Nate is sitting on the front porch, laughing with Chloe.

She's got one of those battery-operated bubble blowers. She's shooting bubbles into the air for Hulk, who is chasing the bubbles down to eat them.

I hesitate behind the screen and listen to them enjoy each other. "Hulk totally loves bubbles," she says, giggling. "Look at her. She loves bubbles *so* much."

Chloe's wearing a tank top and shorts with a winter hat and mittens. Everything about her outfit is weather-incongruous. It's the first day of October. Sunny, slightly cool. She's wearing Wyatt's old cowboy boots, which are two or three sizes too big. Any second, she's going to take off running for something.

She's going to fall, but she won't die. Let it go.

I step out onto the porch.

"Smells good in there," Nate says. He's not here to take the kids, he's here for a *visit*.

Weeks ago, Nate's infidelity was gigantic, overbearing, and inescapable. Like Christmas at the mall. His cheating doesn't seem ubiquitous anymore. I'm not sure what it seems like. Maybe a small, awful gift hidden behind the couch. A ring box full of spiders, their spindly legs glazed and glistening with gonorrhea. Gross and offensive, yet easy to hide. Easy to lose.

"We're going to bring brownies to the neighbors," I say. "Which means, the neighbors will probably get five or six, and we'll eat the rest."

He laughs. "Have you met them yet?"

I sit on the porch beside him. "No. I'm not too worried about it." And I'm not. If they are drug dealers, I'll call the cops on them. If they let their kids beat each other up, I'll say, *Yeah, we don't do that shit.*

Dr. Nasir told me to speak my mind. She said, "People who keep their thoughts and worries bottled up under pressure, under agitation, eventually explode. Mentally healthy people let their thoughts dribble here and there." She also lowered my Adderall dose, added Wellbutrin for anxiety, and wants to see me every three months instead of six.

"The doctor I spoke with last week said you were hallucinating," Nate says, his voice kind and calm. "You thought you saw Ava Boone in the neighbor's house."

Let's be clear. I told a doctor, several doctors, I was hallucinating, but I didn't tell them *everything*. I didn't tell them I broke into Leland's house. I didn't tell them I was having vivid dreams of murdering Leland in a highly orchestrated, well-thought-out, fairly logical manner. You have to be careful with doctors. What they write down they can use against you.

I don't know I'll ever tell Nate all the details. *Speak your mind* is different from *reveal every nook and cranny of your crazy*, but I might be able to gradually reveal myself. I feel like Nate and I are even. I used to cling to my innocence and stick Nate in the naughty corner. Now, we've both slept around, we've both done bad things, but we're also people who want to get better, do better.

"Why didn't you tell me?" he says softly, meeting my eyes.

OK. Now *speak your mind.*

"I didn't want you to take the kids from me."

"Grace, I would never do that." His voice is gentle, his eyes watery. "Who could worry about them more than you? Keep them wearing coats and eating their vegetables? Give them a conscience? You're their Jiminy Cricket. You can tell me anything. I'm not going to use it against you."

"It's not something you want to broadcast, that you're fucked in the head."

"Yeah, I know, but, Grace, so am I."

"You're saying you've been hallucinating?"

"I'm a different kind of fucked. Why else would I have cheated? All my issues from childhood. My parents were cold. There's so much shit I remember. Walking home in fourth grade, and Theo's not there to greet me like he always was. 'Where's Theo, Mom?' 'We put him down.' No fucking warning. That dog was barely sick. He could have lived three more years, maybe five. He was getting old and crapping on the floor, and they didn't like the inconvenience."

I've heard that story before and others like it. I never

thought of it in terms of *messing him up*. Nate always seemed invulnerable to his parents' callousness.

"And medical school," he says. "It was merciless and cruel. I am detached. I don't want to be, but I am." He turns to me. He has the sad, loyal liquid eyes of a retriever. "But I want to be a good dad. I want to be on your team."

Sane people speak up.

"I appreciate what you're saying, but you telling me these things, it doesn't solve everything."

"I know," he says.

I still feel it just under my skin, my rage, like an electric hum. I would have done it, you know. If I were pulled and stretched for seven more nights or maybe three, I would have.

I place my hand on Nate's. His hand pivots and squeezes mine. It's brief, then we both let go. I'm not sure what will become of our relationship, but the connection feels good. The connection drowns out the hum.

For now, a dog has pawed my mind—the snow globe— under the couch, and the insane shitfaced toddler who wouldn't stop fucking with me can't find me and has moved on to breaking other toys.

The garage door rumbles open, and Wyatt's whistling echoes within the garage. He rolls his bicycle onto the driveway while holding the bicycle pump under his arm. He's young, he has a little boy's body, but he's also strong and capable. I sense his impending independence, his imminent bigness. The feeling blows through me like a ghost.

Still whistling, he drops the kickstand and gets to work

unscrewing the valve cap on his back tire. My heart bloats, light and airy, and my shoulders relax. A breezy smile touches Nate's lips and crinkles his eyes. Nate and I, we both know: Wyatt only whistles when he's happy. Peaceful.

Hulk nudges my hand with her nose. I pet her, and she lowers her hind legs, sitting her ass right on my shoe. Glad I'm not barefoot.

Chloe picks dandelions, singing "Three Little Birds" by Bob Marley. The bubble machine, abandoned, drips into the grass.

"What's that you're singing, Chlo?" Nate says.

"Wyatt taught me. He's practicing for a coral concert."

"Chorus concert," Nate says, gently correcting her. "Come here and sing it for me. I want to show Grandma. I'll record." He pulls his phone out of his pocket.

Chloe walks over, dandelion stems strangled in her hand, flowers wilting. "Will you put it on YouTube, Daddy?"

He laughs, lifts his phone, and touches the *record* button. "Maybe. Go ahead and sing your song."

It's precious. It's heartwarming. It's fucking chilling.

ACKNOWLEDGEMENTS

There is a profound gratitude an unknown writer holds for the people who champion her and her first novel. I'm talking about agents, editors, and everyone with the power to greenlight a book.

My agent, Barbara Poelle, has hung in there with me, believed in me and supported me for a long dang time. Thanks for that, sister. BP is my bottle of champagne: she's explosively energetic, always a good time, and frankly, so whip-smart, she leaves me feeling buzzed.

To the entire team at Irene Goodman Literary Agency (especially Maggie Kane and Heather Baror), thank you for your energy and support.

I had ambitious expectations going into my first relationship with an editor. Sophie Robinson surpassed them. Sophie is all warm enthusiasm, sharp insights, and thrilling ideas. Her notes always left me dazed and nodding. Thank you, Sophie, for making my book shinier.

The whole team at Titan has been wonderful. Julia Lloyd,

the book cover you created was haunting and perfect. Natasha Qureshi, your provocative insights made the book stronger. Hayley Shepherd, your copyedits were brilliant. Katharine Carroll in Publicity, Sarah Mather in Press, and all of the people working behind the scenes, thank you.

I am grateful to the people that surround me every day: my family, my friends. Most of them have no idea how supportive they've been. Truth is, the pursuit of art, all those hours spent alone, working on something that brings you joy and gives you life, can feel self-indulgent. If anyone of my family or friends would have suggested that my time spent writing was wasteful, it would have been a sore in my already, occasionally self-doubting mind. They never once did that in all these years. We've laughed, celebrated, and discussed everything but the books. OK, occasionally the books. You people mean the world to me.

My neighbors! Good God, it must be said. My neighbors are nothing like Grace's. My neighbors are the kind who provide onions and potatoes in a pinch and drop off desserts. Although they could complain about the various projects on my driveway (fish tanks, Go-kart engines, the *constant* PVC pipes), they don't. My neighbors are the best kind.

Love to my generous and creative mother, Linda Doering, who always wants to help, always wants to read, and has been catching my mistakes for years. Shoutout into the universe to my dad for his constant love, humor, and support. If he were still with us, he would be thrilled for me.

Chicago Criminal Defense Attorney Tara Pease fielded my

questions. Much appreciated, Tara. Any legal inaccuracies in this book are mine.

Gratitude to Patricia Rosemoor, the first writer who supported me and connected me with other Chicago writers.

Shoutout to all the writers I've shared words with in-person and online, so many of you I now consider dear friends. This writing community is keenly talented, but more importantly, is full of humble, generous, uplifting people. I think the world of all of you. I reached out to some of you, asked you to read my book, and it blew my mind when you reached back and said, Glad to! To those who have said kind things about me or my book, I am deeply grateful. Seriously, like, don't ask me to do anything illegal because I. Well. I just. Please, don't ask.

This year I dipped my toes into social media. Book bloggers and bookstagrammers, you made that experience warm and delightful.

Now, to the lovely creatures with whom I share a roof.

Indy, good dog, oldest lady in the house, thank you for taking care of the children.

Sam, Ed, and Jon, my children, my heroes! You make every day more playful, more interesting, and bursting with love. You are better thinkers and better humans than I ever was as a kid. Love to you, always.

Marc, my brilliant husband, my muse, my personal comedy show. Thank you for two decades of love and laughter.

Lastly, deep gratitude to the readers. If you got to this part, you probably read my book, which is pretty cool. Thanks for that. In the end, it will always be for the booklovers—readers, librarians, bookstore owners. If you're up for it, I'd appreciate an honest review. Online or word-of-mouth, your opinions are powerful magic.

ABOUT THE AUTHOR

Sharon Doering lives in the Chicago area with her husband, Marc, their three kids, and a peculiarly civilized dog, Indy. In her other life, she was a science professor, a biotech stock analyst, and a xenotransplantation researcher. She has also been a good waitress, a mediocre bartender, and a terrible maid. Sharon is working on her next novel.

sharondoering.com
@DoeringSharon

For more fantastic fiction, author events,
exclusive excerpts, competitions, limited editions and more

VISIT OUR WEBSITE
titanbooks.com

LIKE US ON FACEBOOK
facebook.com/titanbooks

FOLLOW US ON TWITTER AND INSTAGRAM
@TitanBooks

EMAIL US
readerfeedback@titanemail.com